DESERT ROSES

Beneath A Harvest Sky

TRACIE PETERSON

BETHANYHOUSE
MINNEAPOLIS, MINNESOTA

Published by Bethany House Publishers
11400 Hampshire Avenue South
Bloomington, Minnesota 55438
www.bethanyhouse.com

Bethany House Publishers is a Division of
Baker Book House Company, Grand Rapids, Michigan.

Printed in the United States of America

Library of Congress Cataloging-in-Publication Data

Peterson, Tracie.
    Beneath a harvest sky / by Tracie Peterson.
        p.   cm. — (Desert roses)
    ISBN 0-7642-2519-7 (pbk.)
    1. Archaeological thefts—Fiction. 2. Tour guides (Persons)—Fiction.
3. New Mexico—Fiction. I. Title. II. Series: Peterson, Tracie. Desert roses.
    PS3566.E7717B465   2003
    813'.54—dc21   2003001454

To Rainy

You are a light and joy in

our lives. May God bless you

and grow you into a beautiful

young woman.

Love,

Nana

Books by Tracie Peterson

www.traciepeterson.com

Controlling Interests
The Long-Awaited Child
A Slender Thread • *Tidings of Peace*

BELLS OF LOWELL*
Daughter of the Loom
A Fragile Design

DESERT ROSES
Shadows of the Canyon • *Across the Years*
Beneath a Harvest Sky

WESTWARD CHRONICLES
A Shelter of Hope • *Hidden in a Whisper*
A Veiled Reflection

RIBBONS OF STEEL†
Distant Dreams • *A Hope Beyond*
A Promise for Tomorrow

RIBBONS WEST†
Westward the Dream • *Separate Roads*
Ties That Bind

SHANNON SAGA‡
City of Angels • *Angels Flight*
Angel of Mercy

YUKON QUEST
Treasures of the North • *Ashes and Ice*
Rivers of Gold

NONFICTION
The Eyes of the Heart

*with Judith Miller   †with Judith Pella   ‡with James Scott Bell

CHAPTER ONE
New Mexico, Late March 1931

W e'll never stick to schedule if you keep putting the Cadillac in the sand," Rainy Gordon teased her twin brother. She cast a glance over her shoulder at the Harvey House tourists, or "dudes," as the staff called them, who waited rather impatiently in the noon sun. Lowering her voice she asked, "How can I help?"

Gabe Gordon, better known as Sonny, looked up from beneath the brim of his ten-gallon cowboy hat and smiled. "Well, if you're done merely supervising, you could get behind the wheel and try to move this beast forward when I give you the okay. I think I've cleared as much sand as I can back here, and those rocks you brought me are bound to help give her a little more traction. But just to be safe, I'll push."

Rainy gave a salute from the brim of her uniform hat. She was grateful the Fred Harvey Company didn't require their women couriers to dress in the overexaggerated cowboy attire. Still, looking down at her Navajo tunic of dark purple velvet, silver concha belt, and squash-blossom necklace, she supposed she

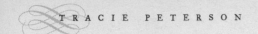

played the role of Indian to her brother's cowboy act.

Sliding behind the wheel of the Harvey touring car, Rainy pushed back her braided strawberry blond hair and waited for Sonny to give her the go-ahead. Getting stuck in the sand wasn't that unusual along some of the wilder stretches of New Mexico and Arizona, but they were only five miles outside of Santa Fe, and this little mishap should never have happened. Sonny hadn't had his mind on business as of late, but Rainy was hard-pressed to know what consumed his thoughts.

"Give it a try—just don't press down too hard on the accelerator. Just ease her out," Sonny called.

Rainy did as he instructed and with a jump and a lurch the Caddy reared onto solid ground, causing the dudes to cheer. Rainy giggled to herself knowing that the teenage daughters of one of their clients would surely see Sonny as their knight in shining armor. They'd positively swooned over him since first joining the tour three days ago. But that was just as the Harvey Company planned it to be.

After three years of working as a Detour courier, Rainy knew the routine better than most. She was in the entertainment business, just as surely as if she starred on the silver screen. Her job was to make people forget their problems and entice them into the wonderful, mysterious world of the Desert Southwest. As a tour guide, Rainy could direct their attention to the subtle and not-so-subtle nuances that shrouded the Indian lands and add intrigue and excitement to their otherwise dull, fearful lives.

For in 1931, there were a great many reasons to fear.

Hard times were upon them as the country was rapidly sinking into a stifled economy. Some claims led folks to believe that good times were just around the corner and that people owed it to their country to open their wallets and spend. At the same time, other predictions were far more discouraging. Doom and gloom hung over the country like an ill-tempered relative who threatened to extend his visit and take up permanent residency.

Rainy worried about her mother and father, who lived in Albuquerque. Her father worked for the university there, and while his job seemed perfectly secure, Rainy knew the economy's failings could easily change that. After all, a college education was a luxury, and many people would forego it in a flash in hopes of securing stable work in its place. If that happened often enough, her father would no longer be needed to teach history and archaeology.

"We need to move out," Sonny called, putting an end to Rainy's reflections. "Why don't you gather your dudes and let me get back in the driver's seat?"

"Only if you think you can keep us out of the sand," Rainy said, sliding from the seat. "I honestly don't know what gets into you sometimes, but maybe you could tell me about it over dinner. We can start with where your mind was when you put us in that hole."

Sonny shrugged and positioned himself behind the wheel, suddenly growing sober. "We should talk, but right now isn't the time."

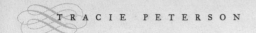

His serious tone caused Rainy's imagination to run rampant. Was something wrong? Did he have some word about their jobs? Was the company about to fold? There had been all kinds of rumors suggesting major changes. Maybe Sonny had more information than she realized.

Plastering a smile on her face, Rainy went to the overweight matronly mother and her two teenage daughters. "We need to get everyone back in the touring car," she announced. The woman, red-faced and perspiring fiercely, nodded and motioned to her brood.

"Mother, tell Miss Gordon to let me sit up front with Sonny," the elder of the two girls whined. The girl had made eyes at Sonny all day long. She'd even tried to throw herself into his arms by faking a fall from a ladder, only to have her sister bear the brunt of her descent.

The woman looked to Rainy as if to comply with her daughter's request, but Rainy gave her no chance to speak. Instead she moved forward to take her place. "Let's hurry, folks. Santa Fe is just over the hill. We have supper waiting for us at La Fonda, and let me tell you, the fare there is not to be missed. Tonight they're offering a variety of choices including some wonderful Mexican dishes, broiled salmon steaks, and roast larded loin of beef with the most incredible mushroom sauce."

She positioned herself inside the front passenger door without actually taking her seat. "And for those of you who haven't yet stayed at La Fonda, you are in for a treat. The hotel has been completely renovated and offers some of the nicest rooms along the Harvey line."

The plump mother consoled her daughters and shooed them into the backseat of the touring car as an elderly couple took the seats directly behind the driver's place. Had the girl not insisted on pouting and causing a scene, the older pair might not have robbed her of at least sitting behind Sonny. Rainy fought to hide a grin as she did a final head count and climbed into the car.

"We're all here," she told her brother.

"Good thing too. We're losing the daylight." Sonny put the car into gear and headed down the road.

Rainy breathed a sigh of relief when they pulled up to La Fonda. The adobe hotel was a home away from home for her tourists, and she was only too happy to turn them over to the Harvey House for the evening.

In order to save Sonny as much grief as possible, Rainy rounded up her charges and led them into the lobby without giving them a chance for argument.

"Your luggage will be delivered to your rooms," she told them.

"I wanted to tell Sonny good-bye," the elder of the teenagers pouted. She threw Rainy a look that suggested the guide had just separated the child from her true love.

"Sonny's very busy arranging for the luggage. You may see him around the hotel later," Rainy replied.

She turned her guests over to the registrar and hurried back to the car to help Sonny with their things. "Give me your bag," she told her brother. They shared a two-room apartment at a boardinghouse very near to La Fonda. Many of the couriers and a few other drivers lived there as well. It was inexpensive and the food was good. Still, it wasn't home. Home was in Albuquerque with her mother and father. She had cherished their little adobe house for as long as she could remember. Her mother had planted a lush garden in the courtyard and Rainy loved to spend hours there just dreaming of the future and all the plans she had.

"Pedro is already taking care of the dudes' luggage," Sonny said, handing her his small bag. He pulled his cowboy hat off and used his oversized kerchief to wipe his brow and sweat-soaked auburn hair. "I thought that tour would never end," he declared.

Rainy leaned into him good-naturedly and giggled. "But you're soooooo handsome," she mimicked in the voice of the teenage tourists. "Your eyes are dreamy." She batted her lashes at her brother and both of them burst into laughter.

"You'd better behave. Seems to me you get more than your share of attention when those dudes come in the unmarried male variety."

Rainy shrugged and hoisted her own bag to balance Sonny's. "If God would just tell me which one He has in mind for me to marry, I'd happily take their attention."

Sonny sobered. "How can you be so sure your husband will come by way of the tourists?"

"I don't know that he will, but it seems as logical a conclusion as any," Rainy replied. "Should I wait to have dinner with you?"

Sonny nodded his head. "Yeah, save me a seat. I'll need to get the car to the garage and get cleaned up. How about giving me an hour?"

Rainy nodded. "Sounds good." She made her way to the two-story adobe-over-brick boardinghouse and made her way upstairs.

"You look exhausted," Maryann, one of the newer couriers, declared as she passed Rainy on the steps.

"It was a tiring group today. Lovesick girls mooning over Sonny . . . and Sonny putting us in the sand."

"I think Sonny is the bee's knees," another girl declared as she came down the oak stairs to join Maryann. "He's so sweet."

Rainy laughed. "That's pretty much how the dudes saw it. Anyway, I need to get this stuff upstairs and get over to La Fonda for dinner." The girls nodded and stepped out of her way.

"We're heading to a party over at Teresa's place," Maryann added. "You and Sonny would be welcome. It's mostly just couriers and drivers."

"I'll think about it," Rainy replied, knowing she and Sonny wouldn't be attending. Neither one was big on parties all that much—unless, of course, it was with family.

Rainy trudged down the long carpeted upstairs hall. The housekeeper, Mrs. Rivera, kept sparsely furnished but very clean quarters and Rainy appreciated it greatly. Juggling the bags, she slipped her key in the door and stepped inside with a sigh.

She deposited her bag by the door and tossed her hat to the bed. Crossing the room, she opened the door that adjoined her space to Sonny's. She left his

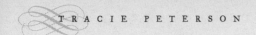

bag on the bed and went to open the window. Sonny liked it crisp and cool at night, and the warmth and stuffiness of the room would only serve to give him a headache.

Stretching her arms overhead as she walked back to her own room, Rainy couldn't suppress a yawn. Indeed, this tour had seemed so much longer than most of the others. Rainy pulled off her silver bracelets, then removed her squash-blossom necklace of turquoise and silver. She placed the items on her dresser, noting her reflection in the standing mirror. No matter how careful she tried to be, it always seemed her fair skin managed to get burned and, in turn, add a few freckles to her already dotted nose.

"Oh, bother," she said, unfastening her braid. "If I didn't come back burned and freckled, I'd run to the doctor to see what was wrong with me."

Her long red-blond hair rippled down her back. "Why couldn't my hair be as dark as Sonny's?" Her twin brother had the most beautiful shade of auburn hair, and for some reason he tanned easily and never freckled. It was simply unfair.

Noting that time was slipping away from her, Rainy hurried to clean up and dress for dinner. Even though she was no longer required to share her dinner with the tourists as the staff had been in the early days of the Detour program, Rainy was still expected to dress nicely to represent the coveted Harvey name. "You are still an ambassador of the Harvey Company!" her supervisor would often say.

"But for how long?" Rainy murmured aloud. She pulled on a clean black skirt and tucked her frilly white blouse into the waistband. First rumor and then newspaper articles had revealed that the Harvey Company was planning to sell the Detours. In fact, it would most likely be Major Clarkson, the manager of the transportation company from its inception, who would buy the company and run it.

With the financial uncertainty of the day, everyone saw the necessity for a bit of belt tightening. Taking the train to the American Southwest and hiring the expensive Indian Detours, as the Harvey Company dubbed the guided tours, was a luxury most couldn't afford. When it came to deciding between keeping food on the table and taking a vacation, travel went way down on the priority list. Yet Clarkson knew a good thing when he saw it. He wouldn't disassociate the company too far from the Harvey reputation. The Detours would still spend their nights in Harvey hotels, eating Harvey food.

Making her way downstairs, Rainy suddenly realized how hungry she was. Her thoughts, however, didn't drift far from the question of whether or not she'd have a job in another six months. No one could be certain of work—especially women. After all, why should a single woman be given gainful employment when a man supporting a family was turned away? It was all a matter of being sensible in a time that seemed to reject all pretenses of sense and sensibility.

"Are you eating with us tonight?" Mrs. Rivera questioned as she rounded the corner with a tray of tortillas.

"No, Sonny and I will be dining at La Fonda." Rainy gave the older woman a smile and bent to inhale the aroma of the freshly fried tortillas. "Although I'm tempted to stay. You are far and away the best cook in all of Santa Fe, Mrs. Rivera."

The old woman grinned. "I'll save you some *sopa-pillas* on the back of the stove. You might need a late-night snack."

Rainy laughed. "I know Sonny will appreciate that."

She took her leave and walked back to La Fonda, where the bustle of tourists and workers was always a wonder to behold. The cool stone interior welcomed her with wonderful artistic drawings and the flavor of old Mexico. The hotel, rich in the furnishings and interior design of Harvey's cherished architect, Mary Colter, was the most sought-after establishment in all of Santa Fe. The rooms were lavishly furnished, the suites incomparable to anything else in the state, and the hotel food was up to the Harvey standards: huge portions and rich ingredients fashioned by the hands of some of the finest chefs in all the world.

Rainy was shown to a table for four in the back corner of the hotel restaurant. It was her favorite place to enjoy her meal. She was rarely pestered by the tourists, and she didn't have to deal with old friends . . . unless, of course, she wanted to. The early evening rush had cleared out, and now there were more local diners and Harvey employees than tourists. Rainy sighed and leaned back against the oak chair. It felt so good to be off duty.

She'd no sooner taken her seat at the elegant table than she spied Duncan Hartford. Her heart seemed to skip a beat as she studied his handsome face and thick dark hair. How she wished she could get to know him better.

Since Sonny planned to join her soon, Rainy reasoned that it wouldn't seem out of line to invite Duncan to join them. He might as well have been one of the Harvey employees since he worked at one of the museums where the company arranged tours, allowing Rainy to see him on a regular basis. He was practically family, she told herself. Never mind that Rainy found herself attracted to this man of archaeology and Indian research.

Her breathing quickened as she tugged on the sleeve of her Harvey waitress. "Would you do me a favor and ask Mr. Hartford if he'd like to join me for dinner?"

The young woman beamed Rainy a smile. "Sure thing." She wove in and around the tables and guests to where Duncan was just about to be led to another table. Rainy watched as the girl appeared to explain the situation.

For one horrible moment Rainy feared he'd reject her offer. *Why did I do that?* She'd never before gone running after a man for company.

She wanted to bury her face in her hands and pretend it had been a mistake. *Maybe if I pretend to read the menu . . . then I won't seem so desperate.* She picked up the menu and considered her choices.

"It was very kind of you to invite me to join you this evening."

Rainy looked up to meet Duncan Hartford's deep brown eyes. She swallowed hard. "I hope it didn't seem too . . . well . . . forward. I mean . . . we know each other . . . pretty well, and my brother will be watching—I mean, he'll be joining us."

He laughed and the sound was deep and throaty. He pulled back the chair while the Harvey waitress filled their glasses with ice water. Rainy felt rather silly. Her words seemed all jumbled, and while they made perfect sense in her head, they didn't seem so accurate when they came out of her mouth.

"Would you like to order now?" the Harvey Girl questioned.

"My brother should be joining us shortly," Rainy indicated. "But I'd very much like to go ahead and start with some tea."

"That sounds good to me," Duncan replied.

The waitress disappeared, leaving Rainy feeling rather uncomfortable in the silence. She'd long admired this man, but how could she make that clear without sounding like one of Sonny's young admirers?

"Oh, there you are," Sonny suddenly said, coming from behind her. "I can't stay. I need to help a friend of mine get his car running. Do you mind?" He looked from Rainy to Duncan.

Rainy swallowed hard. When she'd thought Sonny would be a part of their company, she hadn't felt quite so awkward. "You still have to eat."

"I'll grab a sandwich at home," Sonny replied. He extended his hand to Duncan. "You're Mr. Hartford from the Indian museum, right?"

Duncan shook his hand. "Yes, but please call me Duncan."

"I've seen you at the museum, but since I generally wait with the touring car, I haven't had much of a

2

chance to get to know you." He glanced at his watch. "I'm sorry, Rainy. I really need to get over there."

Rainy nodded and unfolded her napkin to keep from having to meet Duncan's expression. "That's all right. You have a good night and I'll see you in the morning. Oh, and Mrs. Rivera is leaving you some sopapillas on the back of the stove."

"God bless that woman. She always seems to know just the right way to work herself into my heart." He gave a little wave and hurried out of the dining room.

Rainy could only think to smile and apologize. "I'm really sorry. If you feel it inappropriate to stay . . ."

"Not at all. We're both adults and we're obviously both hungry," he said with a hint of amusement in his voice.

"So is Sonny not staying?" the Harvey waitress asked as she passed their table.

"No, he had to tend to another matter," Rainy replied.

"We're ready to give you our orders if you like," Duncan added. He looked at Rainy with an expression that almost seemed sympathetic.

Maybe, she thought, *he understands how I feel. Wouldn't it be marvelous if a man could just look at the situation and comprehend the details of the matter without having to ask a lot of questions?* Rainy had often enjoyed the quiet companionship of her parents. They worked so well together and almost seemed to read each other's minds.

"And what will you have?"

Rainy broke free from her thoughts. She looked up

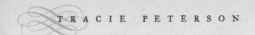

to find both the waitress and Duncan watching her quite intently. "I'll have the beef," she murmured without bothering to look at the menu.

The waitress wrote down their orders, then went off to tend her other tables. Rainy felt the discomfort of not knowing what to say. She knew Duncan Hartford from his work at the Indian Museum and Art Gallery, but she didn't know him all that well. What she did know was that she thought him one of the most handsome men she'd ever seen and she enjoyed his kind and gentle nature when he dealt with the demanding tour groups.

She hesitated, then cleared her throat with a delicate little cough. "I hope I didn't interrupt your plans." She glanced up to find him gazing at her.

"My plans for a quick meal alone were worth interrupting. Especially when I can share the company of one as pleasant as yourself." He toyed with his necktie and smiled.

Rainy felt her stomach do a flip and reached for her water. Perhaps a drink would help to settle her nerves. "I've long admired your Scottish brogue," she said out of desperation when the water didn't do anything to calm her. "My family is also from Scotland. My father was born in Edinburgh."

"Truly?" Duncan asked, his tone revealing his surprise. "I was actually born here in the United States, but my father is a Methodist minister, and the call took him to the land of his ancestors to preach. We moved shortly after my birth and lived there for twelve years. I've refined my speech a bit since returning. I suppose an absence of nearly twenty years should alter the cadence and intonations rather completely, but . . ." he said, leaning in closer, "I can roll my *r*'s in a right bonny fashion if I've a mind to do it." He emphasized his brogue, making Rainy laugh.

The Harvey Girl again appeared, bringing them a pot of English tea. Rainy smiled when she realized Duncan had ordered tea.

"Most American men prefer coffee," she said.

"Can't say I'm not given over to drinking a cup now and again," Duncan admitted. "But for supper, I prefer tea."

Rainy thought it all marvelous. "So your parents are Scottish?" She stirred a bit of cream into her tea and noticed Duncan did likewise.

"Actually we're all American-born. My father's father was a Scot who lived in the borderlands, and his mother was English. Their families strictly forbade them to see each other, but young love refused to listen." He smiled and leaned forward. "They eloped and eventually, because both families refused to accept the marriage, they came to America. My mother's people are Scottish through and through. None of those distasteful English skeletons to hide." He pulled back and drank his tea.

Rainy sipped from her cup for a moment. They had a great deal in common—more so than she might have imagined. "My ancestors are Scottish and English as well. My uncle Sean still lives on a farm outside of Edinburgh. My parents would like to go back for a visit someday. Of course, with the economy as it is now—banks failing and the gold standard crumbling—I think they're almost afraid to hope for such a thing."

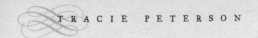

"It is a bleak time, to be sure."

The waitress arrived and in perfect Harvey fashion served their meals. "I must say, the breaded pork tenderloin is my favorite," she told Duncan as she fussed over him and made certain he had what he needed. But true to her job, she turned equal attention on Rainy as she placed the roasted loin of beef in front of her. "And this is my second favorite. I think the chef does it up better than just about any place along the Santa Fe line."

Rainy smiled. "It certainly looks good."

The Harvey Girl made certain they had everything they could possibly need, then left them to the privacy of their meal. Rainy looked up with uncertainty. "Would you like to say grace?"

Duncan threw her a look of admiration. "I would like it very much."

He murmured a prayer and blessed the food, leaving Rainy at peace for the first time in days. *How I've longed for God to send a man into my life who I could seriously consider as a husband. Not only is Duncan Hartford handsome in a rugged and understated way, but he holds to my faith and beliefs. Is he the one, God?* She looked at Duncan even as she poised the question in her mind. He sliced into his pork and extended her a piece.

"Would you like to try it?"

Rainy shook her head. "No, thank you. I've had it many times before. It's also one of my favorites."

They ate in silence for some time before Duncan braved the next round of questions. "So where do your parents live?"

"Albuquerque. My father works for the university

there," Rainy added. "I used to work with him." She immediately regretted the words. Oh, how she'd tried to bury that part of her life.

"Oh? What did you do there?"

Rainy tiptoed ever so cautiously through the memories of her scarred past. No sense waking sleeping dragons. "I worked with him in the history department. He's a professor of history, and I hold a master's degree in history with a special focus on the American Indians—particularly the Hopi, Navajo, Zuni, and Pueblo."

"How marvelous. You truly are the right woman to be leading the Detour trips."

"I love the Southwest," she admitted. She forced herself to sound calm and unflustered when all the while her heart was pounding like a racehorse's hooves in the final stretch.

"As do I. My focus of study is archaeology," he admitted.

"I have a bachelor's degree in archaeology," she said, hoping he'd see how much they had in common. Instead, it led him back to troublesome waters.

"Truly? Did you utilize your degree when you worked at the university?"

Rainy felt light-headed from his question. She wasn't about to get into the details of her past. *Anything but that,* she thought. How could she possibly hope to interest Duncan Hartford in becoming her husband if she had to share the memories she longed to forget? Yet, how could she hope to move toward marriage and not share those details?

No, she thought. *Until I can clear my name, no one else needs to know what happened.*

CHAPTER TWO

A week later Rainy was still contemplating her supper with Duncan when Sonny came into the boarding-house dining room and interrupted her breakfast. The look on his face prepared her for the blow of bad news, even before the words came out of his mouth. They had always been able to read each other like a book.

"You know how we planned to leave tomorrow for a week with Mom and Dad?" he questioned, plopping down in the chair opposite her. "Well, our vacation has been canceled."

She had already started to eat a hearty breakfast of scrambled eggs, potatoes, and ham, and the news didn't set well with her stomach. "What do you mean it's been canceled? We requested that time off months ago. Surely it's just a mistake."

"No mistake," Sonny said, reaching for the coffee-pot.

"Good morning, Sonny," Mrs. Rivera said, coming into the room with a bowl of scrambled eggs. "Are you ready for breakfast?"

"You bet I am," he replied. "I need about a gallon of coffee, then I'll take four eggs over easy, one of those thick ham steaks, and toast." He grinned up at her and winked as she placed the bowl on the table. "That ought to get me started. I'll let you know where we go from there."

She shook her head. "I don't know where you put all that food. You're just a beanpole, and yet you eat like my uncle Gordo."

"Ah, now," Sonny said, lifting her hand to his lips, "it's just that your cooking is the best I've had, except for my mother's. If you were twenty years younger, I think I'd propose." He kissed her hand.

She giggled as if she were twenty years younger. Pulling her hand away almost reluctantly, she picked up Sonny's plate and headed to the kitchen, still chuckling to herself.

"You are such a flirt," Rainy declared. "I don't know what Mother would say if she saw you."

"She'd say I take after Dad."

Rainy laughed. "No doubt. Now explain what's going on with our vacation time."

Sonny took a long drink of coffee, then replied, "There's been a special request for our Grand Canyon trip."

"But that trip lasts over five days—and I thought that with the economy failing they were going to scale it back or eliminate it altogether."

Sonny nodded. "Well, apparently these are friends of the governor—and of the Harvey Company. It's a special group of folks who sound like they're used to getting whatever they want. Money is no object."

"Well, it must be nice," Rainy replied, pushing her eggs around. "Still, I don't know why we have to lead the tour."

"Because we were asked for—by name. We have quite a reputation for quality tours, don't ya know. They get Sonny and Rainy weather with us." He grinned at the long-standing joke. Early on, upon hearing Rainy's given name, their uncle dubbed her twin, Gabe, "Sonny." He said it didn't seem fitting to have one without the other. The nickname stuck.

"When do they want to head out?" Rainy asked.

"Tomorrow afternoon. So at least you'll get to sleep late." He grinned at his sister and then transferred the smile to Mrs. Rivera as she placed his food in front of him. "Thank you! I thought I might well waste away to nothing but teeth and bones."

"And ego," muttered Rainy under her breath.

Mrs. Rivera fawned over Sonny for another minute or two, then made certain Rainy had what she needed before moving on to the other couriers and drivers.

Rainy tried not to resent the intrusion of the Detour company on her plans. She loved what she did as it related to educating the public about the various Indian cultures and about the great American Southwest. But she didn't love the whining dudes who complained about everything—from how hot it was to the color of the touring car. She didn't love the flirtatious men who seemed to think she was just one more item on the Harvey restaurant menu. And she didn't like being told her plans had to go by the wayside because some rich friend of the governor wanted to take a vacation.

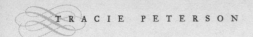

"Why didn't you just tell Sam we couldn't do it?" she asked her brother. "You could have just told him no."

Sonny tried to speak around a mouthful of toast. "I did."

Rainy waited for him to swallow before continuing. "Why didn't he reassign it?"

"He promised us two weeks off when we finished this round," Sonny said, seeming rather proud of this fact, as if he'd somehow negotiated the extra time.

"Two weeks, eh?" Rainy frowned. "You don't suppose they're cutting back even more on their trips, do you? Maybe he made the offer because he isn't going to need us much longer."

Sonny shrugged. "I can't say that it would break my heart. Sure, it's a good job with steady pay, and I'm not scoffing at that in this day and age to be sure. Still . . ." He seemed to be considering something.

Rainy waited a moment, expecting him to pick the conversation back up, but when he didn't she jumped back in.

"So we do this tour and then take two weeks off?" She sighed as Sonny nodded. "I suppose I can wait another week. Still, I was really looking forward to sleeping in my own bed."

"Well, you can tomorrow night. The tour stays over in Albuquerque and we aren't required to sleep at the hotel. We'll just go home and explain the mess to Mom and Dad and enjoy at least a short time with them."

"I suppose you're right," Rainy said, glancing at her watch. "You do realize we're supposed to take that group of older ladies around Santa Fe in fifteen minutes?"

Sonny nodded and started shoveling the food in faster than ever. Rainy gazed at the ceiling and sighed. If they could only see her brother in this, his most natural state, she seriously doubted that many women would fall all over themselves to sit beside him.

The officials seated in front of Duncan Hartford seemed more than a little on the serious side. The man from the Office of Indian Affairs, a Mr. Richland, seemed especially stern with his beady-eyed gaze boring holes in Duncan as though he were keeping the truth from them.

Duncan returned the man's gaze and said, "I assure you, this theft of Indian artifacts is the first problem I've heard of. We've had no trouble here at the museum."

"All of the thefts have occurred on Indian property. Reservation land," the agent told him. "We're hoping you might help us put a stop to it."

"Why me?" Duncan asked. He leaned back in his leather chair and faced the man with what he hoped was his own equally serious expression.

"You are very knowledgeable about Indian artifacts and archaeology. You also know the area. Your background has proven you to be trustworthy."

Duncan questioned, "You had me checked out?" The idea irritated him to no end. "Why would you do that?"

Richland seemed quite exasperated with Duncan's

inquiries. "Because we had to know to whom we could entrust this job. We didn't want to introduce someone from our bureau because their arrival would draw undue attention to them. You, however, are already known in the area, and if you were to suddenly step into the scene, no one would be the wiser."

Duncan further braved the man's ire. "Step into what scene?"

Richland exchanged a glance with his companions. "We're afraid someone is coming onto the reservations, perhaps under the guise of the Detours, and using the tourists to cover up their jobs."

"What do I have to do with that?" Duncan questioned. "I'm not an employee of the company."

"Maybe not yet," Richland replied, "but we've made arrangements for you to become just that. We have our eye on two different teams. One is the team of," the man paused to look at his notes, "a Jeremiah Sotherby and Tamela Yates, and the other is a Rainy and Sonny Gordon. They're sister and brother."

"I know the Gordons," Duncan said thoughtfully. "Not well, but certainly better than the other couple. Tell me though, why have you singled it down to these two teams?"

At this, another man, an agent of some other federal bureau, leaned forward. "The artifacts have only gone missing after one or both of these groups have passed through the area involved. We want to put a man in with each group. Since you know these Gordon folks, we'll arrange for you to be brought in as a driver-in-training. They should be quite comfortable with your presence and would not change their plans, if they are the ones who are stealing the pieces."

Duncan considered the man's comments while the third man, a representative of the Harvey Company and good friend of Duncan's parents, who lived north in Taos, leaned forward. "Duncan, it would mean a lot to me personally if you would help in this matter. I know I can trust you not to get caught up in whatever theft ring is being run. I don't want to have this turn into an even bigger affair than it's already become. This could be bad news for the Harvey Company and the Hunter Clarkson Company. I needn't tell you that times are hard enough without additional scandal. With Major Clarkson having just agreed to purchase the Detours, it wouldn't look good to have this kind of thing go public. Perhaps Clarkson would even attempt to back out of the arrangement."

"I can understand your concern, Mr. Welch," Duncan said, toying with the cuff of his suit coat. "I suppose I could give it a try. It's not like I'm trained as a detective, however."

"But of course you are," Welch said, grinning. "You're an archaeologist. You're trained to go into a situation and ferret out the truth."

Duncan laughed. "I dig in the dirt for bits and pieces of past civilizations. That hardly makes me capable of uncovering something like this."

Welch sobered. "Duncan, it's all we have. I don't want the newspapers getting wind of this, and right now we're barely keeping it out of their hands. This could ruin us. If tourists think there is a threat of danger, they'll stop coming. Robbery is a strong personal threat. If they see the Indians being robbed, they'll figure themselves to be next. I remember many years ago when there was concern about the possibility of a jewelry thief in the midst of the staff at the Alvarado Hotel in Albuquerque. It caused all kinds of panic, and dudes requested we place them in other hotels. Nothing ever came of that rumor, but we still lost money. Now with this being an actual problem . . . can you imagine what might happen? Why, it could very well prompt the tourists to stay home altogether for fear of a widespread ring of thievery."

"So, what will I be required to do?"

"Watch the Gordons and record any suspicious activity," Richland said. "Keep an eye on everything they do. The stolen pieces have been small enough to hide in large suitcases or trunks. If you have passengers with exceptionally large baggage, you might find a way to check the contents."

"How am I supposed to do that? No one is going to want me going through their things."

Richland stared at him with a cold indifference. "I don't care how you do your job; just do it. We need to put an end to this for the sake of everyone involved."

Duncan could see the truth of it and turned to his family's friend. "I'll do it as a favor to *you,* Mr. Welch. When do you need me to start?"

"Tomorrow. We've already arranged it with your boss here at the museum. The Gordons have been hired for a five-day tour that ends at the Grand Canyon. Unless another group wishes to take the same trip in reverse, you'll board the train at the canyon and return here. The Gordons are then scheduled for a two-week vacation after that. If additional artifacts and pieces turn up missing during this trip, but then suddenly nothing goes missing in the two weeks that follow, we'll know we probably have our people."

"You shouldn't jump to any conclusions," Duncan said quietly. He couldn't imagine the beautiful red-headed Rainy stealing anything from anyone. "We'll need to check the rosters and see if the tourists who are on the Detours are the same people who've taken trips before or if they're somehow connected to those who have."

"We've given some consideration to those lists," Welch admitted.

"Yes, this is a thorough federal investigation," the Indian Affairs agent added as if Duncan had somehow questioned their professionalism.

Not wishing to make an enemy of any official, Duncan nodded. "I'm sure it is. I'm just thinking out loud."

This seemed to calm the smaller man, while the other bureau official frowned. "Please keep quiet about this matter. We don't want to scare off our people. We want to catch them red-handed, in the act."

Duncan could see the man was almost pleased with the intensity of the moment. "I'll be careful," Duncan assured them with a casual shrug. "Just remember, you came to me. I didn't ask for this. I'm glad to do what I can to help preserve the Indian relics and ruins, but I'd much rather be doing it through archaeology instead of this cloak-and-dagger intrigue."

"I assure you, Mr. Hartford, this is hardly the stuff of dime novels. We have a serious matter on our hands," Mr. Richland said, his voice rising in pitch.

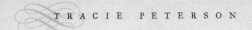

Mr. Welch calmed the situation immediately. "I've known the Hartfords for some time. The family is extremely responsible and law-abiding. Duncan will not let us down."

Welch looked to Duncan with an expression that seemed to plead for assurance on this matter. With little else to do, Duncan extended his hand and shook hands with each man. "I'll give this my very best effort."

After the men had left his office, Duncan allowed himself to daydream a bit. Rainy Gordon hadn't been far from his thoughts since she'd invited him to share her supper table the previous week. Vivacious and carefree, she seemed almost too free-spirited to be someone whom Duncan could give any serious consideration for a future relationship.

She had caught his attention on the very first day he'd met her, almost three years earlier. She'd just taken a job with the Harvey Company and was leading one of her tour groups. They'd come to the museum for a tour and an explanation of the artifacts and art pieces displayed there. When he encountered the group, he had been amused to hear Rainy denouncing the labeling of one of the ancient pieces.

Duncan had immediately made a close examination of the piece and found her to be absolutely right. The piece had clearly been mislabeled. His admiration for her had grown from that first moment. Unfortunately, he'd been too shy to approach her about spending time together. Rainy Gordon was so full of life—she moved from person to person with an infectious smile and charm that seemed to suggest the interests of each person were her foremost concern.

"She would probably never be interested in me," Duncan muttered. "She'd never want to settle down to a life of digging in the dirt or traipsing after someone who did such a thing for a living."

He thought of her physical beauty. Her face seemed so delicately crafted—high smooth cheeks dotted here and there with a few freckles. Her fair skin seemed sunburned when he'd last seen her, but the freckles were endearing. Her eyes, such an icy pale blue, brought back memories of cold highland lakes in Scotland.

Duncan tried to remember every detail, filling in any missing piece with his imagination. He sighed. She was athletic and obviously in great condition or she would not be able to act as a tour guide. She was used to long spells of walking and climbing as she led tourists through various ruins and wilderness lands. Yet at the same time, she cleaned up to be a most fashionable and attractive young woman.

But now there was concern over whether Rainy was a part of this ugly matter regarding the stolen artifacts. Surely she and her brother were innocent of such things. After all, she appeared to be a good Christian woman. She had asked him to pray over their meal.

He pushed back his wavy black hair and sighed. "I suppose there is nothing for me to do but pray. Father always said, 'When in doubt—pray. When not in doubt—pray.' "

He looked to the open door where the officials had exited only moments ago. Tomorrow he'd find himself in the company of Miss Rainy Gordon. They'd

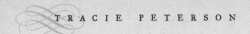

remain together for at least five days. Surely that would give him a very good idea as to the real quality of her character.

"It might also prove detrimental to my heart," he said, shaking his head.

CHAPTER THREE

*R*ainy rolled over in bed and yawned. Pulling the crisp white sheet over her head, she wanted nothing more than to go back to sleep. Disappointment crept in when she thought of how she might already have been at home sleeping in her own bed. It took great resolve to lower the sheet and open her eyes. She glanced at the clock and noted the lateness of the hour and moaned.

"Why do we have to do this tour now?" She had so longed to spend time with her mother and talk about the future. Her mother was the only one who would really understand her feelings—well, besides Sonny.

Sonny always seemed to understand, but at twenty-seven years old he thought himself perfectly lucky to have escaped matrimony, while at the same age, Rainy felt that life was passing her by. Her mother assured her that God had someone special for her—a man of quality and spiritual conviction.

"Sometimes," she could hear her mother say, *"he's right under your nose and you don't even realize it."*

"Well, if he's here," Rainy said, sitting up, "I sure wish God would make him more clear to me—and me to him."

After a long hot bath, Rainy sat drying her hair with a soft cotton towel. Still the thoughts of her future refused to be pushed aside. For so long she had planned to be married—to perhaps have children. She had buried herself in college studies for the early years of her adult life, but even there she thought that surely she would find a proper mate—a man who shared her passion and enthusiasm for history and archaeology. But the men who joined her in those classes only seemed intimidated by her grades and intelligence. The other women, few though they were, avoided Rainy as well. It soon became clear that Rainy made the others uncomfortable with her knowledge, and no matter how she tried to downplay her abilities and intellect, no one wanted to be her long-term friend.

"I can't help it if I'm smart," she said. Sighing, she tossed the towel aside and went to where her suitcase sat half packed.

Rainy picked up her stockings and stuffed them into a corner of the case. "I just want a husband, Lord—one who will respect me and love the things I love. Is that too much to ask for? Are compatibility and shared interests such unthinkable requirements?"

She often prayed like this. Chatting with God as though He reclined nearby in one of her chairs. Her mother had taught her early on that, while God was more than willing to listen to their petitions, people often avoided bringing the details of their lives to Him.

Rainy stuffed the rest of her things into the case and closed the lid. "I'm twenty-seven years old. I'll be twenty-eight in June, Lord. What good are my education and a good job when all I really want is a husband and family?"

But it wasn't all that she wanted. She'd had her chance at a couple of men who worked at the university. Of course, that had been before she'd been forced to resign from helping her father. The memory still left a bitter taste in her mouth.

Another glance at the clock reminded her that she'd have just enough time for lunch if she hurried. They were scheduled to leave at two and there was no arguing with those well-established timetables.

A knock and the opening of her door revealed Sonny. "I came for your luggage."

Even his good-natured smile did nothing to break Rainy from her mood. "I just finished packing. I was about to braid my hair and then get something to eat. Have you had lunch yet?"

Sonny nodded as he retrieved her suitcase. "I just finished. Mrs. Rivera suggested you were sleeping in, and I figured it was probably for the best. Go ahead and get something and meet me at the hotel." He paused at the door. "Oh, and there will be a surprise for you on this trip."

"The trip itself was a surprise," Rainy said as she set to braiding her still-damp hair.

"Well, this one will be a pleasant surprise."

"What is it?" Rainy asked, pausing to look up.

Sonny grinned. "I'm not telling. It wouldn't be a surprise then." He pulled the door closed behind him, whistling as he went on his way. Rainy knew he always whistled when he was pleased with himself. Frowning, she only wished she knew what it was that brought him such satisfaction. Sonny had been acting strange of late, and every time she thought to question him about his mood or actions, it seemed something happened to prevent her from learning the truth. If she didn't know better, she'd think he was in love.

"Strange," she murmured. "We've always been so close, and now I feel as though I'm losing touch with him."

Rainy finished her hair and pulled on her Indian jewelry. The Detour management encouraged the girls to buy and wear as much Indian jewelry as they could. This was in hopes of promoting the very same articles in the Harvey shops. The idea was that the tourists would see the beautiful objects and rush to buy their own copies. Sales were down in the Harvey shops, however, just as they were most everywhere. Rainy thought it almost silly to encourage the purchase of an expensive silver-and-turquoise necklace when the economy was so questionable. Of course, the only people booking passage on the Indian Detours were those who had plenty of money to splurge. The common person had no hope of making such expensive sojourns.

After a quick lunch, Rainy hurried to La Fonda to find Sonny. She saw him standing behind the touring car talking to Duncan Hartford. Her stomach did a flip-flop as Duncan looked up and smiled. He wore a dark blue suit and looked quite stylish with his necktie and felt fedora.

"Here's your surprise," Sonny announced. "Duncan is coming with us. He's a new driver-in-training."

Rainy frowned. "You're working for the Detours Company? Why didn't you say something last week when we had supper together?"

Duncan looked momentarily uncomfortable. "Well . . . that is . . . I didn't know then that I would be hired."

"You could have at least told me you were considering it. We could have talked about the various tours," Rainy replied, feeling as if Duncan had somehow betrayed their friendship. She knew it was silly, but she almost felt as though he'd lied to her.

"It kind of came to me out of the clear blue," Duncan admitted. "I wasn't sure I would ever do anything like this, to be honest."

"He's going to make a great driver," Sonny threw in. "He knows this area like the back of his hand. He's a little sketchier with Arizona and he hasn't done the Puye route, but I told him we could easily teach him the ropes. He'll be mastering the tours before he knows it."

Rainy knew there was nothing to be done but welcome Duncan. "We're glad to have you on board. We've had some real questionable recruits before, eh, Sonny?"

"That's to be sure. One man arrived all decked out in his cowboy attire not even knowing how to drive a car. I'll never know how he put that one over on the company, but he was out of here faster than a jackrabbit crossing the railroad tracks."

"Then there was the guy who kept eating all the picnic food," Rainy said with a teasing lilt to her voice. "You aren't likely to sneak around eating up all the food, are you?"

Duncan laughed and his expression revealed his genuine amusement. "I promise not to raid the picnic basket."

"Oh, and don't forget that one driver who when faced with a tire going flat called back to the shop and said, 'I have a tire going *pssst*. What do I do?' Let me tell you, he was out of a job mighty quick. You have to change a lot of tires in this business," Sonny said, shaking his head. "It's a good idea to get used to that fact up front."

"Well," Duncan began, "I not only can drive, but I can change a tire as well. I've lived in this state nearly twenty years, so I'm pretty familiar with New Mexico. My parents are pastoring a small church in Taos, but prior to that they had a church in Gallup, then one in Socorro, Magdalena, and even Las Vegas. I moved along with them until I decided to settle here in Santa Fe ten years ago."

"Sounds like you should have a good knowledge of the land, then," Rainy admitted. "Are you familiar with the height of various mountains? Can you explain various land formations and weather patterns?"

"Pretty much so. That was one of the reasons I got this job. There are a few routes Sonny was mentioning that I'm not that familiar with, but he promised to help me note the important issues on my map."

Sonny looked at his watch. "Rainy, you'd probably

better go gather our tourists. They're supposed to be at the front desk by one-forty-five. It's that time now."

Rainy realized he was right and turned on her heel to go. So Duncan Hartford was going to share the next five days of her life. Could this be God's way of answering her prayer? She tried not to get too excited. After all, she was forever trying to help God arrange things. Her mother had chided her for such attitudes in the past, but Rainy always thought it a simple matter of being tuned in to what God wanted you to know. *It's not like I'm trying to be God or take His place,* she thought. *I just want to help Him out and make sure I don't miss any subtle direction change He might send my way.*

Rainy spotted the family of five waiting near the front desk in the lobby. A mustached man wearing a tan linen suit and straw hat stood beside a woman of forty-something. The woman was fussing with one of the children, a teenage girl who seemed to be having trouble with her hair ribbon.

"Good afternoon. I'm Rainy Gordon. Are you the Van Patten family?"

The man nodded. "I am Mr. Van Patten. This is my wife and our three children, Gloria, Thomas, and Richard."

Rainy smiled and shook their hands. Immediately the boys, who looked to be about sixteen or seventeen, flooded her with attention.

"Are you the one who will lead our tour?" Thomas asked.

"Will we get to sit beside you in the car?" Richard threw in.

Rainy was used to the flirtatious nature of young

men. She smiled. "I am indeed your courier. I will guide you over the next five days."

"Will there be any other families joining our tour?" Mrs. Van Patten questioned.

"No, but there will be one more Detour employee aside from the driver. Mr. Hartford is training to drive for the company, so he'll be observing us and learning the routine. My brother, Sonny Gordon, will be our driver. He's very knowledgeable about the area, so feel free to ask either of us any questions you might have.

"Now, if you'll follow me, we'll be on our way. Your luggage has already been arranged for," she said as she noted Mrs. Van Patten looking behind them as they moved toward the door. "You will find it's already been loaded, in fact. The company strives to make this a most memorable and pleasant time for its guests. Part of that goal requires that we offer you the finest service available. Do not hesitate to tell us how we might make your journey more pleasant."

"My journey would be more pleasant if you sat by me in the car," Richard said, his dark eyes intense with interest.

Rainy laughed. "I'm sorry, but I have to sit up front with my brother. We can't very well lead from the back of the touring car." It was the only explanation she'd offer him, in spite of his hangdog expression.

Gloria took one look at Sonny and seemed to perk up. Then she noted Duncan and for a moment she seemed to weigh each candidate before returning her attention to Sonny. Rainy knew his rugged outfit was appealing to wealthy easterners. She wasn't sure where this family hailed from, but it was clear they were more city than country, and the cowboy attire was a novelty all its own.

"Is that our driver?" Gloria questioned Rainy as she pushed her brother aside.

"Yes. I'd like to introduce you all to Sonny Gordon. Sonny is my twin brother and the driver for our expedition." Rainy turned and reached out to touch Duncan's arm. "And this is Duncan Hartford. He's training to drive for the company, as I mentioned earlier." She turned back to Sonny and Duncan. "These are the Van Pattens. Mr. and Mrs. Van Patten and their children, Gloria, Thomas, and Richard."

Pleasantries were exchanged; then Rainy directed everyone to seats inside the touring car. Set up to hold as many as twelve, the car had more than enough room for the family to spread out and enjoy themselves. Six swiveling chairs allowed the dudes a full range of motion, while two additional bench seats were available for those who preferred a more fixed position.

The boys, disappointed to find they couldn't sit with Rainy, headed for the very back of the car while Gloria secured the swivel seat behind Sonny and beamed with pleasure when Duncan took the seat behind Rainy.

Although it was nearly April, snow could still pose a problem in the mountains. Generally the Detour trip to the Grand Canyon wasn't offered this early in the year for that very reason, and because of this the regular trip had to be altered slightly. They wouldn't be able to go high into the Sandia Mountains, but they would try to make up for it with a visit to a little native town called Placitas, which was hidden near the base of the Sandias.

Rainy began her speech about the trip and what was expected and not expected of the tourists. She explained the routine and how they should have their luggage ready prior to breakfast each morning.

"Sonny will see to it that your luggage gets on board each day. Tonight we will stay at the Alvarado Hotel in Albuquerque. The Alvarado is a marvelous hotel created in the manner of a Spanish mission. The thick stuccoed walls keep the rooms cool even in the hottest days of summer." She smiled and turned to face the tourists a bit more. "Of course, we're still experiencing very chilly nights, so you'll be pleased to know that they have steam heat to keep the rooms warm.

"While you're there, you'll be able to enjoy beautiful lawns and brick walkways. There are also marvelous verandas upon which you can sit and read. Of course, we'll only be there for the night."

———

Duncan endured the tour with great pleasure. He enjoyed listening as Rainy pointed out various land formations and told of the native peoples. He thought she seemed very much at home as a tour guide and wondered if she meant to make this a lifelong career.

When the group finally arrived at the Alvarado Hotel in Albuquerque, he watched with some amusement as the teenage boys told Rainy how much they'd learned and enjoyed her teaching. Rainy seemed genuinely touched, thanking them each for their special attention and feeding them tidbits of the things to come the following day.

Duncan didn't believe the boys to be half so interested in the trip and Rainy's teachings as they were with Rainy herself.

"So what are your plans for the night?" Sonny asked Duncan.

"I suppose the same as yours. Eat supper and get some rest."

"We're heading over to our parents' house after we get unloaded here. If you'd like to come with us for supper, you'd be more than welcome, and I can bring you back here for the night. We usually just sleep at home."

Duncan considered the situation for a moment. "I wouldn't want to intrude."

"It wouldn't be an intrusion at all. Our mother is a wonderful cook and always makes plenty. She extends an open invitation to our friends and co-workers, so you wouldn't be out of place at all."

Duncan knew it would be of far more comfort to join the Gordons for a home-cooked meal than to eat alone in the hotel. "I'd like very much to join you," he finally replied. If nothing else, he told himself, he'd have a great meal and be able to see Rainy in a more intimate setting. Surely if there were any strange or underhanded deeds going on between the brother and sister, they'd be more inclined to let down their guard at home.

Later that evening, Duncan pushed away from the Gordon table with a groan. "I think I overdid it," he told Rainy's mother, Edrea. She was an older version

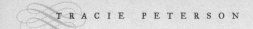

of her daughter, with a winning smile and crystal blue eyes. "It's just that it's been a while since I've been home. I miss my mother's cooking very much."

"I'm glad you enjoyed yourself," Mrs. Gordon replied. "Are you sure now that you won't have another piece of peach pie?"

"I'd surely burst if I did," Duncan replied. He watched Rainy move quickly to help her mother clear the table. The meal had been incredible, just as Sonny promised, and the company had been delightful.

Sonny yawned and stretched. "Duncan, I hate to rush you off, but if you're ready, I'll take you back to the hotel. I'm just about to drop from exhaustion."

"You're welcome to stay here with us, Mr. Hartford," Edrea Gordon said as she picked up an empty bowl.

"That you are," Raymond Gordon added.

Duncan thought for a moment about accepting, then shook his head. If he seemed too eager to stay, Rainy and Sonny might very well become suspicious. "I thank you for the invitation, but I think I should go back to the hotel. After all, my things are there and the company has already arranged a room for me." He got to his feet and noticed that Rainy had failed to return from the kitchen. He hated to leave without saying good-bye, but he didn't want to make a scene.

"I'll be out in the car," Sonny told him.

Mrs. Gordon went to Duncan as Sonny left the room. "It's always good to meet new friends. Please know you're welcome to join us anytime. Raymond would agree with me."

"Because I know better than to argue with her."

His Scottish brogue hung thick in the air. Duncan relished the sound with a bit of homesickness for the land of his childhood. "Now, if you'll excuse me," Mr. Gordon continued, "I need another cup of coffee and I see Rainy has already moved it to the kitchen."

"Good night, Mr. Gordon. I truly appreciate the meal."

"As Edrea said, you're welcome anytime." Raymond Gordon headed off in the direction of the kitchen.

"Oh, dear," Edrea suddenly said. "Your jacket is in the other room. Why don't you go tell Rainy good-bye and I'll fetch it for you."

Duncan nodded, happy for the excuse to see Rainy. He walked toward the kitchen door and paused as he overheard Rainy say something to her father. Duncan glanced over his shoulder to make certain Edrea had gone. Seeing that the room was empty, he delayed his entrance long enough to eavesdrop.

"They'll never believe me. No matter what I do. No one cares what really happened or why."

"Now, daughter, God is with you. We'll be finding a way."

"But it's been three years," Rainy argued. "I don't want to take this guilt with me the rest of my life."

"I know, darling. I know."

Duncan knew he couldn't wait any longer. He pushed open the door and peeked inside. "I just wanted to tell Rainy good-bye." He smiled at the surprised woman. "Your mother told me to and I didn't want to appear the disobedient one."

Rainy smiled at this. "It's for the best. Mother

would never brook any nonsense. I'll see you in the morning. If you've never slept at the Alvarado, then you're in for a treat."

Duncan nodded and headed back through the dining room just as Edrea brought his jacket. "I hope to see more of you, Mr. Hartford."

"I hope you will too."

Duncan pulled on the jacket and made his way to the car. Sonny stood outside, leaning against the driver's door, staring up into the night skies.

"Caught you daydreaming," Duncan teased.

Sonny laughed. "That isn't hard to do." He jumped into the driver's seat and started the car while Duncan took the seat Rainy had used all day.

"So what were you thinking about just then?" Duncan asked, knowing he was being more personal than their brief time together allowed for.

Sonny Gordon didn't seem to mind. "Oh, I guess my mind was in faraway lands. I have some interest in Alaska. Sometimes I contemplate taking a trip north."

"Sounds fascinating," Duncan admitted. "I hope you'll get a chance for it."

"I hope so too," Sonny said, maneuvering the car toward town.

Duncan thought of what he'd overheard Rainy saying, wishing fervently that he had the right to ask what she meant. He supposed it would just have to wait. Perhaps toward the end of the trip he and the Gordons would be much closer and then Rainy wouldn't mind such an intimate question.

CHAPTER FOUR

S onny finished securing the last of the Van Pattens'
ten pieces of luggage in and on the touring car. Mrs.
Van Patten had been particularly difficult that morning, haranguing Sonny about the care of her
matched pieces.

"This is an exceptionally expensive collection of
leather luggage," she told Sonny. "See to it that you
do not allow it to be scratched."

Sonny had smiled, poured on the charm, and
assured her that he was used to handling such pieces.
Mrs. Van Patten looked down her nose at him in an
expression that suggested Sonny must surely be
mistaken . . . or lying.

Once she'd gone, Sonny's thoughts drifted to the
night before. He knew his sister enjoyed Duncan's
company. He also suspected that his sister would
probably love nothing better than to secure a more
permanent position in Duncan Hartford's life.

If I could manage to get the two of them together, Sonny
mused, *I wouldn't feel so bad about my own plans.* And
his plans were extensive. He had just received word

from two college chums who had teamed up for a government exploration trip to Alaska. The government was assessing the area to discover its potential for farming and relocating poverty-stricken families. All very new ideas, his friends assured him, but ones that held great promise—especially as drought seemed to be gripping various areas of the country. His friends droned on about the possibilities as if they needed to sell Sonny on the idea. Then they finally mentioned needing a third member for their team, a geologist, and wanted to know if he was interested.

Interested didn't begin to describe Sonny's feelings on the matter. This venture would fulfill a lifelong dream of his. Geology was a passion to him. He could only imagine the thrill of exploring the frozen north. Now his only problem was how to break the news to Rainy. Sonny knew she depended on him for companionship on the tours. She had said more than once that she might never have taken the job with the Detours if Sonny hadn't been hired on as her driver. Now his plan was to resign his position by the end of summer, and he still hadn't found a way to break the news to his sister.

Thoughts of Duncan Hartford came to mind again. With Duncan training to drive the tours, Sonny wondered if he couldn't arrange it so that Duncan could take over his place with Rainy. He wondered even more seriously if something romantic might develop between the couple. He'd seen the way Rainy had looked at Duncan—heard her talk about him too. There was no denying her high regard for him.

If Rainy and Duncan would fall in love and marry,

Sonny thought, *my troubles would be over. Rainy wouldn't need me anymore. She'd have a whole new life, and her interests would lie with Duncan rather than me and Mom and Dad.*

He thought about this as he double-checked the Van Patten luggage one final time. Rainy certainly had expressed her interest in finding a husband and settling down, though Sonny knew she'd also love to be working in archaeology. Since they'd been young her heart's desire had been to work on great archaeological digs. She'd even thought for some time she might go abroad to the great pyramids of Egypt. The Middle Eastern countries were certain to be full of mystery and intrigue from the past.

Instead, he'd watched Rainy develop a deep love for the American Southwest. She had a passion for the desert and the Indians who lived there. He was amazed at the quick and easy manner in which she'd learned various Indian dialects. Furthermore, he knew she had grown to care deeply about the Indian people.

"The Van Pattens will be out shortly," Rainy called as she came from the hotel. "I left them to conclude their breakfast."

Sonny looked up and smiled. Rainy always brightened his day. They were as close as a brother and sister could be, and being twins, they felt they could very nearly read each other's minds. Given that, Sonny wondered if Rainy had any clue as to his desire to leave the Detour business. He was waiting for just the right time to tell her—praying that the timing would come neither too soon nor too late. She wouldn't be happy with him, for they always discussed major plans and changes with each other. He supposed they filled the void in each other's life where a spouse might have offered counsel. But this time he hadn't shared his plans, and he knew she'd be hurt.

"We need to head out as soon as possible if we're going to make Gallup by suppertime and still see everything in between," he replied.

Rainy straightened her serviceable brown skirt. "I know that. They were nearly finished. If they aren't out here in five minutes, I'll go get them."

"So, Rainy, I saw you eying Duncan Hartford. I think you like him," Sonny said, grinning from ear to ear.

Rainy shrugged. "He's a very nice man. Of course I like him."

"No, I mean you *like* him. As in, you're interested in him for more than friendship."

Rainy's head snapped up at this. She came to stand directly in front of him and lowered her voice considerably. "What makes you say that?"

"Rainy, don't forget I can read you better than most," Sonny replied, leaning casually against the glossy black frame of the car. "I know you want to marry and have a family, and Duncan Hartford has many of the qualities you're looking for."

"Oh, really? And how would you know what I'm looking for?" Rainy asked defensively.

Sonny laughed. "Maybe because I'm your twin brother, or maybe it's because we work together and spend a good deal of our time together, and maybe because you've told me about a million times."

Rainy gave him a sheepish smile at this. "I'm pretty bad, eh?"

"Not bad—just specific." He sobered a bit and took hold of her shoulders. "Look, sister of mine, I want you happy. I know you're putting your future to prayer, but like Mom would say, you have to be willing to leave it in God's hands in order for Him to be able to do anything with it."

"I know. But some things are harder than others to leave behind. I'm fast becoming an old maid. I don't want to spend the rest of my life regretting my earlier choices for school and an education. I don't want to come to the end of my life and find out I was wrong— maybe I can't balance pursuing my passion for archae- ology with the demands of a family."

"That's not going to happen. God has been the one guiding your life. I remember how hard you prayed about college—about when to go and when to stop. Remember how much that one professor of yours wanted you to go for your doctorate, but you said no because that's what you felt God leading you to do. Have you regretted that choice?"

Rainy shrugged and Sonny dropped his hold on her. "I can't say that I regret it because I'm confident it was the right thing at the time."

"Then trust that God has this issue under control. Duncan Hartford may well have come into our lives through the Detours in order for you to know his char- acter even better than before. You've known the man for three years, Rainy. You've seen him conduct the museum tours and have spoken to him on hundreds of occasions. He's always appeared respectable and upright—now maybe God's giving you the opportunity to spend your days with him on the tour so you'll know for sure whether or not his personality fits yours."

Rainy smiled. "And when did you figure this all out, little brother?"

"You're never going to let me live down the fact that I'm three minutes younger than you, are you?"

"Not when it serves my purpose so completely." She smiled.

"Well, it serves my purpose not to give you an answer," Sonny said, laughing. "I suggest you run ahead and get our guests. While you do that, I'll find out what's happened to Duncan, and hopefully we can get on the road within the next few minutes."

Rainy went in search of her charges, realizing that Sonny had gotten out of telling her when he'd given time to plotting a romance between her and Duncan. She had to admit he made a good point. She had prayed long and hard about all of the details regarding a man to love and spend her life with. And Duncan had been a constant in her life for the past three years. He was there for the tours she brought to the museum. He was often in La Fonda for his meals, and when she managed to be in town on Sunday, she saw him at the little community church not far from the Plaza. And now he was going to be on their trip to the Grand Canyon. Maybe God would—

Running into the rock-hard wall of another human being caused all thoughts to fly out of Rainy's mind. She felt herself falling backward. As she fought to regain her balance, she looked up to catch Duncan's stunned expression change to one of intense concern. He reached out to take hold of her but missed her by inches. Rainy smacked down hard on her backside.

"Making friends with the floor?" he questioned good-naturedly. The look of amusement changed to concern, however, as Rainy frowned. "Are you all right? I tried to catch you but . . ."

"I'm fine," Rainy said, trying to gracefully get to her feet. He reached down to help her up and kept his hold on her while she steadied herself. She rubbed her lower back.

"I'm so sorry." He gently rubbed her upper arms.

Rainy momentarily lost herself in his dark brown eyes, his tenderness her undoing. *Could he be the one, Lord? Could he be the man I'm to spend the rest of my life with?*

"It was all my fault," she said, finally finding her voice. "I wasn't watching where I was going. I was a bit preoccupied." Rainy's words sounded foreign in her ears. *What's wrong with me? I'm acting so silly.* She straightened and pulled away. With a much more serious tone, she added, "Sonny's looking for you. He's out at the car. I need to get the guests out there as well."

Duncan's manner became quite formal, almost as if she'd somehow offended him. "Very well. Mind your step."

He moved around her with little fanfare and walked toward the door. Rainy watched him momentarily. *Oh, Father, please show me what to do. Help me to be patient, because I'm not at all sure I have it within myself to keep from charging ahead.*

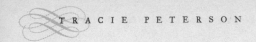

"Miss Gordon, I have my family rallied for the trip," Mr. Van Patten announced as he brought his entourage down the hall.

Rainy smiled. "I was just coming to find you. Looks like we'll have a beautiful day for travel. The temperature has warmed quite nicely but shouldn't get too hot. That's the luxury of traveling this time of year."

"I cannot bear the heat," Mrs. Van Patten said, her chin raised ever so slightly.

Rainy could tell the woman would most likely be a problem guest. Guests came in three varieties. Accommodating—those with easygoing personalities, who rolled with the punches and unexpected catastrophes. Confused—those who were too old, too young, or just too misplaced to enjoy themselves fully. And the problem guests—those who found fault with everything from the food to the transportation to the color of the tour guide's hair. Rainy actually had one woman refuse to take a tour with the Gordons because they had red hair and that was an omen of bad luck for her.

Rainy tried to push aside her fears of Mrs. Van Patten being just such a guest. "I shouldn't imagine it will be a problem this time of year, Mrs. Van Patten."

"And what will you do if it is hot? How will you see to our needs?"

Rainy smiled. "I shall pray for cooler temperatures and find you a fan. But right now we need to be on our way. We have a schedule to keep."

She left without waiting to hear what Mrs. Van Patten might have to say. Sometimes Rainy had a hard time keeping her sarcasm to herself. Again she sent up a petition to God for patience, only this time it was for an entirely different reason.

Along the route of their tour, Rainy told them of rock formations and rivers, of vegetation and wildlife. She pointed out a roadrunner that seemed rather intimidated by the huge touring car.

"I'm sure he's afraid we might eat him," Rainy said, laughing. She glanced at her watch. "We'll be arriving at the San Augustine Church in Isleta in about fifteen minutes. Before we get there, and because the stop is a very short one, I thought I'd give you the history of the church. Something quite unusual has taken place there, and for over one hundred years everyone from officials in Rome to the president of the United States has been rather stumped as to why these things have happened."

With that prelude into the mystery of her story, Rainy realized she had the unwavering attention of everyone in the car, with the exceptions of Sonny and Mrs. Van Patten.

"It is said," Rainy continued, "that a Franciscan friar named Brother Juan Padilla was murdered by a hostile Pueblo Indian in 1756. Now, the Pueblos are generally a very peaceful people, as they were then. The killing took place because the murderer was afraid Brother Juan might betray the Pueblos to the Spanish.

"The Pueblos were terrified at what would happen if the killing were discovered. After all, Brother Juan had been with them for some time and his healing abilities had proven to the Pueblos that he must serve a powerful god. Knowing he was of Spanish descent, they feared Brother Juan's powerful god would bring the Spanish to destroy them." Rainy loved the way the boys seemed to be perched on the edge of their seat, waiting for the rest of the story. She glanced at Duncan and saw that he, too, seemed to be thoroughly enjoying himself. He gave her a smile that warmed Rainy to the bottom of her toes.

"Ah . . . where . . . was I?" Rainy stammered, trying to regain her composure. "Oh yes. The Pueblos, fearing retribution, arranged for four of their swiftest runners to take the body of the friar to Isleta, which was nearly seventy miles to the east. There, they were to bury the friar and return.

"The runners were in a very big hurry, terrified that they'd get caught with the body and the Spanish would find out what had happened. When they arrived at Isleta, they buried the friar without any form of ceremony. They dug a six-foot-deep grave in the dirt floor of the church and buried the friar in front of the altar. They stomped down the ground so that it looked as though it had never been disturbed and fled. Their deception worked, and the tribe bore no retribution for the death of the friar.

"Fifteen years later, a caretaker noticed that there was a bulge in the floor, directly in front of the altar. He thought nothing of it, but over the years it grew and gradually began to resemble the outline of a man's body. The ground cracked and the people tried to fill it with dirt, but nothing seemed to work. Twenty years to the day after the friar's death, the people of the church came in one day to find the body of the friar lying on the ground. He looked newly dead, and his skin was soft and pliable. His robes had rotted, so they reclothed him and reburied him."

"Oh, that's awful. That poor man," Gloria Van Patten gasped. "What a horrible thing to happen."

"That wasn't the worst of it," Rainy stated. She lowered her voice for effect. The boys moved from the back of the touring car and took a seat on the midway bench. "Twenty years later the same thing happened. The friar again resurfaced and again he seemed just as freshly dead as when he'd been buried nearly forty years earlier."

"What a horrible story!" Mrs. Van Patten exclaimed.

"There's no possible way that could happen," Mr. Van Patten stated, as though Rainy had insulted his intelligence. He dutifully patted his wife's hand as if to calm her. Rainy only smiled.

"That's what many people said. So when the people grew fearful and tired of this, and after the padre had resurfaced a few more times, they called on the authorities of the church. The padre was given a proper burial with church rites in 1895. So far," she said with a smile, "Father Juan has stayed buried. But every time I bring a tour group here, I always wonder if this will be the year Father Juan reappears."

"Oh, I hope so," Thomas declared. "This is much more fun than I thought it was going to be."

"I want to be the first one in the church," Richard said, nudging his brother. "I'm the oldest and I should have the first look."

Rainy couldn't help but chuckle at their sudden interest. How disappointed they would be when they found two-inch planks on the floor as an added incentive to keep Friar Juan in the ground.

Sonny pulled up to the church and before Rainy could say another word, the Van Patten boys hurried from the car. Their parents and Gloria followed at a slower, almost apprehensive pace. Mrs. Van Patten seemed quite pale, in fact, almost as if she had begun to worry about what they'd find.

"That was a great bit of storytelling," Duncan said as Rainy climbed from the car.

She straightened her skirt before meeting his gaze. "It's a fascinating story, isn't it? I've always wondered, though. If the Pueblos said nothing about the death, then who learned the truth of what happened to the poor friar?"

Duncan laughed. "You have a strong investigative nature. You'd make a good archaeologist or anthropologist."

"You're kind to say so. I can't imagine anything I'd enjoy more. In fact—"

A girl's scream filled the air, causing Duncan and Rainy to exchange a surprised look before bolting at full speed to the open door of the church.

Rainy couldn't imagine what had happened. She came up behind Mr. and Mrs. Van Patten to find Gloria clinging to her mother. Mrs. Van Patten's face was now a greenish gray, and her tight-lipped expression suggested a true tragedy had befallen the party.

Peering inside the church, almost sure she'd find the poor old friar had resurfaced once again, Rainy found instead that Thomas Van Patten had stretched himself out in front of the altar, hands crossed over his chest, eyes closed. Richard stood to the side laughing hysterically.

"Oh, we scared her good, Thomas," Richard called. "You can get up now." Thomas popped up, giggling.

Rainy shook her head while Mr. Van Patten launched into a reprimand of his sons. Leaving the scene to afford the family some privacy, Rainy looked up to find Duncan barely containing his mirth.

"Oh, so you think that was funny too?"

"Indeed. It was perfect." He leaned toward her. "Did you see the look on Mrs. Van Patten's face? I doubt she'll be any more trouble for the rest of the day."

"If only it were that easy," Rainy replied. "I'm sure we'll hear an earful before the day is done. Remember, we still have hours to go before we reach Gallup."

CHAPTER FIVE

Day three found the tour in the land of the Navajo. Rainy explained how the Navajo people had taken the dry, unyielding land and created life from it. They were able to raise crops by using ingenious manners of irrigation and raised sheep for the wool and meat they could provide. The Navajo jewelry was especially pleasing to Mrs. Van Patten. She bought several pieces before retiring for the night.

Day four brought the group into Hopi land. Here, Rainy's good friends Istaqa and his wife, Una, were happy to see her and happy to share their native stories with the tourists. Istaqa and his wife had actually allowed Rainy to live with them for several months one summer. She taught them better English, including how to read, while they taught her Hopi and lessons of their people.

Rainy had the highest admiration for both the Hopi and the Navajo. The Hopi, too, had taken the desert land and made it into fertile farms. Their ability to dry farm was a marvel that was getting more than a little attention as drought had begun to cause problems in various areas of the country. Perhaps the whites would learn that the Indian nations had something to teach them after all.

They spent the night in Tuba City, an old Mormon settlement that now acted as the western headquarters for the Navajo reservation. Their accommodations were at the Trading Post, which offered comfortable rooms and good food, although both were far simpler than seemed to please the Van Pattens. Rainy was more than a little excited to know this would be her last night of responsibility for the group. Falling asleep that night, she thought of Duncan and the fact that, while they'd been together throughout most of the trip, they'd spent very little time in private conversation. Duncan always seemed preoccupied or busy with questions for Sonny, while the Van Pattens consumed her time with everything from Mrs. Van Patten's concern about Indians growing suddenly hostile and attacking to the boys' pranks.

Finally the morning of the fifth day arrived, and Rainy knew that by evening she'd be able to eat and relax at the Harvey Hotel in Williams and be free of the Van Pattens. That promise was enough to help her endure Gloria's whining and Richard's covert love notes. At least the love notes had offered Sonny, Duncan, and Rainy a bit of amusement. The previous night Richard had accidentally slipped his note under Sonny and Duncan's door instead of Rainy's. Sonny thought the note had come from the Trading Post management and had opened it to read: *My heart is ever yours. You are the joy of all I see. Please know that I will adore you until my dying day. RVP*

Sonny had shown Duncan the note, and knowing Rainy had received similar notes from Richard Van Patten, they risked waking her to show her the missive. Rainy had chided them for being such ninnies but laughed nevertheless. She thought the boy was only toying with her, otherwise she might not have laughed. She had no desire to crush the romantic spirit of the young man. Richard, however, seemed not at all sincere in his attitude but rather appeared to be playing a game with his brother as to who could garner more of Rainy's attention.

Day five passed quickly with tours of the Painted Desert, the suspension bridge across the Little Colorado River, and the Petrified Forest. Soon they were approaching Williams, where the Van Pattens would catch the train for the Grand Canyon. Rainy had never been happier to see the familiar sights of the little town. Exhausted from the marathon trip, she sighed with relief as Sonny pulled up to the train station.

"This is the end of our journey," she announced. "I know from your itinerary that you have a week's stay planned at the Grand Canyon. I think you'll be impressed with El Tovar's service and décor. The hotel has long been admired for its beauty and quality service."

"Anything would be better than what we just endured on this trip," Mrs. Van Patten muttered.

"Now, dear, in all honesty, we knew this trip was more strenuous and less luxurious than most. We all agreed it would be fun to give it a go." Mr. Van Patten seemed to stress the latter with a stern look at his wife.

She nodded and said nothing more, and Rainy

took this as her cue to exit. "I'll go inside and make sure your reservations are in order." With that, she bid the Van Pattens farewell.

───────

Rainy had just finished supper and was enjoying a soothing cup of coffee when Sonny and Duncan joined her. "Where have you two been? I tried to wait to eat but got too hungry. I joined some of the other Harvey staff and ate without you."

"You know how this was supposed to be a dead-end trip?" Sonny asked. "Leave the car here, catch the train home, and so forth?"

"Yes," Rainy said, drawing the word out. "What's happened?"

Duncan took the chair opposite her, while Sonny took the one beside her and whispered, "We've been hired to do the trip in reverse."

Rainy shook her head. "But I'm tired. I don't feel like doing the trip in reverse."

"I think it will be good for all of us. I'm going to let Duncan drive part of the trip and get some practice in."

Duncan looked rather surprised at Sonny's announcement. "I beg your pardon?"

Sonny shrugged. "Everybody has to jump in sooner or later. You might as well do it now. Rainy's a great guide. She can help keep you up and running, and I'll be sleeping right behind you," he said with a grin.

"Not if I can put some pesky four-year-old in the seat beside you," Rainy said, letting her frustration get the best of her. "Or better yet, some teenage girl who thinks you are the most wonderful, most handsome man she's ever seen." She put her hands together under her chin and batted her eyelashes in imitation of the young women who fawned over her brother.

Sonny laughed and got to his feet. "You aren't that mean. Besides, it's not my fault we have to work our way back home. Just remember, we get two weeks to rest up. Look beyond the trip to the goal. Now, if you'll excuse me, I need to go down to the garage and make sure the car is in order for tomorrow."

Rainy watched him go and sighed. There was no sense trying to cover up her obvious disappointment.

"I was just going to take a walk," Duncan said softly. "Would you care to join me?"

Though rather disheartened at Sonny's news, Rainy decided to accept since she'd had so little time alone with Duncan. She smiled at him. "I probably can't stay out long, but yes, it sounds like a nice way to end the day."

Duncan came around and helped her up from her chair. "I found the trip quite fascinating. You have a real gift for dealing with the tourists."

"Sometimes I think I could trade it all," Rainy said, looking beyond Duncan to the street outside.

"But for what?"

Rainy continued walking, considering his question for a moment. "There's no easy answer to that question. There's a part of me that would walk away, without a second thought, for the right incentive." She thought of marriage or the chance to work with a company like the National Geographic Society. Her days at the university had put an end to that, however. Half the staff were members of the Society, and they knew very well why Rainy had left her position.

They walked down the stairs of the hotel and into the twilight of the Arizona skies. The temperature was much cooler than what they'd endured in the open desert lands. Rainy shivered, and before she knew it, Duncan had draped his coat around her shoulders.

"Thank you," she whispered. The golden glow of dying sun against a turquoise sky left her rather breathless and inspired. Or maybe it was just the smell of Duncan's cologne as she hugged his coat close. "I tend to forget that it gets much cooler here at times. I've even been here when there was snow on the ground." She fell silent, uncertain of what else to say.

"So what kind of incentive?" Duncan asked.

"What?" she asked. Though she knew he was referring to her earlier statement, she was hoping to stall for time to formulate an answer.

"What kind of incentive would cause you to leave the Detour business?"

She knew the answer but found it difficult to voice. "I know it might sound funny, but I've always wanted to settle down, maybe start a family."

"I wondered why you hadn't already married and done just that. I thought perhaps you didn't want to have children—or a husband."

Rainy tensed and looked to Duncan but instantly relaxed as she saw the warmth in his expression. He cared about her answer; she could see that much in his eyes. "No, it's not that. I went to school and the years just kind of slipped away. I thought I'd meet someone at school, but that never worked out."

"Why not?" Duncan asked, the breeze blowing strands of wavy black hair across his forehead.

Rainy stared at his hair momentarily. She wanted to reach up and push the tousled strands aside but instead turned back to face the narrow street, lest she give her heart away. "I seemed to intimidate the men in my classes," she finally answered. "I was a very strong student—I caught on quickly and studies were easy for me. They resented that. Especially when they added to it the fact that I was working in a field few women found of interest, much less excelled in."

Feeling uncomfortable, Rainy began to walk back toward the hotel. Duncan followed, easily coming up alongside her. "Some men are fools," he said.

Rainy looked at him, thinking perhaps he was saying more with his words than what was actually spoken. "Some women are too," she replied. Slipping from his coat, she handed it back. "I'd better go inside. I need a hot bath and a chance to get my clothes washed for the return trip. I'll see you tomorrow."

She hurried away from Duncan Hartford. Uncertainty dogged her heels. Why had she grown uncomfortable so quickly? What was it about Duncan's quiet manner that had put her so off guard?

———————

"Rainy!"

It was Sonny, and he was knocking on her door loudly enough to awaken the people in the rooms on either side of her.

"What?" she asked, opening the door.

"Are your bags ready?"

She yawned. As much as she'd tried to sleep and rest up for the day, it had been a fruitless effort. "They're ready. I just finished packing them. I washed my things out last night and had to wait until they were dry. I needed to iron out my skirt at the last minute." She motioned to the brown skirt that fell just below her knees.

Sonny looked at her hard, almost as if he were trying to figure out how to deliver some kind of horrible news. "What's wrong?" she asked. "Did I miss a spot?" She tried to twist and turn to better see her skirt.

"I need to tell you something, but you aren't going to like it."

She stilled in her actions and looked her brother in the eye. "I haven't liked much you've come to tell me these last few days."

Sonny nodded. "I understand that, but you're going to like this even less."

Rainy yawned again. "Just tell me, Sonny. You know it's the best way."

"The Driscolls are among our passengers today."

"Please tell me this is a bad joke," Rainy said, shaking her head. "You can't be serious."

"I am, I'm sorry to say, and Chester is traveling with his parents. If it's any consolation, we have a famous movie star traveling with us too. Phillip Vance. Remember? He's the one who starred in that western movie you liked so much last summer. Anyway, he's with his sister. She happens to be a writer who lives in Santa Fe."

"Why is this happening?" Rainy said, putting her

hands to her head. Chester Driscoll was one of those ill-fitting pieces of her past. A piece that she had tried to force into place, only to have it pop back up.

"I'm sorry, sis. If I could do the trip without you, I would."

"Maybe I could tell them I'm sick. Surely there's another courier around here," Rainy said, desperately trying to think of how she might get out of this situation.

"I don't know. I suppose you could check into it."

Rainy doubted there would be anyone who could take her place, however. Most of the other couriers were short-run girls. They wouldn't want to drive all the way to Santa Fe and spend five days out on the road.

"No, just take my bag," Rainy said in resignation. "I'll be down shortly. I still can't believe this is happening." Sonny nodded, seeming to realize further conversation would be useless.

After Sonny had gone, Rainy sat on the edge of her bed and prayed. "Lord, I don't want to talk with those people. I don't want to be with them. I don't want to pretend to be friendly after the way they stabbed me in the back."

Rainy was momentarily taken back to Marshall Driscoll's office at the university. His position gave him a great deal of authority, and he'd had the final say on what happened to Rainy after valuable Indian artifacts were stolen and later found in her office. She could still picture the look on his face.

"If you leave quietly, the board has agreed not to press charges," Driscoll had told her.

"But I'm innocent. Someone placed those artifacts in my office. I didn't steal them." Rainy had protested her innocence for half an hour until finally Driscoll had to leave for another meeting and quickly dismissed her. He didn't care about the truth, and it was for this that Rainy faulted him.

"I'll need your answer by morning," he had stated without emotion or even the slightest hint of compassion.

Of course her answer had been to leave. She had no choice. To push the situation would have brought shame upon her family, and her father was a professor at the university. She couldn't allow him to bear any of the blame. Worse yet, Mr. Driscoll had suggested her father's position would be in jeopardy if this matter were brought to public attention.

So she left. Quietly. She left without a word to anyone—except Chester Driscoll. Chester had purported to be in love with Rainy, but all that changed when the artifacts were found in her office. He had come to say good-bye to her, promising that in time this would be behind them and they could start their love anew.

"I'm not in love with you, Chester. I have no desire to start anything—anew or otherwise," she had told him, even as she packed the bits and pieces of her life into a small box.

"Darling, you're just upset. Don't worry about this mess. No one really believes you stole those artifacts."

When she looked into his eyes, she suddenly knew the startling truth. Chester knew she hadn't stolen the artifacts. He knew it for a fact. His eyes betrayed the truth even as she stood there with tears flowing down her cheeks.

"What do you know about this, Chester?" she had asked angrily.

"I don't know what you're implying. I know nothing about the theft."

"Then how are you so certain of my innocence?"

He smiled. "That's easy. I know your character. I know you'd never do this thing."

"Then why didn't you tell that to the board?"

He'd had no answer, just mumbling about how no one would have taken seriously a man who was in love with the defendant.

"Why must I endure this man again, Lord?" Rainy now prayed, pushing the memories aside. "Why must I face his father and mother and the others? I've no desire to be their courier. I've no desire to make a pretense of enjoying their company for the sake of the Detours. Oh, God, please help me with this. This is so hard to deal with."

Thirty minutes later Rainy found herself face-to-face with the Driscolls. Mrs. Driscoll, a dour little woman, had not changed much in the three years since Rainy had last seen her. Marshall Driscoll had put on at least fifty pounds, however, and Chester looked quite sporty in his top-of-the-line single-breasted coat of brown check.

"Why, Rainy Gordon," he murmured, "you look simply marvelous. If I weren't a married man, I would definitely be in pursuit of rekindling our romance."

"We never had a romance," Rainy said, refusing to shake his hand. "I congratulate you on your marriage.

I understand you married Bethel Albright, the niece of my father's good friend Professor Albright."

"I should have known you'd keep track of me," Chester said with a hint of a smirk.

"Like I would any other snake," she murmured.

"I absolutely insist on being introduced to this marvelous young woman." The voice came from a dashing blond-haired man who came up to stand at Rainy's left side.

Chester laughed. "This is Rainy Gordon, an old love of mine. Rainy, this is Phillip Vance, famed legend of the silver screen."

Phillip smiled warmly and lifted Rainy's hand to his lips. "I'm positively charmed to meet you."

"It's nice to meet you, Mr. Vance," she said, barely keeping herself from adding that she'd never been a love of Chester Driscoll's. She allowed herself a moment to study the screen star's smooth jaw, straight nose, and startling eyes.

"I'm hoping you can help me," Phillip said, his voice honey smooth.

"I'm not sure I can," Rainy replied, "but I'll certainly do my best."

Phillip beamed her a smile. "I've come to the Desert Southwest to learn more about the Indians. If you're familiar at all with my work, you'll know that most of my films are westerns. I want to make them more realistic. I'm starring in a new film called *The Mystery of Navajo Gulch.* I'm hoping to see the real Navajo people—to learn about them and better understand them. I want the movie to be as accurate as possible because I'm putting some of my own money into the making of this project."

"How very noble of you," Rainy said, not feeling at all interested in his cause.

"You think me insincere?" He looked genuinely hurt and Rainy immediately regretted her reply.

She was grateful that Chester had lost interest and had now joined his mother. He was deep in an animated conversation that included all kinds of hand gestures. *Same old Chester,* Rainy thought. Turning back to Phillip, she drew a deep breath. "I'm sorry. I'm afraid I didn't sleep well last night, but that is still no reason to be harsh with the guests. Please accept my apology. I'll do what I can to help you."

Phillip immediately perked up. "Wonderful. Now, you must come and meet my sister, Jennetta. She lives in Santa Fe and is one of those madly tortured authors who sleeps all day and writes all night. Some day she'll be famous—but right now she's just grumpy."

Phillip immediately put her at ease and Rainy couldn't help but giggle at this reference. She'd met many of the writers who frequented Santa Fe's cafes and other gathering places. Artists and writers made up a growing number of people who had embraced Santa Fe as their undisclosed place of residence. The community was branded as positively inspiring for those of an artistic nature.

Phillip led Rainy to where his sister stood talking with Marshall Driscoll. "Jennetta, dear, this is our guide, Rainy Gordon. Miss Gordon, this is my sister, Jennetta Blythe." The woman looked mousy compared to Phillip's vibrant appearance. Plain brown hair had been bobbed short and she wore a gray wool skirt and jacket that allowed only a hint of a blue blouse to peek from the top.

"Will we be leaving soon?" Jennetta questioned in a tone that suggested boredom. The look she offered Rainy seconded this emotion.

"Yes," Rainy said, forcing a smile. "If you'll all make your way down to the car, we'll head out immediately."

"Marvelous," Phillip declared. "I can hardly wait to get to know you better."

"I thought you were here for the desert and Indians," Jennetta said, scowling at Rainy. "She doesn't appear to be either one."

Rainy immediately disliked the woman but put it aside. *Five days,* she told herself. *I only have to endure them for five days.*

CHAPTER SIX

Duncan immediately realized that the Driscolls and the Gordons shared some kind of past. Rainy particularly avoided the younger of the Driscoll men, while conducting herself in an overly formal manner with the elder Mr. Driscoll. Duncan couldn't help but wonder what secrets the past held. Mr. Driscoll seemed to hold Rainy in some kind of contempt, while Chester appeared to go out of his way to speak in intimate whispers with her whenever the situation presented itself. Chester had put his hand on Rainy's waist only to have her elbow him sharply. But it wasn't the action so much as the look she gave him that left Duncan little doubt as to her disdain. Her glare could have frozen water at noon in the middle of the desert.

They reversed the order of their trip, spending the first night in Tuba City. Duncan, as always, helped to unload the luggage and didn't see any suspicious packages or additional suitcases. He shared a room with Sonny and saw nothing in his demeanor or actions that suggested he was about the business of stealing artifacts.

Leaving Tuba City, Sonny turned the driving over to Duncan. He hesitated, knowing that he wasn't truly interested in becoming a courier driver. Of course, he would have to at least pretend to be about the business of learning the route. The drive was a fairly easy one. They took the Kayenta Road, and because the weather had been dry, the road was decent.

"You'll want to take the lower road to the left," Sonny said, leaning over Duncan's shoulder.

"Yes, unless you want to put us in the sand, as Sonny delights in doing," Rainy teased. Duncan nodded and maneuvered the car to the left while Rainy turned to her passengers. "The body of water you see is called Sheep Dip. After we cross a sandy stretch we'll reach a lake called Red Lake. It's called this because the sand at the bottom of the lake appears red."

They passed the lake and headed on their way across the dry wasteland. At one point Rainy again turned to the guests and smiled. "This area of ruins is full of pottery and arrowheads. Little is known about the Indians who once lived here. There are several archaeologists who intend to study the area, but they feel confident the findings will prove the tribe to have been Navajo." Duncan enjoyed her comments but could tell by the way she frowned whenever she turned back to face the road that she wasn't happy at all. He couldn't help but wonder what was making her so miserable.

At midday they paused to share a picnic lunch that had been packed for them back in Tuba. Duncan felt ravenous as he settled in beside Rainy to share in the sandwiches and fresh fruit. Rainy was nearly finished with her food, but helping Sonny resecure some loose luggage had delayed Duncan's lunch.

"So how do you like driving the touring car?" Rainy asked.

Duncan unwrapped a ham and cheese sandwich and shrugged. "It's an adventure, I will say that much."

"Are you sorry you gave up the museum?"

He felt a twinge of guilt. There was no way he could explain that he hadn't given up the museum. He couldn't very well tell one of the prime suspects of the investigation that he was only along to spy on her and gather information.

"I don't want to spend my life living in a museum," he finally said. "I have other plans."

"Truly? Maybe you could tell me about them sometime," Rainy said, seeming quite interested in him.

"Miss Gordon," Phillip Vance interrupted, "I wondered if you might take a walk with me and tell me about the landscape."

Rainy smiled up at the handsome man. "Of course." She quickly got to her feet and dusted off the backside of her skirt. "What would you like to know?"

They walked away with Phillip casually putting his hand on the small of Rainy's back as they ascended a slight incline. Duncan couldn't help but notice there was no sharp elbowing of Mr. Vance. On the contrary, Rainy seemed to enjoy Mr. Vance's attention very much. Duncan wanted nothing more than to run after them and insist he join the walk, but his appetite was fierce, and besides, he knew he had no business interfering in the matter.

Why does it have to be so hard to wait, Lord? I feel as though most of my life has been spent waiting for one thing or another to happen. Rainy Gordon is a beautiful and exciting woman, probably too much so for my simple life, but still I find myself drawn to her in a way I can't explain.

"You don't understand."

Duncan perked up at the statement. The voice of a man speaking in low, hushed tones carried over from the other side of the rock where Duncan ate.

"I understand better than you think," came another male voice. The second voice had to belong to Marshall Driscoll. It sounded much too refined and old to be his son's. Since Chester Driscoll was the only other man on the trip, besides Phillip Vance, the other voice must belong to him, Duncan reasoned.

"But Rainy is still determined to see the truth come out about those artifacts."

"Shut up," Driscoll told his son. "This is not a matter for discussion."

They moved away from the rock, leaving Duncan feeling rather ill. What did they know about Rainy and artifacts? The situation didn't look at all good for Rainy. First the Office of Indian Affairs believed her a possible thief, and now Driscoll's comment seemed to suggest there could be good reason to hold her accountable for the disappearing artifacts.

The sandwich settled heavily on his stomach. Swallowing hard, Duncan tried to figure out what he should do next. He could always take Chester aside and try to get the man to talk. It was doubtful he'd say

anything, however. After all, the man didn't know Duncan and would have no reason to confide in him.

Maybe I should talk to Rainy and just ask her up front what his comment was about. But what if she is involved with stealing from the Indians and my questions ruin the investigation? There seemed to be no easy answer.

———————

That evening, after the work of pitching tents and setting up cots had been completed, Rainy was surprised to find Phillip Vance at her side once again.

"I wondered if we might walk together?" Phillip asked. "I know I monopolized your time at lunch, but I do have more questions for you."

"Given the fact you were so willing to help us set up camp," Rainy began, "it would be uncharitable of me not to at least share a walk with you." She smiled and moved away from the gathering of tents. "So where would you like to walk? It's growing dark and we shouldn't go far. The desert is full of dangerous creatures."

"I'm sure that's wise counsel." He joined her, matching her long-legged strides with equal pacing. "I wondered if you would tell me about the Hopi people we visited today—about your friend Istaqa and his wife, Una. I liked them."

Rainy smiled. "They are wonderful people. Istaqa is one of the Indian police who keep law and order on the reservation. At first his people resented him, but they've come to discover over the years that they'd prefer to have another Hopi tell them what's right and wrong rather than have a white man do the deed. Of course, the authorities really don't hold him in very high regard, and they certainly would pull rank on him should they dislike his performance. Una is his wife of some fourteen years. They have three boys who attend the government school and do quite well."

Phillip took hold of her elbow and guided her toward an outcropping of rock. "I cannot imagine living the life they live. Do they really enjoy living in the pueblos?"

Rainy laughed. "Where else would they live? You certainly don't see any palatial mansions awaiting them, now, do you?"

Phillip appeared flushed in the fading light. Rainy realized she'd embarrassed him with her teasing. "I'm sorry," she said softly. "I shouldn't have answered in such a manner." She noticed that he continued to hold on to her arm even though they'd stopped walking.

"It's just that I feel people don't take me seriously when I say I want to learn. My sister thought me mad when I suggested this trip. She had come to visit me in Los Angeles, and when she mentioned traveling through Indian country and that souvenirs and such were available . . . well, I knew I had to see it for myself."

"And what do you think so far?" Rainy asked, warming under his intense scrutiny. The darkness robbed her of a chance to clearly see his expression, but she knew he had fixed his gaze on her.

"I'm deeply moved by the desert. It appears so harsh and lifeless, yet there is life out there. I look at the pueblos, so much like a natural outpouring of the earth, and marvel at the shapes and the sensibility of their creation. I see the people and know I shall never be as strong and worthy as they."

Rainy thought his attitude and feelings a refreshing change from so many of the tourists. His comments suggested a depth of feeling that did him honor. "The Hopi are a proud people. They can date their existence here back to A.D. 1050. They are very much as their name suggests: good, peaceful, and wise."

"I want to know everything," he said, pulling Rainy closer. He didn't even seem to notice what he'd done, yet Rainy was now only inches from him.

"Ah . . . well . . . they grow maize as a basic food. It's a type of corn. In fact, they raise over a dozen different kinds of corn—adding new varieties all the time."

"I had no idea there were so many varieties."

She found herself hesitant to speak. The words stuck in her throat. Here she was with a famous movie star. Her friends would have fainted dead away to be this close to Phillip Vance, and yet Rainy stood her ground—a bit light-headed, perhaps, but nevertheless, she was standing.

"What's it like to play a character in the movies?" she asked without thinking.

Phillip laughed. "Harder than some might think. It's mostly an endless chore of lighting and scenery details or dealing with some incompetent who has forgotten half his equipment. I actually like the acting part, but it's so different from the stage.

"But enough about me. I'm so glad you aren't like

those poor girls who lose their heads at the mere mention of a celebrity name. Sometimes I begin to find a woman halfway interesting and she swoons at my feet. Terribly hard to discuss matters of importance when the other party is unconscious."

Rainy laughed out loud at this and stepped away from Phillip. "I assure you I'm not one of those women. However, you must admit no matter where you go, someone is bound to recognize you and desire to share in your glory."

He sighed and Rainy thought he sounded very sad when he replied, "Yes, it makes my life very difficult. I've often wondered if it might be possible to find friends now who are truly interested in me as a person and not me as a star."

Rainy thought about this for a moment. "You're very personable, Mr. Vance."

"Oh, please, call me Phillip," he said, moving closer to her once again.

Rainy smiled. "All right, Phillip. You have a genteel quality that I find refreshing, and yet for all your fame and fortune, you seem quite down to earth."

"Exactly!" he declared and once again took hold of her arm. As he began walking them back toward camp he added, "I knew you were different. I could see in your eyes that you understood my plight."

Rainy stumbled on a rock, but Phillip easily kept her upright. He steadied her, then stopped Rainy and turned her toward him. By the light of the campfires, Rainy could see his expression had grown very somber. She feared perhaps she'd made him overly morose.

"Rainy," he said, then paused. "May I call you by your first name?"

"Of course." She trembled slightly as he rubbed his fingers over her hands.

"Rainy, I find you the most delightful woman I've ever known. You are so very genuine and refreshing. I'd like very much to know you better, and I hope that during my stay in Santa Fe, you'll allow me to call on you."

Rainy swallowed but the desert dust left her choked. "I . . ." She cleared her throat with a little cough. "Excuse me," she apologized, then regained a bit of her composure. "I think it would be very nice to get to know you better, Mr. . . . Phillip. But after we return, I will be going to Albuquerque for two weeks. You see, my parents live there and my brother and I plan to have an extended visit with them."

"Oh, well . . . how unfortunate."

Now he really sounded sad, and Rainy could hardly bear that she'd caused it. Especially when her heart continued to suggest that perhaps this was the man who would sweep her off her feet. Perhaps this was the very man she had nagged and pleaded with God to give her for a husband.

"I could postpone my trip for a day or two," she said.

"Oh, would you?" he questioned, his voice taking on the same animation she'd heard when she'd first met him. "I think that would be absolutely delightful. We could have a chance to get to know each other that way. Perhaps to even consider something more permanent in our relationship."

Rainy felt a quiver start at her toes and work its way up her body. "Phillip, we hardly know each other well enough to think on something that serious."

"I'm sorry, but I'm used to going after what I want." He drew her hands up to his lips. "I'm not impetuous enough to rush in and say that you're what I want. . . ." He kissed her hands gently and then just held them under his chin. "But I feel fairly confident that the next few days will make up my mind for me."

Rainy realized she was getting caught up in his romantic manners. She gently disengaged her hands and smiled. "I leave my fate in God's hands. I've no doubt He will show me the way. I must retire now, Phillip. I hope you have a pleasant rest."

She moved away quickly, hoping he wouldn't follow her. He didn't and although it was what she really wanted, Rainy felt rather disappointed.

Later that night as she struggled to fall asleep, Rainy wondered if Phillip Vance was the husband God had in mind for her. *He's handsome and compassionate,* she thought. *I loved the way he treated Istaqa and Una as equals.* So many of the tourists treated the Indians as if they were merely staging and ornamentation—not real people with honest feelings.

Phillip seems to care about the Indians and their lives here in the desert. He seems to understand the complexity of their culture and to respect it. Could he be the one?

But then it dawned on Rainy that if God had sent Phillip into her life for the purpose of matrimony, she would most likely have to leave the Southwest and her desires to be a working archaeologist. Phillip would have to be in California making his movies. His lifestyle and needs were completely different from hers—much more complex.

She'd overheard Jennetta and Mrs. Driscoll talking about the lavish, newly built mansion Phillip owned in a small community outside of Los Angeles. Jennetta told of the house having over twenty-five rooms. Rainy had thought surely the woman was exaggerating, but she began naming them off with such detail that Rainy began to believe the story.

Jennetta had concluded by describing a huge swimming pool and gardens with marble statues that had come all the way from Italy. Apparently the depressed economy had not caused harm to Phillip Vance's life.

Rainy tried to imagine wearing lavish gowns and acting as hostess for Phillip. Would his friends willingly accept her because she was Phillip's wife? Or would they turn her away because she wasn't of their social class?

Lord, I don't know what you have in mind here. I don't know if you've sent Phillip to me for a purpose beyond the tour, but he does seem to like me. What do I do?

She wrestled with the thought of Duncan. Duncan understood her love of New Mexico and Arizona, and as far as she knew, he had no plans to leave the area. Still, for all the attention she'd shown Duncan, he hadn't seemed inclined to return her interest. He talked to her when they were together and he had asked her to walk with him in Williams, but that hardly constituted affection.

Why does this have to be so hard?

Just as Rainy felt her mind grow clouded and her

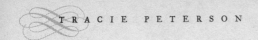

eyes become heavy, a scream split the silence of the night.

"What in the world is happening now?" she moaned, feeling her heart race just as it had when Gloria Van Patten had been scared by her brothers.

Bolting upright, Rainy pulled on her boots and began lacing them up. The woman screamed again, and this time Rainy was positive that it had to be Jennetta Blythe.

CHAPTER SEVEN

*R*ainy wasn't the first one on the scene of Jennetta's hysterical display. Duncan stood outside with a lantern, while poor Sonny bore the brunt of the woman's tirade as she dragged him into her tent. Rainy stood back and watched with some amusement as Sonny escorted an uninvited gopher snake from Jennetta and Mrs. Driscoll's tent. The older woman stood patiently to one side while Jennetta looked as though she might kill them all as she flailed her own lantern and ranted about the conditions.

"You'd think for the price of this tour we could at least stay in a real hotel!"

"Now, now, Jennetta," Phillip said, patting her arm reassuringly. "We knew part of this trip would be spent in rustic environments. You mustn't get yourself all worked up over a little snake."

"He wasn't little," she replied angrily. "I'll not be treated as a child!" She jerked her arm away from Phillip's touch and marched into her tent. It was clear she wanted nothing to do with any of them.

Rainy smiled at her brother. "The handsome

knight rescuing the lady fair," she murmured as he passed by her.

"Ha!" It was the only comment he had on the matter.

Rainy laughed and headed back to her tent.

"You hardly seemed fazed by that," Phillip declared as he came up beside her.

She looked up and smiled. "But of course not. The snake wasn't poisonous, and even if he were, there are ways to take care of the situation without resorting to hysteria."

Phillip grinned. "Perhaps she'll write a poem about it. She does that, you know."

Rainy shook her head. "I knew she was a writer of some sort, but I didn't realize Jennetta was a poet."

"Oh yes, she writes about her life. Dark, brooding, end-of-the-world kind of poetry. The more it suggests misery and torment, the more she loves it." He cast a glance back at Jennetta's tent and chuckled. "Poor Jennetta."

"Poor snake," Rainy replied.

———

Travel the next day was even more torturous than the day before. Jennetta was in a sour mood that kept the others at a distance. Phillip spent his time consoling her, which left Rainy alone until Chester Driscoll decided to seek her out.

"You know, Rainy, there's no need to play standoffish with me," he said while the others spent a bit of extra time wandering around the Navajo displays and goods. Mrs. Driscoll seemed to give her purchases little thought as she pointed to first one thing and then another.

When Rainy gave no reply, Chester reiterated, "I said that you needn't play standoffish with me."

Rainy met his gaze. "I wasn't playing."

Chester smiled. "Now, now. You owe my family too much to maintain this façade of anger."

"I *owe* your family? Neither you nor your father would defend me in the truth, and you think I owe you something for that?" Her anger was getting the better of her. She tried to remind herself that Chester was a guest of the Detour Company.

"We could have prosecuted you for the theft."

"Just because the articles turned up in my office—"

"In your desk," Chester interrupted.

Rainy scowled. "I didn't take those pieces, and you know that full well. Your father did too. One word of defense from either of you could have cleared my name with the university board. Now I'm still trying to do that on my own."

"You shouldn't waste your time. No one will ever believe you. You left quietly and didn't protest the charges so long as they were dropped. What do you suppose that meant to the board?"

Rainy tried to do a mental count to ten, but it was no use. "Exactly what I presumed they would think— that I was guilty. But I'm not."

Chester reached out to take hold of her shoulder. "Now, Rainy, you are getting upset over nothing. No one even cares about that ordeal anymore. It's already

behind us. You and I, however . . . now, that's a topic that still begs discussion."

"What of your wife?" Rainy questioned, trying to pull away from his touch. He tightened his hold so that it became painful. "You're hurting me," Rainy muttered from behind clenched teeth.

"That isn't my intention, but you must hear me out. My wife would never need to know about us."

"There is no 'us.' Leave me be."

"Just hear me out for a moment," he said, eyeing her with a pleading glance.

Rainy stilled. "You have one minute and then I scream for Sonny."

Chester chuckled. "I know what you want out of life. You want a position with the National Geographic Society. You want your own dig and I can make that happen. In return, you can be my mistress and I'll buy you a wonderful house in Santa Fe. We could have a lovely life together."

"Just you, me, and the little wife, eh?"

Chester was completely unmoved. "People do it all the time. Wealthy men are allowed a level of living that other men are never given."

"Wealthy? I thought the Driscolls were more show than substance."

"That might be true for the Driscolls in general, but not for this Driscoll." He puffed out his chest and loosened his hold. "I've married into money and have no worry about the future. Oh, certainly the economy has made things more difficult. Already the cities back East are filling with unemployed beggars. But that has nothing to do with us. I can get you what you want. I can get you your dream."

"Your time is up," Rainy said, pulling away abruptly. "I have no interest in your proposition, Mr. Driscoll, and I do hope you will keep from embarrassing yourself further by refraining from future references to this conversation. If not, I'll be compelled to have a conversation of my own—with your wife."

She walked away as quickly as she could without causing a scene. Mrs. Driscoll, shopping concluded, stood patiently under an Indian-blanket awning. Jennetta Blythe stood at her side.

"Are you ladies enjoying yourselves?" Rainy asked in as pleasant a manner as she could muster.

"I won't enjoy myself again until we're in Santa Fe," Jennetta declared.

Rainy couldn't help the smile that overcame her. "My mother used to say that if you're determined to feel a certain way, you'll most likely succeed."

Phillip's sister scowled. "Whatever do you mean by that?"

"Just that if you intend to be miserable, you will be. If you decide to be happy, then you'll find a way to achieve it. You seem determined to be miserable no matter what takes place on this trip, so you are welcome to it. Just don't expect the company to love misery."

"Well! I've never encountered such rudeness."

"I guess that makes two of us," Rainy replied, matching Jennetta's hard gaze with one of her own.

Mrs. Driscoll eyed Jennetta for a moment, then

turned to Rainy. "How much longer will we be detained?"

Rainy nodded. "I believe we'll be here another five or ten minutes."

"Oh, I see."

Rainy tried to think of something to say that might draw the older woman into a conversation. "Mrs. Driscoll, were you able to hold your annual Christmas party for the college faculty?"

"Yes."

Rainy had hoped she'd elaborate. "And was it a success?"

"Yes."

Mrs. Driscoll shifted her purchases from one hand to the other but otherwise showed little sign of life. Rainy thought her the most completely boring woman in all the world.

"So are you having a nice time on the tour?" Rainy questioned, trying a different angle.

"It's much too hot for this time of year," Mrs. Driscoll replied.

Rainy thought the weather had been perfect. Many times tourists came to the desert in the cooler months, hoping to avoid the piercing heat of summer. "I thought it quite lovely today."

"I'm sure someone lacking in the more refined things of life would find this day enjoyable," Jennetta chimed in. "But it really is appalling. I won't rest a moment until we're back in Santa Fe."

That evening they spent the night in Gallup, New Mexico, enjoying the hospitality of the local Harvey hotel, El Navajo. Jennetta finally seemed at peace and

Mrs. Driscoll disappeared shortly after their arrival.

Rainy was glad for the reprieve but found the quiet to be short-lived when other guests began recognizing Phillip Vance and pleading for autographs and conversation. Rainy watched, with Sonny and Duncan, as the entourage of people came to pester Phillip.

"That poor man—he won't have a chance to eat his meal while it's still hot," Rainy declared, craning to the right to see past Duncan.

"He's a grown man," Duncan said. "I expect he understands by this point in his career that this is a part of the game. He'll either send them away or bask in the glory."

Rainy frowned and straightened in her chair. "What's that supposed to mean?"

Sonny laughed. "The man isn't a movie actor because he values his own company is what Duncan is saying. Mr. Vance seems pretty happy with the attention."

As if to accentuate her brother's point, Phillip let out a booming laugh that filled the air. Duncan met her gaze with raised eyebrows, as if to say, "I told you so."

Rainy lowered her gaze and poked her green beans around the plate. "He's just too sweet to send them away. He's kind to everyone."

"He's certainly been kind to you, sister dear. Maybe too kind. Maybe I need to have a private talk with Mr. Vance."

Rainy looked up at Sonny and cocked her head to one side. "I don't know what you're implying with that comment, but I assure you Mr. Vance has been nothing but a gentleman. He even treated my Indian friends with great civility and open admiration."

Sonny laughed, but it was Duncan who leaned in to say, "Your defense of Mr. Vance isn't helping your case at all."

Rainy pushed away from the table. "You're both being silly. Phillip has been very charming and, well . . . yes, he has shown me some special interest. But it's my business—not yours," she told Sonny. She then looked to Duncan and added, "Or yours."

She started across the dining room just as Phillip and his entourage rose. "Miss Gordon," Phillip called and motioned.

Rainy froze midstep. She was afraid to acknowledge him and afraid not to. Finally she looked over her shoulder to where Phillip stood alongside Chester Driscoll. "Do join us. We're retiring to the Writing Room, where Jennetta has agreed to read us a couple of her poems and I am to do a scene from my last movie. Please say you'll come."

Rainy opened her mouth to reply but found Sonny speaking instead. "Is the invitation extended to everyone?" She turned around and found that he and Duncan were only a few paces behind her.

"But of course. The more the merrier. We artists are nothing without our audience to appreciate us," Phillip replied.

His response was not what Rainy had hoped to hear. She had thought perhaps her invitation was a summons to a private, exclusive time of privilege. There was just something about Phillip Vance that made her easily forget herself.

She followed with Sonny and Duncan as the growing party moved to the Writing Room. She took a seat toward the back, hoping it would afford her a quick getaway should the need arise. Much to her surprise, Duncan took the seat beside her, while Sonny went up closer to the impromptu stage.

Chester had been appointed the host and soon several other participants had been encouraged to join in showing off their talents.

There were several recitations of speeches that were followed by a bleak soliloquy by Jennetta Blythe entitled, "The Despair That Haunts My Soul." For Rainy, the despair was that the poem went on for twelve stanzas. Gloom and sorrow dripped from every word. The woman was clearly not a happy person.

Finally Phillip stood and gave a rousing speech from his last movie. The speech dealt with a cowboy's plea to his dying father to forgive him for past indiscretions. The audience applauded with great enthusiasm and the women rushed to plant kisses on Phillip's cheeks and lips. Rainy was rather stunned by their reaction. Phillip, in the meantime, seemed quite content with the attention. The situation confused her.

Lord, if you've brought him into my life as a potential husband, then why is he acting like that? The question surprised even Rainy. She looked at Duncan and found his gaze fixed on her, almost as if he were awaiting some response or reaction.

She got to her feet, unable to figure out her heart in the matter. Duncan had a way of making her weak in the knees, but then, so did Phillip Vance. Duncan's smile had aroused thoughts of marriage and happily ever after. But then, Phillip Vance had mastered the art of the enticing smile, too.

Suddenly she realized she was still staring at Duncan. "I suppose I'll retire for the evening."

"It's been a rather tiring day," Duncan said, getting to his feet.

Sonny came bounding toward them, shaking his head. "Have you ever seen such a fuss? I nearly had two different women sitting on my lap as they fought to get past my seat. And all for that," he said, motioning over his back.

"It was calmer back here. I didn't have any threat of ladies in my lap," Duncan replied with a grin. "But I did get a good looking over."

Rainy felt her cheeks grow hot. "I'm going to bed."

———————

Duncan wasn't sure what to do with his feelings. He had thought of Rainy all night as he slipped in and out of sleep. And then when they gathered with the dudes at the car the next morning, he watched her with such intensity that she asked him twice if something was wrong.

He wanted to tell her about the investigation. He wanted to tell her that his feelings for her were getting . . . well, out of control. He wanted to explain everything that mattered and yet knew there was nothing he could say. At least not at this point.

"Rainy!"

Duncan looked up to find Phillip Vance making his way to where Rainy stood with Sonny. Duncan picked up a road map and ambled toward the threesome, pretending to study the route.

"When I saw the glorious sunrise, I thought of you immediately. Your hair is like the ribbons of color that unfurled across the sky," Vance said with a smile.

Rainy, who had seemed discouraged all morning, perked up at Phillip's greeting. "Well, you know what they say. Red skies in morning, sailors take warning."

"Well, there certainly aren't any sailors in this part of the world, so maybe there are others who should heed the signs," Phillip said in a teasing manner. "Anyway, I wanted to catch you before we started out for Albuquerque. We had no time to talk privately last night. Did you enjoy my performance?"

Duncan wanted to laugh out loud, but instead he touched Sonny on the shoulder and held up the map as if to suggest directions be given. Sonny darted behind the map and exchanged a grin with Duncan. Together they lowered the map just enough to watch Rainy and Phillip.

"I enjoyed it very much," Rainy told Phillip. "I remember that scene in the movie brought mc to tears."

"Truly? How marvelous!" Phillip declared. "I knew you were a woman of great passion. I have a very poor relationship with my father, and I drew on that to support my character's reaction. The scene conjured all sorts of memories for me . . . but, of course, such a scene would never be allowed in real life. My father believes in grudges."

"How very sad."

Phillip sighed. "You are very understanding of my

situation. So often the world leaves little room for honesty, but I find that you are a woman of not only impeccable truth but also incredible beauty."

Sonny coughed to cover a laugh. Rainy glanced their way, but it was Duncan's gaze she met. She frowned and looked back to Phillip. "Was there something else I could help you with?"

"Absolutely." Phillip oozed charm, and Duncan personally wanted to wring his neck. "I know we'll stay the night in Albuquerque. I wondered if you would be my personal escort and give me an evening tour of the city. I'd love to see all the special places—just you and me."

Rainy smiled and looked away. Duncan thought she looked rather nervous. "I'd love to," she told him.

This caused both Sonny and Duncan to drop the map. Duncan knew, from what she and Sonny had both shared, that nights in Albuquerque were always devoted to family. From the look on Sonny's face, Rainy was acting completely out of character.

"Rainy, what about Mom and Dad?" Sonny asked.

"They'll understand. Take Duncan home with you. Give them my excuses."

Sonny looked to Duncan and shook his head. "I think it's time to get on the road. You want to drive?" he asked.

Duncan nodded, although he really didn't feel like taking on the chore. At least it might help to keep his mind occupied. It might—but he doubted it.

CHAPTER EIGHT

J've really enjoyed our evening together," Phillip said as he strolled with Rainy.

"I have too," Rainy admitted. She'd known nothing but his complete attention and generosity this evening. Phillip's genuine kindness and interest in her life and the things around her proved him to be a man of integrity and consideration. Her only real frustration was that she still knew so very little about Phillip Vance, the man. He was openly delighted to talk about his life as an actor, but when it came to anything more personal, he seemed to easily avoid her questions.

"I must say, I've learned a great deal about your Indian friends. I think it marvelous that you know so much about them. You'd be a tremendous asset to the movie studio. You really should give it some thought."

"Move to California? But I don't know anyone there," Rainy said without thinking.

"You would know me," Phillip said, stopping to take hold of her hand. "And by then, well . . . who can say?"

Rainy felt a surge of frustration. These were hardly the kinds of words she wanted to hear. She wanted to know if Phillip had any real interest in deepening their relationship, of course, but she wanted to know much more. Rainy needed to know if he was like-minded—if he honored the truth, honored God. She'd always respected her mother's admonition to not get involved with nonbelievers. Rainy had worked hard, in fact, to avoid such heartaches. It was definitely something that had allowed her to keep Chester Driscoll at arm's length.

Overhead the night skies twinkled with diamond-like stars. The moon, a lazy crescent, offered little light. Rainy wanted so much to know Phillip Vance's true self, yet he never seemed able to tell her much more than who he was as an actor or public figure. Even his interests and concern about the Hopi were more related to his work than to his personality—at least that was how it seemed at times.

"Isn't it marvelous how God so intricately created the universe—so beautiful . . . so perfect?" Rainy said, hoping perhaps this line of questioning would give Phillip cause to respond and share his heart. She continued gazing into the night sky, waiting for his response.

After a moment he replied, "It's beautiful here, to be sure."

Rainy waited for him to say something more, but he seemed completely content to remain silently at her side. Frustration coursed through her veins. "Phillip, you've really said very little about yourself. I feel like I know all about Phillip Vance the actor, but what of your personal life? What did you do with yourself before getting into the movie business?" she asked, suddenly breaking the intimacy of the moment. She pulled away and continued their stroll back to the Alvarado Hotel.

Phillip quickly followed. "There really isn't much to tell. I was born and raised in New York. I went to school and developed an interest in movies from the first time I viewed a silent picture." He smiled down at her as he again claimed her arm. "I knew then that acting was for me."

"But surely you had other plans and dreams as a child."

Phillip grew momentarily thoughtful. "My mother took me to my first play when I was only five. I regularly attended after that—whenever she was to attend. My father despised the theatre, so we never told him of our destinations." He shrugged as if he'd said too much. "I suppose there was the thought to become something studious—you know, a lawyer or banker. I believe my father hoped I might follow in his footsteps and help with the family business."

"Which was?" Rainy asked, finally feeling she was getting somewhere.

"He made tools," Phillip murmured, as if ashamed. "Jennetta hated our life there and often spoke of moving from New York to California—Los Angeles, in particular. I thought it sounded marvelous. I knew it would allow me to be exposed to all that I would need to get me into movies. That's where my real passion lies."

Movies. Rainy sighed. So they were back to that topic. How was she supposed to know him better? How was she supposed to know if this was the man God intended for her to marry if he wouldn't discuss the truly important aspects of life? Still, he seemed so interested in being with her. He could have taken his pick of beautiful women, yet here he was with her. That had to mean something—didn't it?

They'd reached the hotel veranda, and Phillip stopped and pulled Rainy around to face him. "I have a surprise. I've arranged a carriage ride to take you home," he said, his expression suggesting he was quite pleased with himself.

Rainy thought the gesture very sweet. "How marvelous. It's been a long time since I've ridden in a carriage. With the Harveycars—well, I guess now that Major Clarkson has purchased the Detours they're being called courier cars—but nevertheless, with the touring cars I've had plenty of non-equestrian transportation."

"I thought this would be rather . . . well . . . romantic," he whispered.

"Romantic?" Rainy asked, her voice squeaking a bit. Was this the sign she'd been waiting for? Was God finally going to show her the truth about Phillip Vance?

Phillip laughed and led her toward the carriage. "I think you're absolutely marvelous."

Rainy didn't know what to make of his comment. Was he laughing at her? Did he think her naïve? *Why did I have to make that comment?* She moaned inwardly.

He probably thinks me quite immature and completely un-sophisticated.

Rainy allowed Phillip to help her into the carriage. As a young girl, her family had used horse and carriage exclusively. Her father hadn't the inclination toward nor the money to spend on an automobile. But the 1930s seemed to demand more and more attention toward change. Horses and carriages were giving way to the motorized car and quicker modes of transportation. Lindbergh had flown across the Atlantic, and air travel was rapidly becoming an acceptable alternative to the slower-paced trains. Automobiles were even more accessible with their makers desiring to produce a product that every American family could afford to buy.

Still, there was something very romantic and lovely about an evening carriage ride. Rainy settled back against the leather upholstery and sighed.

"I hope that was a sigh of contentment and not boredom," Phillip whispered.

His nearness made Rainy straighten a bit. "It was the happy kind," she replied. "I always enjoy coming home to Albuquerque. My folks . . . our house . . . well . . . it's just very nice to be around the things and people you love. I've cherished growing up here. My mother always made our house a home. She has the most marvelous gardens in the inner courtyard. You'll have to see them sometime." Rainy found that she never quite realized how much she loved it here until after she'd been gone for a time. "I've enjoyed working with the Detours, but I also like the idea of taking time away from my job. I'm going to greatly enjoy my two weeks off."

"But you will still consider postponing for just a few days, won't you?" he asked so sweetly that Rainy couldn't do anything but nod.

"I suppose I can postpone my vacation by a day or so to show you around Santa Fe." Rainy couldn't believe she was agreeing to do such a thing. She could easily remember the disappointment she'd felt when Sonny told her of the trip to the Grand Canyon. Now, however, the idea of delaying wasn't at all unappealing. With Phillip Vance in the picture, in fact, the delay seemed quite promising.

"Phillip, may I ask you something?" Rainy decided the only way she'd get answers would be to ask very specific questions.

"Of course you may," he said, taking hold of her hand.

"What are your plans for the future? I mean, do you always intend to work as a movie star? Will you stay in California?"

He chuckled softly and turned a bit to better face her. "I see my future only getting better. I see the movie industry booming like a gold rush, and I see myself in the midst of that boom. California is a perfectly lovely place to live and my new home is marvelous. But without the right woman to share it all . . . well . . ." He looked away momentarily. "I want a wife and children. I want a closeness of family that I never experienced growing up."

"I thought from the way you spoke that you and your mother and sister were all very close," Rainy said, not giving any thought to how personal the statement might seem.

Phillip's expression seemed pained. "No, it wasn't as it might seem to an outsider. What I want is nothing like what I had growing up. I want honesty and love—compassion and open-mindedness."

Rainy thought she'd never heard anyone sound so sad. She trembled as he returned his gaze to her face and reached up to gently stroke her cheek. "I've been searching for the right woman," he murmured. "A woman who wouldn't be intimidated by the fanfare and nonsense that accompanies me. A woman who would understand the attention I'd be given by my fans. A woman who would take all of that in stride and still manage to give me the support and love I need."

Rainy felt as though time stood still as he softly spoke of his desires. Could she be that woman? Would she want to put herself into that life—take herself away from the world she knew and loved? A tiny voice in the back of her mind questioned, *What about the support and love* you *would need?* Rainy quickly pushed the thought aside. There would be time to figure that out later.

The driver slowed the horses to a stop in front of her parents' house. The sudden lull caused Rainy to look up, almost startled. "We're here."

Phillip nodded. "I hope I didn't bore you with my talk."

"Not at all," Rainy said, more confused than ever.

"I'll walk you to the door." Phillip climbed down from the carriage and reached back up to help Rainy. As her feet touched the ground, Phillip's arms went around her and he pulled her close for a kiss.

Rainy was too surprised to really enjoy the kiss. She was so shocked that Phillip would take such a liberty with her, and yet at the same time she couldn't help but wonder if this, too, was a part of God's plan to show her the truth of His choice.

Phillip pulled away, a hesitant look on his face. "I'm sorry. I shouldn't have done that."

Rainy shook her head. "I would have preferred that you had not. We barely know each other."

He laughed. "I tend to forget myself. I have women throwing themselves at me all the time. I suppose it seemed strange not to have you respond in the same manner."

"That's who I am," Rainy defended. "I'm not like your throngs of fans."

He released her and took a step back. "Please forgive me. Don't let my ill manners spoil our evening or our future."

Rainy couldn't be angry with him. "Of course I forgive you." She smiled sweetly. "Thank you for the wonderful evening, but now I really need to get to bed. Tomorrow is the final day of our tour, and you'll want to get your money's worth."

"I think I already have," Phillip said, laughing.

———————

"Where have you been?" Sonny asked as Rainy came through the door.

"You know perfectly well where I've been. I've been out with Phillip Vance." She pulled off her dress jacket and tossed it aside. "Where are Mom and Dad?"

she asked, looking around the room.

"They went to bed about an hour ago. It's ten o'clock, Rainy."

"Goodness, I didn't realize it was so late."

"That much is obvious," Sonny said, trying not to allow his worry to turn to anger. "Rainy, I really was starting to worry. First you take off with Phillip instead of spending time here at home with us, and then you don't return until ten. It's not at all like you."

Rainy sat down opposite him. "No, I suppose it's not. I just felt it was something I had to do, however. I couldn't help but wonder if God had brought Phillip Vance into my life for more than just a tour."

Sonny got a sinking feeling inside. "What do you mean?"

"Well, I wonder if he's the man God will have me marry."

"What about Duncan?" Sonny questioned. He knew his sister's feelings for Duncan Hartford were more than a passing interest. How could she so easily trade one man for another?

"What about him? I've tried to show him interest and make it clear that I find his company enjoyable, but he doesn't seem to have the slightest interest in me." She leaned her elbow on the table, then shrugged. "I suppose Duncan Hartford has too many other interests to consider me."

"I wouldn't be so sure. I also wouldn't expect him to show his true feelings and compete with a movie star."

"But Phillip Vance wasn't even in the picture when

I first showed Duncan my interest in him. You can't blame Phillip."

"I'm not blaming anyone," Sonny replied. "I just think you should be cautious about this. Phillip Vance seems to be the kind of man who's used to dallying with women. I'd hate to have to straighten him out over his dalliance with you."

"I'm a grown woman, little brother. I know how to handle myself."

Sonny smiled. "I'd like to believe that, but actions speak much louder than words."

"Oh, go on with you. Stop worrying about me. I'm just trying to seek out God's will for my life," Rainy replied. "God doesn't expect me to just sit around and wait for Him to drop a husband in my lap."

"Oh, He doesn't? When did He tell you this?"

Rainy squirmed a bit and shifted in her chair. She refused to meet Sonny's eyes and looked to the table instead. "I just can't imagine that He wants me to do nothing. I've prayed about it, and I just figured it was partly up to me to do something about it."

"If God wants you to marry Duncan Hartford or even Phillip Vance, don't you think He can handle the task of bringing it about, without you having to work double time to see it to fruition? It's not like you've been asked to take on an extra tour shift. We're talking about God's ability to do infinitely more than we can ask or imagine. Remember?"

"I remember."

"Besides, what if God has called you to be single?"

Rainy glared at him for this. "He hasn't. I know without a doubt that God wants me to marry and have a family. I've prayed about it. I have real peace that this is His will for my life."

"If that's the case, then why not rest in it and wait for Him to act? It's not like He's going to forget you."

She yawned. "I know all of that." Straightening a bit, she asked, "So how did you spend your evening?"

Sonny laughed. "Changing the subject, are we?"

"Yes, please. What did you do?"

Now it was Sonny's chance to grow uncomfortable. "I met with some old friends of mine. They came here to the house and we visited for a couple of hours."

"Truly? Who were they?"

"You remember Jess and Richard, my friends from college?"

Rainy nodded.

"Well, they've gotten themselves involved in an Alaskan Territory exploration group. It's a government project."

"How exciting for them. When will they head to Alaska?"

Sonny straightened, knowing he had to tell her his plans. Finalizing his departure without letting her in on it seemed almost criminal. "Part of the team is heading up at the end of August. The other part will leave in September."

"Seems like the wrong time to head up north," she said, laughing. "Don't birds usually fly south in the winter?"

He smiled. "Well, a team of thirty scientists can hardly be mistaken for birds. They're doing a winter study."

"Oh, well, that makes sense—if you like that kind

of thing." She yawned again and got to her feet.

"There's more. It has to do with the team and I want to tell you about it," Sonny said, a desperate tone to his words. He knew he needed to tell her the truth of his plans. He didn't want her to accidentally learn it from someone else.

"Oh, Sonny, not now. I'm completely spent and want to go to bed. You can tell me about your friends tomorrow." She came around and kissed him atop his head. "I'm sorry I worried you."

"I just want you to be safe and happy," Sonny said as she walked from the room. She didn't reply, so he wasn't even sure she'd heard him.

Sonny felt a sense of guilt and knew it was silly. He was a grown man with every right to plan to travel to Alaska with his friends. A job as a government geologist was something he simply couldn't pass by. Rainy would understand and be happy for him, but he knew she would also be hurt that he hadn't discussed it with her early on.

"So did you talk to her?"

Sonny looked up to find his father standing in the dining room doorway. His well-worn robe was the same one Sonny had seen him wear since he and Rainy were kids. "I tried. She was tired though and wanted to get to bed."

His father nodded and joined Sonny at the table. "There will be time."

"I'm worried about her," Sonny said, shaking his head. "She's so caught up in trying to figure out whom God wants her to marry. Then there's the whole issue of wanting to figure out who framed her and got her fired at the university."

"I'd like to get to the bottom of that myself," Dad replied. "Seems senseless that a young innocent girl should be singled out like that and blamed for something everyone knew she couldn't possibly have done. I've tried to talk to Marshall Driscoll several times, but he won't even discuss it."

"He was on our tour this last trip," Sonny began. "I was stunned to see him and Mrs. Driscoll but even more surprised to find Chester with them. Rainy feels confident that Chester was somehow behind the entire incident. She said he spoke with too much familiarity regarding the matter. Yet when she's tried to talk to him about it, he turns the tables on her and reminds her that his father kept her from prosecution."

Dad nodded knowingly. "I've never understood it. Rainy was always so very conscientious about anything regarding the artifacts. I know she would never have taken them for any purpose—not even for cleaning them, as Chester suggested."

"Chester showed way too much interest in Rainy then *and* now. Even on the trip this week he was always finding ways to be alone with her. Duncan and I tried to keep that from happening very often, but it wasn't easy. Between Chester and Phillip Vance, we had our hands full."

"Well, your sister is a grown woman and times are changing. Women are able to vote and to speak their mind. Certainly they're able to choose the company they keep."

"I suppose," Sonny said, feeling rather deflated.

"But I don't think at this point she knows what's good for her."

His father laughed. "I guess I could wonder if running off to the frozen north was good for you, but you'd give me some long discussion about it being your lifelong dream and how"—he got up from the table and looked down at his son—"you'd waited forever for a dream position like this to come along." His father smiled. "Hmm, on second thought, I guess we had that conversation."

"I know what you're saying, Dad." Sonny got up and stretched. "I'll try to just pray it through."

"That's the best you can do, son. Rainy knows better than to plunge into anything without taking it to God first. She'll do all right."

CHAPTER NINE

I can see why Jennetta loves it here," Phillip declared as he strolled the streets of Santa Fe with Rainy. "There's a feel of the ancient here. Almost as if another world existed inside this plaza center."

Rainy smiled, feeling at the moment that she'd never been happier than being on the arm of Phillip Vance. "It's a wonderful town full of Spanish and Indian influence. I love the architecture, especially— the red tile on the roofs and the courtyard gardens. I adore the adobe and wrought iron, the arched doors and windows and adobe fireplaces. It's all so very pleasant."

"And romantic," he whispered against her ear.

Rainy trembled. "Yes, definitely that."

"I feel so honored," Phillip began, "that you would agree to cancel your vacation and spend some time acting as our courier. I knew if we requested you, they would somehow find a way to persuade you."

"They didn't have to persuade me," Rainy admitted. "When the matter came up, I just felt it was the right thing to do. I prayed about it and felt even more confident of my decision."

"You put a lot of stock in prayer, don't you?"

Rainy stopped and looked up. Phillip's expression was one of curiosity laced with concern. "I do put a lot of stock in prayer. Don't you?"

Phillip shrugged and looked away. "I suppose it's never been that important to me. I didn't grow up religious, and therefore I've just never had any real use for such matters."

Rainy felt as though she had plunged from a three-story building. She might be foolish about matters of the heart, but she could never ignore the warning regarding being unequally yoked with a nonbeliever.

"But what of standards to live by?" Rainy questioned. "How do you gauge those standards?"

Phillip shoved his hands in his pockets and leaned back against the adobe face of one of the Plaza stores. "I suppose I make my own."

Rainy had heard this argument before. "Based on what?" The wind whipped her hair across her mouth as if trying to hush her.

Phillip smiled and reached out to push back her hair. "I want people to treat me well, so I treat them well."

"That's Jesus' command to 'Love thy neighbour as thyself.' " Rainy replied. "Nothing self-made in that."

Phillip laughed. "No, I don't suppose it's a new concept." He pushed off the wall and motioned to the café across the street. "Jennetta tells me the Mexican food at that café is the best in town. Why don't we have lunch there? We can sit and eat and wax theological."

Rainy allowed him to take hold of her arm but couldn't help replying, "I don't want to wax theological, Phillip. I just wondered how you—"

"Aren't you Phillip Vance?" a young woman who looked to be no more than twenty questioned. She'd come to stand directly in front of them and refused to move.

Phillip flashed her a smile and lowered his voice to match his cowboy characters. "That I am."

The girl squealed and motioned to several friends who stood in absolute awe on the opposite street corner. "It's him! It's him!"

Rainy was quickly nudged out of the way as the gaggle of giggling, screaming girls swooped in like vultures to the prey. Leaning back against the porch support, Rainy thought long and hard about the scene. *This is what it would be like to spend the rest of my life with Phillip Vance. No matter where he went, people would recognize him. Sometimes that would be good and sometimes it would be bad. But it would always be inescapable.*

She listened to Phillip talk in his soft-spoken manner. He seemed to take a genuine interest in each girl, listening as they poured out their delight in having seen him. He answered their questions and allowed their adoration—basking in the glory of it, as Sonny had suggested.

Bored with the situation, Rainy crossed the narrow street and took a seat on one of the Plaza benches. No one even seemed to notice she'd gone.

"Quite the display, isn't it?"

She looked up with dread. "Hello, Chester."

Ignoring her obvious displeasure with him, Chester

took the seat beside her. He pretended to dust the pant legs of his gray suit before adding, "It's like this everywhere he goes. If there are people about, especially women, Phillip Vance doesn't wait long for a crowd."

"You speak like such an authority," Rainy said, trying hard to be civil.

"Oh, I suppose I am somewhat of one. You see, my wife has been good friends with Jennetta Blythe for some time. That's why we were out in California to begin with. Bethel's parents lived only two doors down from the Blythes. Jennetta suffered a stormy marriage to a man who never understood her. Do you want to know something really awful?"

"No!" Rainy interjected. "I don't. I have no interest in such matters."

"Ah, I suppose not," Charles said, sounding quite disappointed. "Well, where was I? Ah, yes. When Jennetta began to hear of the wonders of Santa Fe, well, she didn't wait long to make her way here. The art community has been quite rewarding for her. She found people who could understand her heart."

"I'm glad someone can understand her," Rainy murmured.

"Phillip is really quite the Casanova. He has no trouble securing a woman to keep him company. After all, look at yourself. You've cancelled a two-week furlough just to be at his side."

"I did not cancel just to be at his side," Rainy protested. "He needed a courier." She knew the excuse was lame, but she refused to have Chester suggesting she was no different from all the other silly women who flocked to Phillip Vance.

Chester laughed. "And you were the only one in the entire fleet who was available? Really, Rainy, you needn't pretend with me. Not after our past together."

"We have no past together, unless of course you count the fact that you let me be blamed for something I didn't do."

"Oh, we aren't going to talk on that tiresome subject again, are we?" He leaned closer and Rainy cringed, all the while watching the women flirt with Phillip.

Chester's breath was stale as he whispered, "Rainy, there are so many things I could do for you now. I can get you what you want. The past doesn't need to control your future. I have friends in high places, and believe me, they can move heaven and earth for me if I give them the word. You have only to agree. After all, you don't want to spend your entire life leading tourists around the desert. Why, there may not even be an Indian Detours after this year."

Rainy scooted to the far end of the bench and looked at him hard. "Why do you say that?"

Chester had the good sense to stay where he was. "I'm often privileged to overhear information. You know the financial markets have failed and that America and Europe are both suffering tremendous setbacks economically. Luxury items, such as tours and vacations, can't hope to survive. If things go as poorly as some of my friends believe they will, it would be wise to have a nest egg to bank on. I myself believe in setting up a wide reserve—diversification is the key."

"But you've not heard anything in particular to

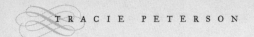

suggest the company plans to stop offering the Detours, have you?" Rainy questioned, hating to have to use Chester for information.

"Well, there is of course the obvious situation of the Harvey Company selling the Detours to Clarkson. They take their cues from the Santa Fe, and the railroad has obviously tightened its belt and wants the Harvey Company to do likewise. Clarkson may have run the transportation company, but I doubt he has the Santa Fe Railroad in his pocket as tightly as the Harvey Company does. I wouldn't be at all surprised to see him eliminate all but the most lucrative and most commonly requested tours from the rosters. As they do that, they'll obviously need fewer and fewer people."

"But people like Phillip Vance and other movie stars continue to come," Rainy protested. "Why, just last week we had three different tours with movie stars. They all raved about the tours and their plans to return and enjoy the hotels. Surely things can't be all that bad if they're willing to do that."

"They will probably be happy to share time at the resort hotels like La Posada and El Tovar, even La Fonda, but they won't want to be dragging around out in the desert for pleasure rides. And let's be realistic here—if the economy fails as my friends believe it will, even movie stars are going to be cutting way back on their spending. After all, if the general public can't afford to go to the movies, the producers of those movies certainly aren't going to have money to pay their stars. No, mark my words, the Detours won't be long for this world."

Rainy immediately thought of Sonny. It wasn't so fearful for her to be out of work. She could always live with their mother and father and no one would think less of her. An old maid living at home was perhaps pitied but never condemned. But Sonny's situation was different. Sonny was a man, and for a man to be out of work and living with his parents, well, that wouldn't be good for him. People already talked of how Sonny was approaching thirty years of age and had no steady girl. Some of the couriers had even teased him about living at home, being a "momma's boy." It was unfair and insensitive, but Sonny bore it well.

"I can see I've given you much to consider," Chester said, following Rainy to the far end of the bench. "But you needn't worry about the future. I have more power now than I did three years ago. I can keep you safe and well cared for. You don't need Phillip Vance— not that he'd give any real consideration to you when he can have his pick from important, wealthy daughters of society. Phillip is toying with you—enjoying the good time you can give him." Chester paused and got to his feet. "He does this everywhere he goes. He finds one vulnerable, needy woman and plays on her sympathy and desire."

Rainy didn't want to believe his words but was unwittingly drawn back to his gaze. Chester's sandy brown hair peeked out from beneath his straw hat, almost as if to remind him he was long overdue at the barber's shop. She would have laughed had the moment not been so serious. Chester studied her for a moment then narrowed his eyes.

"How long do you suppose you'll keep your job if the company were to find out about the university scandal?"

Rainy jumped up. "You have no call to threaten me, Chester. I did as I was asked. I left quietly. Now uphold your end of the bargain and leave me alone."

"I don't recall leaving you alone to be part of the agreement," Chester said, smiling maliciously. "But if you don't want to be a part of the National Geographic Society, suit yourself."

Just then Phillip managed to disentangle himself from the women and came bounding across the road. "I'm so sorry, Rainy. Sometimes it just can't be helped. Fans need to be pampered a bit from time to time."

"I was just explaining that to her," Chester replied. "I told her you deal with this all the time. I was just about to tell her of that poor lovesick Harvey Girl back at El Tovar. What was her name, anyway? Colleen? Collette? Co—"

"It was Caroline and is clearly not worthy of discussion," Phillip declared, not appearing too happy with Chester's comments.

"No matter. The real reason I'm here is that your sister has asked me to fetch you. Seems she has designs for heading north to Taos and needs you to join in on the plan," Chester told Phillip and added, "She told me she wouldn't accept any excuses for you not returning with me to her home."

Rainy felt only moderately disappointed to have Phillip taken from her. There was a part of her that needed time to process the events of the day. But there was also a part of her that very much wanted to sit down to a quiet lunch with Phillip Vance. She had so many questions to ask him—questions about God and faith. Maybe if she explained it better he would understand how important it was to have faith in God.

Phillip laughed. "I suppose I have no choice. But, Rainy, why don't you come along, too? Jennetta seldom allows anyone to come to her home, but if she's calling us there now, then the spirits must be favorable. She won't mind an additional person."

Rainy couldn't help but wonder what he meant by his comment about the spirits, but she had no desire to sit down to conversation with Jennetta Blythe. "I haven't had lunch yet. . . ." she began as a means to excuse herself.

"I'm sure Jennetta will have some monstrous-sized fruit platter, along with cheese and breads," Phillip countered.

Chester laughed. "Yes, indeed she does. I was there when the food arrived."

Phillip nodded as if that made all the difference in the world. "She does that on the few occasions when she has people in. We can feast there."

Rainy wasn't about to join their happy little enclave. "No, I really shouldn't. If your plans involve one of the Detour trips, just let me know."

Phillip lifted her hand to his lips. "But of course it will involve you. After you gave up your vacation for me, I must endeavor to make it worth your efforts." Rainy smiled, losing herself momentarily to his movie-star charm. He kissed her hand, then released his hold.

Feeling completely overwhelmed with her emotions, Rainy turned rather abruptly and hurried down the sidewalk. She couldn't even think of something witty or casual to say in reply. *What a mess I am. Losing control just like those silly girls I watched. They made cow eyes and fawned all over Phillip and I'm really no better.*

"There you are!" Sonny declared as he came walking out of La Fonda. "Where have you been? I looked for you at the boardinghouse, then went through La Fonda and still couldn't find you."

"I've been . . . well . . . I was showing Phillip a bit of Santa Fe," Rainy said defensively. She didn't care at all for the look of concern on her brother's face. How dare he treat her like some wayward child?

"I heard something rather disturbing and I need to know if it's true," Sonny said, the seriousness of his tone leaving little doubt that this was of utmost importance to him.

"So ask me," Rainy said, feeling annoyed.

"Is it true you've cancelled your entire vacation to take on the job of baby-sitting Phillip Vance?"

Rainy crossed her arms and lifted her chin defiantly. "And what if it is? I've been requested to courier the group. I'm being offered the two weeks at a later time and a handsome bonus as well."

"But we're generally a team," Sonny threw out. "Why didn't you talk this over with me?"

Rainy realized how inconsiderate she'd been. "I'm sorry, Gabe," she said, reverting to his given name. "I didn't think. I just figured you'd want us to take the job."

Sonny shook his head. "No, I don't want to take the job. I didn't want to take the last two jobs, but I let

Sam sweet-talk me into it. I need the time away more than I need the extra money. I have plans and things to prepare for."

Rainy had no idea what could possibly be so pressing. "Look, it's just for a couple of weeks. They couldn't promise me that they could reschedule the time off immediately following this tour arrangement, but we'd get the time off before June for sure."

"I need the time now, Rainy," Sonny replied. "And I'm taking it. I already figured you'd respond exactly this way. I've asked Duncan to be your driver for what I thought was only going to be a day or two, but I'm sure he'll drive you the entire two-week period if necessary."

"You arranged it without asking me first?" Rainy questioned.

"Just like you accepted the Blythe/Vance tour without asking me."

Rainy calmed at this and saw the logic of his reasoning. She couldn't argue with the truth. "Well, I suppose Duncan is safe enough."

"I trust him to take care of you and keep you out of trouble," Sonny said, stepping forward. He took hold of Rainy and sighed. "This time off is important to me. My friends Jess and Richard are in town and . . ."

"Sonny! I hate to interrupt you, but Sam told me to talk to you before I left for the day," Duncan Hartford stated as he emerged from La Fonda. "I've been looking all over for you."

"Seems everyone is looking for someone," Rainy muttered. She noted that Duncan carried the driver uniform. Ten-gallon hat, khaki jodhpurs, plaid shirt, and silk neckerchief were neatly stacked in the bundle Duncan held. "So you're going to be my driver," Rainy added before her brother could respond.

"He told you, huh? Hope you don't mind," he said, smiling rather nervously.

Rainy laughed. "Of course I don't mind. I was surprised, but Sonny deserves to take the time off."

Duncan watched her, almost as if studying her for some further response. Rainy grew a bit uncomfortable under the scrutiny. She knew if she looked deep into his eyes, she'd probably lose herself just as she had with Phillip Vance.

Maybe I'm just in love with the idea of being in love, she reasoned and moved her gaze to Sonny, where she knew she'd be safe. But the worried expression on Sonny's face did little to settle her nerves. Why was he so upset with her? And what was it that was making him suddenly act the part of the worried brother?

CHAPTER TEN

Duncan felt rather apprehensive as he waited for the tour group to gather. He knew the route to Taos but was less familiar with the side roads of the touring sights and Indian dwellings. He studied the map Sonny had given him and read the little notes that Sonny had penciled in.

> *Watch for the turn at this point.*
> *Sand is bad on the left-hand side.*
> *Got stuck twice in this area.*

All the notes were given as little warnings to keep Duncan from putting the dudes in danger, but it all seemed a bit overwhelming. After all, he wasn't here to be a driver—he was a spy. Duncan's mind went to Rainy as he glanced over the top of the map. She stood only about ten feet away, explaining something to one of Jennetta's friends. The woman seemed quite disturbed, and Rainy was doing her best to calm the situation.

She's really a remarkable woman, he thought. *She's so good with people and tolerates their moods with ease. How could she possibly be a suspect in a crime?* It just didn't fit the woman he thought he knew.

Still, the information given him just that morning left little doubt that there was still a big chance that Rainy and her brother were responsible for at least some of the thefts. The Hopis were missing several important pieces, and the artifacts hadn't gone missing until after Rainy's tour group pulled out only days ago.

Duncan had been on that trip, but he'd had no way to watch everyone at the same time. He couldn't help but wonder how the thieves could have spirited the pieces away. They would have had to load them onto the touring car, yet Duncan had checked and rechecked the luggage and storage areas. There had been no sign of anything out of place.

The law officials had been convinced he was mistaken. They'd chided him for not being observant enough or for overlooking something. But Duncan knew how closely he'd watched Rainy and Sonny. Neither one seemed at all interested in sneaking around or keeping him from knowing their business. In fact, they seemed only too happy to have Duncan tag along and often included him.

"No, we can't do it that way," Rainy protested. Duncan again raised his eyes to peer over the map. "There are rules we have to abide by, ma'am. That's just one of the many."

"Well, I find it very inconvenient," the woman huffed, then stormed off to where Jennetta stood arguing with one of her other friends.

Duncan smiled as Rainy looked his way. She took

the smile as an invitation and joined him.

"The tourists are misbehaving, I take it?"

Rainy gazed heavenward. "You have no idea how silly they're being. First, one wants to be allowed to sit up front. Then another wants to bring her parrot."

"Her what?" Duncan began folding the map, but his gaze was fixed on Rainy's rosy cheeks.

"Her parrot. Seems the woman's best friend in the world is a parrot and she never travels without him. I told her I couldn't have a parrot traveling with us, that sometimes special provisions were made for dogs— small dogs—but that a parrot was not going to be allowed." She motioned over her shoulder. "And that one wanted us to take a different route to Taos so that she could stop by her housekeeper's mother's house, where she's been promised a large bundle of herbs."

Duncan grinned. "But you've managed to keep them all in line. I'm proud of you. It couldn't have been easy."

Rainy took off her hat and fanned herself with it. "I'm really getting tired of it all. I almost wish I hadn't promised Phillip that I'd be their courier."

"Speaking of Mr. Vance, where is he?"

Rainy shrugged. "I have no idea. Jennetta said something about an herbal cleansing. I'm not at all sure what exactly that means, but I'm hoping it won't delay us past eight."

Duncan looked at his watch. "That gives him two minutes." He glanced around the gathered group. "Say, weren't there supposed to be six guests joining us?"

Rainy grinned and leaned forward. "Mrs. Dupree

has her moon in the seventh house or maybe it was the fifth house and one of the planets is not aligning as it should with her . . . hmmm . . . I forget."

Duncan laughed out loud, causing the entire group to look at him momentarily. He ignored them and looked back to Rainy. "And all of this means . . ."

"She isn't coming," Rainy replied rather conspiratorially. "She's not going anywhere until her moon straightens out."

"I'm sure that's for the best." Duncan couldn't help but be amused by the entire situation. "Ah, here comes the elusive Mr. Vance. Perhaps his moons were out of order as well."

Rainy giggled. "Let's hope not, for the sake of the tour."

Duncan watched as Phillip greeted his sister and her friends, then made his way to Rainy. "I apologize if I've held the party up. My sister insisted I partake of an herbal steam bath, and I must say it did much to refresh me."

As Rainy began complimenting the color and texture of Phillip's blue cotton blazer, Duncan glanced down at his uniform and knew how ridiculous he looked. He couldn't believe the Harvey Company had ever started such a uniform. There were rumors that Clarkson planned to tone down the outfit, but it wouldn't matter to Duncan. Right now he had to wear the outlandish gear in order to fit his role as driver.

"Phillip, can you help me get everyone into the courier car?" Rainy asked sweetly. "We really need to be on our way. This isn't our usual trip to Taos, and if we're going to make it to Chimayo and then the Puye ruins by lunchtime, we're going to have to be going."

"But of course." He raised her hand to his lips and kissed her fingers.

Duncan wanted to punch him and tell him to keep his hands to himself, but he knew Rainy was enjoying the attention by the look of pleasure on her face. She followed Phillip as he went to announce to the other ladies that it was time to go, while Duncan stood stock-still and watched the entire situation.

This trip was important. If artifacts disappeared on this trip, then it would be determined that Rainy had something to do with the thefts. Still, Duncan thought, if anything of value goes missing, there's also the fact that Jennetta and Phillip are on the tour. They were on the last tour as well. Of course, he didn't suppose they'd been on the previous tours when pieces had been stolen. But it was food for thought.

Desert flowers were blooming in their bold, vibrant shades. Flowers elsewhere might well delight the land-scape with pastels, but here the shades were brilliant, almost as if they were competing for attention. Over-head, the sky was a deep blue without so much as a hint of a cloud. The day couldn't have been more per-fect.

As they set out, Duncan tried to keep his gaze fixed to the road, but his mind kept wandering as they made their way north to Chimayo. From time to time he couldn't help glancing at Rainy, who told the travelers tidbits and tales from her Harvey Company monologue.

The guests were less than interested. Most talked as though the area had been their home for several years, leaving Duncan to wonder why they'd bothered to pay good money for the trip via the Clarkson Detours when cheaper modes of transportation could have been found. In fact, it made him wonder a lot, but he'd known the wealthy to do even more ridiculous things than take expensive tours. When he'd lived in Las Vegas, he'd heard of a wealthy woman who had huge quantities of ice brought in by train on a daily basis during the hot summer months. It was said she had a penchant for ice baths and filled her tub several times a day with ice and water for relief from the heat.

His mother also mentioned a woman who lived in Albuquerque who paid for the upkeep of seven automobiles so that she wouldn't have to ride in any one car but once a week. He supposed the wealthy were given over to all kinds of quirks and idiosyncrasies. Maybe taking this tour was just their way of being eccentric and lavish.

They arrived at Chimayo a little before ten. The road had been perfect and Sonny's instructions proved to be accurate. Duncan allowed Rainy to direct him to where he might park the touring car.

"Just head up this road," she told him, "then turn left at the first intersection, then turn immediately to your right."

The dirt street was lined with small whitewashed homes. Long strings of chilies hung from poles on the porches, drying in the sunshine until they were needed for cooking. Here and there a dark-skinned woman sat before a loom, a riot of color woven upon its frame. The colors reminded Duncan of the desert flowers.

Warm, spicy aromas drifted through the air, causing Duncan to wish he'd eaten a more substantial
breakfast. He stopped the car and secured the brake
before looking to Rainy for further instruction.

"As you know, Chimayo is famous for weaving.
We'll watch several weavers as they work on foot looms,
and you'll have an opportunity to purchase blankets or
other woven goods," Rainy announced.

She opened the car door and nodded to Duncan.
"Go ahead and open their side door," she told him.

Duncan had forgotten that Sonny generally did
this task. It was such a well-established routine with
Sonny and Rainy that he hadn't given it much
thought.

Duncan opened the door and helped the first two
ladies from the car. Both were very thin and seemed
intent on exploring. He stepped back to allow Phillip
Vance to emerge. The man smiled at him and nodded
as if they shared some special secret; then Phillip made
his way to Rainy and took hold of her arm.

Duncan refused to let the situation defeat his true
purpose, reminding himself that he needed to keep an
eye open for anything out of the ordinary. The only
problem was, he wasn't really sure what was ordinary
and what wasn't.

Rainy led the group along a short cactus-lined
path. Not knowing what else to do, Duncan followed.
He felt rather out of place and remained silent. Perhaps he'd go wait back at the car after he found out
whether or not Rainy would need him for anything
else. He didn't want anyone trying to sneak something
back to the car in his absence.

Rainy introduced the group of tourists to a short, plump Mexican woman named Maria, then stepped back as Maria began discussing the woolen yarn they used and the plants they procured for dying the various colors. Duncan noticed Phillip's interest in the information and took the opportunity to separate his hold on Rainy.

"If you'll excuse us for a moment," he said to Phillip, "I need to speak with Miss Gordon."

Phillip willingly stepped aside while Rainy allowed Duncan to lead her away from the group. "What's wrong?" she questioned.

"I don't know what I'm supposed to be doing," he said rather sheepishly.

Rainy laughed. "I'm sorry, Duncan. I didn't think. This is a rather special tour. Maria will have us busy for about thirty minutes. She's going to show them all about the weaving they do and then take them to another couple of weavers. After that the tour group will be ready to leave for Puye."

"Oh, I see." He glanced up the street toward a small adobe chapel. "Are we free to explore, then, or do you need to remain with the group?" Since Rainy and Sonny were the ones under suspicion, maybe he would just remain at Rainy's side and see what happened.

Rainy smiled. "I see you've spotted Santuario. Come on. Let's walk over. They usually have someone to give a tour and tell about the church."

Duncan smiled. "I'd like that."

"The ground where the church is built is said to be endowed with healing powers. People come and dig up bits of it for a kind of tea they make. It's amazing. They sometimes even take dirt to use as a charm to keep them safe from harm."

"I suppose we've both seen a great deal of superstition among the Indians and Mexicans in the area. I have to say that sometimes the cures seem worse than the curse they fear."

"As in drinking dirt tea?" Rainy asked.

Duncan laughed. "Exactly."

Santuario offered them shelter from the brilliance of the sun. Inside the air was cooler and the silence heavy.

"Welcome," an old man said in greeting. Duncan noticed his weathered brown face and toothless smile.

"We've come to see the church," Rainy explained.

"*Sí*, it is good that you do. This church was built by my ancestor Bernardo Abeyta. He was a poor farmer who had a vision to dig in the earth for his reward. As he dug here, he found a wooden cross and pieces of cloth that belonged to two martyred priests."

Duncan noted the wall niches where unusual native wood carvings made decorative offerings from artists now long gone. Below these and lining the walls on either side of the chapel were crutches and braces, cast off as proof of the healing powers of the church.

The man showed them around, talked of the miracles he'd seen, and then suggested a small offering might be in order to help with the maintenance of the shrine. Rainy produced some change and Duncan followed suit. The old man rewarded them with a gummy smile and thanked them profusely for their generosity.

"We need to get back to the car," Rainy said,

noting the time. "They should be returning in about five minutes."

Duncan couldn't believe how quickly the time had passed. "I really enjoyed that," he told Rainy as they made their way back.

"This part of the country is so full of history and interesting stories. I can't imagine ever leaving it—at least not for a long period of time."

Duncan wanted to comment about Phillip Vance's interests and how she would have to leave the Southwest if she followed after him. But he didn't. Rainy was a smart woman; no doubt she had considered all of those details.

The passengers returned with their purchases, and Duncan had to admit to being surprised by the stacks of blankets purchased by Jennetta Blythe. He raised a brow in question, but she refused to make so much as a single comment. Instead, she thrust the pile into his arms and walked away. Duncan didn't like the feeling of being dismissed, but he said nothing and worked to pack the blankets in the storage area of the touring car.

Once they were all back in the car, Jennetta made an announcement. "We've talked among ourselves and have decided that rather than stopping in Puye, we'd like to go straight to Taos."

Duncan looked to Rainy, wondering what her response to this would be. Rainy didn't seem in the leastwise disturbed by this announcement.

"Since this is a custom tour and you are all in agreement, we'll proceed for Taos. Of course, we would have taken lunch at Puye."

"It's of no concern. We'll eat a late lunch in Taos," Jennetta replied.

Rainy turned. "And you are all in agreement about this?"

Duncan heard murmurs of affirmation. Rainy turned to him. "Let's go."

Heavy clouds were moving in by the time Duncan pulled up to the Don Fernando Hotel in Taos. The adobe structure seemed something of familiar territory to the group as they commented about one thing or another. He pulled to the front of the hotel and looked to Rainy once again for instruction.

"In a moment you may make your way inside. I'll go ahead and see to your reservations," Rainy instructed. She opened her door and began to step out. "Oh, and one more thing." She paused and looked back over her shoulder. "I'll speak to the manager and arrange lunch. Shall we say in half an hour?"

Again the murmurs of affirmation were thrown out between animated female chatter. Phillip Vance had been surprisingly silent, but Duncan had no doubt that would change.

Duncan made his way around the car as Rainy entered the hotel. He opened the door and helped the ladies once again from the Cadillac, remembering this time to smile and make pleasant small talk as he'd seen Sonny do.

Phillip was the last to depart from the car. He stepped from the vehicle and yawned. "Just in time for a siesta," he said, smiling at Duncan.

Duncan had to admit a nap sounded like a wonderful idea, but he said nothing. He wondered instead what Rainy planned to do with her free time. Duncan's first choice would be to make his way to his parents' house and enjoy spending as much time as possible with them. But what of Rainy? If she were involved in some sort of thieving, he would be giving her all kinds of extra time to plot and consort. He was torn about what to do.

He began unloading the luggage and his heart grew heavy. *What if she is the guilty party? Just the idea of worrying about what she'll do with her free time must suggest that deep down inside I question her innocence.*

He hated the thought. He didn't want to believe Rainy capable of any wrongdoing. She always seemed so positive—so honest. Still, the words of the law officials rang loud and clear. *"Rainy and Sonny Gordon are the only ones who have been consistently available when objects of value have disappeared from various sites. We'd like to catch them in the act, however, and see if others are involved."*

Taos was full of priceless pieces: artwork, Indian crafts, church icons. Duncan knew the possibilities were limitless.

"Well, we have lunch arranged," Rainy said as she came around the car to join Duncan. "And here's a list of the room numbers and where each person is supposed to stay. They're a bit shorthanded right now, so I'll help you get the luggage up to the rooms."

"No, that's all right. I'll carry it myself. You've worked hard enough today."

She opened her mouth to reply, but it was then that Phillip Vance made an unwelcome entry. "Rainy, we're getting together tonight for a marvelous party.

One of Jennetta's friends is throwing it. He lives just a short distance from here. I'd like for you to join us."

Rainy looked to Duncan and he wanted very badly to advise her against it. Instead, he diverted his attention to the luggage and tried not to play eavesdropper.

"I'm sorry, Phillip. I really must decline. I'm tired, and tomorrow I'm to lead you and some of the others on a tour of Taos. I need my rest."

"But I promise to bring you back in plenty of time for a good night's sleep."

Duncan placed two bags directly in front of Phillip. Any closer and they'd be on the movie star's toes. Phillip stepped back a pace but said nothing.

"I can't go with you, Phillip," Rainy said. "Thank you for the invitation, but perhaps another time."

Phillip's expression was one of pure disappointment. Duncan wondered if he were merely acting or if his feelings for Rainy were such that he was truly devastated by her answer. Duncan had a hard time believing the man was capable of true feelings and decided it was all a show. He waited, however, until Phillip went inside the hotel before commenting to Rainy.

"The man is really good at what he does."

Rainy looked up, her expression betraying her confusion. "What do you mean?"

"I think he performs the part of wounded suitor," Duncan replied with a shrug. "I just think he's acting when it comes to the way he treats you."

"I take it Sonny asked you to look out for me," Rainy said, sounding slightly offended. "Well, you can tell him for me that I'm a grown woman and know very well how to take care of myself."

Duncan realized they were heading into dangerous waters and held up his hands in truce. "I don't want to fight with you. In fact, I was kind of hoping you'd agree to meet me later tonight. I'm going to go visit my parents for a time when I finish up here, but I'd like to have some time to talk with you. There are some things I need to tell you."

Rainy arched her brow. "Such as?"

"Not now. There are far too many details. Why don't we just say eight o'clock at the Plaza?"

"All right, if it's that important." Her expression remained doubtful.

"It is," Duncan promised. He had been given permission to leak a certain amount of information to Rainy. The plan was to feed her the information and see what her response might be. He hated the deception but knew of no other way to test the situation.

"Eight o'clock at the Plaza," Rainy repeated. "I'll be waiting for you."

Duncan nodded. "Thanks. I really appreciate it. And thanks, too, for the lovely day. I enjoyed our time at the church. It was a right bonny kirk," he said, exaggerating his Scottish burr.

Rainy turned to go and laughed. "Aye, 'twas indeed."

He watched her walk away. "And a right bonny lass to keep me company," he murmured. *She can't be guilty,* he told himself. *She just can't be guilty.*

CHAPTER ELEVEN

*R*ainy walked along the Plaza corridors, enjoying the crisp cool air. There was a bit of a bite to the wind, but she hardly minded it. The smell of pine filtered down from the trees, along with the undeniable aroma of woodsmoke. It would be a perfect night to curl up in front of a fire and read a book. Even better to share that spot with someone she loved. Her thoughts went immediately to Duncan. Did she love him? Or did she just love the idea of being in love? It was a question that came back to her over and over.

Surely this longing in my heart isn't just my own doing, she reasoned. *God must have put the desire there—otherwise I would go on being content to be single, just as I have been up until now.* But love? What did she know of love?

She knew she loved her mother and father and Sonny too. She knew she'd give her life for them, just as the Bible said: " 'Greater love hath no man than this, that a man lay down his life for his friends.' " The fifteenth chapter of John had always been one of

Rainy's favorites, but that thirteenth verse in particular touched her deeply. She loved her family and they were indeed her friends. Duncan Hartford made her feel weak in the knees and giddy, but so did Phillip Vance. But Phillip didn't love God and Duncan did. That fact, in and of itself, seemed to make the choice clear.

But Duncan hasn't shown any real interest in having us be anything more than friends. Surely he would have mentioned something—something to state his position if he felt that we should be more than co-workers and acquaintances.

Scanning the small adobe-lined square for any sign of Duncan, Rainy couldn't help but wonder why he'd asked to meet her here. Her mind, already cluttered with the confusion of her own thoughts regarding husbands and romance, refused to sort through any additional details. Even at supper she'd been a poor companion to those around her.

She'd wondered about Phillip and the party he'd invited her to. She'd observed the group departing for the gala and marveled at the finery and expense of their clothing. Phillip looked dazzling in his black tuxedo. He'd slicked back his blond hair, leaving only the slightest hint of a side part. His blue eyes were sparkling in the candlelight as he glanced across the room and caught sight of her. He had started to walk toward her table when Jennetta and a friend of hers named Sylvia latched on to him and practically dragged him out the front door of the Don Fernando Hotel.

Rainy thought he might have asked her again to accompany him to the party, and at that point, she probably would have said yes, although she could never have come up with an outfit to equal those of the women in Phillip's gathering. Jennetta wore a blood red gown with a deep plunging neckline. One of the other women, dressed in a full-length black velvet sheath, commented on the gown being designed by Chanel, but Rainy had little knowledge to determine whether the woman was right or not.

I've filled my mind with archaeological terms and phrases, spending hours poring over artifacts and pieces of clay while these women have made for themselves worlds of glittering jewels and fashionable attire. Rainy paused to look into the window of an art gallery. The painting displayed in the front window was of several nearly nude women lounging in a clothing-strewn dressing room. The title given was "Before the Show."

"Not exactly something you'd buy to hang in the living room," Duncan commented over her shoulder.

Rainy turned on her heel so quickly that she practically fell headlong into Duncan's arms. He reached out to take hold of her shoulders and smiled. "Glad you could meet me."

"I thought maybe you'd decided against coming," Rainy replied. "After all, it's almost quarter past the hour."

"I know and I do apologize. My mother was well into a second story of my great-aunt Tillie's birthday party when I realized how late the hour had gotten." He dropped his voice. "Do you forgive me?"

Rainy shivered, but not from the cold. She looked into his eyes and lost all rational thought. For years she'd admired Duncan from afar. It should have been so easy just to tell him that. But instead she couldn't even force her lips to form words.

"Rainy? Are you all right?"

Duncan's expression changed to one of great concern. Rainy forced herself to stop acting so childish. "I'm fine. Why did you want to see me?"

Duncan looked away and let go of his hold on her. "I've something to share with you. Something that I can't talk about in front of the guests."

"Sounds ominous. Why don't we take a seat and you can explain."

Duncan nodded. "I'm sure that would be best."

Rainy sat on one of the benches and waited while Duncan seemed to consider whether to sit close to or far away from her. He finally sat down fairly close and glanced around. With his hands affixed to his knees, Rainy longed to reach out and cover his fingers with her own. She held back, fighting her feelings. How silly she was, pining first over Duncan and then over Phillip.

Of course, she chided, *my feelings for Phillip could never go any further without him first coming to God.* The thought seemed to make clear her choice between the two men and she looked up at Duncan with a new perspective.

Maybe he'd asked her here to share his heart with her. Maybe he wanted to suggest their relationship deepen. She looked away and licked her lips. *What if he kisses me? Lord, is he the one?*

"I wanted to talk to you about something that's happened," Duncan began. "I was at the museum when I overheard talk about the theft of Indian pieces from the Hopi. In particular, some ceremonial flutes are missing."

Rainy's illusions were shattered. The memories of that long ago day when she'd stood accused of stealing from the university left a tremor in her voice. "Someone . . . stole flutes . . . from the Hopi?"

Duncan nodded. "It happened on our trip. There's some concern that one of the guests took the pieces."

Rainy cleared her throat nervously. "But you and Sonny packed and unpacked the Harvey . . . I mean courier car. You would have noticed if something were amiss."

"That's what I said."

"You mean they confronted you?" She felt a wave of nausea overcome her. It was as if the past had reared up to destroy her hope for the future. She felt light-headed and pressed her fingers to her temple.

Duncan suddenly looked very uncomfortable. Rainy couldn't help but wonder what had transpired to make him act in such a manner. "Duncan?"

He shook his head. "The thing is, I think we would do well to keep our eyes open and see if we can spot anyone in our group who might be trying the same thing here in Taos."

Rainy felt her stomach continue to churn, and she lowered her hand to comfort her midsection. "Jennetta and Phillip are the only ones with us this time who were also present on the last trip." She thought immediately of the Driscolls. Chester! He had been her bane once before. She tightened her hands into fists, wanting nothing more than to punch the arrogant little man right in the nose.

Duncan gently covered her hand with his own. "You planning to hit me?"

Rainy shook her head. "No, but I'd like to hit someone else."

"Because of the thefts?"

"That and so much more. There is one person in particular. . . ." She paused, suddenly realizing she was going too far. "I'm sorry, Duncan. I'm afraid I'm tired and not feeling very hospitable."

"Is that why you chose not to go with Phillip Vance and his friends?"

She looked at his face momentarily, then to the place where his hand still covered hers. A moment ago she was longing for such contact, and now all she wanted to do was get away. Before she could comment, however, Duncan continued.

"He's showing you a great deal of attention. Sonny is worried about it."

"Sonny should mind his own business."

"He just wants to see that you're safe—protected."

Rainy nodded. "I'm perfectly safe and protected. I have God as my shield and defense."

"Still, God doesn't want us to put ourselves in foolish situations," Duncan countered.

Rainy felt him gently stroke the side of her hand with his thumb. His touch was doing things to her mind—clouding her ability to reason. Without warning she pulled away. "I've asked God to send me a husband. If he's sent me Phillip Vance, what business is it of Sonny's . . . or yours?"

She started to walk away, but Duncan quickly

joined her. "So you plan to marry Vance?"

She stopped and looked at Duncan. His eyes seemed to darken, even as his Scottish burr became more pronounced. The look he gave her left Rainy trembling from head to toe. It seemed so consuming—almost as if he could see inside to her soul.

"I . . . well . . . I have no plans . . . I mean, he hasn't asked me."

"But you'd like for him to?"

Rainy tried to steady her nerves and looked away. She wanted to scream, "No, I'd much rather have you ask me." But the very thought of that concerned her more than anything else they'd discussed. Did she care more for Duncan than she realized? Had she grown so much closer to him in the last few weeks that her heart was ready to accept him as something more than a friend? Why couldn't it be a simple matter? She'd heard her friends tell tales of love at first sight—of being certain of the man they were to marry. *Why can't I feel that way? Why can't I know for certain that Duncan Hartford is to be my husband?* She looked up rather startled. Why had she put Duncan's name into that question rather than Phillip's?

Duncan still studied her, almost as if he could will the truth from her with his stare. Rainy straightened her shoulders and drew a deep breath. "I want to do whatever it is God wants me to do. I've prayed and asked Him to send me a husband." She felt her cheeks grow hot. "I don't even know why I'm telling you this."

"I think you do," Duncan said, his voice low and steady.

Rainy stepped back a pace. Being too close to Duncan Hartford just might well be her demise. "I don't want to discuss this any further. Some things should just be left unsaid."

"I disagree. I think there's a great deal between us that needs to be said," Duncan replied, moving toward her.

Rainy froze. She'd long considered the possibilities that might exist between her and Duncan. Was he the one God had sent? Would he tell her now of his love for her—of his desire to be a part of her life?

"I know that you realize Sonny wants me to keep an eye on you," Duncan began. "He worries, and probably because he knows you're so determined to find a husband, he knows that you're vulnerable to those who might use you to their own advantage."

Rainy swallowed hard. Her mouth had taken on a cottony dryness.

"I'm trying my best to help Sonny in this situation, and I think you really want my help. I think that's why you blurted out that revelation regarding a husband. If you're wise, you'll listen to the counsel of those who care."

"You?" The word came out more like a squeak than a real word.

"Of course, me. Getting to know you and Sonny, I can't help but care. I wouldn't want to see someone like Vance take advantage of you. Men like him are used to having what they want, and it doesn't really matter if what they want is a new suit or another human being. They'll take what they desire and never give the matter another thought."

Through the haze of her own confusion, Rainy was slowly but surely coming to realize that Duncan wasn't about to declare his feelings of love—but was instead proclaiming a brotherly warning of caution. The idea began to irritate Rainy. How dare he step into Sonny's role just because he'd taken on the job of driving!

"God has a plan for you," Duncan continued. "But you needn't rush it or try to manipulate it for your own desires. There shouldn't be such a sense of urgency in something that God ordains. You don't have to chase after it—He'll bring it right to you if you let Him. Maybe . . ." He paused and looked at her with such longing that Rainy almost felt startled. She edged back and he continued. "Maybe God just wants you to let go of your urgency for a mate and trust Him to be what you need."

Rainy's anger began to build. "What I don't need is for you or Sonny to lecture or preach at me. I know that God is in control, and further, I know that He has a plan for my life. I believe that plan includes a husband and children and when the time is right, God will show me the mate He has chosen. If that man is Phillip Vance, so be it. If not, then that is perfectly acceptable as well."

She walked away, surprised that Duncan didn't follow after her. Tormenting thoughts raced around inside her brain, giving her a headache and deep desire to run away from Taos and leave the whole tour group behind.

Father, I'm trying so hard to be obedient—to hear your voice rather than my own. I wouldn't choose a husband without being completely certain that he was the man you'd sent me. *I don't want to do anything to displease you. I kind of figured you sent Phillip into the picture when Duncan showed no interest. Of course, I suppose I haven't really given Duncan time to show true interest.* She toyed with that thought momentarily. With a heavy sigh, she sat down on a small rock wall and looked to the starry skies overhead.

Father, she continued her prayer, *I hate that Duncan treats me like a child—like a little sister—in Sonny's stead. I hate that Phillip's lifestyle leaves no room for you. I thought perhaps you'd brought Phillip into my life to be my husband. Then when I heard he wasn't interested in you, I wondered if maybe I was to help point him to you, and then he'd be ready to be my husband.*

Now Duncan suggests that I stop trying to work this out and rest in you—to let go of worrying after a mate and let you be my husband. I know that's biblically sound advice, but still it hurts. It hurts deep inside because I'm lonely and because I see other women around me enjoying marriage and children. And, Lord, I want that so very much.

She thought of the past and how much she'd always hoped to clear her name so that she might go forward in her career. Now that thought seemed so secondary to the issues of husband and babies.

Father, I want to clear my name as well. I don't want anyone to go on in this world thinking me a thief. And now there's this situation with the missing Hopi flutes. Will I be suspected again? Will someone from the university get news of this and suggest me as a suspect? A sickening dread coursed through her. The Driscolls! They were connected to Phillip and his sister. If word got out about this, they would most definitely stir up trouble.

"Oh, God, please help me," she moaned.

CHAPTER TWELVE

*S*onny moved through his parents' house carrying a large birthday cake that read, "Happy Birthday, Gunther." Gunther Albright was his father's best friend at the university. They'd been friends from the start of Raymond Gordon's teaching career in New Mexico. Gunther, a funny sort of man, was also the uncle of Chester Driscoll's wife, Bethel. Because of this, Gunther was, of late, quite often seen in the company of the Driscolls.

Sonny thought the combination a rather strange and complicated one. The Driscolls were really no longer welcomed in his parents' circle of friends. Their refusal to help clear Rainy of the ridiculous charges against her was the main reason for the falling-out, but Sonny suspected there were other problems as well.

Entering the dining room, where tables and the sideboard stood overflowing with finger foods, Sonny was immediately set upon by Bethel Driscoll.

"Why, Sonny Gordon," she fairly purred, "I'd know you anywhere." She reached out to touch him

and traced his jacketed arm down to where his hand held the cake tray. She toyed with the back of his hand for a moment, stroking her fingers over his knuckles as she smiled sweetly into his face.

She wasn't all that pretty, Sonny thought, but there was something about her manner that demanded attention. "My mother pointed you out to me. I understand you're Dr. Albright's niece and Chester Driscoll's wife."

Bethel laughed. She stepped away and raised her hands as if for emphasis. "I'm also very much my own person. Don't think to limit my identity to my uncle and husband."

Sonny nodded, rather mesmerized at the way her silver gown shimmered. She moved again, this time twirling in front of him as an animated child might do. "I purchased this dress in Los Angeles. Do you like it?"

"It's very nice," Sonny answered, not at all sure what else to say.

"My uncle and husband hate it. They said I paid too much for it and that it's much too revealing. But, as I mentioned, I'm my own person and I make my own decisions. I think women have long been oppressed in being prohibited from choosing their own fashions. Why should our choices be dictated by men? Do you realize that all of the most famous creators of women's clothing are men?"

"No, I suppose I didn't."

She nodded. "Well, I'm sure few people realize that. If so, they probably imagine that these male masters of style are being advised by women, but it simply isn't true. They choose the fashion and design and have all the say over how it comes together. Women are stuck with wearing whatever men throw their way. It's no different for the poor woman whose husband allows her only a few dollars for a new dress and shoes or the wealthy matron who fills her closets with new clothes twice a year. We are all following along under the guidance of men."

Sonny nodded, still unsure of what she expected him to say. Sometimes conversations with strangers were easy. At those times each person seemed to have an understanding of their lines, and the conversation took place with as much ease as could be mustered between people who had no intention of intimacy.

Conversing with Bethel Driscoll wasn't that way, however. Sonny felt completely confused. Not only that, but the cake tray was starting to feel pretty heavy.

"I'm afraid," he began, "that I need to deliver the cake."

"Of course." She smiled rather coyly. "We each must do what is assigned us."

Again he nodded, but he had no idea what she meant to imply. Was she making some kind of subtle comment about clothes again?

"Oh, there you are," Sonny's mother said as he came into the living room. "I was beginning to think I'd have to hunt you down." She smiled and took the tray from him. Sonny couldn't help but wonder what his mother would have had to say about Bethel's comments. He looked at her simple navy-colored dress. She seemed simple but elegant. Bethel just looked . . . well . . . cheap.

"Look at the cake, Uncle Gunther," Bethel said as she swept into the room to stand at Sonny's side. "I'll bet they had this marvelous confectionery made at that little bakery just down the street."

Sonny's mother seemed surprised by this statement but said nothing. Sonny felt the need to rush to her defense. "Mom made the cake. She's quite remarkable in the kitchen. We never feel the need to use the bakery."

His mother flashed him a look of gratitude as she said, "We hope you are enjoying your party, Gunther. You've been such a good friend to Ray and to me."

Gunther Albright wasn't a tall man. He stood only a few inches taller than Sonny's mother's five-foot-four-inch frame. But it was the pockmarks on Gunther's face that made him seem more foreboding. Smallpox had marred him as a teenager, but he seemed hardly concerned with the scars at the age of sixty.

With his snowy hair and bushy white eyebrows, Gunther looked much older than Sonny's father, yet Sonny knew them to be rather close in age. Gunther, however, wore the weight of his years.

"I can't thank you enough for the party," Gunther said, leaning forward to kiss Sonny's mother on the cheek.

"Hey, now, what is this?" Sonny's father called out as he joined the party. "I see you kissing my best gal."

The partiers laughed and Gunther smiled. "She's the prettiest in the room and she cooks like an angel. I couldn't let her go without thanking her."

"Well, I don't know that angels cook," Ray Gordon

stated, "but I do know Edrea makes the best food I've ever eaten."

"Hear, hear!" Sonny joined in. "It's one of the biggest reasons I've remained at home for this long." He wanted to take back the words as soon as they were spoken, for he'd inadvertently invited talk of his personal life.

"I wondered why you hadn't married yet," Bethel said, moving in for the kill. She lowered her voice so that only Sonny could hear her words. "Had I met you prior to meeting Chester, I might have given his proposal less consideration."

Sonny stepped back and tried not to look shocked. "Where is Chester? Is he here tonight?"

Bethel's expression took on a look of boredom. "I haven't any idea where he is. He talked of going back to Santa Fe to help my friend Jennetta with a special project."

"I thought Jennetta Blythe was going to Taos with her brother and some friends. They were hiring a courier car and my sister to guide them."

Bethel laughed. "Well, perhaps that's where he went, then."

Sonny tried not to worry about Rainy, but it was hard. He felt that he was responsible for protecting her from harm. *I should have given up my vacation and stayed with her. I shouldn't have given my responsibility over to Duncan.* He wanted to kick himself. Now he'd just worry about Rainy until he heard that she was safely back at the boardinghouse in Santa Fe.

Sonny heard his mother question Bethel about something, but he paid no attention to the words.

Instead, he chose that moment to move across the room and take up conversation with another of his father's friends from the university. He wasn't about to get caught up in another conversation about fashion.

"It's an outrage if you ask me," the man declared.

Sonny looked hesitantly at the man. He didn't want to nose into the conversation and so thought maybe it would be better to leave. He turned, but the man put his hand on Sonny's shoulder.

"What are your father's plans?"

"Excuse me?" Sonny said, shaking his head. "His plans for what?"

"The university is planning to eliminate a large number of their staff. They're asking for the older faculty to retire or step down. I was just wondering what your father planned?"

Sonny looked to where his father stood talking with Gunther. "I don't know. I can't speak to the matter because he has not discussed it with me."

"I suppose I've gone and let the whole messy ordeal out of the bag," the man said, his tone apologetic.

"What mess is that?" a younger man asked.

"Oh, you know. This matter of employment in times of trial and tribulation. The university situation."

Sonny was surprised to find Gunther Albright suddenly take up the conversation. "It's ludicrous, that's what," he called from the other side of the room. Sonny's father took a step back as Gunther continued. "How dare the university ask its older, more experienced members to leave? I've worked hard to establish

a good career and to benefit the school with my exper-
tise—and this is how they reward me? By putting me
out to pasture?"

Ray Gordon shook his head. "Now, Gunther, I'm
sure that's not what they intended. I would imagine
they're merely considering that younger men might
well have families—children to provide for."

"That's no excuse. I have plenty of expenses to see
to. They needn't rob me of my income and lifestyle in
order to benefit another. This idea that men with families are somehow more deserving of steady work holds
no credence with me."

"So you don't plan to retire, I take it," the man
who'd brought up the entire matter commented in a
rather lame fashion.

"I certainly do not. I will never retire for those reasons. Let someone else step down."

The somber spirit and intensity of the moment
seemed to steal away the party gaiety. Sonny's mother
worked quickly to retrieve the goodwill. "Let's have
some cake. I happen to know that this is Gunther's
favorite."

Sonny took the opportunity to slip from the room.
If anyone asked where he was going, he'd tell them he
was just getting a glass of water, which was exactly what
he planned to do. He would not mention that he'd
rather go hide in his bedroom and read the government reports on Alaska. If he tried that, his mother
would just hunt him down and force his return. So,
instead, he stood in the silence of the kitchen trying
hard to figure out what was to be done.

"My uncle is a bit of a killjoy," Bethel announced

as she came into the room. "But you have to understand. He lost a good deal of money during the crash
of '29."

"I'm sure he feels quite threatened," Sonny
replied, wishing Bethel would go back to the party and
leave him alone. He poured himself a glass of water
and drank.

"Yes, well, he needn't worry. I have enough money
to keep him in cigars and brandy until he dies. He's a
dear man who's cared greatly for me over the years. I
could never let anything bad befall him."

Sonny toyed with the glass for a moment. "Yes,
family should take care of each other. That's what the
Bible says."

"Oh, so you're one of those stuffy Christians who
has a list of rules and regulations a mile long," she
commented, moving closer. "Don't you ever want to
just have some fun?" She walked her fingers up his
arm.

"I have lots of fun, Bethel, but it never conflicts
with how I feel about serving God."

She feigned a pout. "But you could have so much
more fun if you just pretended that God wasn't looking."

Sonny shook his head. "Nope, I don't think I
could. You see, I know God is looking. He's always with
me, no matter where I go or what I do. He's in my
heart because I asked Him to be there. I want His company no matter the journey."

She shook her head and moved away. "A real man
wouldn't need a governess to watch over him."

Sonny chuckled. "No, indeed, but a real man can

always benefit by looking to his father for direction and companionship."

———————

Later that night, after the party had dispersed and the cleanup had been completed, Sonny sat alone in the living room. He thought about the evening and about his father and Gunther Albright. How terrible to have depended on a job—to have expected that job to last a lifetime—only to have it stripped from you.

"You seem deep in thought, my boy. Anything you care to discuss?"

Sonny looked up to find his father standing in the archway. "I guess I'm just concerned for you and Mom."

His father studied him momentarily before taking a seat in his favorite blue brocade chair. "And why is that?"

"Well, you heard the discussion regarding the university. Why didn't you say anything to me about this? I mean, I know you don't owe me any explanations, but I care what happens to you. Are you going to retire?"

His father seemed to consider the questions for a moment before leaning back and lacing his fingers behind his head. "I've given it a great deal of thought, and I've talked it over with your mother."

"And?" Sonny hated that his father was dragging this along at such a slow pace, but it was his father's way.

"And I believe I will retire. There are hard times coming, son. I have a bit of money saved—money that

I managed not to lose when so many others lost everything. It's not a lot, but enough. I also have the property in Scotland and your Uncle Sean would like to see us come back. He'd like help with the farm. And since you're moving to Alaska to work with your friends, we've decided we might as well go."

"Scotland? Truly? What about Rainy?"

His father nodded slowly. "That has been a concern of ours, but we trust God to work out the details. Rainy is welcome to come with us. Aye, in fact, she'd be quite good company for your mother. If I know Sean, and well I do, he'll have me working from sunup to sunset, and your mother could grow quite lonely."

"I worry about Rainy. She's so vulnerable."

His father leaned forward at this. "How so?"

Sonny shrugged. "I suppose I don't even know the answer to that as well as I'd like to. She's caught up in her feelings. She thinks God is leading her to marriage, but she doesn't know which man is the one God has picked out for her. She fancies that movie star Phillip Vance. But she also likes Duncan Hartford."

"Tell me about this movie star. He must have been pretty special for her to go canceling on her mom and me."

"He's smooth, that's for sure," Sonny said. "He's too smooth. He's all glitter and glamour. Women flock to him and girls adore him. He's shown Rainy a bit of extra attention and she seems quite intrigued. I'm sure I don't understand what she's experiencing, but . . ."

"No, there aren't any 'buts' in this matter. You can't know your sister's heart. As close as you two have always been—finishing each other's sentences and always seeming to know what the other one was thinking—you can't know her heart. Rainy is a woman, and that will always stand as a mystery between you two."

"But she isn't making sense. Duncan Hartford cares for her and his interest in archaeology is exactly what Rainy desires. He's caught her attention and she finds him handsome, intelligent, and in general what she's looking for. At least she did until Phillip Vance came to town. I'm just afraid that Vance will sweet-talk her into giving up the things most dear and precious to her, and then he'll hurt her."

"Rainy is an adult. She'll have to make some of these choices for herself. She's a good woman who loves God and knows to put Him first. If she does that and seeks His will in the matter, she should be just fine."

"And if she doesn't?" Sonny hated to even voice the question, but it had to be asked.

"If she doesn't, she'll bear the consequences of her actions, just as we all do. Satan is good at deceiving people. He comes as an angel of light and offers what looks to be a good and proper path. If he came as an unattractive monster with death and destruction written clearly on his face, no one would fall prey to his schemes. It could very well be that God does intend for Duncan Hartford to be your sister's husband. Perhaps Duncan and Rainy would accomplish wonderful things for the Lord. Do you suppose Satan will sit by and allow that?"

His father got up and looked down at Sonny with great compassion. "Pray for her, son. Pray the good

Lord will give her strength in adversity. She has to be able to determine what's of the Lord and what isn't. Rainy alone can make the choice, but we can support her in prayer . . . and offer advice when she allows it." He squeezed Sonny's shoulder. "Like I said, pray for her. She'll come through just fine."

"I hope so, Dad. I just don't want to see her hurt."

"Son, you can't keep that from happening. We all suffer in this world. Jesus said it would be so. That's why our faith must stand firm—otherwise we fall."

Sonny thought on his father's words long after he'd gone to bed. The next morning he was still considering them when a knock came on the front door. Opening it, Sonny found himself face-to-face with Bethel Driscoll.

"Hello, Sonny," she said, smiling in her coy manner. "I wonder if you might do me the tiniest favor."

CHAPTER THIRTEEN

*A*fter a week in Taos, the ensemble headed back to Santa Fe via the earlier forgone Puye ruins. The Puye Cliff Dwellings, carved into rock formed from compressed volcanic ash and cinders, stood as a reminder of the long heritage of New Mexican people. The Indians had built into the rock for protection, eventually stretching out to build adobe houses on the slopes and on top of the numerous mesas. The marvel of Indian pueblos fascinated Jennetta, who immediately declared upon arriving that she would write a poem devoted to the site.

Rainy directed the party to their outdoor lunch of chicken sandwiches, fruit, cheese, and coffee before taking her own lunch to a more secluded spot. Here, the scattered sage shared company with the buffalo grass and prickly-pear cactus. The varying shades of green gave a look of life to the desert land. From place to place a mouse or ground squirrel skittered across the parched ground in search of food and water.

At times this area seems so desolate and desperate, Rainy

thought. The ruins gave proof to a life that had once existed. Who were the people who had carved these homes of rock? Where had they gone? Had some enemy come to snatch them away? The archaeologist in Rainy demanded answers. She longed to forget the tour and just set out on her own to study the ruins and the legacy left behind.

There was so much she desired and so little that she seemed to truly be able to grasp. *How has my life become so completely contrary to what I had planned?*

Sitting there gazing across a landscape dry and pleading for moisture, Rainy thought of her own pleadings before God. Duncan's words haunted her. So much so that she began to pray with those comments in mind.

She truly sought her heart and realized there was a great deal of truth in what Duncan had said. She knew the urgency was not of God. At first, she believed the pressure had indeed been something divinely given in order to motivate her in the direction God desired her to go. But after Duncan spoke of God's timing and there being no need to rush into a relationship, Rainy truly began to reconsider.

I don't love Phillip Vance, she told herself as she nibbled on her sandwich. *And as fond as I am of Duncan, I cannot truly say that I love him either.* Although she knew that given Duncan's love of the Southwest and of archaeology, they would have much more in common than she and Phillip would share. Plus there was the most critical situation of all: Phillip did not share her faith. Duncan did.

But my feelings are so volatile where Duncan is

concerned, she thought. *He makes me feel* . . . She let her emotions surface for once. *He makes me feel cared about. He makes me feel safe.* She sucked on her lower lip and considered what such feelings might mean.

"I hope you don't mind if I join you," Phillip said, coming to sit beside Rainy.

Rainy smiled and stuffed her feelings down deep. "Not at all. Are you enjoying the ruins?"

"Very much. I had no idea such places even existed prior to coming on this trip. I think I shall miss it very much."

"When do you leave for Los Angeles?" she asked.

"Tomorrow. I'm scheduled on the afternoon train. I won't be able to get back for a while—probably not any sooner than a month, maybe two. But, Rainy, I want to come back and see you. Will you let me do that? Will you wait for me?"

Rainy felt a strange stirring as she gazed into Phillip's blue eyes. "I . . . well . . . I don't know if that's at all wise."

Phillip seemed genuinely startled by her response. He put down his lunch and looked at her for a moment as if trying to ascertain how honest she was being with him.

"Have I done something wrong?" he asked.

Rainy shook her head. "No, but I find my life turned upside down. I'm not at all sure what God would have me do."

"Don't hide behind God, Rainy."

She tensed at his words. It sounded very much like something Chester Driscoll had once said. "I'm not hiding behind God," she replied stiffly.

Phillip reached out and took hold of her hand. "I'm not insulting your faith. I'm simply trying to say that I've met people who pretended to be steeped in concern for what God wanted in their life, but rather than truly being of a spiritual mind, they were using the concept to avoid making decisions and commitments. I wouldn't want you to do that merely because the potential choices are frightening."

Rainy calmed a bit. Phillip couldn't possibly understand how she felt about her faith, but at least he wasn't trying to be harsh with her. "I don't believe I'm hiding behind God so much as hiding in Him. There's a big difference."

"Is there really?" He lowered his face but looked up at her in a manner Rainy had seen him do in the movies. It was done for effect—there was no doubt about it. She wondered if he did it consciously or if the action had been performed so many times before that by now it was a natural part of how Phillip Vance responded.

"Of course there is. The Bible is full of verses that talk about God being our shelter and refuge and about hiding in Him. He's the source of my strength and my hope. To consider any other way would never work for me." Rainy straightened and put down her sandwich. "I suppose we've all known people who didn't truly revere or honor God yet they used Him. But the Bible says God will not be mocked. I would imagine those people who have acted thusly will find a very difficult path ahead of them."

"You really believe that, don't you?" It was Phillip's turn to straighten and put aside his act.

"I do believe that, Phillip. God has too often shown himself in my life for me to believe otherwise."

"And He's never let you down? Never seemed indifferent to your pleas?"

Rainy looked away rather quickly. Phillip's words stung. Of course she had felt God rather indifferent in what had happened to her at the university. After all, He still hadn't seen fit to clear her name.

"I can tell by your reaction that you have felt God's absence at times. What happened?"

Rainy felt her breath quicken. "I'd rather not talk about it. It's rather painful."

Phillip squeezed her hand. "But perhaps we can ease that pain together."

Rainy shook her head. "Not until I find a way to right the wrong done me." She met his handsome face and offered him a weak smile. "Perhaps when that happens, then I'll share it."

"But why wait? I care deeply about you; surely you must know that," Phillip said, almost pleading.

Rainy remained unmoved. She had no desire to tell anyone what had happened. She didn't want pity or sympathy, and she certainly didn't want to be falsely judged. No, silence was the better choice.

"Look, Phillip, we have very different lives, you and me. I can't expect you to understand that, but it's true."

"There is no difference that can't be overcome," he said softly "if the parties involved desire to over-come."

"So you would give up movies and move to New Mexico in order to get to know me better?" Rainy asked, knowing the answer before he even spoke.

"A similar question might be asked of you, my dear. Would you give up New Mexico and come to California in order to better know me?"

Rainy knew in her heart that the answer was no. She couldn't see herself gallivanting off to the coast, dressing in stylish fashions and lingering until all hours at one party or another.

"Your silence tells me that you are uncertain," Phillip spoke before she could say a word. "So don't give me an answer just yet. Think about it. Think about it for a month, and when I return we can discuss this again. Then maybe you can give me an answer."

Rainy pulled away from Phillip's touch and began gathering up her lunch. "I'm not sure what the question really is."

"The question is, will you stay at my place in California and get to know me better? The house is positively huge and there are always other guests. You could come out with Jennetta, if nothing else. Please say you'll at least think about it. Please?"

Rainy felt that same sense of urgency wash over her. There was no peace in dealing with Phillip Vance. "I can't make any promises." She got to her feet and looked back down at where he sat. "I'm sure I'll be around, but I can't say that I'll be any closer to an understanding of this situation then than I am now."

She walked away feeling peace come back in little showers of hope. *God truly has this under control. Phillip Vance doesn't hold the answers to my future—God does. And furthermore, Phillip cannot understand this. It's not something he has experienced or looked at with any real depth of*

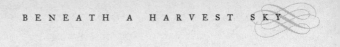

consideration. Perhaps I should have told him that I would consider spending more time with him if he would spend more time with God.

But was it fair to bargain with one person's desires and force a relationship with God as a means to a more beneficial end?

She wished her mother or father or even Sonny might have been present in order to discuss the matter more thoroughly. She desperately needed guidance.

"You seem quite down in the mouth," Duncan said as he caught up with her. "Are you feeling all right?"

Rainy looked up at him ready with an angry retort, but instead she held her tongue. His expression showed genuine concern and it softened her heart. "I'm fine. Just tired."

"The days are getting warm," he offered. "The heat is enough to wear anyone out." He kicked at several rocks, and Rainy watched them dance away and settle into their new location. The desert was easily disturbed, but just as easily it readjusted itself to the disturbance. Would that human beings could do as well.

Rainy and Duncan walked back to the car in an awkward silence. Rainy wanted him to go away, but at the same time she wanted to pour her heart out to someone. "Do you ever feel confused about choices you have to make?" she finally asked. "You told me the other night that God has a plan for me—for everyone," she said, suddenly feeling rather nervous. "You also said I shouldn't feel the need to rush or manipulate the situation. But we do have to act sooner or later. We make a choice, even in deciding not to choose."

"That's true enough," Duncan said somberly. "I never suggested choices didn't have to be made. I simply said I didn't believe there should be such a sense of urgency in something so entrusted to Him." He glanced to the skies and momentarily Rainy did the same. The color was a soft turquoise with threadlike wisps of white clouds. How serene it all seemed. Rainy would have loved nothing better than to lose herself in the vast open expanse and never deal with another single problem.

"But . . ." she hesitated. She felt certain Duncan expected her to continue the conversation, but what could she say? How could she explain what she was going through? How could she explain her despair about the past at the university, her shock over the news of the missing Hopi flutes, and her desire to find a mate? How could she hope Duncan could understand that she knew Phillip Vance was a liability she couldn't afford, yet at the same time he was so very attractive and . . . *Forbidden fruit.* The thought came to her in a flash. Was that what this was about? Was God somehow testing her? Testing her desire to stay true to Him?

"But what? You never finished your thought," Duncan said softly.

Rainy caught the intensity of his gaze. It left her feeling almost breathless. My, but he was handsome. She noted how the sun had darkened his skin to a honey gold.

"Oh, goodness, look at the time," Rainy said. "We need to get back to Santa Fe." She hurried off to gather the others, leaving Duncan looking rather stunned by her exit. She couldn't explain herself to him, so she decided it was just better to walk away. *No sense in letting him get in the middle of this when God so clearly has allowed this entire situation to test my trust in Him.* She would simply devote more time in prayer for the entire matter. Once they were back in Santa Fe, she'd put in for her time off and return home for a good long think. God clearly wanted her attention, and Rainy didn't want to ignore her heavenly Father—even for a moment.

The next day Rainy packed her bags. She felt confident that the best thing for her to do right now was return home to Albuquerque and take some time for quiet reflection and prayer. No Phillip Vance. No Duncan Hartford. Just the peaceful sanctuary of her parents' home and their sweet company.

Her mother would help her to better understand her mixed-up feelings, and Sonny and their father would keep her from becoming too maudlin. Her father might also have some ideas about what she could do to get the Driscolls to clear her name regarding the university thefts. He seemed to be the only one who really understood that it was more than a matter of letting the issue fade away. She wanted to be vindicated. There were still people out there who believed her a thief, and Rainy could not bear this.

Making her way downstairs, she paused to speak with Mrs. Rivera. "I'm leaving now. I will be gone for two weeks, so don't be giving my room away," she teased the older woman.

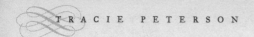

"I wouldn't dream of it. You and Sonny are my best boarders."

Rainy grinned and handed her the month's rent. "Here, this will ensure it, just in case you forget us. Sonny should be back next week, unless he's made other plans that he hasn't shared with me."

"How will you get to the train station?" Mrs. Rivera asked.

"The touring company promised to send someone for me." Rainy shifted her bags and looked at her watch. "I'd better hurry. The driver is probably here already."

Rainy hurried outside, noting as she went through the door that the black touring car was waiting for her at the end of the walkway. She looked around for the driver and was taken off guard when Duncan appeared at her side. He took hold of her arm and escorted her without a word to the car.

"I was asked to drive you to the train. You're leaving in a mighty big hurry. What's the rush?" he asked as he took her bags in hand. He seemed to consider the larger of the two for a moment, then tossed both cases onto the backseat and helped Rainy into the front.

"I wanted to spend time at home. You know I was scheduled to take a two-week vacation. Sonny's time is nearly up, but I felt it was important to go anyway. Sonny can either work with another courier or he can do odd jobs for Major Clarkson until I get back."

Duncan started the car and eased it into the traffic. Rainy noticed he'd dressed rather smartly, leaving his tour-driver uniform at home. He looked quite handsome in his trousers and jacket of charcoal gray. A crisp white shirt accented with a red-and-gray striped tie made Duncan look more like a railroad owner than an employee. His fedora was the perfect touch.

"You're certainly dressed up," Rainy said before she realized the words were out of her mouth.

Duncan seemed uncomfortable with her analysis. "I was called to a meeting. It seemed appropriate attire."

"Oh." Rainy looked at him and saw that his jaw had tensed. There was the slightest tick in his cheek, suggesting he wasn't at all happy. "You seem upset."

"I am upset."

"Oh." Should she ask why? Should she try to pry into his affairs as he had done with her? Before she could question him, however, Duncan pulled the car to the side of the road and turned to her.

"Two very expensive paintings disappeared from Taos. Did you by any chance hear anything about it?"

Rainy shook her head. "No. Should I have?"

He fixed her with such an intense look that Rainy lowered her gaze to her blue cotton skirt. She trembled when he reached out and took hold of her chin. He raised her face to meet his gaze and leaned forward. For just a moment Rainy thought he might kiss her.

"If you do know something about this, you must come forward."

A sense of confusion washed over Rainy. "Why would I know anything about it?"

"Because they disappeared the day we left—or rather the night before."

Rainy shook her head. "I hadn't heard so much as a single bit of gossip suggesting it. Was that what your meeting was about?"

Duncan stiffened and dropped his hold. He gripped the steering wheel tightly. "Why are you leaving Santa Fe?"

"I told you," Rainy replied. "My work for Phillip and his sister is done, and I need a vacation. Phillip is heading back to Los Angeles this afternoon, so there is no reason to stay here."

Duncan looked at her with an expression that suggested disbelief. "No reason?"

Rainy shook her head. "No working reason. Duncan, what is this all about? I don't understand your anger. I don't know what I've done to make you feel so hostile toward me, but—"

"Rainy, I don't feel hostile toward you." Duncan took hold of her hand. "I'm worried about you."

The sinking feeling that there was something more to this than met the eye caused Rainy to pull away. "Why are you worried about me, Duncan?"

He sighed and leaned back against the car door. "There are so many reasons to worry about you. I feel like, even though we've gotten to know each other better through the Detours, I don't know you at all. I'd really like to, but you seem far more interested in other things."

"Other things or other people?" Rainy shot back in defense. "Is this about Phillip?"

Duncan clenched his jaw again. Rainy could see the muscles in his neck tense. He started the car back down the street. For several blocks he said nothing, then finally he glanced over. "I don't want to see you hurt."

"I don't want to see me hurt either. That's why I wish you'd just tell me what this is all about."

"I can't," Duncan admitted.

"Can't or won't?"

"I can't. There are things going on that I can't talk about."

Rainy watched him for a moment longer, then turned her attention to the passing scenery. She could barely contain her frustration at Duncan's riddles. Why couldn't he just speak the truth and let her be responsible for whatever needed to be addressed? She hated it when people thought they were protecting her and instead only ended up hurting her more. Chester had been that way. He had told her it was for her own good that he hadn't shared with her all that he knew about the missing artifacts.

The missing artifacts.

The words stuck in Rainy's head. Duncan talked about the theft of the Hopi flutes and now the paintings from Taos. Her stomach churned and dread settled over her like a wet blanket. *How could I have been so dense? Dear Lord, do they really think I'm responsible?*

The sudden revelation perfectly explained Duncan's attitude. "You think I stole the paintings and the flutes, don't you?"

Duncan continued to drive, his gaze fixed on the road ahead. "No. *I* don't think that."

He had emphasized the word "I," leaving Rainy even more certain of the situation. "But someone else does. Is that right?"

Duncan pulled into the station and parked the car. He sat for several moments before turning to Rainy. "I have to say I'm far more concerned about the situation with you and Phillip Vance."

Rainy shook her head. "But why? That's a matter that is clearly none of your concern."

"Maybe not directly, but since Sonny asked me to look after you while—"

"Leave Sonny out of this," Rainy said, opening her door. "If you have some reason to care about what happens to me, then stop hiding behind Sonny and tell me so. Otherwise, leave it alone."

She slammed the door, startled at the boldness of her words. She grabbed her bags off the backseat and rushed to the depot. *Oh, Lord, I'm always making a mess of things. Put a guard on my mouth and keep me from false accusations. You know I've had nothing to do with any of the missing pieces. You are the only one who can clear me of these suspicions. I don't know if someone other than Duncan considers me to be involved, but I am worried. Worried enough that I know I'll never have a moment's rest at home unless you take the matter from me and I yield it in turn.*

At the depot door she turned. Duncan remained in the car, the look on his face suggesting a bit of shock. *Good,* she thought. *Let him stew over this as I have.*

CHAPTER FOURTEEN

*T*he beady-eyed Indian Affairs official sat opposite Duncan's desk at the museum. "I want to know everything you did and saw while in Taos," the man said.

"I saw nothing that would help you with the recovery of the two pieces of art that disappeared from Taos," Duncan replied. "I checked and rechecked the luggage as best I could—though I obviously was not able to look inside. Not that two large oil canvases would have fit in any of the bags I loaded."

"Canvases can be rolled," the Taos deputy sheriff offered. He sat to Mr. Richland's left and seemed quite anxious about the entire matter. Duncan couldn't even remember the man's name, but his anxiety and nervous twitching made him seem an unlikely candidate for law enforcement.

"I'm sure you may not be aware of what else is going on in the world," Richland began in his condescending manner, "but this country stands on the brink of a financial disaster. People are stockpiling money and goods—at least those people who seem to

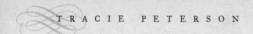

understand what's happening. Someone has no doubt taken the Hopi artifacts and paintings in order to sell them to the highest bidder."

Duncan asked what seemed a logical question. "But if everyone is hoarding, who will be buying?"

"The wealthy will always find a way," Richland answered. "There are plenty of well-to-do people who intend to stay that way. They know that diversifying their holdings will be the way to stability."

Duncan shook his head. "It doesn't make any sense. There are pieces here in Santa Fe that are worth far more than those on the reservations. Why steal a few historically important artifacts that probably have very little monetary value—except to museums?"

"People have collections," Richland responded. "Collections that include all manner of items. Don't play naïve with me, Mr. Hartford. You may have no idea of the true financial status of this country, but surely you understand that there are those who would steal such artifacts to sell to museums or personal collectors."

"Of course I understand that, Mr. Richland." Duncan fought back his irritation with the man. "I'm merely suggesting that financial gain may not be the reason why those pieces are missing."

"What's your theory on the matter?" the deputy sheriff asked.

"I've given some thought to this while driving for the tours. You both realize, don't you, that the Harvey Company recently sold the Indian Detours to Major Clarkson."

"What of it?" Richland questioned.

"Suppose this isn't about the money or the Indians or even the oil paintings. What if this is about the transfer of the company? What if we're dealing with a disgruntled former employee or even someone in the Harvey Company who doesn't want to see Clarkson succeed?"

"That makes very little sense, Mr. Hartford," Richland said. The deputy nodded in agreement with him.

"I think it could make perfectly good sense. Think, gentlemen. If you were angry because you'd lost your job after the sale of the Detours business, what might you do to settle the score?"

The men stared blankly, so Duncan continued. "You'd do whatever it took to make the business look bad. You'd arrange for things to happen that could be blamed on the company. I think it's completely possible that someone has a grievance against Major Clarkson or the Harvey Company and they've set this up to create mistrust with the Indians and cities involved with the Detour business."

"But the thefts have been going on longer than Clarkson has owned the business. More information has surfaced to prove that smaller articles have disappeared from the reservations during past tours," Richland stated coolly.

"So that might help us narrow the field," Duncan replied. "Maybe we need to focus on employees who were fired from the Harvey Company before the thefts began."

"I think you're grasping at straws," the nervous deputy sheriff announced.

Duncan shrugged. "You asked me to check into

this situation. I've done a great deal of thinking and observing. I saw nothing to suggest that either the employees or the guests of the Detours have stolen a single article. Of course, my experience is limited to only a handful of trips, but that's my observation."

"Then perhaps the employees or guests are arranging for the theft and then are accomplishing it through another person—someone not on the trip. This would be very easy for an employee to pull off."

Richland's determination to pin the matter on the Gordons made Duncan all the more determined to fight.

"Maybe some of your Indians are involved. After all, the United States government hasn't exactly been fair with them at times. Now that the country is in the midst of this financial downturn you mentioned, perhaps the Indians have joined together to create this mishap for their benefit."

Richland stiffened. "Mr. Hartford, that accusation is even more ludicrous than your previous suggestion."

"I'm not accusing anyone—and neither should you. I see no evidence to suggest any real culprit. That's why I want you to consider every angle before deciding who's to blame. Sonny and Rainy Gordon have no reason to steal from the Indians. They've been on good terms with them for years. In fact, Miss Gordon has close friends among both the Hopi and the Navajos."

Richland stood. "But the pieces are missing nevertheless! I need answers, Mr. Hartford. Solid, dependable answers that may be defended in a court of law."

"And I'm telling you that I have no answers for you—only speculation. I've seen nothing to offer as proof. You'll have to wait until I do before I allow you to accuse friends of mine."

"Oh, so now the Gordons are friends?"

"You can hardly work around the clock with some-one and not have them become either a friend or an enemy. Sonny and Rainy Gordon are decent God-fearing people. They come from a good family. I've even shared dinner in their home. They're simple people who show no evidence of wealth—ill-gotten or otherwise."

"If they're such good people, then why have they covered up the real reason Rainy Gordon left her posi-tion with the university?" Richland asked, the sneer on his face leaving Duncan little doubt that he had already determined Rainy was guilty.

"And what would that reason be?" Duncan ques-tioned, his Scottish brogue thickening with emotion.

"It's not on the official record, mind you, but I have a very dependable source who has told me in confidence that Rainy Gordon was responsible for the theft of several university museum pieces. They found the articles in her desk, in her locked office."

Duncan felt the wind leave him momentarily. Could it possibly be true? Was this the thing that stood between Rainy and the Driscolls? He knew Marshall Driscoll was a powerful man with the university. Per-haps this was the real reason Rainy appeared to despise the man.

"I can see I've silenced you with this news," Rich-land said. He pulled out his pocket watch and popped open the case. "I have to leave now or I'll never make my train. I want evidence, Hartford. We aren't paying you to ignore facts."

"I'm not ignoring anything," Duncan said, feeling sick to his stomach. Surely Rainy was innocent. "And so far," he added, "I've not been paid a cent."

Richland pushed an envelope across the top of the desk. "Here, this should satisfy you for a time. I just want to know that I'm getting my money's worth."

Duncan looked at the envelope—his thirty pieces of silver. At least that was how it felt. "I didn't accept this job for the money." Duncan pushed the envelope at Richland. "I don't want your money. I only want the stealing to stop. I was willing to help you because of the request of my family's friend, Mr. Welch. But I'm not taking your money."

"Suit yourself—so long as the job is done properly. The Gordons will be on vacation the remainder of this week. While both are gone, we can keep an account of whether or not any other artifacts or valuables disappear. Meanwhile, I will expect you to nose around and ask questions. I'll return within the week and expect to see something more concrete."

Richland hesitated a moment, then picked up the envelope. He watched Duncan the entire time, as if expecting him to change his mind. When Duncan did nothing but watch him, Richland motioned to the deputy sheriff and headed for the door. "Remember that what I've told you goes no further than these walls. There is no doubt those who are involved would sell such details to the wrong person."

Duncan nodded. Who could he possibly tell this

to? Sonny? Rainy? There was no one he could share this with—except his heavenly Father. *Oh, Lord,* he began to pray, *I need clear direction on this. I need understanding.*

———

After spending his lunch hour in prayer and working well into the evening hours on the backlog of work he'd promised the museum, Duncan finally left for his small house on East Palace Avenue. The tiny territorial-styled house was a haven away from the busyness of his life. His one-story home had a lovely stone porch with five simple roof supports. Above this, the roof parapet was trimmed in a fired-brick crowning that gave the house a little bit of charm and personality. Inside, the furnishings were simple yet solid. He'd purchased only those pieces necessary for his comfort, despising clutter and unnecessary bric-a-brac, though at times the house seemed empty and rather lonely. He couldn't help but wonder what a woman might do with the place.

As he walked toward home Rainy's smiling face came to mind. He could almost smell the scent of her perfume. What would she suggest doing with the house? Would she want to add pieces of Indian art? Maybe she'd prefer to make it over in a manner less Southwest in nature.

But she loves the Southwest, he thought. That much he'd come to realize. She might have her secrets from the past, but she loved New Mexico and all it offered. He'd never known any woman to so thoroughly enjoy

herself while sitting among ruins and desert landscape.

She can't be responsible for the thefts. Rainy isn't like that.
He felt confident in his thoughts—so confident, in
fact, that his only real concern was not how to prove
Rainy innocent but rather how to find the guilty party.

Humming to himself as he made his way up the
road to Palace Avenue, Duncan was surprised to catch
sight of Jennetta Blythe. Actually, her laughter had
caught his attention first. The woman had an annoy-
ing nasal laugh that set Duncan's nerves on edge.

He glanced across the street to see Jennetta in the
midst of a small gathering. She seemed to be showing
off some new find. Duncan couldn't really see what
she held, but her circle of friends seemed more than
a little impressed. He slowed his walk, hoping for a
glimpse.

He paused beside a stand of honey mesquites,
whose pale yellow blooms offered a sure sign that
spring was upon them. The fragrance wafted on the
breeze, but Duncan couldn't take time to truly enjoy
it. He watched Jennetta move toward the house, her
flock gathered around her as tight as could be. But
then, just before she followed her friends into the
house, Duncan caught a glimpse of a long cylindrical
object in her hands. Laughter filled the air as the party
disappeared one by one into the house.

Still uncertain of what Jennetta had held, Duncan
couldn't help but wonder if it might be one of the
missing Hopi flutes. From the description given him
earlier, it was the right size. He wished he could have
gotten a better look. With a sigh, he headed up the

street as the last of Jennetta's entourage disappeared into the house.

How am I going to figure this out? I can hardly go up to that house, knock on the door, and demand to know what Jennetta was showing everyone. He gritted his teeth in frustration. There had to be an answer, but none seemed to present itself to him.

"If I don't learn the truth and do it soon," he muttered, "they'll blame Rainy and maybe even charge her with stealing. I can't let that happen."

The intensity of his feelings startled Duncan. He knew he couldn't deny the thoughts that flooded his mind—his heart. He was falling in love with Rainy Gordon.

He laughed out loud. "Falling is hardly the word for it. I've already fallen—and hard."

———

"It really was the strangest thing," Sonny told Rainy as they cleared away the breakfast dishes. "I couldn't believe Bethel Driscoll was asking me to drive her to Gallup. I mean it just didn't make sense. She offered me an enormous amount of money and told me it was vital that she get there and that she didn't trust anyone else."

"What did you do?" Rainy put the dishes in the sink and turned to face her brother.

"I told her no. I couldn't see putting myself in the position of being alone with her for several hours. It just didn't make sense. I thought the appearance of it would be damaging to her reputation and told her so. She laughed this off and insisted she absolutely had to get to Gallup to pick up something. I suggested she take the train but she refused, saying the car was the only way that would work. I have no idea what it was all about, but when she saw that I would have no part of it, she left quite angry."

"That is really strange. You don't suppose . . ." Rainy's words trailed off into thoughts. She'd always believed Chester had something to do with the university artifacts showing up in her office. Maybe Bethel and Chester were involved in the missing artifacts and oil paintings. It seemed a long shot, but Rainy thought it entirely possible.

"What were you about to say?"

Rainy shrugged. "It isn't important. Just a fleeting thought. Anyway, I'm so glad you extended your vacation. It's been very pleasant here with you and Mom and Dad. I really hate to go back."

Sonny shifted and looked at the floor. "You wouldn't have to go back."

"Why would you say that?" Rainy questioned as she took heated water from the stove and began making herself a cup of tea. "Want some?" she asked, holding up the pot.

Sonny shook his head. "I only meant that maybe you should consider going to Scotland with Mom and Dad."

Rainy replaced the pot and eyed her brother in curiosity. "Go to Scotland?"

"Sure, why not?"

"Are you planning to go to Scotland?" Rainy noted the sudden change in Sonny's features. "You are, aren't you?"

"Now wait just a minute, Rainy. I am making plans, but . . ."

"No, I can't believe this. You're planning to leave. Why didn't you tell me you were going to go with Mom and Dad?" She felt betrayed—deserted. "I can't believe you wouldn't talk this over with me before making such a serious decision. I know we're adults, but I thought we had a closeness that allowed for such confidence."

Sonny stepped forward. "We are close, Rainy, but you're misunderstanding."

Rainy raised her hands. "Stop. I'm not going to discuss this any further." She left the kitchen and walked out into the courtyard. Here her mother's lovely garden offered comfort as the world seemed to crumble around Rainy's feet. The security she'd once counted on was seeping through the cracks a little at a time. Why was this happening? How could Sonny make plans without consulting her first?

Because he's a man and fully capable of choosing his own path, her mind suggested.

But we always talk things over. We always make certain that we get each other's advice, she argued with herself.

Oh, and that's why you consulted Sonny before getting all wrapped up in Phillip Vance? That's why you discussed putting off the vacation in order to cater to Phillip and his rich friends? Rainy immediately felt awash in guilt. Her own conscience spoke against her.

What will I do without him? She turned back to the house. "What will I do without all of them?"

Rainy knew it was silly to be so alarmed. She wasn't a child anymore. She was nearly twenty-eight years old.

Maybe she wouldn't be feeling so abandoned if she had already married and had started a family of her own.

She sat down and toyed with one of her mother's rosebushes. The plant had many buds on it, and while most hinted at the rich pink color to come, some were so tightly formed they offered nothing but their green casing.

My life is just like this, she thought, gently fingering the hard green cover of one bud. *I'm wrapped up tight, so unaware of the possibility of a future outside my little shell. I've so much to learn—so much to do—and yet here I sit, afraid of what's to come, angry because my life is changing.*

She glanced up and caught sight of Sonny watching her from the kitchen window. *I should apologize, I suppose.* But she turned away rather than motioning for him to join her. No doubt he would be wounded by her actions, but she was wounded as well. And sadly, she couldn't even truly understand why.

I know he's entitled to make plans without consulting me. I know he's a grown man and well past the age of going off on his own. If he wants to live with Mom and Dad in Scotland or anywhere else, that's completely his right. She sighed. *So why do I feel so lost and empty? Why does it hurt so much to know they're all going away?*

CHAPTER FIFTEEN

The time following their return to Santa Fe was filled with a flurry of visitors and tourists. Apparently, just as Major Clarkson had hoped, the rich still desired diversions from their daily jobs and the ever depressing news of the economy.

Rainy sat in a meeting for the couriers and their drivers. Clarkson wanted to make certain each person was advised as to the plans for the scaled-back Detour services, and so he had arranged meetings where the supervisors would be able to convey the important details of their changes in business.

Rainy gave only halfhearted attention to one of the newer supervisors, Mrs. Lehman, as she addressed the workers. "We have several fixed routes that we will offer on a regular basis. Some of the specialty trips we offered in the past can still be had on a person-by-person basis. These customized trips will be expensive, however, as our costs are up quite drastically. There are those of you who have proven to be much requested as couriers and drivers, and of course we will continue to accommodate those requests whenever possible."

Rainy sighed and shifted uncomfortably. She caught Sonny's sympathetic gaze from across the room and looked away quickly. Sonny had attempted to discuss the family's move to Scotland several times, but Rainy refused to hear him out. The idea still disturbed her in ways she couldn't explain. Before he could get a word in, she'd told him that it was better to leave it in the past—that she was trying hard not to hold on to her anger and frustration. She'd even told him that he was entitled to do whatever he pleased with his life— yet everything she said seemed to frustrate him further.

"The Taos trip, of course, will continue to be offered," Mrs. Lehman announced. "The costs are minimal and the three days offer a well-rounded tour for most tastes. It has proven to be our most popular tour by far, and so to show that we sympathize with the American worker, we've lowered the price by ten dollars. Instead of sixty-five dollars, we'll be charging fifty-five dollars for the three-day tour and only thirty-five dollars for the two-day tour."

The mention of the Taos tour caused Rainy's mind to drift again—this time it went to Phillip Vance and his continued absence. He should have been back by now, but Rainy had heard nothing. She had only received one short letter since he left for Los Angeles. In it Phillip had maintained an ardent passion for Rainy and the fervent desire that she join him in California. Rainy never gave serious thought to the arrangement, although she did check the train schedule to Los Angeles on more than one occasion. But after that brief note in the early days of his absence, there had been no other communication. A month came and went and still there was no sign of Phillip, and Rainy had no desire to look up Jennetta Blythe to ask where her brother might be. Perhaps this was God's way of keeping Rainy from a painfully wrong decision.

Of course, the only real decision Rainy had made in her very real battle of the wills was to let go of the matter and let God take control. She still earnestly desired a husband and family and still kept her gaze on Duncan and Phillip both as potential mates; however, she wasn't feeling the same frantic desire that had haunted her not so long ago. It was difficult to trust that God had everything under control. She supposed it was more difficult for her than most because of what had happened at the university. Why would a just and fair God allow her to be blamed for things that weren't her fault? God loved her and cared about her—but He didn't seem to love and care *enough* about her to keep bad things from happening to her.

Even as she'd discussed the situation with her father, Rainy had known an odd kind of resolve. Her father said matter-of-factly that a person wasn't entitled to know why God worked things in a certain manner—that God has His ways and they are so far removed from man that they make little sense. He called it the "foolishness of God" and showed her verses of Scripture that backed up his reasoning.

Rainy could accept that God's ways were often confusing and indiscernible, but she still didn't understand why He'd allow her to lose the one thing that mattered most. She had held a wonderful position with the university. She was to have been awarded a special grant from the college to study the Hopi. She would have eventually been asked to teach a class or two and, in time, might have become a professor. It wasn't fair that she should have to lose all of that.

Then again, nothing seemed fair at the moment. Her family was leaving for Scotland. By autumn, they would be heading for the East Coast by train. From there they would take a ship to England and then take another train to Edinburgh. So it was up to her; she could either give up her driving desire to see her name cleared and go to Scotland with her family, or she could stay here in her beloved Southwest and live alone. Resignation left a bitter taste in her mouth.

"We will also offer an overnight trip," Mrs. Lehman said in a tone that seemed a bit elevated. Rainy looked up to find the woman staring directly at her.

Straightening in her seat, Rainy forced her mind to stay focused. There would be adequate time to figure out what was to be done in regard to her reputation and future.

"The overnight tour will include an itinerary that takes the dudes to the Puye Cliff Dwellings and the Santa Clara Indian Pueblo. The fare of fifteen dollars will cover three meals and one overnight stay with private bath. And, of course, the transportation itself is covered. Are there any questions?"

One young woman raised her hand and Mrs. Lehman quickly acknowledged her.

"Will the tours continue to start here in Santa Fe at La Fonda?"

BENEATH A HARVEST SKY

"Yes, the hotel will remain the central starting point. The tours will start promptly at nine each morning. This is a convenient hour for guests coming in from the station at Lamy. The only exception will be the overnight trip, which will also leave from La Fonda but will delay until 10:30 A.M. Other questions?"

No one offered any comment, so Mrs. Lehman dismissed the group and Rainy left the room as quickly as she could. With her heels click-clacking on the stone floor of the hotel, she made her way outside. The only real interest she had was to distance herself from her friends and Sonny. She wanted to be alone, as she had so many times recently. She knew her personality seemed altered as she withdrew and sought solitude, but she couldn't help it.

I'm confused, Lord. I thought I would feel better once I got back to work and into the swing of things, but I don't. Phillip hasn't written, Duncan has been completely absent, Sonny plans to go away, and everything is changing. I want my peaceful life back—the life I had before the university incident. I need direction for my life, but I seem to be walking in circles.

She strolled along the Plaza walk, noting that at the Palace of the Governors the Indians were beginning to pack up their wares. Every day this faithful collection of natives brought handmade jewelry and baskets to sell. They would gather here under the protection of this ancient porch and put out their wares for the tourists to purchase. Then every day, like clockwork, the evening hour would come upon them and they would gather their things and go home.

Rainy looked at her watch and realized the dinner

hour was upon them. The meeting with her co-workers had taken most of the afternoon. Funny, but Rainy could barely remember anything they'd discussed.

Turning from the preoccupied Indians, Rainy glanced up again and caught sight of Duncan. He was sitting on the opposite side of the Plaza and seemed to be watching her. Not knowing what else to do, Rainy offered a little wave. She hadn't spoken to Duncan since their falling-out. She wondered if he still worried about her guilt or innocence regarding the Indian artifacts.

She waited as he got up and made his way across the Plaza to her. A trembling went through Rainy as he offered her a smile. Apparently he wasn't mad at her. Rainy took his smile as her cue and smiled in return.

"I thought maybe you weren't speaking to me after the way I acted when we were last together," she offered by way of apology. "I regret that I treated you so poorly."

"I'm the one who owes you an apology," Duncan replied. "I'd like to take you to dinner to make up for it."

Rainy nodded, trying hard not to show her surprise. "I'd like that very much. Where shall we go?"

"If you don't mind a bit of a walk, I know a marvelous place over on Alameda. It just opened up and is run by a Frenchman."

"Sounds wonderful, and I don't mind the walk at all," Rainy assured him.

They headed off in the direction of Alameda Street, and it was Duncan who once again picked up the conversation. "How have you been?"

His voice was melodic, like liquid pouring over stones. "I've been . . . well . . ." She didn't want to lie to him, but how could she explain? "I suppose the best I can say is that my life is in turmoil. I've been trying to take your advice and give it over to God, but at times that's not as easy as it sounds."

Duncan chuckled. It wasn't exactly the response Rainy had expected. "You don't have to tell me. I'm terrible at taking my own advice. It's hard for me to place my burdens at the feet of God and leave them there."

"It's a relief to hear someone else feels that way," Rainy declared. "Sometimes I feel that I must be God's biggest disappointment. I sat in church last week listening to the pastor teach on all things being possible with God, and not moments after leaving I once again felt that things seemed impossible."

Duncan nodded. "Indeed. I can relate very well, but I always rest in the fact that no matter how many times I fail, God never will. And He'll forgive my mistrust and help me to start over. He desires only that we draw near to Him—to love Him and yield our lives to Him."

"And that's what I want most of all," Rainy admitted. "I don't want my own way. . . . Not really. There are things I hope for—long for—but I won't demand them of God anymore."

"Like a husband?"

Rainy felt embarrassed by the question and looked away. "Yes," she whispered.

Duncan reached out and took hold of her arm.

"You know, my father, being the preacher that he is, once gave the example of a man whose boat was capsized in a storm on the ocean. The man can't swim, but as fortune would have it, he finds himself next to a rusty old buoy. He clings to that buoy out in the middle of a stormy sea, praying and pleading that God will rescue him. He grows more weary by the minute, but still he holds on to that buoy for fear of drowning. Then, much to the man's surprise and answered prayer, a rescue boat draws up alongside and a sailor reaches out a line to rescue the man."

Rainy stopped walking and turned to look at Duncan. He continued. "The sailor throws out the rope over and over, but the man won't let go of the buoy. It's almost as if the meager safety he has as he clutches the buoy is better than the hope of what safety he might have in the ship. The sailor pleads with the man to let go of the buoy and be rescued, but the man's fears refuse to let him trust. The storm worsens and the boat moves away to safety, leaving the man to drown."

"How awful," Rainy said, forgetting momentarily that it was just a story.

"Yes, but my father said we're the same way with God. He's offering us safety and rescue and we hold on to what we have in front of us—believing that it will somehow save us instead of God."

The silence engulfed them momentarily, and then Rainy nodded slowly. She was just like that man. She was clinging with her own strength to that which she thought would be beneficial—her pride, her self-reliance. She looked to Duncan. "Yes. Yes, we are very much like that. I believe God sent you to me for the very purpose of sharing this story. I can't begin to explain it, but I almost feel as if a veil has been lifted from my eyes. I thought all along that I was clinging to God, but I have been clinging to earthly things, self-centered things, the wrong things."

"We all make that mistake from time to time. Some things look very much like they've been divinely provided, when in fact they are offering only a temporary solution. God has a complete plan, and often we settle for only part of it."

They had reached the little restaurant by this time, so Duncan ushered her inside and waited until after they'd been seated at a highly polished walnut table before commenting further.

"I'm glad I could be of help. Glad, too, that you agreed to have dinner with me. I remember what you said about hiding behind Sonny—"

"Oh, please don't hold those words against me," Rainy interrupted. "They were so awful and spoken more out of my own misery than any truth."

"I'm not holding them against you. I'm thanking you for them," Duncan said, his voice low and his gaze intense. "I do have reason to care that has nothing to do with Sonny."

The words thrilled her heart and Rainy lost herself in his gaze. She longed to reach out and touch his wavy black hair, to run her fingers along his jawline. A slight sigh escaped her and she knew by the expression on Duncan's face that he somehow understood.

"Have you decided on what you'd like for dinner?" the waiter asked.

Rainy felt enormous frustration at the interruption. She looked away. "Why don't you order for us both," she murmured to Duncan.

He ordered veal Bourguignonne and stuffed mushrooms after marveling at the enticing selection and sharing small talk with the waiter. Rainy listened to the conversation, trying hard not to make Duncan's declaration into something more than he intended.

"I really think you'll enjoy the food here," Duncan said as the waiter left them.

"I take it you've eaten here before?" Rainy questioned.

"Yes. I've come here twice now. I had the lamb on one occasion and chicken Maciel on the other. Both were absolute perfection."

Rainy picked up the linen napkin and noticed the fine silver that lined her plate. Harvey standards to be sure, she thought. She glanced around her, finding that the waiter had placed them in a most private part of the dining room. Only a few other tables were occupied, and those were at the other end of the room— well away from where she sat with Duncan. Perhaps the waiter thought them to be young lovers who were courting.

She looked back to Duncan and smiled. "I'm very impressed."

"So am I," he murmured. "That's why I asked you here tonight."

Rainy was about to ask him what he meant when a voice from her past interrupted the moment. Chester and Bethel Driscoll stood not a foot away.

"I thought that was you, Rainy. We haven't seen anything of you in weeks."

"Hello," Rainy replied, offering nothing more. She kept her focus on the candles at the center of their table.

"We couldn't help but notice that you'd just arrived," Chester continued. "I could scarcely believe my eyes. How marvelous that we're all here together."

Duncan, who had gotten to his feet, motioned to the table. "Would you care to join us?"

Rainy wanted to throw something at him for inviting them to invade her evening, but she knew it was only polite to offer. Perhaps Chester would have the good sense to realize he was unwanted and leave.

"We'd be delighted," Chester replied, pulling out a chair for his wife. As soon as he had seated Bethel he snapped his fingers for the waiter. The man rushed to his side. "We'll have our usual," he told the man.

Then seating himself, Chester turned to Rainy. "Jennetta introduced us to this wonderful place. Do you come here often?" He looked from Rainy to Duncan and back to Rainy.

Rainy toyed with her knife. "No," she answered flatly.

Duncan quickly took up the conversation. "What brings you to Santa Fe?"

"Oh, we're here to see Jennetta and Phillip," Bethel oozed.

Rainy stiffened. Phillip was in town and hadn't bothered to get in touch with her? She said nothing, but her desire to demand answers nearly overwhelmed her good manners.

Bethel leaned forward. "In fact, they were to have met us here tonight, but Phillip had friends arrive from Los Angeles, and Jennetta, after spending much time in meditation, decided to cook for them all. She does that from time to time, don't you know."

Rainy wanted to run from the restaurant but instead gave Bethel a forced smile. "Why, no, I didn't know Mrs. Blythe could cook."

Bethel laughed like Rainy's comment was some great joke. "Oh, Jennetta is a mystery. She's an expert at a great many things but prefers to be known for her writing."

The food arrived along with a stilted silence. The couples ate and murmured comments about the quality of the meal, but little else was said until the empty plates were cleared away and strong coffee was poured. Chester immediately pulled a silver flask from his pocket and poured a generous amount of amber liquid into his coffee, then offered the flask to Bethel. Bethel did likewise, then offered the flask to Rainy.

"I don't use spirits—besides, they're illegal," Rainy said, fixing Bethel with a stare.

Bethel giggled. "Well, hopefully not for long. Uncle Gunther says that given the poor economic condition of this country, they'll have to repeal Prohibition and give folks something to live for."

"They could live for God," Rainy suggested.

Bethel's amusement faded. "What fun would that be? All those stuffy rules and dour Sunday faces. I would definitely need a drink then."

Duncan interceded before the conversation could turn ugly. "So what's the news from Albuquerque?"

Chester stirred his coffee and shrugged. "Not much that would interest anyone. I will say this, however. I had an opportunity to ride up here with one of the railroad officials. It seems those mysterious thefts of artifacts have stopped. It's been . . . what did he say, dear?" He looked to Bethel. "Over a month now, right?" She nodded and sipped at her coffee. Chester smiled and looked at Rainy. "About the time you went on vacation the whole thing seemed to stop."

Rainy knew he was goading her. She knew he wanted her to feel uncomfortable. Her eyes narrowed as she met his smug expression. "Well, thank the Lord they've stopped. The Indians have suffered enough without someone stealing away important pieces of their heritage."

"The timing's strange, don't you think?" Chester questioned.

Rainy felt her stomach churn. She raised her napkin to her lips and dabbed lightly, trying hard to think of what she should say or do.

Duncan, however, came to her rescue. "Speaking of timing, it's getting late, Driscoll. I'm afraid I have a tour to drive tomorrow and Miss Gordon also has a tour to direct. You'll have to excuse us."

Rainy could have kissed Duncan for his smooth way of dealing with Chester. He didn't need to make a scene or even acknowledge Chester's question. He merely dismissed the man.

"But we haven't even had time for dessert," Bethel said, sounding like a disappointed child.

"I'm afraid Duncan is absolutely right. I need to get ready for tomorrow. Good evening," Rainy said without meeting the expression of either Bethel or Chester. Instead, she turned to Duncan and accepted his help as she rose from her chair.

After he paid the bill, Duncan held fast to her hand, showing no sign that he desired to turn her loose. They were nearly halfway back to the Plaza before either one spoke.

"I'm sorry for the way he acted toward you," Duncan began.

"Is it true that the thefts stopped when Sonny and I were on vacation?" Rainy asked, needing to know the truth.

"They stopped after the oil paintings were taken in Taos. There haven't been any further reports of missing articles."

Rainy trembled, but this time it wasn't from Duncan's touch—it was from the fear of the obvious connection. "So will I be arrested for the thefts?"

Duncan stopped and turned her toward him. He held on to her shoulders and gazed intently into her eyes. "You aren't guilty of stealing those articles, so you have no reason to fear being arrested."

"Do you really believe that?" Rainy prayed it was true—that he truly knew her to be innocent, but her fears from the past were creeping in to haunt her.

Duncan reached up and gently touched her cheek. "I believe in you."

CHAPTER SIXTEEN

*R*ainy closed her eyes and leaned back into the front passenger seat of the courier car. She'd given all the regular information needed for the tour and found her dudes were barely paying attention to what she had to say. They were much too caught up with comments and concerns about the economy and the conditions of the world.

"Germany is suffering," one man began. "I have a friend who lives there. He said that banks are failing there and in Austria. Industry is suffering, and their only hope is to find some way to stabilize the economy. It's worse there than here."

Another man chimed in. "I've heard great things about that man Hitler. I heard that he blames the bankers—most of them Jews, you know. He feels they've been reckless in their business dealings. They're all in cahoots with the Bolsheviks, as I hear it."

"How can they be Bolsheviks and bankers at the same time?" the first man questioned.

"Don't be foolish; it's all a plot for world

domination. Bolshevism is just a smoke screen. The Jews are using Bolshevism to hide their real intent and confuse things."

"And what is their real intent?"

Rainy couldn't help but wonder at this as well. She'd heard a great deal of anti-Jewish sentiment among the wealthy tourists who traveled with the Detours, though she had never understood the great disdain such people held for the Jews. She found herself turning around to view the two men. They gave her perusal no consideration whatsoever.

The heavier of the two men shrugged and bore an expression that suggested the answer was elementary in nature. "World domination through economic control, of course. Look at all the properties that are being foreclosed upon. The bankers are getting wealthy, even if they claim the banks themselves are failing."

"So you believe this man Hitler has all the answers for Germany?"

"He seems to have a clear understanding of what the Jews are up to—not that others haven't spoken of the same thing. In fact, I believe Hindenburg knows the truth as well, but he doesn't have the power to do anything about it. Hitler shows strength as well as courage. That alone will allow him an edge in overcoming the problem. He seems to speak for the people of Germany."

"We could sure use a man like that here in America. Hoover is a waste in the office of president."

The man nodded in agreement, but his wife reached out and patted his arm. "Now, dear, must we talk politics? This is our vacation. The first we've taken this year."

The man smiled at his wife and nodded. "But of course, you're right." He gave the other man an apologetic nod. "Forgive me if I conclude my thoughts."

The first man nodded and turned to his own wife. "So where would you like to dine tonight?"

Rainy turned back to watch the road and ignored their chatter about places to eat in Santa Fe. She couldn't help but wonder if the problems in the world would escalate to make matters in the U.S. even worse. Maybe the economy would be better in Scotland. After all, farms were very self-sufficient. Her mother and father were beginning to talk with great anticipation about the move. Rainy wanted to get caught up in their excitement, but it was difficult. She still hadn't decided what she would do.

Ever since Duncan had rescued her from Chester's accusing comments, Rainy had felt more certain of her feelings for him. He said he believed in her. He didn't think she'd taken the artifacts or the oils. He had touched her with such tenderness and said that he cared—and not because he was doing a job for Sonny.

Rainy touched her hand to her cheek. Her original longing to know Duncan better resurfaced with the memory of that night. Phillip Vance seemed a distant memory. Apparently Chester had been right on that account. Phillip seemed only to have toyed with her affections. She knew from the Driscolls that Phillip had been in town for over a week now, and still he had done nothing to get in touch with her.

Sonny maneuvered the car into a spot directly in

front of La Fonda. Rainy watched him help the passengers from the car, even as she gathered her things. She needed to talk to Sonny and clear the air between them, but she didn't know what to say. Her own confusion over the problems with the Indian thefts had caused her to take out her anger on him. He was entitled to his own life and she had made such an ugly scene about it.

"Can we talk when you get back from the garage?"

Sonny seemed genuinely surprised at her question. "Why, sure. You mean at the boardinghouse?"

Rainy nodded. "I'll take our things and walk on over now. I'll wait for you there."

She walked the short distance from La Fonda to Mrs. Rivera's, all the while thinking of how silly she'd been to put Sonny at arm's length. *I'm trying to protect myself,* she reasoned. *I'm trying to keep the world at a safe distance so that I won't get hurt. But instead, I'm hurt all that much more.*

Stepping up onto the porch of the boardinghouse, Rainy nearly fell off backward when Maryann came bursting out the front door.

"I've been positively dying for you to come home. You have to come see what arrived for you!" she declared, pulling Rainy toward the lobby. "You won't believe your eyes!"

Rainy walked into the welcoming cool of the house and found an enormous bouquet of red roses waiting for her on one of the front receiving tables.

"Look! Didn't I tell you?" the girl at her side commented. "We tried counting them and lost track after the first three dozen."

Rainy shook her head. "They're for me?"

"Yes, look at the card." The girl pulled Rainy to the table and pulled a card from the bouquet.

Rainy took hold of the card and read:

Rainy, I know I've been unforgivably delayed in corresponding, but please know you've never been far from my thoughts. Please have dinner with me at La Fonda tonight at 7:30. We have much to discuss about the future. I'm more certain than ever. Phillip

She folded the card and pushed it into the pocket of her skirt. "Well, I must say, he certainly knows how to get a girl's attention."

"I'll get one of the drivers to carry these up to your room," Maryann said with giddy delight. "They weigh a ton, and you wouldn't want to risk falling and breaking this lovely vase."

Rainy noted the exotic vase. Patterned in blues and purples, the Indian-styled piece had an opening of at least twelve inches to accommodate the massive bouquet.

Maryann sighed and leaned into Rainy. "He sure must be in love with you."

Rainy thought of the girl's words and frowned. Phillip Vance was a mystery to be sure, but Rainy seriously doubted that real love was a part of the situation. Still, the flowers were beautiful and definitely caught her attention. She would join him for dinner and then maybe she'd have the chance to hear him explain his feelings.

"What if he proposes?" Maryann said, dancing

around Rainy as a couple of the other couriers joined them.

"Is Rainy getting married?" one of them asked, nearly squealing the question.

"Oh, how exciting! Who are you marrying?"

"Phillip Vance, the movie star," Maryann declared.

Rainy shook her head. "I'm not marrying anyone. The flowers are from Phillip Vance—and no proposal came with them."

"But if he asks, you'll say yes, won't you?" the other courier questioned. She looked at Rainy with such an expression of anticipation that Rainy wanted to burst out laughing.

"He's not going to ask me to marry him," Rainy said matter-of-factly. She hoped her disinterested tone and firm resolve would silence the matter for good.

"But he might," Maryann murmured, delicately fingering one of the many roses.

The other girls nodded. "Yes," they said in unison. "He might."

Rainy felt a heaviness in her stomach. Maybe she should avoid dinner and just send Phillip a note explaining how she felt and why they were all wrong for each other. She could start with the fact that she loved God first and foremost and always would. Then she could ease into the fact that she didn't love Phillip—and probably never would.

———

Rainy waited for Sonny in the boardinghouse lobby for as long as she could. Hot and sweaty from her miserable day, she trudged upstairs carrying her bags—a driver behind her trying to balance the huge bouquet. Her room felt stifling, so Rainy quickly put the bags to one side and went to open the windows.

"Just put those flowers anywhere you can find a place to fit them," Rainy instructed.

"These must have cost a pretty penny," the driver said. Rainy turned from the window in time to see him create a spot for them on her tiny desk.

"Thanks, Joe. I really appreciate it. I expected Sonny to meet me after he took the car in, but he never showed up. Guess I'll catch up with him later, but in the meantime, I'm really grateful that you handled those for me."

"No problem, Rainy. And I wouldn't worry about Sonny. The garage manager was keeping all of today's drivers in for a meeting. He talked to the rest of us earlier."

"I see. Well, then, I guess I won't fret over it." She showed him out, then gathered her things in order to clean up.

After a long tepid bath, Rainy felt cooled down and much more capable of dealing with Phillip. She dressed carefully in a cotton dress of lemon yellow. Pale white flowers with tiny orange centers and lacy-leafed stems dotted the skirt of the dress.

Spending extra time, Rainy took the trouble to pin up her thick strawberry blond hair and fashion it into a stylish bun at the back of her head. She wanted to be cool as well as look attractive, yet she was determined to tell Phillip that this would be their last night together.

Her bath time had allowed time for reasonable

thought and consideration of the problem. Phillip, while attractive and romantic, did not love God. In the past Rainy had put this aside, believing that it was possible that God had brought them together in order for her to lead him to salvation. But now that idea seemed silly. She knew from experience that it was much easier for her to be dragged down by someone who held no respect for God than for her to pull him up into an understanding of the Bible and God's laws. It wasn't that she couldn't share the hope of Jesus with Phillip, but she couldn't use that as a reason to see him romantically.

When Rainy had first seen the flowers and heard Maryann's excitement, she wondered seriously if her own excitement would emerge. She thought of Phillip and his gentle spirit, his kindness to her, and all that he offered. But instead of feeling something more intense, Rainy was very much aware of her lack of feeling. There was not even a glimmer of love or hope of a future that came to mind when she looked at the enormous bouquet. Phillip had been an interesting diversion, but in more ways than one, Rainy could see that he had interfered with her life in a way that could have proved to be most destructive. She needed to put an end to it tonight—to explain that his life and ways held little interest for her.

She prayed her motives would be pure. She didn't want her words to come across as sounding like punishment for Phillip's inconsiderate attitude. He needed to understand that the absence of God in his life was the true reason that she couldn't allow herself to fall in love with him. Of course, there was also Duncan.

Rainy's feelings for Duncan were stronger than ever. She tried not to focus on whether or not Duncan would return her feelings and be the man God ordained for her husband. But it was hard. Not only that, but Duncan had seen her reaction to Phillip. He might have been deeply wounded by her attitude. Her actions reminded her of something that had happened when she'd been a child. They'd had a family dog—Shep. He was more loyal than most dogs, and Rainy had loved him with all her heart. Then one day her father brought home a stray puppy. Rainy immediately gave her time and attention to the pup and completely abandoned Shep. A few weeks later the pup ran off leaving Rainy heartbroken, but Shep, ever faithful, was there to console her and lick away her tears.

She smiled at the memory. Duncan certainly wasn't to be equated with Shep, but Rainy's actions with Phillip had been the same as when that pup had come into her life. The new, exciting adventure of meeting and spending time with a movie star, a wealthy man who could give her any material thing, had temporarily distracted her. But as Rainy had told Duncan that night, a veil had been lifted. She was growing up spiritually and realized that trusting God meant something more than just saying the words. She had to live it by her actions.

Making her way to the dining room at La Fonda, Rainy gave a quick glance about the room for Phillip. It was exactly seven-thirty—he should be here. She spotted him standing by the entry. Beside him were several well-dressed men and women. Phillip was the center of attention, as usual.

Rainy made her way to the gathering, confident that these were more of his fans and that soon they could break away to discuss their relationship. She smiled when Phillip looked her way. He returned her smile and gave her an appreciative nod.

"You look wonderful," he whispered as he broke away from the crowd to take hold of her hand. "Come join us. We were just about to be seated."

Rainy tried not to look confused. "I thought it would be just you and me."

"I'm sorry," he said, looking rather chagrined. "These are some writer friends of Jennetta's. They want to talk about writing for movies and I couldn't send them away."

Rainy could think of nothing to say, so she only nodded and allowed Phillip to guide her as their table was finally ready.

Sitting beside Phillip and listening to the comments made by the ever growing party of people, Rainy felt very stupid for ever imagining that she might hold a special and solitary interest in Phillip Vance's life. She also felt more confident of her decision.

Phillip was a people pleaser. He thrived on attention and basked in the praise and devotion of his fans. Beyond that, he was eager to make himself invaluable to others, just as he was doing tonight.

"Phillip, darling, you don't mind if we squeeze in two more, do you?"

It was Jennetta, dressed in a skimpy black beaded gown that seemed overly dramatic for a quiet evening in Santa Fe.

The men quickly rose, but it was Phillip who spoke. "Of course we don't mind. We'll simply scoot in."

The waiter brought two more chairs while Jennetta took the seat on Phillip's left. Obviously he had reserved it for her, as the group surrounding them had never even attempted to take this place for themselves. Rainy felt more than a little irritation. First there had been no word from Phillip, and then he finally tried to make amends by sending her five dozen roses and inviting her to dinner—a dinner that quickly turned into a party for anyone and everyone who had an interest in Phillip Vance and the movies.

"I fail to see why it should be a problem to allow the true language of the people to be portrayed in a film," one balding man said as he leaned closer to Jennetta.

Phillip nodded. "The average person thinks nothing of swearing, but the censors will not allow that. They consider it crude and vulgar. Never mind that it is commonplace."

"But it isn't commonplace," Rainy declared. "At least not in my world."

Everyone turned their attention to her, and Rainy instantly wished she'd thought before speaking. Shifting uncomfortably, she looked to Phillip and added, "I'm sure swearing would hurt your audience numbers."

Phillip shook his head. "But must we sacrifice realism because of an oversensitive minority?"

"What makes you so sure only a minority would be offended by swearing and vulgar language?" she asked.

"Because I hear it all the time. From the common dock worker to the railroad worker to the newspaperman who interviews me to the calf-eyed schoolgirls who follow me around town, it's the common language of a people who are in despair and who find the world difficult to endure."

"So why not offer them hope instead of cursing?"

"I suppose you mean offer them God and religion."

Rainy noticed that their conversation held the attention of everyone else at the table. "Offer them God, yes. Offer them an understanding of what God desires for them—of His love for them. Offer them a way out of their despair."

"I find the entire matter of God to be a worthless pursuit," the balding man declared.

"Oh, well said, Samuel," a black-haired woman sitting opposite Phillip agreed. "I grew up in a positively hideous home where religious nonsense and piety were all the rage. My father wouldn't drink liquor, even when it was legal, and he certainly saw no use for entertainment and parties. Every Sunday," she said, leaning close as if to share a great secret, "we were all forced to attend church and then to spend the rest of the day fasting and praying for forgiveness. It was awful. As a child I would sneak out of the room on the pretense of relieving myself and would make a fast run to the kitchen, where Cook always kept me something to snack on. She always knew I would be coming and she'd have it all ready for me. It was wonderful fun to fool them all."

Rainy eyed the woman momentarily and was about to speak when Jennetta added her thoughts. "I find that a need for religiosity is stifling to the mind." The group rapidly agreed with her. "I couldn't work in my writing if I was constrained by the limitations demanded by the Christian faith. I'm sure I'm seen as the worst of sinners by our Miss Gordon here, but in truth, her beliefs will never allow her to understand the mind and soul of a true artist."

A chorus of murmured affirmation rose up from the gathering. Rainy ignored it and spoke out. "I suppose I do understand what you're saying, Mrs. Blythe. You write from the emptiness and darkness that consumes your soul. You write of despair and of hopelessness and lace it with platitudes of ambition and call it art. Because, I believe, the emptiness you feel comes from your alienation from God, then yes, a relationship with God would drastically alter and limit your art."

"I would expect that reply from the uneducated masses," a man with a pencil-thin mustache threw in.

Rainy got to her feet, unable to contain her temper if she remained in the pompous group for even a moment longer. "Sir, may I inquire as to your educational background?" she asked.

The man lifted his chin and stared down his long thin nose at Rainy. "I have a degree in literature from the University of New York." His companions nodded as if to confirm this truth.

"Anything else?" Rainy asked, knowing she

shouldn't be goading the man.

"That's entirely enough," the man responded.

She nodded. "Well, given your response about uneducated masses, I presumed you might lay claim to something more. As for myself—just so that you understand I do not speak as one of the uneducated masses—I hold a bachelor's degree in history and one in archaeology. Furthermore, I hold a master's degree in history and speak four languages fluently." Most of the group straightened in unison, as if stunned by Rainy's declaration. Only Phillip and Jennetta seemed unconcerned.

"Sit down, Rainy dear. Our waiter is coming and we'll need to place our orders."

Rainy shook her head. "No, thank you, Phillip. I believe I've had my fill of this evening."

She left without another word, not surprised that Phillip remained with his friends. Making her way outside, Rainy could only shake her head at her own foolish thoughts that she might have ever fit into Phillip Vance's world.

"You look like a woman with a purpose," Sonny declared as he came alongside Rainy.

"My purpose is to get away from this place as fast and far as I can," Rainy replied, stopping her stride to take in the sad-eyed gaze of her twin. She immediately felt horrible for the anger she'd held against him. "We should talk," she said softly.

"I'd like that very much. I'm sorry about not meeting you at the boardinghouse. We had a meeting."

She nodded. "Yes, Joe told me." She motioned to

one of the Plaza benches. "Why don't we go over there and sit down?"

Sonny smiled and followed her to the bench. They sat down, and Rainy breathed deeply, enjoying the cool evening air. "It was so hot at the cliff dwellings today. I'm glad Santa Fe is cooler."

Sonny yawned and leaned back against the bench. "Me too. Makes sleeping a whole lot easier."

Rainy knew it was silly to continue with mindless chitchat. "I want to clear the air between us. I know for these last few weeks we've just tolerated each other and, Sonny, I'm sorry. I should never have lost my temper when you told me about Scotland. I just panicked. I thought of all of you going away, and I didn't think of how it might make you feel for me to respond in such a manner. Please forgive me."

"You know I do," Sonny said gently. "But you really have misunderstood the entire matter."

Rainy nodded. "Then please explain and I'll hear you out."

"I did make plans without consulting you. Actually, the plans fell into place without me having much time to really consult anyone—anyone but God, that is. It's true that I plan to leave by the end of summer, but I'm not going with Mom and Dad. I plan to go to California first and then to Alaska. I'm going to work for the government on a survey party with my friends. I tried to explain this several times, but we always got into other matters or someone came to interrupt us or . . ."

"Or I got mad," Rainy said, stunned by her brother's news. At least when she'd thought of him going with their parents to Scotland, there was the possibility of her going along as well. "I'm happy for you, Sonny, but I'm also upset over the matter. You'll be miles and miles away from all of us—especially if I go to Scotland with Mom and Dad."

"I know. I've already thought a lot about that. I just feel it's the culmination of a lifelong dream. You know how I love geology. This is the perfect job for me."

Rainy took hold of his hand and patted it. "Of course it is. You'd be silly not to go. Besides, we're both a bit old to still be clinging to Mother's apron strings. I guess our homelife was just such a joy that leaving permanently never seemed like a very good idea."

"But what about you? I'll obviously be breaking up our Detour team. What will you do? Will you go to Scotland with Mom and Dad?"

Rainy dropped her hold and looked out across the Plaza. "I don't know. I've prayed and asked God to show me what the future holds—what I'm supposed to do—and I feel that He's only giving me silence in return."

"Maybe you aren't really listening," Sonny suggested.

Rainy looked at her brother and saw the compassion in his eyes. "Maybe I'm not, but I truly want to. I want to put my selfish desires aside and really heed God in this matter."

"If that's the case, Rainy, God will honor your attempt and guide you. You have to trust that to be true."

"I know."

"So what did you do about Phillip Vance?" Sonny

asked, changing the subject. "I heard about the flowers. Did you have dinner with him tonight? Did he
propose as Maryann hinted he might do?"

Rainy laughed. "Maryann is a hopeless romantic.
She had me dressed and down the aisle before I could
even consider what was happening. But to answer your
question, yes, I joined him and about ten other people
for dinner. I thought the dinner would be just between
Phillip and me. I had planned to tell him that I
couldn't see him anymore—that there was no future
for us because he had no room for God in his life."

"I see. So you didn't get a chance to tell him
because of the other people?"

Rainy nodded. "But I did make a statement. I'm
afraid I wasn't a very good witness. I got angry and
spouted off after one of the men implied that my faith
in God was somehow related to my being uneducated.
I told them all just exactly how well educated I truly
was, then stormed out of there like a child who hadn't
gotten her own way. I feel ashamed and yet at the same
time I can't bring myself to go back and apologize."

"Maybe there's no need. That prideful bunch
probably got no more than they deserved."

"Maybe so," Rainy said sadly, "but it was my desire
to show them the love of Jesus instead of revealing my
wounded pride."

"I'd imagine God understands the desire of your
heart. He put it there, after all. Cheer up, Rainy. I'm
sure it will be all right. Sometimes people like that
won't listen to anything else."

"Yes, but my anger was an issue of pride," Rainy
admitted. "All of my problems have stemmed from

issues of pride. Being falsely accused of stealing, dealing with Duncan and Phillip, getting mad at you. It's just a case of prideful nature, and I must learn to control it. Otherwise, I fear that I'll end up destroying more than I manage to mend or rebuild."

Sonny chuckled softly. "Everything is changing for us. I'm going to miss these talks."

"I know some folks think it strange that a brother and sister should be so close, but, Sonny, you've always been there for me. When my girlfriends grew bored with me and left for more exciting companions, you were there to comfort me and keep me from feeling too sorry for myself."

She sighed and shifted just enough to see him better. The streetlights gave off enough of a glow to reveal the compassion in her brother's expression.

"I will always cherish what we have. You and Mom and Dad mean the world to me," Rainy declared. "I couldn't have asked for a better family, and even now that you're going so far away, I know we'll still be a family. That won't change. We'll have our memories, but we'll also have the liberty and freedom to be the individuals that God intended us to be. Sooner or later, I'll have a family of my own—you'll probably do the same. Together we'll blend that group to give Mom and Dad grandchildren, and the cycle will go on and on. I know now that I'm not losing anything—I'm gaining a great deal."

"I'm glad you feel that way," Sonny said, giving her a smile. "Because I feel that way too."

Rainy nodded knowingly. She sensed his deep commitment to her, while at the same time she knew it was well past time for them both to break from the nest and fly.

"I'll visit you in Alaska," she said, tears coming to her eyes.

"And I'll visit you wherever you end up," he said, laughing. "Even if you manage to get yourself on the moon. And given your determination—that wouldn't surprise me in the least."

CHAPTER SEVENTEEN

The following morning Sonny came to Rainy with their assignment for the day. "We're doing an overnight trip to Taos," he told her as he shoved a strip of bacon into his mouth. He reached to the serving dish for more only to have Mrs. Rivera chide him to sit and eat like a normal human being.

Rainy pushed away from her half-eaten breakfast of bacon and eggs and smiled at her brother. "That should be easy enough. Quick tour of Puye and Santa Clara. Overnight in Taos and back to La Fonda tomorrow, with the rest of the day to ourselves."

Sonny nodded. "Jennetta Blythe and Phillip Vance are going to be our passengers." He quickly finished the remaining bacon.

Rainy felt the wind go out of her. "Them? Again?" She got to her feet and motioned to Sonny. Grabbing her hat, she paused by the door only long enough to pick up her bag and hand it to Sonny. Walking to La Fonda, Rainy couldn't help but voice her concerns again. "Why are they taking this trip again?"

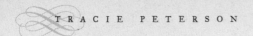

"I don't know, but that's not all. They're bringing a bunch of their obnoxious friends along as well."

Rainy shook her head. "I don't know why they do this. For the money they waste on these Detour trips they could buy a car and take themselves."

"I know. I thought it kind of crazy too. I thought of giving them over to Duncan and his courier, since they're making a trip to Taos as well, but they're full up."

Rainy could hardly believe that she was going to have to spend the next twenty-four hours dealing with those people. What was God up to? Why would He allow her to be forced into the company of Phillip and his sister when they and their friends so clearly despised her values?

"Look, the car's being serviced. I'll bring it around to the front in about an hour. We're supposed to be on our way by ten-thirty. That gives you plenty of time to take care of other things if you need."

"I'd like to take care of arranging another courier," Rainy admitted. "Maybe I'll talk to Mrs. Lehman. She might be able to get us off the hook."

"It's worth a try," Sonny replied.

Rainy walked into the hotel lobby and went in search of Mrs. Lehman. But the meeting gave her no reprieve. The other couriers were already on the road, nine o'clock having been their starting time. Only one other team was left in-house besides Rainy and Sonny, and they were heading to Gallup to pick up some passengers who had requested a customized tour to the Grand Canyon.

"But Sonny and I could take that tour instead," Rainy protested.

"I'm sorry," Mrs. Lehman replied, "but you and Sonny were specifically requested for this tour. You know we like to meet the request of the touring dudes whenever we can."

"Yes, I realize that," Rainy replied, knowing at that moment that she had no recourse but to follow through with the trip.

Walking back across the lobby, Rainy spotted Jennetta Blythe. She fervently hoped she might make it outdoors without Jennetta seeing her. Rainy had no desire to even acknowledge the woman, much less suffer any conversation. Not that Jennetta ever seemed interested in talking with Rainy.

Jennetta surprised Rainy, however, by moving away from her friends to greet Rainy as though the animosity at the dinner table the night before had never happened.

"Hello, Miss Gordon. I suppose you know you'll be taking my party to Taos today?"

Rainy drew a deep breath. "Yes. Although I must say it surprises me. You took this very tour not so long ago."

"Yes, well, these are friends in from the East Coast. They've never had a chance to see the ruins," Jennetta replied. "I must say, however, the real reason I've stopped you is to applaud your efforts last night."

Rainy stared at her quizzically. "What do you mean?"

"Well, I was beginning to have serious doubts about you being a suitable wife for Phillip. You seemed so mousy and weak-willed, never standing up for yourself and such. Phillip's world demands a woman who is strong and capable—one who won't shrink away from challenges. Until last night, I thought you completely incapable of such fire and endurance. I'm ready to concede that I misjudged you. You very well may make Phillip the perfect wife. It won't be easy for you to stand up to the crowds and parties required of Phillip, but at least I know you're made of something more than I previously thought."

Rainy stood speechless as Jennetta walked back to her friends. She supposed Jennetta somehow believed herself to have paid Rainy a compliment, but Rainy certainly didn't see it that way.

How dare she assume that I plan to marry Phillip. What in the world has he said to her to bring her to such a conclusion? Rainy walked outside the hotel and paced the strip of sidewalk in front.

Jennetta certainly didn't apologize for her attitude last night. In fact, she apparently saw nothing wrong with the way she and her friends acted, Rainy seethed. *They insult me and think nothing of it—certainly not enough to warrant an apology.*

Then, as if that weren't bad enough, Jennetta presumes upon the kind of life I would have if I married her brother. She has it all figured out in her mind. She probably has the wedding planned and the caterers hired and . . . Rainy forced herself to calm down. She drew a deep breath and leaned back against the cool stone wall.

Why am I so upset? Those people have proven themselves to be rude and insensitive. They have their world and ways and I have mine. The two do not mix, but I already knew

*that. So why should I be so upset just because Jennetta wants
to presume upon a relationship that will never be?*

Rainy smoothed down her purple velvet tunic and
straightened her silver concha belt. Calm was gradually returning. *I'm just being silly. I'll find a chance to talk
to Phillip later, and then I'll set everything straight.*

An hour later they were on their way north. Phillip
had tried briefly to get Rainy away from the crowd, but
she refused. She also encouraged the seating so that
Phillip would be at the far back and she'd be free of
him during the trip. She wasn't about to try to explain
herself to him in this crowd.

They left a trail of dust behind them as they
headed out across the desert land. Rainy talked of the
history of the area, giving her standard speech. She
spoke of the Indians who had lived in the area for
hundreds and hundreds of years, and while her guests
didn't interrupt or try to talk over her, Rainy could see
they were bored and indifferent.

They stopped first at the Santa Clara Pueblo, where
the Tewas, a gentle Indian people, were going about
their affairs. Rainy explained that for the brief visit
they should be mindful of their manners. Rainy
remembered that it hadn't been so long ago that one
of the other tours had a mishap that found some of
the dudes climbing on the pueblos. Rainy quickly
explained the houses were off limits and rounded her
people up after only fifteen minutes. Not long afterward they stopped for lunch and exploration at the
Puye Cliff Dwellings, and after a couple of hours there
they were on their way once again.

The heat of the day made Rainy wish she could

wear a lightweight cotton blouse instead of her tunic. Even Sonny had it better, as his shirt was cotton and his white hat tended to reflect the sun rather than absorb it. She fanned herself lightly as the temperature inside the black Cadillac climbed.

By the time they pulled into Taos, Jennetta was already instructing her friends about their evening.

"Have a nice cold bath first and then we can gather for dinner. I know some marvelous places to eat, and we can get anything we want to drink," she advised. "The only place in town that doesn't sell some form of liquor is the church." Her friends laughed and commented on the sensibility of the town ignoring the laws that robbed them of a pleasant time.

Rainy helped Sonny to pull out the luggage and recognized Phillip's touch the moment he reached out to tap her shoulder. She looked up and met his somber expression.

"Are you angry with me?" His tone sounded concerned.

"I don't really have the time to discuss it right now," Rainy said softly, almost shyly. It was almost like the first day they'd met—all awkward and uneven, not quite knowing how to treat the situation. She didn't want to say things in front of Sonny or the others who still lingered near the car. Humiliating Phillip wasn't her desire. "We could talk later this evening."

"I'm afraid Jennetta has the night completely planned out. Could we meet at breakfast?"

Rainy shook her head. "Don't worry about it. It really isn't that important. I'll catch up with you sometime." She reached in to pull out the suitcase she'd often seen Jennetta carry. It felt incredibly light. In fact, if Rainy didn't know better, she would have thought it was empty.

"Please don't be angry with me," Phillip pleaded. "I didn't mean for last night to turn ugly. I was very upset that you got hurt."

Rainy put the case on the ground and looked into Phillip's warm expression. "You could have been more supportive," she said, though she had not intended to be drawn into a conversation.

"I know and I'm sorry."

Rainy nodded. "You're forgiven. I hope you have a wonderful time this evening."

"Come with us."

Rainy saw Sonny give her a raised eyebrow, but he remained silent as he pulled the last of the bags from the car. "I'm busy, Phillip. You know how it is. Now if you'll excuse me, I have to make sure everyone got checked in without any trouble."

She left him looking rather dumbstruck. Maybe he thought this was just a game she was playing, but Rainy had little interest in such forms of entertainment. A game was more Jennetta's speed. Jennetta—who was already planning for Rainy and Phillip to marry.

Jennetta.

Rainy's thoughts went back to the empty suitcase. Was it really empty, and if so, why? The idea of the missing artifacts came to mind. Rainy felt her breath catch in the back of her throat. She stopped midstep and looked back through the doorway at the touring car. She felt as if she held all the clues to a great mystery, but they were out of order and, as such, made no sense.

"Hello, Rainy."

She whirled around to find Duncan. "What are you doing here?"

He smiled and it seemed to light up his whole face. His wavy black hair looked windblown and his dark eyes seemed to assess her with extreme interest.

"I had a tour," he explained. "I wondered if you'd like to join me for dinner tonight. My mother is a great cook, and she's promised wonderful beef roast and fresh bread."

Rainy lost her thoughts of Jennetta and nodded. "That sounds wonderful. Do I have time to freshen up?"

He grinned. "You look fresh enough, but of course. Dinner isn't for another hour."

Sonny trudged into the lobby with the last of the luggage. Duncan immediately offered his help, but Sonny waved him off.

"I've got these things stacked just so," Sonny said. "I'm going to deliver them, take a bath, and go to bed. I'm bushed."

Sonny mastered the stairs in short order, and only after he'd disappeared from sight did Rainy turn her attention back to Duncan. Before she could speak, however, a woman's shrill laughter filled the air. Phillip Vance came in from the street with a woman on each arm. Both of his companions wore heavy makeup and tight dresses that seemed to accentuate their every curve. Phillip leaned first one way and then the other as the women whispered in his ears. He laughed at their comments, then ushered the women upstairs.

Rainy had no idea where they were headed or why. The entire scene just made her glad she had determined to remove herself from Phillip's influence. Looking to Duncan, she found him with an expression that suggested sympathy.

"Oh, Duncan. Why can't more men be like you?"

———————

Duncan watched Rainy with intense interest as his mother asked her question after question about her work for the touring company.

"I've loved being able to share history with people who generally have no clue about the Southwest. The tourists, or 'dudes,' as we call them, often come out here with this image of the Wild West and of Indians and cowboys shooting it out over the next hill. I've heard women worry over having the windows of the cars down for fear an Indian arrow might come through and kill them all."

"Oh my," Joanna Hartford declared. "You would think they would know better."

Rainy smiled. "You would think so, but I'm always amazed at the general lack of knowledge and understanding. One woman tourist we had stood in the midst of several Indian children and asked me if they would bite her if she were to stroke their black hair." Rainy's facial expression changed to one that showed sadness over the memory. "I told the woman they were children, not wild animals, and she reprimanded me, saying that everyone with even the tiniest bit of education knew they were savages."

Duncan's father nodded. "I've encountered that attitude many a time. It's the same mentality that says the Indian cannot be saved for eternity because they have no soul."

Rainy shook her head. "How can people be so blind? I truly had hoped that the Detours would help people better understand the Indians. I have friendships that span across several tribes and those have been hard made—simply because of attitudes like that."

"Father has endured the same problems gaining the trust of the Indians as he works to share his faith with them," Duncan threw in.

"I admire what you do here," Rainy said, pushing around a piece of roast with her fork, "but do you ever feel it's much too little—too late?"

Lamont Hartford laughed in a deep hearty manner. Duncan knew his father had been asked this question many a time. He watched his father's dark eyes narrow slightly as he sobered. "Do you believe," he asked, "that God's timing is ever too late?"

Rainy smiled. "I've wondered that very thing from time to time, but I don't really think His timing is ever too late." She glanced at Duncan, her cheeks reddening slightly. Duncan immediately thought of her desire for a husband and family. "I often feel that God is delayed in answering my prayers," she continued, "but from my own upbringing and growing faith, I know that isn't the case. Sometimes, however, I wish He would hurry things along for my sake."

Duncan's father smiled and nodded. "I've wished it often myself. I can't blame you for your desires, but

I would encourage you to trust that He has your best interest in mind."

———————

The weeks passed by and then a month and then nearly two, and still Duncan found himself remembering the details of the dinner at his parents' house. Rainy had come dressed in a simple dress of pale lavender. She'd pinned her hair up and Duncan thought it looked very fetching, but he longed to see it down, flowing across her shoulders to her waist. Rainy had treated his parents as though she'd known them for years.

After he'd returned home from walking Rainy to her hotel, Duncan's mother had commented that Rainy seemed to be a very special young woman and that God clearly had His mark on her. Duncan's father had also noted his complete approval of such company for Duncan. Both of his parents encouraged Duncan to share his feelings about Rainy, but he wasn't yet ready to speak on the matter.

Now, as the summer months melted away, Duncan felt a sense of frustration in that he hadn't seen much of Rainy. She and Sonny had been quite caught up with their courier duties, and rumor had it that both planned to resign their positions at the end of the month. Duncan worried that Rainy planned to move to Scotland with her parents. He wanted very much to talk to her and let her know his feelings, but it seemed they were never in Santa Fe together. Today he'd been told over the lunch hour that Rainy would be in town that night. She was to have the next day off and

Duncan decided he would use the time to his advantage.

He knocked on the front door of Rainy's boardinghouse and waited, with card in hand. He had decided he would leave an invitation for Rainy to join him for dinner. He knew her routine would bring her home before she headed off for supper. Rainy had mentioned more than once that she absolutely had to wash off the day's dust before sitting down to enjoy a meal.

"Sí?" the heavyset Mexican woman who answered the door questioned.

"I'd like to leave this note for Rainy Gordon. Would you please see that she gets it?"

The woman nodded and took the envelope. "You are Mr. Vance, the movie star who sent the flowers?" Her words stabbed at Duncan even while her smile stretched from ear to ear.

"No, I'm not Mr. Vance. I'm Duncan Hartford. We work together—sort of."

The woman's smile faded. "Sí, I will give her the letter."

"Thank you." Duncan desired nothing more than to get away from the woman and avoid any more questions. He tried to console himself with the fact that at least Phillip hadn't come calling here at the boardinghouse—at least Duncan figured he hadn't. Wouldn't the woman have known he wasn't Vance otherwise? Still, just the thought of her delighted expression when she thought he was Vance gave Duncan cause for worry.

Hours later, Duncan was not at all pleased to find himself once again face-to-face with Mr. Richland from the Office of Indian Affairs. The matter of stolen artifacts was definitely not the kind of thing he wanted to give his attention to when the supper hour was so close at hand and visions of Rainy in her lavender dress kept coming to mind. No, he'd much rather go find Rainy and share a meal than sit here and listen to Richland tell him how guilty the Gordons were.

"Three important brass statues disappeared from Taos while the Gordons were there with their tourists," Richland began.

"But the time you've outlined proved to have other tours there as well. My tour group was there and so was at least one other group that I know of," Duncan offered. "Could have been more."

"Be that as it may, there were no thefts for over two months—including the two weeks Miss Gordon was on vacation."

"So you're still determined to blame the Gordons for this?"

Richland looked down his nose at Duncan. His expression seemed pinched, almost pained. "I'm determined to arrest the guilty parties and put a stop to this nonsense. The other driver and courier we were considering prior to this have both resigned and gone elsewhere to work. The Gordons remain, and now the stealing has begun again."

Duncan had hoped Richland's recent lack of communication meant that the matter was resolved or at least put aside for lack of evidence, but he supposed he should have known that the problem was not resolved since he was still driving for the Detours. "As I mentioned to you before, you might want also to consider the fact that in each of the tours where articles have disappeared over the last few months, the Detour passengers in the Gordons' care have been the same. Or they have been connected in some way."

"We considered it but find that it's not relevant."

Duncan pushed down his anger. "Of course it's relevant. You have chosen to blame the Gordons because they had the opportunity to perform the thefts. I'm saying they weren't the only ones who have had the opportunity. You can hardly rush in accusing and arresting with nothing more than this."

"I think perhaps you've gotten too close to this, Mr. Hartford. You don't seem to be willing to look at the facts. Perhaps your usefulness has reached its limits."

"I never set out to be a part of this to begin with. You came to me. The Gordons are my friends, and I won't see them falsely accused." Duncan raised his hand. "Hear me out. I've seen some strange things, things that suggest that perhaps Jennetta Blythe and her brother, Phillip Vance, are to blame for the disappearance of the artifacts."

Richland leaned forward. "Why do you say this?"

"I saw Jennetta showing off a piece that very well could have been one of the ceremonial flutes. I couldn't get a good look at the item, however. Then I overheard Phillip Vance comment on the original oils he took back to Los Angeles. It seems very likely that the missing Taos paintings could be the very oils to which he was referring."

Richland suddenly looked interested. Leaning back in his chair, he rubbed his chin. "All right. So let's say that's a possibility. What do you suggest we do about it? You can hardly expect me to rush ahead and have Phillip Vance arrested. The man is famous. It would be in all the newspapers before we could even determine if the paintings were the ones we were looking for. We have been good about cooperating with the various companies involved to keep this quiet. Charging Vance would eliminate any hope of continuing that silence."

"I realize that," Duncan admitted. "That's why I propose to set a trap for them. I've talked to my superiors here, and they have agreed to cooperate. I suggest I talk privately with Jennetta Blythe. I'll talk to her brother as well if he's in town. I will tell them that I have a variety of articles here at the museum that I would be willing to sell to the highest bidder. I could even make something up about the history of the pieces and such."

"The museum would put actual artifacts at risk?"

"No, the pieces would be insignificant pieces made to look like the real thing. I can replicate them well enough that Mr. Vance and his sister won't be any wiser. If they take the bait, then you can let the charade play out. I'll sell them the pieces and you can arrest them with the items in hand."

Richland shook his head. "But that wouldn't work. The pieces wouldn't be authentic, and proving the intent to purchase stolen goods would be difficult. They could just as easily say that they knew the pieces were of no significance and that you had assured them they were legally for sale—perhaps even out of your own private collection. No, if you can get the museum to agree to put genuine artifacts at risk, then perhaps it might work, but otherwise I cannot agree to this."

"But you have to admit that these circumstances do raise questions. When I was with the Gordons, I watched them every step of the way—I barely slept in order to keep a continuous eye on them. Jennetta Blythe and her brother have had every opportunity to slip around unnoticed. If found in areas where they shouldn't be, they could easily have feigned ignorance or being lost. I think the situation is such that you should have someone follow them and keep track of their activities."

"Perhaps you're right. Maybe I'll take you off of watching the Gordons and have you watch this Blythe woman instead."

Duncan breathed a sigh of relief. At least Richland was being reasonable about the matter. With his eyes narrowed, Richland studied Duncan a moment in silence, then nodded. "Go ahead and set your trap. Approach them if you can get the museum to allow you to use real artifacts. I'll get someone to watch them and see what they do. You send word to me as soon as you have word from them one way or another."

"Of course," Duncan said, getting to his feet as Mr. Richland did likewise. "I can't help but believe we're on to something here. I wouldn't have suggested it otherwise."

"I hope, for your sake, you're right. I would hate to be made the laughingstock of New Mexico. It wouldn't sit well with me, Mr. Hartford."

"Nor with me."

As soon as Richland departed, Duncan immediately went to his superiors. It took some convincing, but they finally agreed that Duncan could offer three pieces of museum art. One was an intricately detailed squash blossom necklace. Another piece was a wooden statuette of the Madonna and Child. Last was a beautifully designed silver tray. All three pieces were chosen because of their durability. Duncan knew that even if he had to go forward with some sort of exchange, the pieces would probably remain unharmed in the process.

With that matter taken care of, Duncan then began to consider how he might approach Jennetta and Phillip. He would have to handle the matter delicately. If they were to blame, then a bold approach might scare them off. But if Duncan was too subtle in the matter, they might not take the bait. It was also possible that if they were completely innocent, they might run to the legal authorities and expose the investigation, and that was the last thing he needed.

He thought of Rainy and wondered if she could get him an audience with either Jennetta or Phillip. Surely there was a way. He pulled on his coat and hat and set out to find Rainy. With any luck at all he could avoid explaining himself and still accomplish what was needed. Once he managed to prove Rainy's innocence, then maybe he could tell her about his feelings for her. Maybe he'd even let it be known that he'd worked hard to keep Richland from jumping to conclusions and having her arrested. If she knew how much he cared, how he'd tried to protect her from the law officials, how he'd even set aside the job he'd worked so hard to get, then maybe she'd understand how deeply he'd come to love her.

He smiled to himself. Yes, it would be best to wait until her name was cleared, and then they'd both be at liberty to reveal their true feelings.

He glanced at his watch and headed for La Fonda, knowing Rainy would probably be there checking her dudes in. If not, he'd head back to the boardinghouse and wait for her there.

The bustle of the crowd in the lobby of La Fonda made Duncan worry that he'd missed Rainy. He asked several of the couriers he knew if they had any idea where Rainy might be. No one had seen her since she'd dropped her travelers off at the registration desk nearly thirty minutes earlier.

Duncan was just about to give up when he rounded the corner to find a young couple in a tight embrace. They were kissing rather passionately, but all at once the woman pushed the man away. Duncan quickly ducked into the shadows.

The woman was Rainy and the man was Phillip Vance.

CHAPTER EIGHTEEN

You had no right to do that!" Rainy broke from Phillip's embrace and headed for the hotel door.

Phillip followed and took hold of her before she could rush outside. "I only kissed you."

Rainy nodded. "Yes, but you had no right."

"But you're the woman I love . . . the woman who loves me."

"Oh, half the world loves you, Phillip Vance," Rainy said, then stormed out of the hotel. She could hear Phillip hot on her heels. Once outside, Rainy turned around and met Phillip head on. "But I'm not one of them."

"Not one of what?"

"I'm not one of the masses who love you."

She could see his expression contort. It was almost as if he couldn't comprehend what she was saying. He'd been adored for so long, Rainy figured he probably had no idea how to deal with rejection.

"But I thought you would marry me. I thought it was understood. You seemed quite happy in my company."

Rainy sighed. How could she make it any clearer to him? "Phillip, we've hardly seen each other in the last two months. I presumed you'd put aside any interest in me because I didn't have so much as a letter in that time."

"I wanted to write, but I was busy with my work. Surely you can understand that. You travel all the time and know there is hardly a chance for lengthy communications."

"I think if I were of a mind to marry someone, I would have made the time for 'lengthy communications,' as you put it."

Phillip's expression contorted. "But I thought you cared for me. You seemed so happy in my company."

Rainy wanted to roll her eyes. How very self-centered this man could be. Even now he seemed to have no idea that more than once she'd been miserable sharing his companionship.

"To be honest, Phillip, at first I thought you were the type of man I could love. I'll admit I was definitely enamored by your movie-star charm and handsome features." She smiled and reached out to touch Phillip's arm. "But we're too different. I've had a lot of time to think about this. We're from two different worlds. You have a lifestyle I could never hope to be happy in."

"You don't know that," he protested.

"Oh, but I do." She squeezed his arm and felt her heart ache at the pleading in his voice. "At the end of August, I plan to go to Scotland with my parents." She hated the thought of leaving New Mexico, but there didn't seem to be a better answer.

"Please don't say these things, Rainy. Please."

Rainy began to walk toward the Plaza. She hoped that by doing so she might clear her mind. She hadn't been prepared for Phillip's emotions, and now she felt guilty for the way she'd just blurted out her thoughts. She supposed it was because, after weeks and weeks of not seeing him, she just wanted to get the message across before he was called back unexpectedly to California.

"Rainy, you're just afraid of the unknown," Phillip argued as he followed behind her.

"No, it isn't that. I can't make you understand this, but my first allegiance, my first love, is to God. You have no desire for God in your life, and we would always be at odds over this. I thought maybe you'd come into my life so that I could share the joy I have in Jesus Christ. But you want no part of that—in fact, you scoff at such things."

His expression grew more desperate. He took hold of her and shook her ever so gently. His blond hair fell forward, making him look more like a little boy pleading for his own way than a man in love. "But I would never deny you the right to worship your God in any fashion you desired."

"But my faith is the foundation of who I am. Everything about me—everything you claim to love—is a product of that foundation. So long as it was just a matter of 'my God' versus 'your god'—never to be 'our God'—we couldn't be happy."

"But I have no god . . . so there would be no conflict."

Rainy felt tears come to her eyes. "Oh, Phillip,

you've made for yourself a god of fame and fortune. You have a god, but you simply refuse to understand the hold it has on you. I'm sorry, but I know deep in my heart I could never fully love or respect any man who didn't love and respect God first."

"Then it's truly over?"

Rainy smiled as a tear glistened in her eye. "It never really began, Phillip."

Phillip cast his gaze to the ground. "Then I suppose I should go."

"Yes," Rainy said softly. "I'm sure that would be best."

Phillip turned to go, then stopped. He looked around in true movie-star fashion, dropped his gaze to the ground, then slowly looked up. "I really do love you."

Rainy had a vague recollection of this scene from a movie, but instead of rushing into his arms as the screen heroine had done, she shook her head. "Goodbye, Phillip."

He walked away, leaving Rainy with her sorrow. She wasn't sad for what they might have had, but rather she was grieved by the fact that Phillip cared nothing for God. She walked along the Plaza, ignoring the couples that surrounded her, wishing she could sort through her feelings.

Should I have tried harder to help him understand, Lord? Should I have worked more diligently to bring him to an understanding of the Bible? The more she questioned her actions, the worse she felt. So much of her life was in turmoil, and this scene with Phillip, although necessary and overdue, was more than she wanted to deal with. Maybe he really did love her. Maybe it wasn't just a game to him.

She sat down on one of the benches not far from the obelisk that stood in honor of the fallen dead from various battles. The memorial only served to remind Rainy that life was fleeting and the choices you made were ones that often changed the course of your life forever. Would Scotland be one of those choices? Was there a strong, God-fearing Scotsman who waited in her future? Did she even care anymore?

Putting her hands to her face, Rainy tried to fight back her tears, but it was no use.

"Rainy?"

It was Duncan, but she couldn't bring herself to look at him. "What do you want?"

"Are you all right?"

She wiped at her tears and steadied her voice. "I'm fine."

"You don't look fine. You look like you're crying."

"Well, that's because I am crying."

Duncan sat down beside her. "Why?"

Rainy bit at her lower lip as a sob broke from her voice. "Because I've just hurt Phillip deeply. I didn't want to hurt him, but I did."

"How did you hurt him?"

She finally met his gaze. "I refused his proposal of marriage." She broke down and cried in earnest. "I just don't know what to do anymore."

Duncan surprised her by pulling her into his arms. "Just cry if it makes you feel better."

"But it doesn't. It doesn't help at all," she sobbed. "I'm confused and frustrated and I don't know what

God wants of me. I try to do what I'm supposed to. I pray and get a peace about things, then something comes along to wreak havoc with my life." She cried even harder.

"Shhh, it'll be all right—you'll see."

"I try to make the right decisions, Duncan, really I do. But I'm no good at it. I just keep making the wrong decisions and everyone always thinks the worst of me."

"I don't understand. Who thinks badly of you?"

Rainy pulled away just enough to see his face. "Everyone. Just think of it. You yourself were concerned about whether or not I'd stolen Indian artifacts and oil paintings. When I worked at the university I was falsely accused of stealing artifacts too. It's like a bad dream repeating itself again.

"I've never stolen anything in my life, but because someone put artifacts in my desk and locked my office tight, I was blamed for the theft. Now I fear it's happening all over again and I'm being blamed for something I didn't do. And every time I try to figure a way to clear my name, something happens to keep me from succeeding. I'm so weary. I don't know what to do anymore."

Duncan pulled her back against him. "Just have a good cry and you'll feel better."

Rainy warmed to his embrace but stated, "No, I won't. You don't understand. I love God, but I don't seem to be able to let go of my fears and let Him control my destiny. I'm always pushing and pulling and trying to make things go my way. Even now, even telling you all of this, in the back of my mind I'm still trying to figure out who really took the artifacts. I think Chester Driscoll had a hand in my being blamed at the university, so I can't help but wonder if he isn't involved in the thefts on the trip. After all, he has either accompanied us on those trips or he's had friends who have. Then I think to myself, just forget the whole thing and move to Scotland, where no one knows you."

She reached up and wiped her eyes, then just rested against Duncan's shoulder. "Why can't life be simple?"

Duncan chuckled. "I've asked myself that many a time. But seriously, Rainy, if you think there's some good reason to believe Driscoll has had a hand in the thefts, you should let someone know."

She rose up and pushed away. "No one would believe me. They'd just think I'm trying to take the focus off of myself. Until I have some real evidence or can get Chester to admit whatever role he played, I suppose I'll just have to bear the misery. And since it's already been three years, I doubt clues and evidence are just going to pop up for the taking. No . . . I think getting as far away from here as possible is the answer." But her tone said otherwise, and she knew she was far from convincing.

With regret, she eased out of his arms, immediately missing their comfort. Duncan had proven himself to be quite kind and considerate, but she didn't want to take advantage of that.

"I'm sorry for all of this. I shouldn't have told you that stuff about the university and Chester. I've never

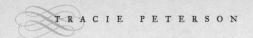

told anyone outside of my family. Please promise me you'll keep it between us."

Duncan nodded. "Of course. I would never do anything to hurt you."

They sat in silence for several minutes. Rainy drew a deep breath as she sat back against the park bench, feeling foolish for breaking down and crying. *Duncan must think me a real ninny. He's probably sitting there right now trying to figure out a way to leave gracefully.*

Then, as if to prove her wrong, Duncan asked, "What did you mean that day when you asked why more men couldn't be like me?"

CHAPTER NINETEEN

*R*ainy was taken aback by Duncan's question. "What?"

Duncan grinned. "You heard me. Why did you make that statement about wishing more men were like me? It was the night we were in Taos and Phillip Vance came into the hotel with a couple of floozies hanging all over him."

"I remember." Rainy had already spilled the truth about her deepest, darkest secret. Why not tell him the real reason for her words? "I suppose . . . well . . . because you've always been kind to me. Even when you hardly knew me. In fact, I see you being kind to everyone."

"What do you mean by 'kind'?"

Rainy stretched her legs out in front of her. "Do you mind if we walk while we talk? I'm weary from sitting."

Duncan nodded and followed her as she got to her feet. Rainy crossed the street and walked past the Palace of the Governors and on up to Washington Street. The summer skies overhead were fading in the twilight. The air held a definite flavor of red chilies and other spices. Rainy felt the gnawing in her stomach and wished she'd taken time to eat supper.

"You're a kind and gentle man, Duncan. I saw that right from the start. When I brought my first group of tourists to see the museum you were very attentive and . . . kind." She smiled. "There's really no other word for it."

"You pointed out the museum's mistake on the label of an artifact, as I recall," he said with a smirk.

"Yes, but you handled it very graciously. You didn't just dismiss me because I was female or because your pride wouldn't allow you to believe the museum capable of mistakes. You listened to me, observed the item, and agreed to further research the matter. I appreciated that. It was prideful of me to point that error out in the middle of a group of dudes, but you handled it with great ease and . . ."

"And kindness?" he asked.

Rainy nodded and after walking three blocks north on Washington, she crossed the street to head back to the Plaza. She didn't want to get too far away from the safety of her room at the boardinghouse. Should the situation with Duncan prove to become uncomfortable, she wanted the option to flee. As childish as that sounded, she simply couldn't bear to deal with another embarrassing or painful encounter. Hopefully Duncan would understand her situation and keep his distance.

"You've been kind in many ways over the years. I remember the extra care you gave the tour groups. I remember once when I had dropped a stack of boxed lunches, you appeared out of nowhere and helped me pick them up—then you carried them for me. We hardly even knew each other except for the museum and tours."

"I remember that," Duncan said thoughtfully. "I never thought of it as an act of kindness—but merely a gentleman's response to a lady in trouble."

They were back to the Plaza and their pace had slowed considerably. Rainy paused in the shadows of a shop portico. "You are a kind man in so many ways, Duncan Hartford. You rescued me at dinner when Chester was making his little innuendos about the stolen relics, and you were kind just now to offer me a friendly shoulder to cry on." She met his gaze and lost herself for a moment in the depths of his brown eyes. She longed to reach up and touch his cheek, to put her hands in his hair, to hold him close.

Duncan appeared just as captivated. He turned to speak, but he remained silent, almost as if understanding her feelings—her need.

Rainy felt the skin on her arms tingle as Duncan closed the inches between them. "Would you like me to be kind to you right now?" he murmured, gently reaching out to touch her arms and then her shoulders.

Rainy could bear her longing no more. She reached up to touch his hair, just as she'd wanted to do. "Oh, yes, Duncan," she breathed. "Be kind to me."

Duncan's mouth came down on hers in a passionate kiss that took Rainy's breath away. She wrapped her arms around him tightly, fearful that if she didn't, she might very well melt right into the ground. Duncan made her feel at peace—and at the same time he had her heart racing. He seemed to reach inside her and pull out all the bits of doubt and hopelessness. She felt her strength return as his kiss deepened. Now there was no doubt in her mind—the infatuation, the silly schoolgirl crush . . . had turned into something much more persuasive. Dared she call it love?

Duncan pulled away, his hands lingering on her face. Rainy opened her eyes to find the questioning look in his expression. She wanted to speak, but the words wouldn't come. Surely he couldn't doubt how she felt about him. Scotland seemed a remote possibility now.

"I'm sure sorry to interrupt this, ah, moment," Sonny said. He cleared his throat nervously. Duncan let go of Rainy rather quickly and stepped away while Rainy met her brother's amused look.

"What's the matter?" she questioned.

"I just got a bit of news and I knew you'd want to know about it right away. We've been booked to do a one-way tour to the Grand Canyon. We're to leave tomorrow morning, take a customized route through the reservations so that the dudes can see the Hopi Snake Dance, then head down to Flagstaff and finally over to Williams, where they'll take the train to the canyon."

Rainy nodded, but Duncan seemed confused. "I thought they'd cancelled all the longer drives."

"Anything can be bought for a price," Rainy replied. "You know how people are. Major Clarkson said so long as the dudes were willing to pay, we'd take them where they wanted to go. We just don't openly advertise the longer trips.'' She looked at him strangely. "Didn't they tell you this in the drivers' meeting?''

"I guess I forgot," Duncan replied. "How long will you be gone, Sonny?''

"We leave tomorrow morning, and it will take us five days to get to Williams. But there's something else to this. Something Rainy needs to know." His expression grew sympathetic. "Jennetta Blythe is the one who set up the tour. She wants to take some friends on the ultimate Wild West trip. She's also bringing Chester and Bethel along.''

Rainy felt the wind go out of her. She swallowed hard and shook her head. "No. I won't do it. I'll go talk to Mrs. Lehman right now, but I will not lead that tour group.''

"Don't bother. I've already argued the point. She said we were specifically requested and the clients are willing to pay double the usual price for us. They would take no substitutes, and Mrs. Lehman and Major Clarkson said it was of the utmost importance that we please the customer.''

"Well, I'll resign my position now instead of waiting until the end of the month," Rainy said in anger. "I'm not traveling another mile with that collection of ninnies.''

Duncan reached out and touched her arm. "You might get the answers you're looking for—especially if Chester is on the trip.''

"What are you talking about?'' Sonny questioned.

Duncan held her gaze, and Rainy realized he was

absolutely right. She might very well uncover the clues to her vindication. It was a long shot—none of the other trips had borne fruit—but it was always possible. She shrugged in defeat and sighed.

Rainy turned to Sonny. "He knows about the past. I told him about the university and how I have always believed Chester had something to do with what happened."

"So now you figure going on this trip is somehow going to give you the answers?" Sonny looked first to Rainy and then to Duncan. "Why now?"

Duncan shrugged. "I'm just suggesting it might be beneficial. It might offer her nothing but frustration too."

Rainy felt trapped, and yet a part of her was eager to see if this trip would somehow be different. Maybe Duncan's intuition was God-given. Maybe it was a sign that she would be able to learn the truth once and for all. Defeated, she said, "I guess there's no real choice but to go."

Sonny gave her an apologetic smile. "I tried, sis. Really I did."

Rainy knew he spoke the truth. "I'll be all right. After all, you'll be there to help me." Her stomach rumbled loud enough for everyone to hear. "Right now, I think I'd do well to get some supper. I'm famished."

"I haven't eaten either," Sonny admitted, then looked to Duncan. "Want to join us?"

"No, I have some business to take care of," Duncan murmured. He let go of Rainy and touched his hand to his hat. "I'll catch up with both of you when you get back from the tour."

———

Duncan watched Rainy and her brother walk past La Fonda and disappear down the street before trying to decide what to do next. He wanted very much to locate Phillip and his sister and tell them about his museum artifacts. The timing was critical. If they were involved, perhaps his offer of artifacts would keep them from stealing anything on the Grand Canyon trip and Rainy wouldn't look so bad.

Going in to the hotel registration desk, Duncan asked for Phillip Vance's room number. He knew Phillip always stayed at La Fonda when in town. He'd checked out that much. He wasn't sure why, however. With Jennetta situated not far from the Plaza and the main thrust of activities, he couldn't imagine why she would send her brother to a hotel.

Bounding up the stairs, Duncan tried to think how he might approach Phillip. He didn't want to appear too eager. After all, if they weren't guilty of stealing, they might well believe him to be out of his head and report him to the police. The last thing Duncan needed was that kind of interference. Worse still, they might tell their friends what had happened and ruin the entire investigation.

He paused outside the door, whispered a prayer, then knocked loudly. He could only hope that Phillip was inside. It wasn't quite the hour for parties to begin their entertainment. To his relief, he heard voices coming from the other side of the door. In a moment, Phillip Vance opened the door. He stood there

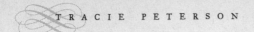

wearing a red satin smoking jacket, a cigarette in hand.

"Oh, hello . . . Mr. . . . Hartson?" Phillip said hesitantly.

"Hartford. I wondered if you had a moment to talk to me."

"Well, my sister is here," Phillip began, "but I'm sure she won't mind. We're making an early evening of it because she's heading to the Grand Canyon tomorrow."

Duncan nodded. "Yes, I'd heard that. What I have to say won't take long, and I'd be happy to share the information with your sister as well."

Phillip nodded. "Then please come in."

Duncan entered the lion's den—at least that's what it felt like to him. He tried to appear as though this were something he did on an everyday basis. Jennetta Blythe slinked into view. She was dressed in a rather dowdy manner, just as she'd been the first time Duncan had met her. Her hair had recently been cut and seemed not to have adjusted well to the trim. She looked nothing like the socialite he'd seen before.

"I'm glad I could find you both," Duncan said, smiling. "I must say, however, I thought it rather odd that Phillip would have a suite here at the hotel while you live right in town, Mrs. Blythe."

Jennetta seemed indifferent to his observation. "My home is my sanctuary where I create. I can't have a lot of people running about. It would cause problems for the spirits. They would be disturbed," she said matter-of-factly.

"The spirits?"

Phillip chuckled. "Jennetta fancies her house is haunted."

"It *is* haunted, and the spirits help me to write. I have absolutely no one in unless I'm convinced the spirits would approve. Often they do approve, but not for overnight—I never have guests sleep over. I know the spirits would find that much too disruptive."

Duncan nodded as if he'd heard this before.

"So what brings you here, Mr. Hartford?"

Duncan coughed, trying to cover his sudden case of nerves. "Well, the truth is, I remember Mrs. Blythe purchasing some Indian trinkets and thought perhaps you were both connoisseurs of the Indian culture and their artwork."

"I suppose we are," Phillip replied. "I, of course, first came here to better my understanding of the American West. I wanted to utilize it for my movies. Jennetta came here to write. You do know that Santa Fe is a writer's community, don't you?"

Duncan nodded. "I'm very familiar with that aspect of this town. I also know it to have a strong community of painters. The stories surrounding the Cinco Pintores are notorious."

Jennetta gave a scoffing laugh. "The Five Painters, indeed. Writers are much more of an influence here. Painters go to Taos—at least painters of any real repute. My dear friend Mary Austin lives on the Camino del Monte Sol. She's been published many times. She's even working right now on a book that deals with the Indians and some of their 'trinkets,' as you called them. There are far more writers than you

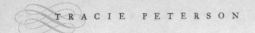

would guess. We're a quiet bunch overall and prefer not to be disturbed."

"I stand corrected," Duncan said, smiling. "I do recall several years ago that Willa Cather came to the museum for information on the Archbishop of Santa Fe. Seems she was putting together a fiction book."

Jennetta nodded enthusiastically. "Yes, exactly! That's what I'm speaking of. You cannot discredit the strong influence of writers."

Duncan nodded. "Well, I should get back to what I originally came for. The truth is, I've seen your interest in Indian artifacts and I wondered if you would be interested in purchasing some pieces that will not be offered to the general public."

Jennetta moved closer, her eyes widening, while Phillip sat down and took a long drag on the cigarette. "What kind of pieces?" she asked.

Duncan felt his heart begin to race. He described the three pieces and their value and meaning. He hinted at the fact that they were museum-owned and were soon to be changed out from their exhibit and put into storage.

"They probably won't be missed for years," he added.

Neither Jennetta nor Phillip acted in any way distressed by the idea of Duncan selling stolen merchandise. Their reaction, or lack of it, gave Duncan hope that he was definitely on the right trail. "I could have the pieces right away."

"I'm particularly interested in the squash blossom necklace," Jennetta said, her eyes gleaming. "I don't suppose you have set a price?"

Duncan shook his head and shrugged. "I know what the pieces are worth from working with them; however, given the circumstances, we both know that negotiating the price will benefit us both."

Jennetta stared him down like a hunter going in for the kill. "I think we could probably come to some arrangement. You'll have to wait until I get back from our trip, however. I positively cannot do any business until I consult . . . the spirits."

CHAPTER TWENTY

*R*ainy was uncertain as to how she'd deal with Phillip Vance when she saw him, but when the dudes showed up with Jennetta, Phillip was strangely absent. Jennetta offered no explanation, and she seemed rather moody and silent. Her friends chided her for her misery and teased that no doubt great poems would be born out of such bleak moments. Still Jennetta said little.

The trip was to be different than most. The route was customized, starting with an early morning departure from Santa Fe and no stops, except for food and gasoline, until they stopped for the night in Gallup. The dudes in this tour had already seen the little side ventures and were more focused on making it in time for the annual Hopi Snake Dance.

Rainy endured the first twenty-four hours with as much grace and consideration as she could. Chester made a nuisance of himself, commenting that he'd heard Rainy was resigning at the end of the month and wondering about the reason for the sudden departure. Rainy ignored him as much as she could, but as they arrived at the Hopi reservation, he seemed to be in prime form.

"I don't suppose the fact that you're leaving for Scotland has anything to do with the missing artifacts, would it?" he asked, coming up from behind Rainy.

She turned around to face him with a grimace. "Chester, you have continued to annoy me on this trip. Why not give us both a rest? I have no interest in hearing anything you have to say, and frankly, although my resignation was going to be turned in at the end of this month, I wouldn't hesitate to up the date and quit early if it meant I would be free of listening to you."

"But you must admit it seems strange."

"Why should it seem strange? The university has asked my father to take an early retirement. The economy of the country is failing fast and hard. My father owns property in Scotland, we have family there, and it seems the logical place to go. I have no reason to remain behind."

"I thought you and Vance had some sort of understanding."

"Well, you thought wrong," Rainy replied and turned back to her paper work.

"Look, you're always misunderstanding my motives," Chester whispered as he leaned close to her ear.

Rainy moved away. "I don't believe I've misunderstood anything you've said or done. When I was falsely accused of stealing the artifacts at the university, I knew you had the information I needed to clear my name."

Chester looked rather shocked. His face paled. "I . . . had nothing of the kind."

"Your words are far from convincing. I asked you one night prior to the university's final decision why you didn't go in there and fight for me. You said it would result in your own dismissal. Why was that, Chester, if not for the fact that you had more information than you were allowing anyone to know? Wasn't it you who took the artifacts and placed them in my office? After all, you had a key."

Chester seemed to regain his composure. "You can't pin this on me. My family is well respected."

"So was mine until you and yours did us wrong."

Noting the time, Rainy gathered her things. "We leave for the snake dance in ten minutes. I suggest you be ready unless you plan to miss it, which is just as fine by me." She could barely contain her anger. She knew by the look on his face that she'd hit pay dirt with her suspicions, but Chester wasn't about to jeopardize everything by admitting his participation.

Lord, help me in this. I know he holds the key to the past.

To Rainy's disappointment, ten minutes later Chester was present, along with his wife. Bethel and Jennetta looked positively miserable and Rainy could only suppose it was due to the heat. Someone told her it might well reach one hundred degrees. She didn't mind the warmth, but these poor creatures of luxury and ease seemed unable to endure the sun's intensity for long.

Hiding behind her huge straw hat, Jennetta dabbed herself with a cloth and remained silent while Rainy ushered her clients into the car so that they could drive to the mesa where the dance would be held.

Rainy gave the same speech she gave every year. "You need to understand how very important this ritual is to the Hopi. The government once tried to put an end to the celebration back in 1923. They said time could be better used by working instead of celebrating. They wanted the Hopi to move the event to the winter, not understanding that the snakes would be hibernating then.

"The dance has its basis in the myths and legends of the Hopi people. It's said that Ti-yo, a hero god who is often seen in Hopi legends, wanted to follow the river at the bottom of the Grand Canyon and see where it would take him. His father helped him build a boat and made gifts for the people he would meet along the way.

"The first place he came to was a small hole in the ground where he knew Spider Woman lived. Spider Woman welcomed him and because of his gift, she offered to go along with him and advise him as he made his journey. She took along magic potions that would calm the snakes and other wild animals so that Ti-yo would not be harmed.

"The journey continued and Ti-yo went even deeper into the canyon, where he met other beings. He offered his gifts and was given gifts in return. When he reached the Woman of Hard Substance, he found she lived in a kiva of turquoise and coral. As they sat talking, the Sun came in and landed on the kiva roof. Ti-yo gave him gifts, and the Sun told Ti-yo to take hold of his girdle and Sun would take him around the earth.

"When Ti-yo's journey ended, he spent time in the Snake House and learned what songs to sing and how to paint his body so that the rain would come. He was then given two maidens. One to be his own wife and one for his brother. Spider Woman made a special basket for him and the women to bring back to his home. Later, Ti-yo and his brother married the women.

"After this, the village had trouble with snakes coming in to eat their corn. The legend says the maidens reverted to snakelike beings that bore small snakes that attacked and killed the children of the village. The mothers of these children forced their men to migrate, and in migrating they taught the snake ritual to their Hopi brothers and sisters as they traveled."

"What a marvelous story," Bethel declared. "I love Indian lore."

Others quickly agreed with her. Rainy let them chatter a bit more while Sonny drove on. Finally she interrupted. "We will not be allowed to see the entire ceremony of the snake dance. Prior to our arrival there is a gathering of rattlesnakes by the priests. The snakes are then brought into the kiva and dumped on the floor. The priests will take their choice of snakes, although it is said the snakes actually choose their men. Each priest takes his snakes home and washes them in cold water and yellow root medicine. Then the priest throws away his clothing and washes himself. He must then fast a day and dance all night. He will feed the rattlesnakes before even feeding himself, and when the time for the dance comes, he will gather his snakes, one in his mouth and one in each hand."

"Oh, that sounds absolutely vile," Jennetta said, actually looking a bit green.

"You will see for yourself that the actual dance has its vile moments," Rainy declared. "There have been times when the snakes have bitten the men and yet still they dance and pay little attention to their wounds. They appear to suffer no harm from the venom."

"How does that work?" one man questioned. "Have they pulled the fangs out of the little beasts first?"

Rainy shook her head. "No, you can clearly see the rattlesnakes still maintain their fangs. No one is really certain why the Hopi survive unaffected. During the dance you'll see the men tickle the head, neck, and mouth of the snakes with a ceremonial wand. This seems to stupefy the snake. Some observers claim that the wand must have some sort of potion or herb that sedates the animal, but I cannot say this is true."

They finally arrived at the mesa, where a great many other tourists had gathered as well. The Hopi Snake Dance was not to be missed.

Rainy positioned her people and reminded them to remain silent and do nothing to interfere with the dance. As the ceremony played itself out, she couldn't help but think of how this would be the last time she'd see the snake dance. The thought saddened her, but no more so than the thought of leaving Duncan.

Now that he's kissed me, perhaps I should delay my plans. Maybe things will come together for us, she thought. Rainy glanced to the skies overhead. There were clouds in the west. The dance was said to bring rain and often the dancers finished in the midst of a downpour. Rainy couldn't help but wonder if it would be that way today.

The dancers went through their routine, and at the conclusion the priests offered a prayer and the snake dancers took up bundles of snakes and ran back to level ground below the mesa. Here they let the snakes go in four different directions. This was so that the snakes could deliver their prayers to the underworld and the rain gods would hear and answer.

A purification ritual took place afterward and ended with the Hopi men taking an emetic and vomiting over the side of the mesa. At this point, Jennetta and Bethel both blanched and moved back to the car. Other dudes were not so fortunate and soon joined in the purging ritual without intending to.

Rainy smiled to herself and made her way to the touring car with her stunned dudes. Sonny helped everyone load up and they headed back to their lodging in near silence. It generally went this way, so Rainy didn't offer much chatter. She told them they would remain at the reservation for an extra day before heading to Flagstaff and that the Hopi had agreed to share more information about their culture and beliefs. If anyone wanted to talk to them, Rainy could arrange a private meeting. No one took her up on the offer, much to her surprise.

That evening Rainy went to have dinner with her friends Istaqa and Una. When they first met, both had welcomed Rainy with open arms when she had demonstrated her desire to understand and know them better. In turn, Rainy had shared her faith in God, and Istaqa and Una had accepted Jesus as their Savior.

"We're so glad you could eat with us," Una said, embracing Rainy. "Where is your brother?"

"He was having some trouble with the car and needed to check on it. He said to give you his apologies."

Una nodded. "He will be missed."

They gathered and prayed, and Rainy didn't know when she'd enjoyed herself more. For a time she actually stopped worrying about Chester and the artifacts. She chose instead to listen to Una talk about their boys and how well they were doing in school.

"I don't think I'll have a chance to see you again anytime soon," Rainy explained as dinner concluded and they sat sipping coffee. "I'm resigning my job at the end of the month and will probably move to Scotland with my parents."

Una and Istaqa exchanged a strange look, and Rainy couldn't help but ask them what was wrong. Istaqa looked at his cup, refusing to meet Rainy's eyes. She studied the man and his blunt features. His hair was cut in Hopi fashion, straight and just below the ear. He wore a band around his head as many of his people did. He generally was very straightforward with Rainy, but now he suddenly seemed uncomfortable.

"What is it? Have I done something to offend you?"

Una reached out and patted Rainy's hand. "It is not you. There have been problems and Istaqa worries."

Rainy thought of the thefts. "Yes, I know about the problems."

Istaqa looked up. His dark eyes seemed to scrutinize

her with more interest. Rainy felt uneasy and continued. "I've been told there were thefts and that the Detours trips seemed to correspond with those thefts." Outside, thunder rumbled as the rains moved in. The snake dance had apparently done its job.

Una nodded. "It hasn't been good."

"I actually came here not only to share supper," Rainy admitted, "but in hopes that you'd help me in this very matter. There are people out there who want to blame me for these thefts."

Una looked to Istaqa. For a moment neither one spoke, then Una nodded and gave her husband a nudge. Istaqa finally spoke. "There has been trouble and your name has been given many times."

"But why? You know me. You know I wouldn't steal from you. You know I respect the Hopi."

"We know," Una said, looking to her husband. He nodded as well.

"I did not believe their words," Istaqa stated. "But the Indian agent and his people have been quite convinced of your guilt."

Rainy slumped back in defeat. "I'm trying so hard to find the real culprit, but if everyone else is determined to blame me, I'll be working all alone and never get anywhere."

"You won't work alone," Una said. "You'll work with God."

"He seems to be my only friend."

"No," Istaqa said. "We are your friends. You have been a blessing to us, and we will not believe these lies against you. That is what I told Mr. Richland when he suggested you were to blame. You and Sonny."

"Who is this Mr. Richland?"

"He is the man from the Office of Indian Affairs. He has been so convinced of your guilt he has hired someone to watch you—to get close to you so that they can know the truth."

"Hired someone? Who? What's the name of this person?" Rainy asked, feeling angry at the thought that her every move was being watched.

"I shouldn't tell you this," Istaqa said. "But I am supposed to watch you too." He smiled and shook his head. "It's all worthless to me. I know you are not guilty."

"I appreciate the fact that you believe in me," Rainy said, reaching out to touch both Istaqa and Una. "You have been dear friends. But now I need to know who Mr. Richland has hired to watch me."

Istaqa sighed. "Very well. His name is Hartford. Duncan Hartford."

————

Rainy left shortly after this declaration. She felt that if she didn't leave, she might very well repeat the vomiting ritual viewed earlier that day. She felt a cold numbness creep over her body. Duncan was nothing more than a spy sent to keep track of her comings and goings. No wonder he always seemed to turn up when she was alone. No wonder he invited her to dinner—walked with her—kissed her.

Rainy felt sick. "Oh, God, how can this be? I knew he was aware of the situation. He shared with me that others thought me guilty. Now I can see he only did that hoping I'd talk." She moaned as she remembered that she'd told Duncan about the situation at the university.

The hopelessness of her dilemma washed over her in waves. "Oh, God, where are you?"

CHAPTER TWENTY-ONE

Things went from bad to worse for Rainy. First was the declaration from Istaqa regarding Duncan's involvement in the investigation; then Sonny arrived while Rainy was eating breakfast to tell her that Jennetta Blythe had disappeared. The latter didn't really surprise Rainy—the woman had been moody and unresponsive since the trip first began. All sorts of images ran through her head. Had Jennetta fallen into harm? Had she run off with some new love?

"What do you mean, disappeared?" Rainy asked, forcing herself to remain calm. Maybe it wasn't as bad as she thought.

"I mean she left the hotel shortly after the snake dance and no one has seen her since."

Rainy sighed. "She didn't return to her room last night?"

"No, apparently not. Bethel is beside herself and wonders if we can delay the trip until Jennetta's return."

"I suppose we could consider it, since Jennetta arranged this trip, but we are expected to keep to our schedule. Perhaps I should talk to Jennetta's friends and see if anyone knows what's become of her."

Sonny shook his head and gave his hat a twirl. "I did that as soon as Bethel came to me. No one has seen her. They all admit that something was bothering her, but no one has a clue as to what it might be."

Rainy pushed back from the table. "I suppose I'll go talk to Istaqa and see if he can nose around and find her. She couldn't have gotten that far."

"No, I don't suppose so. You don't think it has anything to do with the missing artifacts, do you?"

Rainy startled at this. She'd talked very little to Sonny about the situation and it seemed strange that he should comment on it now. "How much do you know?"

Sonny shrugged. "Quite a bit. I've talked some to Duncan and I've also talked to several other people. I've wondered about Jennetta and Phillip because of their continued trips. It just doesn't make sense that they would take trip after trip. The Detours are costly and, while entertaining and fun, I don't see those two as benefiting from it."

Rainy couldn't agree more with her brother. "Let's walk around a bit. You can go with me to Istaqa's and tell him what you know."

They walked along together and Rainy felt an overwhelming sorrow as she thought of Duncan. How could he do this to her? How could he kiss her and comfort her, then use her for information? Her hurt went beyond anything Rainy could explain to Sonny.

They didn't go far before they ran into Istaqa. He

waved as they approached and listened to their concerns about Jennetta.

"I'll see what I can find out," he told Rainy.

"We need to leave tomorrow morning," she said. "But obviously I can't ignore the fact that one of my dudes is missing."

Istaqa nodded. "I'll talk to you this evening. You can both come to dinner. Una will be happy."

Throughout the day there was no word of Jennetta and by evening's dinner with Una and Istaqa, they were no closer to knowing her whereabouts than they had been that morning. Jennetta's disappearance made Rainy even more suspicious of her involvement with the missing artifacts. Rainy could only imagine that Jennetta had latched onto goods that she couldn't hide in the touring car and perhaps was making provision for their return to Santa Fe by some other means.

"Is anything missing—has anyone reported missing artifacts?" she asked Istaqa.

"No. Nothing has been mentioned."

Rainy shook her head. "It's possible that Jennetta is secreting something out of the reservation. She has enough money to pay people off and get pretty much whatever she wants."

"I've asked around about her. One woman mentioned having seen someone who fit her description, but she couldn't be sure it was Mrs. Blythe."

"I'm still willing to bet she's up to no good. I think Jennetta has something up her sleeve and this little disappearing act of hers is to cover it up or take care of business."

By the next morning, Rainy was even more convinced as they pulled out of the Hopi village without Jennetta. Istaqa promised to continue looking for the missing woman and to get her to the train once found. It was all they could do.

It wasn't until they left the car in Williams and prepared to return by train to Santa Fe, while their dudes went to the Grand Canyon with Chester and Bethel, that Rainy learned the truth. Istaqa wired the depot to say word had come that Jennetta had gotten sick and had arranged for someone to take her to the train in Winslow. She had ridden the rails back to Santa Fe so she could see her doctor.

Rainy was relieved to know the truth but was still suspicious. It could all be a ruse after all. Just a plot to keep the others from knowing what Jennetta was truly up to. Besides, why hadn't she at least explained the truth to Bethel?

Taking her seat on the train, Rainy immediately pretended to sleep. She figured Sonny would want to discuss Duncan after the kiss he'd witnessed, but she didn't want to talk about him or the missing pieces. She'd already decided enough was enough. She wasn't going to wait until the end of the month to resign her position. She would do it as soon as she returned. Maybe then she could avoid ever having to see Duncan again.

I can't bear to think of him kissing me . . . that it was part of a scheme to spy on me. I can't believe I've lost my heart to him and he's played me for a fool.

The thoughts churned in her head, leaving her with a tight pain in her chest. How could she have

been so taken in by him? His kindness was her undoing. When people treated her poorly as Chester and
his father had, she could handle it. She could deal
with the unruly guests who joined the tours. She could
bear up under irritated travelers, surly supervisors,
and irrational hotel management, but just let someone
be nice to her and . . . well, the effect was obvious.

Rainy dozed off and on, but she was very much
aware of her pain, even in her sleep. Her dreams were
laced with accusations and ugly scenes of confronta-
tion. She would question Duncan only to have him kiss
her again and tell her that he was taking her to jail or
that he knew she was innocent but that he had to get
evidence against her. The thoughts were jumbled and
confusing, and Rainy always woke with a start, sweaty
and hot from the close confines of the train. Her head
ached from a throbbing pain that had started when
they were somewhere around Holbrook.

By the time they arrived in Albuquerque, Rainy
had decided to stay overnight with her folks. "I don't
feel well, Sonny. Take me home. I want to see Mom
and Dad."

"What's wrong?" he asked, his tone revealing his
concern.

"I don't know exactly. I have a horrible headache,
though, and I don't think I can sit another minute on
this train. Please just take me home so that I can take
a cold bath and sleep."

Sonny did just that. When they arrived, their
mother greeted them in surprise but quickly escorted
her daughter upstairs. "Take your bath and I'll bring
you something for your headache," her mother

promised before drawing the drapes.

Rainy went through the paces, feeling no real relief from the tepid water. She sank into the tub and tried to push aside the thoughts that raced through her head.

When done, Rainy quickly dressed in a nightgown of lightweight cotton. She threw herself across her bed and pleaded with God for answers. Clinging to her pillow, Rainy let loose the tears that had threatened to flow all day. She didn't want her mother to find her crying, but the tears were impossible to stop. Her emotions demanded the purging.

"Oh, God," she whispered, "how could this happen? Why should I be accused? You know my innocence. Why can't I be free of this? I love Duncan, but now I learn that he's only been interested in me because of the investigation."

She buried her face in the pillow and cried in earnest.

"Rainy?"

Her mother gently touched her shoulder. Rainy raised her face and shrugged. "I'm sorry."

Her mother put a glass on Rainy's nightstand and sat down beside her daughter. "What's wrong? What has happened to cause these tears?"

"Oh, Mama, it's terrible. I feel so silly and so used." She struggled to sit up and accepted the glass of water from her mother.

"I've put some headache powders in the water, so drink it down," her mother instructed.

Rainy did as she was told, then wiped her eyes.

"I've fallen in love, but I've done so with the wrong man."

Her mother's gentle nature immediately calmed her. "Why don't you tell me all about it?"

Rainy nodded. Her mother's graying red hair and careworn face reminded Rainy that the years were passing by much too quickly. She took hold of her mother's hand and held it to her face. "I fell in love with Duncan Hartford."

"Why, he's a very pleasant young man. Why do you say he's the wrong man?"

"Because he's only kept company with me in order to watch me. He was hired to keep track of me and see if I was the one responsible for the missing Indian artifacts."

She dropped her hold on her mother's hand and shook her head. "I can't believe the way this is all happening again. I didn't take those pieces. I've done nothing wrong, and yet, once again, I find myself in the middle of the same type of controversy. How can this be God's will for my life?"

Her mother smiled. "We don't always know what God is doing. We have to trust that He sees the injustice of this moment, however."

"Well, I'm finished with Duncan and everyone else in Santa Fe. I'm going to stay here until I feel better, then I'm going to Santa Fe to resign early. I know they expected me to finish out the month, but I can't. I don't want to ever see Duncan again."

"You aren't going to confront him with this new information? Let him explain it himself?"

Her mother's words were like a slap in the face. "Why should I?"

"You don't like being falsely accused without people seeking the truth. Shouldn't you seek the truth from Duncan?"

Rainy didn't like hearing her mother's suggestion, but it pierced her conscience immediately and she knew without any question that her mother was right. "But it hurts so much. Seeing him will only compound the pain."

"But it might also ease it," her mother declared. "If you learn the truth, it might very well change everything."

"But what if this is the truth? How do I deal with it then? How do I face up to falling in love with Duncan if he's only been nice to me in order to pry into my past?"

"God will give you grace to deal with whatever comes your way. Trust Him, Rainy. That's all I can say. There is nothing I can do or tell you that will ease your misery. Only the truth can do that for you—but you won't learn the truth if you don't ask."

"I'll think about it," Rainy promised.

The next day Sonny went back to Santa Fe while Rainy stayed in Albuquerque. She continued to consider her mother's words. Perhaps she was right. Maybe talking to Duncan would help her to understand his position. But did she want to understand his position? What if he apologized and told her he was indeed sent to spy on her? What if his kiss meant nothing?

"Will you pack some dishes for me while I run to

the market?" Rainy's mother asked as Rainy sat moping in the living room.

Rainy looked up to find her mother adjusting a small straw hat. Her mother's inner contentment gave her a more youthful and radiant appearance this morning. Rainy wondered how her mother managed to bear up under the stress of life.

"Rainy, did you hear me?"

Rainy startled as if she'd been in a dream. "Oh, sorry. Sure. I think I can do that without causing too much damage."

"I've no doubt you can handle the job admirably. Just use the crates on the far wall. They have packing materials already in them. I've been wrapping things in newspaper first, however, and then I put them in the packing."

Rainy nodded. "If you're picking up food for supper, I heard Dad say he was hungry for mashed neeps."

"I heard him say it, too, so turnips are on my list."

Her mother had been gone no more than ten minutes when a knock came at the door. Rainy, in no mood for company, seriously considered not answering. After all, she wasn't usually in residence and no one would know that she was there. But the knocking was so persistent that Rainy worried it might be some kind of emergency with her father or mother, so she opened the door to find a rather rumpled-looking Gunther Albright smiling back at her.

"I didn't know you were in town," he said.

Rainy smiled and opened the door wider. "I've only been here a day. I'm afraid you've missed both of

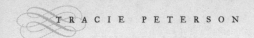

my parents. Dad is at the university dealing with last-minute details, and my mother has just gone out to the market."

"I knew your father was away. I tried to catch up with him at the school. I have a few things I need to discuss with him and thought perhaps he'd already arrived home. If not, I can wait for him." He leaned down and lowered his voice. "I also want to discuss a going-away party for your father. I want to send him into retirement on a good note. Perhaps you and I can conspire on this?"

Rainy immediately felt at ease. Planning a party for her father would be a great deal of fun and perhaps just the thing to bring her out of her self-pitying mood. "That's so kind of you, Gunther. I think it would bless Dad's heart to have such a party. Why don't you come in? We can discuss the details and I'll give the information to Mom."

"That sounds just fine." He handed his hat to Rainy.

Rainy placed his hat on the receiving table and moved toward the front room. "Can I get you some refreshments?"

Gunther joined her in the living room. "No, I'm just fine. Oh, I see the packing has already begun."

"Yes. I'm afraid they aren't taking much. They've given a great deal away and sold off other pieces. Mom said they were taking only what they couldn't bear to leave behind."

"Probably wise, given the distance of the journey. I understand you're thinking about going with them."

"Yes. It wasn't an easy decision. I love New Mexico

and the thought of leaving makes me quite sad." She sighed and forced a smile. "But I felt it would be for the best in the long run. I'm going to resign my position with the touring company tomorrow and help them prepare."

"I wonder if you might have time for another adventure or two before you leave. The departure is still set for September first, correct?" Gunther said, surprising Rainy. He toyed at smoothing a wrinkle in his well-worn tan trousers. "I would really appreciate your help in a matter. We should be able to work it in prior to your leaving."

Rainy sat down and urged Gunther to do the same. "I never consider propositions standing," she teased. In truth, Gunther looked quite tired and Rainy wanted him to relax and rest.

Gunther did as she suggested, then leaned forward, hands on his knees. "I want to organize a dig in a remote area of the Hopi reservation northwest of Winslow. The area shows great promise according to some old manuscripts I've located. I was hoping you could help me negotiate the terms of the dig and help me get permission."

Rainy felt rather awkward, for Gunther's request had taken her totally off guard. "What would the purpose of the dig be?"

"Education, of course."

Rainy considered the matter for a moment. "Well, there are all the rules and paper work to be dealt with, of course. It won't be easy, but I think if we explained the purpose isn't for selling the pieces but to substantiate history, it would probably be better received. And

we cannot, in any manner, disturb burial sites."

Gunther nodded. "No, of course not. I knew you'd understand. I'd actually like to write a book about the area and the people. You can also help me in that matter. Set me up with your friends and such. They'd probably be more willing to tell me their legends and histories if they knew I was a friend of yours. And since you'll be gone, I can't very well seek out your help in the future."

"Yes, that's true. The Hopi are generally suspicious of most whites. They've suffered much at the hands of our race. I would hate for them to endure any more. You would have to agree to be as unobtrusive as possible, but of course you know all of that."

"Indeed I do. What say we agree to meet on Friday? We can take the train to Winslow, where I'll arrange a car for us. I'll take care of all the expenses," Gunther stated. "And I'll be happy to pay you for your time."

"That won't be necessary. I'm happy to help—you know my passion for educating people about the Southwest."

Just then her mother returned and to Rainy's surprise her father followed in close on her heels.

"Look who's here, Mom . . . Dad. Gunther was just telling me about a book he wants to write about the Hopi. Isn't that marvelous?"

"I'm sure if anyone can do the Hopi justice, it would be Gunther," her father said.

"I was also hoping to talk to you," Gunther stated, getting up from the sofa. "I tried to catch you at the university as I heard you were there sorting through some of your books and such, but alas, I missed you. There are a couple of details I need to go over with you before you leave the country."

Rainy's father nodded. "Why don't we head into my study, then? We can talk and maybe Edrea will bring us some tea and cookies."

Rainy's mother nodded. "I'd be happy to do just that."

Gunther lifted Rainy's hand to his lips as she'd seen him do with her mother. "Until Friday?"

"Yes, that will be fine."

The two men went off down the hall while Rainy slipped over to her mother. "Gunther wanted to talk to you about a retirement party for Dad as well. I didn't have a chance to get much information out of him. We had just started to talk when you came in."

Her mother laughed. "Gunther is usually all business. His birthday party must have softened his edges. I'll be sure and speak to him when the chance presents itself. Maybe when they've finished talking you could pull your father into the courtyard on the pretense of needing to talk to him about something, and then I could talk privately with Gunther. Would that work?"

Rainy giggled. "Our great conspiracy. Of course we'll make it work."

———

Finally Rainy knew she could no longer put off her trip to Santa Fe. She had to resign and collect her things, and after two more talks with her mother, she was almost convinced that she should speak to

Duncan. On the train ride, she considered how she might approach him on the topic.

I could just blurt out what I know and confront him, she mused. *Or . . . I could tell him that I love him and see what his reaction is.* Both seemed impossible to do.

Rainy poured over the details of the matter all the way to Santa Fe. When she resigned her position she wasn't at all regretful of or sorrowed by her action because she was still thinking about how she might confront Duncan. By now her curiosity drove her on. *Let him explain himself,* she thought as she climbed the stairs at the boardinghouse. *Let him tell me why he thought his actions were worthy of a Christian man. I should just tell him how much he's hurt me—make it clear that my heart is broken. That will show him.*

But revenge wasn't really what she wanted. She wanted Duncan.

She entered her room, knowing that she had to get ready for her departure the next morning. There really was a lot to tend to and very little time. Glancing around the room she would soon be leaving for the last time, Rainy had never felt more alone. Unable to bear it, she left her packing and knocked on the adjoining room door to see if Sonny was in.

When he didn't answer, she presumed he was working. If anyone could understand her plight, it would be Sonny. She thought maybe he could offer her some advice. She hadn't told him about Duncan's connection with the law officials, but she knew Sonny liked Duncan and he might very well have some idea of how she could deal with the matter. Discouraged, Rainy went back to her packing.

Sitting alone, Rainy tried to pray for wisdom but felt as though her petitions were bouncing off the ceiling. When she tired of packing, she took a long bath to clear her mind, but even that didn't help much. She curled up in front of the open window and combed out her long hair.

Gunther's request came to mind, and Rainy tried to focus on his plans instead of Duncan. She hoped the old man would be fair and kind to the Hopi as he wrote about them. Gunther seemed an evenhanded sort. He'd never questioned her as to why she'd quit the university to go to work for the Harvey Company, and he'd always been very good to her family.

With her hair nearly dry, Rainy decided to send a note to Istaqa via one of the touring groups. She wanted to explain Gunther's plans ahead of time and give him a chance to discuss the matter with the tribal elders. She briefly considered trying to get through by phone, but knew it would be difficult at best and very expensive. Of course, she had no idea if any of the couriers were scheduled for a customized trip through the Hopi village, but she had heard that one was headed for Canyon de Chelly. That wasn't so terribly far from the Hopi reservation. Perhaps someone could arrange to get the note to Istaqa from there. It would just offer him a little advance warning before she showed up with Gunther. It might even allow for him to have all the terms and conditions in order and save them time.

Taking out a piece of paper and a pen, Rainy was suddenly overwhelmed by a feeling of nostalgia. She'd had this room as her own for nearly two years now.

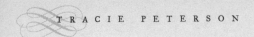

She'd been born and raised in America and now faced the possibility of living in Scotland for the remainder of her life. What would that be like?

She pushed the thoughts aside and addressed her letter to Istaqa and Una, but seeing their names on the paper brought tears to her eyes. *How can I leave New Mexico and the Southwest? How can I take myself away from the people and places I love? Scotland is a world away. Will I find a museum to work in—a dig site to join?* The situation discouraged her more than ever.

A knock on the door startled her momentarily. She glanced at her watch. It was nearly five-thirty. Perhaps it was Sonny. She crossed the room and opened the door to find Duncan Hartford standing in front of her.

CHAPTER TWENTY-TWO

Duncan's mouth dropped open as Rainy grabbed hold of his arm and dragged him down the hall of the boardinghouse. Her hair was flying in wild strawberry-blond ribbons behind her as she led him into the street.

She continued to pull him along until they reached the Plaza. They crossed to the opposite side and were halfway across the park when Rainy stopped just as quickly as she'd started. When she turned abruptly, Duncan wasn't sure what to expect.

"We need to talk."

He nodded, still mesmerized by the way the wind whipped at her hair. He'd never seen her wear it loose. He felt entranced and wanted only to reach out and touch the strands, but the fiery look in her expression caused him to stand stone still.

"I've heard something very troubling, and rather than misjudge the situation and make matters worse, I feel it only appropriate to ask you about it."

"All right," Duncan replied, finally feeling able to speak.

Rainy pushed back her hair and drew a deep breath. "Were you hired to keep track of me—to spy on me and get close to me—so that you could learn whether or not I was stealing Indian art pieces?"

Duncan felt his breath catch. His mouth went dry. "I . . . well . . . I was hired to investigate the thefts . . . yes."

Rainy narrowed her icy blue eyes. "That's not what I asked. Were you hired specifically to watch me?"

Duncan knew that he had to be honest, but at the same time he knew without a doubt it would forever change their relationship. "I . . . uh . . ."

Tears came to Rainy's eyes. "So it is true. I can't believe it. You led me to believe . . . Oh, I won't even say it. I can't believe this is happening. I wanted to give you the benefit of the doubt as my mother said I should do, but now . . ."

"Wait," he said, taking hold of her arms. "It's not as it seems."

"Of course not," she said snidely. "It never is. You were just doing a job."

"I was trying to get to the truth. They wanted me to watch you and Sonny and to prove you were the ones stealing the artifacts. I wanted to prove you were innocent. I was trying to figure out what was going on."

"Oh, really? And just what was it you were trying to figure out when you kissed me?" She lifted her chin defiantly, tears coursing down her cheeks. "I don't want to hear any more. Whether you believe me or not, I did not take those artifacts. I would never do that. I didn't steal the pieces at the university and I'm not responsible for the thefts of the last few months. I really don't care what you think or believe, but it's the truth!" She jerked away from him and ran back across the park.

Duncan sighed and sat down on a nearby bench. Betrayal was the only word for what he knew she must feel. He had no idea how she'd found out about his involvement, but her reaction definitely didn't bode well for their future—unless he could get her to listen to his explanation.

Duncan sighed again. How could things have gotten so out of hand? All he wanted to do was support her, to clear her name. Hadn't he fought for her over and over? Hadn't he worked hard to convince Richland that he couldn't just storm in and arrest the Gordons?

It didn't make sense that she wouldn't listen to him. He knew she cared about him—she would never have kissed him the way she did if she didn't have feelings for him. *So what can I do about it now? How do I make her listen to me when she clearly isn't willing to hear anything I have to say? If I went after her, she'd only think I was making things up to excuse my actions.*

Duncan wished fervently he'd never been asked to look into the Indian thefts. He thought of Jennetta's promise to look him up when she got back to town, but the tour had returned yesterday by train and still there had been no word from Jennetta. He'd thought to ask Chester Driscoll if he had seen her when he'd run into him at La Fonda, but the opportunity never arose and Duncan let it go for the time.

The entire matter was much messier than he'd

ever believed it would be. Maybe the only way to prove to Rainy that he believed in her innocence, however, was to prove Jennetta guilty.

He leaned back against the bench and tried to reason out his next step. He thought of his father's counsel to trust God to make the truth known. He also understood Rainy's frustration, however, when she'd mentioned the length of time she'd waited to clear her name.

"God's timing is never too early or too late," his father had often said.

As a child, Duncan had tried to disprove this with logic and reasoning. He could still hear his conversations with his dad. "But if God is never too late or too early, then why didn't God keep Jesus from having to die on the cross? If Jesus was willing to be a sacrifice for our sins, why wasn't that enough? Why would God make Him go through all that pain and suffering? Why not just say, 'Poof—it's done. You have taken on the sins of the world and now everyone who comes to me through you will be forgiven'?"

Duncan's father had been patient with his tender-hearted son. "Suffering has always been with man since the fall in the Garden of Eden. When people stepped out of God's will for them and decided to take matters in their own hands, there had to be consequences. The consequence of sin was pain and suffering."

"But Jesus didn't sin. He only took the sin on in order to see that we could have forgiveness," Duncan had argued with all his fifteen-year-old authority.

"Jesus had to become the sacrifice for our sins. It

wasn't enough that He took on the guilt of the world—there had to be a consequence for it. If there was no sacrifice, it would make God unjust. Jesus couldn't just take on the sins and not suffer the punishment. It wasn't a matter of God's timing being off, Duncan, it was a matter of God remaining sovereign and just."

Duncan had considered his father's words for a long time. He could see the truth of them, but the timing issue still bothered him, and it didn't seem fair. In the events of human lives, God's timing often seemed skewed.

His father then said, "Duncan, we can't know the mind of God. We can't always understand the result or reason of the things that take place in our lives. The fifty-fifth chapter of Isaiah says, 'For my thoughts are not your thoughts, neither are your ways my ways, saith the Lord. For as the heavens are higher than the earth, so are my ways higher than your ways, and my thoughts than your thoughts.' Sometimes God allows things that make no sense to you or me. We may never know why, but we have to trust that He does and that it's the right way for things to be."

Duncan knew he would have to do the same now. He would have to trust that God had the matter under control. He'd done nothing wrong. His motives were pure. He had set out on a mission to do nothing more than find out who was stealing from the Indians. Rainy just happened to get in the middle of it.

———

In Albuquerque, Rainy tried to help her mother

with a glad heart. She forced herself to get enthusiastic about plans for her father's party, but no matter what she did, Duncan was always in her thoughts. Even as she planned to help Gunther with his project, Rainy thought of Duncan and wondered if he'd just see her as doing whatever she could in order to steal more artifacts.

By Thursday evening Rainy had spent a great deal of time in prayer and felt almost ready to let go of the past, when Sonny surprised them with a visit. The look on his face told Rainy it wasn't good news.

"What's happened?" she asked, hanging her colorful apron to one side.

"It's Jennetta Blythe," Sonny said, pulling out a dining room chair to sit down.

Their parents came into the room, both wearing broad smiles. "Sonny, it's so good to see you again so soon," their mother said and kissed him atop his head.

Rainy saw his frustration. "Sonny has come with news of one of our tourists, who disappeared while traveling in Arizona with us. Remember I told you how Mrs. Blythe couldn't be found and then we had to leave without her?"

Their parents nodded in unison, and Sonny picked up the conversation. "Well, it seems the reason she disappeared was to visit some old Indian medicine woman. She wanted to . . . end her pregnancy."

"I didn't even know she *was* pregnant," Rainy said in surprise.

"No one did. Not even Phillip," Sonny admitted.

Rainy thought of the situation and shook her head. "Why would she want to kill her baby? I mean, I know

Jennetta was divorcing her husband, but they might have worked things out for the sake of the child."

"I don't know about that, but Jennetta's in the hospital. She nearly died from whatever medicines that old woman gave her. She lost the baby, but she could still lose her life as well. Phillip is beside himself. I asked him if he wanted me to bring you to talk to Jennetta, but he said no. He said he couldn't bear to see you just now, but I thought maybe you should go anyway."

Rainy felt torn. She had plans to travel with Gunther in the morning. She hadn't told anyone because she didn't want to be lectured about it. No doubt her father wouldn't like her going off across the desert with only an old man for protection and help in case their automobile broke down. Her mother would no doubt worry about it as well.

"I don't know that it would be such a wise idea for Rainy to go," her father said thoughtfully. "If Phillip has asked that she not come, then we should honor his wishes."

Sonny shrugged. "I just thought she could share Jesus with Jennetta and Phillip."

"Phillip needs a man to guide him in these spiritual matters," Rainy finally said. "I tried to talk to him about God, but I don't think he heard much of what I had to say." She ached for Phillip. It was her fervent wish that he might find salvation—not so that he might be eligible husband material, but rather so that he might find the peace that he desired.

"Why don't you go to Phillip and share the Gospel, son?" their father questioned.

Rainy quickly agreed. "I think he might very well listen to another man. Phillip's life was seemingly perfect when I tried to talk to him. Maybe hearing God's truth would mean much more now."

"But I don't really know him like you do. Maybe we could go together."

Rainy felt a twinge of guilt. "I really feel I would do more harm than good, given our past. I might just end up hurting him even more. Please do this for me, Sonny. It's God he needs, not me."

Their father put his hand on Sonny's shoulder. "Your sister is right. He doesn't need to be clouding his thoughts right now. Seeing Rainy again might make matters all the more difficult. The important thing is to support him while he awaits word on his sister."

"Well, when you put it that way it does make sense. Sure, I'll go back and stay with him at the hospital," Sonny offered.

Rainy reached out and squeezed his hand. "Tell him that I'm praying for Jennetta and for him as well. If he wants me to visit, I will."

Sonny started to get up, but his mother said, "Stay where you are. You can't go back until you have some supper. I still have some tamales on the back of the stove."

Rainy moved away as her father began talking with Sonny about how to handle the situation with Phillip. The evening air felt refreshing as she moved into the courtyard, yet guilt became her companion. There was a part of her that wanted nothing more than to go back to Santa Fe and comfort Phillip, but at the same time she wanted to run as far away as possible. She was actually glad Phillip had asked that she not come.

Lord, I need you to help me through this, she prayed. *I need to be strong in my resolve and I need to trust that you are in control. Please be with Jennetta and heal her body. Heal her on the inside as well.*

The thought of Jennetta taking the life of her own baby angered Rainy. Slipping into a chair, she tried to reason it all out. She knew Jennetta's way of living was self-centered and spoiled, but she couldn't imagine how anyone could reach such a decision.

"Rainy, are you all right?" her mother asked softly.

Rainy turned and nodded. "I was just trying to pray for Jennetta and Phillip, but . . ."

"But what?"

"But why would she kill her baby? Just imagine it."

"I can't because I've always loved being a mother. From the first moment I knew I was expecting you two, I rejoiced." She came and sat beside Rainy in the garden. "Don't be angry with Jennetta. She must have been very scared."

"I know that in my heart and I do feel bad for her. But I can't help but be convinced that she also did this because the baby was an inconvenience to her. Jennetta is an arrogant, self-absorbed woman. A baby wouldn't fit into her lifestyle."

Her mother reached over and patted Rainy's hand. "She needs God. The things of God make no sense to her. She can't understand the value of her child's life because she doesn't understand the value of her own life. You've said yourself that she seems to be miserable most of the time."

Rainy realized her mother was right. "Yes, she is. She's always writing the most depressing stuff—at least to hear Phillip tell it."

"Well, when your soul is lost in sorrow, it's hard to write anything uplifting. My guess is that Jennetta's life is in shambles. There is a great deal of ugliness involved in any divorce. She very well may be overwhelmed with her emotions over that. The baby was probably too much for her to even consider. Be compassionate, Rainy. We cannot approve of what she's done, but we can pray for her and show her love. That's what being a woman of God is all about."

Rainy nodded. "I'll keep praying about it. I know I have so much to do in my own life that I have no right to look at another's person's life with expectations of perfection."

"Sometimes the hardest thing is to deal with the log in our own eye," her mother said sympathetically. "If you look to God, He'll help you to put your own heart in order, Rainy. Then you'll be better equipped to pray and understand the lives of those around you."

CHAPTER TWENTY-THREE

*B*ut you said nothing about this," Rainy's mother argued as Rainy tried to explain her mission with Gunther.

Rainy had purposefully waited until her father and Sonny had both gone before springing the news on her mother. "Gunther just needs my help in arranging matters with the Hopi. He has a couple of dig sites that he wants to research to see if the finds will confirm other findings or offer new evidence."

"I understand the purpose of the trip, but I don't like the idea of my daughter going off across the desert without proper help. If you broke down, Gunther would never be able to make repairs to the car or even change a tire."

"Mother, I know that very well. I can change a tire if need be," Rainy protested. "Look, I promised him I'd help. He'll be here any minute and he's already purchased train tickets."

"So you'll go by train most of the way?"

Rainy shoved another blouse into her bag. "Yes. We'll take the train to Winslow."

303

"Well, I suppose there's nothing I can say to change your mind. I don't like the idea, however." Her mother pushed back an unruly strand of graying red hair and sighed. "Why can't you wait until Sonny has time to go with you?"

"Because Gunther, knowing that we planned to leave on the first of September, wanted to work through this now. He may not even be able to accomplish it all before we leave, but at least I can help him have a good start." Rainy stopped what she was doing and took her mother's hands in her own. "I promise to be careful. We'll take extra food and water when we go into the desert, and I'll make sure that everyone knows our route."

Her mother nodded. "All right. Look, I've made a batch of cinnamon cookies. I'll wrap some up for you."

Rainy grinned. "Thanks, Mom. I know Gunther and I will enjoy them."

Rainy finished her packing and had just brought down her bag when Gunther arrived. "Come on in." She shoved her thick braid up under a wide-brimmed straw hat.

He shook his head. "There's no time. I'm afraid I was delayed this morning. We'll have to hurry if we're to make our train."

Rainy turned to her mother and kissed her on the cheek. "I should be back in a few days. Don't worry about me."

"You take good care of her, Gunther. I don't like the idea of you two setting off on your own. She's just

BENEATH A HARVEST SKY

a young woman and you are not capable of running marathons anymore."

Gunther laughed awkwardly. "I don't intend to run any marathons, my dear woman." He kissed her hand, then reached for Rainy's bag. "We'll take it slow and easy. You'll see. Everything will work out just fine."

Rainy's mother thrust the cookies into her daughter's hands, then kissed her soundly. "You send word if you have any trouble at all."

"I will, Mom."

————

Sonny didn't know how to deal with Phillip Vance. The man was used to people adoring him and falling at his feet. How would he respond to Sonny's words? People generally didn't like hearing that they were living in a manner that was less than acceptable to God. How could Sonny approach the situation, tell Phillip about Jesus, and not offend him?

He found Phillip sitting alone, much to Sonny's surprise. He looked haggard and rumpled. He'd obviously slept in his linen suit, as the wrinkles bore evidence. It made Sonny less self-conscious about his own casual attire.

"Hello," Sonny said, coming into the waiting room.

"Oh, hello." Phillip started to get up but Sonny waved him off.

"Please don't get up. You look like you've had a bad time of it. How's your sister?"

Phillip sighed. "It looks like she's going to make it

through, but she had to have surgery. The doctor said she'll never be able to have children."

"I'm glad she's going to make it . . . but sorry for the situation," Sonny offered.

"I don't know why she did it. I would have helped her in any way I could."

"Sometimes people do things that make no sense to us. They're desperate and needy and they just don't give it much thought."

Phillip stared off into space as though the answer to all his questions might materialize before him. Sonny wished he could ease his pain, but there was nothing he could do but pray. Pray. The thought struck him.

"You know, I took the train to Albuquerque yesterday and I told my family, including Rainy, what had happened. They're all praying for you and for Jennetta. They started last night."

"The doctor said she'd lost so much blood that she probably should have died. She was very weak by the time he operated, but she made a turn for the better early this morning." Phillip rubbed his eyes for a moment and shook his head. "Is Rainy here?"

"No," Sonny said softly. "You said you didn't want her here, so she stayed home. She did send her wishes and prayers that Jennetta would recover and that you would be strengthened."

"It's for the best." Disappointment rang clear in his voice. "I thought she might have married me," Phillip said, again staring off into space. "I thought being with her—having her for my wife—would make everything better . . . different."

Sonny sat down beside Phillip. "How so?"

Phillip shook his head. "I don't know." He seemed so out of place in the sterile confines of the waiting room. He looked to where a crucifix was nailed to the wall opposite them. Sonny's gaze followed suit as Phillip continued. "She trusts God and she couldn't be with me because I don't."

"Why don't you trust God?" Sonny asked.

"I don't know. I suppose because it never seemed necessary to me. Then, too, I've heard the uproar from the religious masses about how movies are sinful and people are going to hell because of what I provide them. I make my living as an actor, and I'm condemned because of it." He seemed so lost and hopeless. "Rainy was the first woman to really make me feel alive. She didn't care about my status as an actor and didn't care about my money." He sighed. "She didn't care about me, period."

"That's not true. I probably shouldn't say this, but Rainy was pretty taken with you at first."

Phillip looked up. "She was?"

Sonny didn't know how much he should say. He didn't want the conversation to be about Rainy, but rather about God's love. "Rainy thought you were very charming. She's taken with men who show manners and consideration for other people. You were like that and so she thought highly of you."

"Then why . . ."

"You know the reason, Phillip. Rainy has given her life to God. She trusts Him for direction and she desires to serve Him as best she can. If that's through her work for the Detours or through archaeology, then so be it. If it's as a wife and mother, then she's just as glad to do that too. But God must come first, and Rainy knew you'd never play second fiddle to anyone."

Phillip leaned back and stared at the cross on the wall. "She's a wise woman. I wouldn't have liked being second to anyone, not even God. Religion has so many rules and regulations, and I'm sure I'd never have been able to stand up to that kind of perfection. I'm a disciplined man, but not in that way. I like my fun."

"So do I, but I also like the peace that comes from holding myself accountable to God."

Sonny watched as Phillip got up and walked to the cross, then reached out and traced the wooden image of Christ. "How can peace come out of something so violent as this?"

"The peace doesn't come from the act of killing Jesus. It comes from His willingness to take the blame and burden of sin in our place. My peace comes daily in knowing that He rose from the dead and that He's interceding for me with the Father. It comes because I know that even if death takes this body, my soul has eternal life in heaven, where all things old will pass away. All things here will fade to dust. Nothing here will matter. Not what I do as a geologist—not what you do as an actor. What will matter then is what we did for God."

"If that's true," Phillip said, turning to face Sonny, "then I've nothing to show for my life."

"But you can change all of that. See the error of your way and repent of it. Turn to God and seek His will for your life. He wants to welcome you into His care—He wants to be there for you."

"How can you be so sure of that? How can you trust that He listens and truly cares?"

Sonny got up and went to where Phillip stood. He reached out and touched Phillip. "You said yourself that the doctor figured your sister would die. But she didn't. I believe our prayers to God were heard and answered."

"But would God demand that I give up my acting? Would He take from me the very things I love?"

"If you loved them more than Him, He might well ask you to give them up."

Phillip shook his head. "I just don't know that I could ever do that."

Sonny felt a deep sadness for the man. It reminded him of the story of the rich young ruler. The man had come to Jesus proclaiming to do everything taught by scriptural law. Jesus told him then to sell everything he had and follow Him. The man couldn't do it because too much was at stake. He was very wealthy—how could he give it all up? Now Phillip was up against the same thing. Sonny had no idea if God would call him to give up acting, but he did know that God required one hundred percent of your heart. Phillip clearly couldn't or wouldn't give that up just yet.

"Think about it, Phillip. Just think on it. Let God speak to your heart and tell you what's true and necessary and what isn't. You might be surprised at the outcome."

"I will think about it," Phillip replied. "After all, it gives you and Rainy a great deal of peace and confidence. It must not be all bad." He smiled weakly.

"I need to go," Sonny said, noting the time. "But

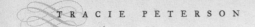

I'll come back this afternoon before I leave for Albuquerque."

Phillip nodded and reached out his hand. "Thank you for coming and give Rainy my . . . my best."

Sonny shook Phillip's hand. "I will."

That afternoon, Sonny concluded his business as quickly as possible. He turned in his resignation, packed his things, and made arrangements to head home. He was just about to head to the hospital again when Duncan Hartford caught up with him.

"Sonny, I'd hoped to run into you. Well, actually I was hoping to run into Rainy. I've looked all over for her, but they told me she'd resigned and moved out of the boardinghouse. Is that true?"

It seemed the day for desperate men. Duncan looked almost frantic in his search. "She's in Albuquerque. She did resign early and now she's helping Mom pack for the trip to Scotland."

"So she really plans to leave America?"

"I suppose so," Sonny said rather thoughtfully. "I know her heart isn't in it, but there aren't a whole lot of options for her."

"I desperately need to talk to her. I don't want her to leave. . . ." He paused and looked away. "At least not without explaining the truth."

"Did you two have another falling-out?"

Duncan pushed back his hat. "You could say that."

"Why don't you walk over to the hospital with me and tell me about it? I wanted to check in on Jennetta Blythe."

"Sure, I'll walk with you. It'd probably do me good

to explain the situation, but I hope you'll hear me out before you judge me."

Sonny raised a brow. "Sounds really serious."

"It is."

———————

Three hours later, Duncan sat beside Sonny on the train to Albuquerque. Sonny had listened to Duncan and, instead of reacting in the emotional way Rainy had, had understood and accepted Duncan's explanation. He'd also believed Duncan when he spoke of how much he loved Rainy.

"You need to tell her yourself," Sonny had said. "Come back with me to Albuquerque and spend the night with us. With you under the same roof, she'll have to listen. Besides, Dad would never allow her to go on pouting and refusing to hear you out."

To Duncan it seemed the reprieve he'd prayed for. He only hoped that Rainy saw it the same way.

"I tried to lay a trap for Jennetta Blythe and her brother," Duncan admitted. "I promised Mr. Richland I'd try to bait them with museum pieces and see if they were willing to buy them."

Sonny seemed interested. "What happened?"

"Jennetta told me she'd be in touch after the trip," Duncan replied. "But now I suppose we'll never know if she was the one who was arranging to steal the missing pieces."

Sonny grew thoughtful. "Given everything you've said, I just can't help but wonder if Rainy wasn't right. Maybe it is Chester Driscoll. He's had plenty of opportunity, and even if Jennetta had one of the missing

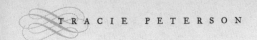

Hopi flutes, she just might have gotten it from Driscoll."

"It's worth considering," Duncan agreed. "I just don't know how we go about proving it one way or another. Chester's no fool."

"Let's talk to Rainy about it. She may have an idea since she's thought him guilty—or at least involved—from the very start."

"All right," Duncan said. "I just hope she doesn't slam the door in my face."

Sonny laughed. "Well, just in case, maybe I'd better go in first."

CHAPTER TWENTY-FOUR

*R*ainy and Gunther planned to spend the night at La Posada, the magnificent Harvey hotel in Winslow, Arizona. Rainy always enjoyed coming to La Posada. The gardens were refreshing and beautifully set against orchards and fountains. No expense had been spared on the marvelous creation.

Bordered on one side by railroad tracks and by Highway 66 on the other, the hotel had been created to look like an ancient hacienda. The stone floors and arched entryways gave the hotel a Spanish look. Rainy had to admit the architects and builders had done their jobs well.

"Rainy Gordon!" a thin, dark-haired woman declared as Rainy entered the dining room. "When did you get here?"

Rainy embraced the Harvey Girl and laughed. "Daisy! I didn't know you were working at La Posada. I just got here. I arrived with my father's good friend Gunther Albright. He's that older man just across the hall." She motioned and the younger woman craned her neck to see. Rainy had first met Daisy Kincaid at

La Fonda, where she worked as a Harvey waitress. Nearly a year earlier, Daisy had transferred to Chicago but now, apparently, she was back in the Southwest.

"I was going to ask if he might be a younger, single friend of your father's, but I can see for myself he's not," Daisy giggled.

"No, definitely not. So when did you come to La Posada? I thought you were up Chicago way."

Daisy directed her to the counter. "Sit here and I'll bring you something to eat. You are hungry, aren't you?"

"Famished. Gunther had to look into a problem with the car he requested, so he told me I might as well get a bite. We're going up to the Hopi villages, where we plan to discuss an archaeological dig that Gunther wants to begin. I have friends up there who just might be able to help him get the permission he needs. But enough about me. Tell me everything you've been doing."

"Well, it's hard to tell everything," Daisy teased. She placed a glass of lemonade in front of Rainy and laughed. "I almost got married."

"No," Rainy said, leaning in. "Why only almost?"

Daisy rolled her gaze to the ceiling and laughed. "He was flighty, as my mother put it, and he was a vacuum cleaner salesman. Mother said you just couldn't trust a man who's always working in dirt."

Rainy grinned. "I suppose that leaves archaeologists out as well." Determined to have a pleasant visit with Daisy, she tried not to think of Duncan. "So is that why you're back in the desert? Baking your brain in order to forget your failed encounter with love?"

Daisy shook her head. "Goodness, no. I found myself pining for the desert as much as anything. Crazy as it sounds for this Michigan girl, I just couldn't stay away."

After an hour of chatter and a pleasant lunch of chicken salad and cantaloupe, Rainy got up to leave. "I never fail to be amazed at these lovely blue-and-yellow Spanish tiles," she said, running her hand along the counter top. "What a wonder. The entire hotel is like an oasis in the desert."

"It is," Daisy agreed. "We've had so many movie stars come here. You'd be very impressed. We even had Phillip Vance."

Rainy smiled and nodded. She didn't even begin to feel like explaining Phillip to Daisy. "Well, look, I should continue to make preparations for our trip. We plan to head out early in the morning."

"I'll be working the breakfast shift. Come see me before you go. You'll want to take some sandwiches and fruit. I'll pack you something special."

Rainy hugged her friend and thanked her for the kind offer and the conversation. Making her way upstairs, Rainy saw nothing of Gunther. She hoped he was able to figure out what had become of the car. He'd certainly been angry when he'd learned it wasn't waiting for him as requested.

Rainy's room was simple but charming. The windows had been opened to let in the evening breeze and there was a pitcher of water and a small bowl of fruit on the wooden desk beside the window. Rainy sat down and began undoing her bootlaces. Again, feelings of nostalgia washed over her as her gaze fixed on the handwoven Indian rug beneath her feet.

"Oh, Lord, this is so hard for so many reasons," she murmured and pulled off her boot. She couldn't help but think of Duncan and wonder what he was doing. She visualized his wavy black hair and brown eyes, his firm jawline and gentle lips. She touched her hand to her mouth, remembering the feel of his kiss.

"I don't want to stay mad at Duncan Hartford. I want to forgive him and rush back to Santa Fe and tell him that I will love him forever." She sighed. "But I can't. He would never believe me. Not after I acted like a spoiled child. Someday I may learn to keep my mouth shut and not jump to conclusions, but I fear it's too late for Duncan and me."

She pulled off the other boot, then went to unpack her belongings. Spying her Bible, she began to read through a few psalms. They were always comforting to her, but today she couldn't concentrate long enough to feel anything but confusion and frustration.

"Lord," she prayed aloud, "I've tried hard to let this go. I know I've done a poor job in many ways. I know I should never have let matters get out of hand. I thought I understood your will for my life and I thought you'd given me a clear and easy path to attain that will. But none of this has been easy, and I feel rather beaten and depleted."

She put the Bible aside and stretched out on the bed. On her back with her hands beneath her head, Rainy stared at the ceiling and tried not to imagine Duncan's face or his touch. She tried not to hear his voice or see his eyes. She thought she'd almost managed the matter as she began to doze off to sleep, but her dreams betrayed her.

In her mind, she saw herself Duncan's wife. They were happy. They were working together on a dig and she had found something of great interest to show her husband. Duncan had nodded approvingly and had lifted her in the air to whirl her round and round. The action took her breath away and Rainy awoke with a start, gasping for air.

The silence of the room reminded her that she was all alone. The dream had been a pleasurable moment and now, in its absence, Rainy felt only empty loneliness in its place.

Tossing and turning in her bed, Rainy argued with herself and then with God. "I can forgive him, Lord. I can forgive the fact that he wormed his way into my heart in order to spy on me. I really can. But if he's the man for me, then why did he not believe me innocent? Why did he get involved with the investigation and try to prove me guilty?"

Or was he trying to prove you innocent? A voice from deep within seemed to challenge her.

That thought had never come to mind. Maybe Duncan had put himself into the position of assisting the authorities because he didn't believe her guilty, just as he'd said. Rainy sat straight up in bed at this thought. *Have I misjudged him?* Were his actions meant to save me instead of condemn me? Just then she remembered Duncan's words that day in Santa Fe. *"I wanted to prove you were innocent."*

Rainy suddenly felt ill. *Have I ruined everything, Lord? Have I put an end to my one chance at happiness with Duncan?* She got up and began to pace. "Oh, God, please take this misery from me. I long to do whatever it is you want me to do. I can't bear the way I feel." She pressed her hand against the soft folds of her skirt. "Deep inside, I want to do the right thing. I just don't know what it is."

She threw herself to her knees. In the middle of the room, she prayed as she'd never prayed before. "I know I've not always listened for your voice. I know that I've often tried to take control of situations and work them out in my own way. I see how I did that with Duncan and even with Phillip. I charged into those situations without allowing you to work. But, God, in all honesty, I love Duncan. Please forgive me and show me that I haven't ruined my only chance for love with him. Please give me a sign—show me a verse—something, Lord."

She prayed for what seemed an eternity, begging and pleading for God's forgiveness and direction. By the time Rainy fell back into bed, she was exhausted—wearied from struggling to understand God's will for her life. Would it always be this hard?

———

"She went where?" Sonny questioned, more than a little upset.

"Calm down, son. I wasn't any happier than you to hear what she did," his father stated, "but you know your sister and her headstrong ways."

"But this goes even beyond her usual nonsense. To go out on a trip like this with no one but your friend for a companion is . . . Why didn't you insist she have someone else go along? Why didn't she wait for me? I would have been happy to help."

Sonny paced back and forth as Duncan watched and waited for someone to answer. He wanted to know the same things. He felt more than a little frustrated that he wouldn't be able to talk to Rainy and explain his actions. He didn't want even one more day to pass between them without her hearing the truth.

"I tried to suggest that she wait for you," Sonny's mother said. "But Gunther needed to get the cooperation of the Hopi as soon as possible, and I had no idea you would return so quickly. I guess she just felt she needed to do Gunther this favor on behalf of us."

"But she won't be able to dig them out if they get stuck. Those roads up from Winslow can be really bad at times. What if she's in a sandstorm? She could forget about the arroyos and get caught in a flash flood. After all, this is the rainy season and they've already had several heavy rains over that way."

Sonny's father held up his hands. "You're only serving to worry your mother. If it's all that much of a concern, why don't you take the train out tomorrow and go after her?"

"That's it!" Duncan declared, getting to his feet. "Let's go after her. Let's help them. Two vehicles would be better than one. If one gets stuck the other one can pull it out."

"Rather like the verses in Ecclesiastes, eh?" Ray Gordon said with a smile. " 'Two are better than one; because they have a good reward for their labour. For if they fall, the one will lift up his fellow: but woe to him that is alone when he falleth; for he hath not another to help him up. Again, if two lie together, then they have heat: but how can one be warm alone? And if one prevail against him, two shall withstand him; and a threefold cord is not quickly broken.' Together, you two will make Rainy a threefold cord and she's sure to be safe."

"I can arrange a car in Winslow with Clarkson's company. I might even be able to get us free passage on the train," Sonny said with a grin.

"If not, I'll pay for it," Duncan replied. He turned to Ray and grew rather embarrassed. "You might as well know that I plan to marry your daughter—if it meets with your approval."

Ray looked to his wife and both exchanged broad smiles. "It's more important that it meets with Rainy's approval. Perhaps," Ray said, putting his arm around Duncan, "we need to have a little talk."

————

Duncan had never known more frustration than waiting for the morning train. He had longed to leave the night before, but there was no way to get passage to Winslow. Sonny had even tried to get them on a freight train, but that hadn't worked at all.

Now as they stood waiting to board their train, he could hardly force coherent thought. *What if she's in danger? What if they've gotten stuck in the desert and had to spend the night?* He paced on the platform while Sonny sat nearby, hat in hand.

"Well, Sonny Gordon," Bethel Driscoll announced as she approached them. "What brings you here?"

"Catching a train," Sonny said rather sarcastically.

Duncan immediately suspected that Sonny wanted

to keep their mission under wraps. He gave Bethel a tentative smile and tipped his hat. "Good morning."

"Mr. Hartford, isn't it?" She smiled rather coyly.

"Yes, ma'am."

"Are you two traveling together?"

"Yes," Sonny said matter-of-factly, getting to his feet. "What are you doing here? I thought given Jennetta's medical condition you'd be at her side in Santa Fe."

"I was with Jennetta until yesterday. She told me to leave her alone and demanded I go, so I did." She shrugged as though the incident meant nothing to her. "I'm to meet some friends coming in from Santa Fe. They're going to stay with me while Chester is away."

Sonny didn't seem to have the time or interest to get into Bethel's affairs with Jennetta, so he chose to keep the subject on Chester's travels. "And where has he gotten off to this time?" Sonny asked.

Bethel laughed. "Oh, he's on some fool expedition with my uncle."

Duncan forced himself not to react. He held his breath momentarily for fear of making a scene. Sonny seemed to be taking the same track.

"Chester and Gunther are working together?" Sonny asked.

"Oh, mercy, yes," Bethel said. "They've been involved in several projects these last months. I've never seen a man so enthusiastic about working with Indian artifacts as Chester. Sometimes I think he might be part Indian. We have the silly things all over the house."

Sonny and Duncan exchanged a look. Duncan knew exactly what Sonny was thinking. Duncan would love to see the pieces in Bethel's house, but in order to do so, even if she were willing, they'd miss their train.

As if on cue, the train whistle sounded from a mile down the track. "Here she comes," Sonny murmured.

Duncan nodded. "I guess we'll be saying good-bye, Mrs. Driscoll."

She laughed. "Well, you could both delay your trip and have breakfast with my party. We're quite a lively bunch, don't you know."

"Thank you, no. We have some pretty urgent business," Sonny replied for them.

Duncan thought it an understatement. To him, the business had just become a matter of life and death. Especially with Chester Driscoll involved.

CHAPTER TWENTY-FIVE

*M*ore coffee?" Daisy asked as she picked up left-over breakfast dishes from the places on either side of Rainy.

"No, I figure Gunther will be here any minute. He's not one to be delayed when he's ready to go. He was livid that we had to spend the extra day here as it was. He expected the car to be at his beck and call and when it wasn't, well, he was very unpleasant."

"I can believe that. He seemed angry when he came down for breakfast. Just shoveled his food in and left," Daisy said, leaning forward. "And he didn't leave a tip."

Rainy shook her head. "Sounds like him. Anyway, he's probably just preoccupied with the car situation. When they didn't have a car here when we arrived—or yesterday—he had to make calls and get things taken care of, and he's not at all happy about that. Then I had the audacity to suggest that I was going to drive. You would have thought I'd told him he would be hog-tied to the hood for the duration of the trip."

Daisy giggled and Rainy laughed. "He assured me that either he would drive or he'd hire a driver whom I could direct." Rainy finished the last of her toast. "I figure the latter would be better. At least I know it would put my mother's mind at ease. She worries that we'll break down and not be able to fend for ourselves."

Daisy reached under the counter. "I have a lunch packed for you. Sandwiches, fruit, cheese, and some pie. Oh, and I have a jug of ice water."

Rainy reached down to the pack at her feet. "Would you mind filling my canteen as well? No sense taking it empty." While Daisy was gone, she slipped a quarter under her plate. *That should make up for Gunther's lack of tipping.*

Daisy returned just as Rainy got to her feet. "Thanks, Daisy," she said, tucking the canteen in her bag. "I should be back tomorrow, the next day at the latest. I can't imagine our work taking much longer than that."

Daisy nodded. "Are you going up to Polacca?"

"Well, that was the original plan, but Gunther actually talked last night of taking the cutoff just north of Egloffstein Butte. I don't know if he means to head to Keems Canyon, however, or Oraibi. Frankly, I'd rather just stick with the main road. It can be perilous enough if you aren't careful."

Daisy cleared away her dishes as they said their good-byes. "Be careful. You know the weather has been rather unpredictable. We've had some bad rains and more are no doubt coming our way. There were even a couple of the smaller bridges that washed out."

"I'm sure we'll be just fine, especially if Gunther hired a local driver."

Rainy took up her bag and found room for the lunch Daisy had packed. With this arranged, she made her way to the lobby. Gunther had apparently just settled their bill and was tucking his wallet into his pocket when he spied Rainy.

"Oh, there you are. Good. I was afraid if we waited much longer to start, we'd be in a bad way."

Rainy couldn't imagine why he was so concerned with the time. "Well, I'm here and ready. Did you get the car situation settled?"

"Yes, but it wasn't easy," Gunther said rather brusquely. His face contorted as if the entire matter were an uncomfortable memory. "We should be set now."

He headed for the door that would lead them away from the tracks and out into a small circular drive on the Route 66 side of the hotel. Rainy noted he wore the same crumpled linen suit that he'd worn on the train. She ventured a guess that he'd probably slept in the thing as well.

She, on the other hand, felt very fresh and smart in her tan-colored skirt and white cotton blouse. She'd worn long sleeves to keep from burning in the sun, but the weight of the material was light enough to let the air blow through and keep her cool.

Gunther took her bags and threw them onto the backseat while Rainy secured her straw hat. She tied it loosely so that she could push it back off her head if she chose. Most likely she'd wear it even in the car because it shielded her eyes from the sun and kept her from getting a headache, something she'd learned early on in her years in New Mexico.

To her amazement, Gunther motioned her to the back. "You'll be more comfortable there." He held the door for her.

"Oh, did you manage to get a driver?" she questioned.

"Yes, in a manner of speaking."

He didn't wait long at all before closing the door behind her and getting into the front seat. Rainy adjusted her bags, then looked up to find Chester Driscoll staring back at her.

"Hello, Rainy."

"What is he doing here?" she asked Gunther.

"My niece was worried that I was too old to be traipsing out across the desert alone," he replied as Chester started the car. "She talked to your parents and they all thought it would be a good idea if Chester drove for us."

Rainy found it difficult to believe that her parents would suggest Chester for any activity that involved her. They knew how she felt about him. As Chester eased the car onto Highway 66 and headed east, Rainy knew she'd have to make a scene in order to get him to stop and let her out. And that would certainly ruin Gunther's plans.

Settling back against the seat, she folded her arms against her chest. Something didn't seem quite right, but she couldn't put her finger on it.

Chester glanced back at her and smiled. "You don't really mind, now, do you? I mean, we're old friends."

"I don't suppose I really have a choice in the matter," Rainy replied.

They drove in silence for a time, but when Gunther motioned Chester to take the turn-off from the highway and head north, Rainy felt her uneasiness grow. It was one thing to be stuck in the desert with Gunther, but it was an entirely different thing to have to stomach Chester's company.

Rainy watched the dry desert landscape for some sign that all would be well. The early morning light was already sending the night hunters and scavengers into hiding. A coyote paused in his lope to look back at their car, almost as if he were checking to see if the noise had scared up something to eat. Seeing that the car was much too large a beast to take on his own, the coyote continued into the rocks and disappeared.

Rainy wished she could disappear. In the front, Gunther and Chester had begun to discuss Gunther's autumn classes. He planned to teach about the Civil War, including the lesser-known battles such as the Battle of Glorieta, which took place some thirty miles east of Santa Fe. He also would be teaching classes on the Crimean War and pre–Civil War England and presenting a session of lectures on New Mexico.

"The university will finally have a rich selection of quality classes," Gunther said, seeming to forget that Rainy's father had had an active part in choosing which classes would be offered. "I believe your father and the board will be pleased with the changes. By eliminating some of the less experienced men, we should have a vast improvement in the history department."

"Yes, it took some convincing to get the board to listen to Father's suggestion that they fire those newer employees, but he shared with them the concerns you had."

Rainy could hardly believe her ears. Had Gunther really found a way to manipulate Marshall Driscoll? Maybe she should have enlisted his help in trying to clear her name.

"I'm concerned that further dismissals will be in order," Gunther said, "but of course, we can deal with that at a later date. The important thing is that I will be in charge."

Rainy felt that Gunther was betraying her father. After all, her father had been in charge of the department prior to this. For Gunther to insult the selection of classes, he might as well insult her father. But that was ludicrous. Gunther treated her father like a brother.

Rainy leaned back and closed her eyes. They had a long way to go, and given the fact that Chester was driving, they might well be even longer than was typical. She tried not to think of his comments about the university or of him as guilty of the Indian artifact thefts, but the suspicion kept resonating in her mind. *I know he has something to do with it. He's been on the tours or has had friends on the tours. What if he's paying them to smuggle the goods to him when he can't be on the trips as one of the dudes?*

"So did you manage to secure that crate?" Chester questioned.

"Shut up, you imbecile," Gunther hissed.

Rainy was momentarily startled but forced herself

to feign sleep. They might well go on discussing whatever it was Gunther wanted hushed up if they thought
she was asleep.

"Sorry," Chester apologized. "I figured with her
sleeping it wouldn't do any harm to discuss business."

"But she could just as easily have woken up," Gunther replied. "Let's leave it be and discuss business at
a later time."

Rainy, although disappointed, tried hard to remain
still. The heat was steadily growing, however, and her
forehead was beginning to drip with sweat in spite of
the fact that Gunther had his window down.

She shifted restlessly, hoping the men would be no
wiser to her ruse. They went on talking quietly, in
hushed voices that Rainy couldn't make out. With the
droning rhythm of the car, Rainy managed to doze.
She again dreamed of Duncan, but the images weren't
as pleasant. She was saying good-bye at the railroad station—leaving Duncan behind. She tried to hear what
he was saying, but a loud noise kept her from understanding. Suddenly Rainy felt herself falling. She
awoke to find the car swerving madly to the right.

"Hold her steady, you fool!" Gunther yelled. "Do
you want to flip us over?"

Rainy sat up just as Chester managed to put the car
into deep sand. The engine died as they came to rest.
Yawning, she straightened her hat and looked around.
She recognized their location immediately. She hadn't
slept long at all, because they were not far from Winslow—maybe fifteen miles.

"Now look what you've done!"

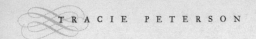

"Gunther, I didn't cause the tire to blow," Chester said defensively.

Gunther was already getting out the car. Rainy had never seen the man so angry. He slammed the door and kicked sand at the car. "Well, don't just sit there! Get out here and change the tire."

Chester looked to Rainy. "I don't know how to change a tire. I have people to do those kind of things."

"I can change a tire, Chester," Rainy said, pushing her bag back in place.

She eased out of the car. The vehicle slumped hopelessly to the right side. Not far from them the rocky outline of red sandstone threw short gray shadows across the desert floor. Rainy shielded her eyes.

Sighing, she turned back to where Gunther and Chester stood. "Well, where's the spare tire?"

"We seem to be without a spare," Gunther declared.

Rainy raised a brow. Looking at Chester she said, "You came into the desert without a spare tire? Next I suppose you'll tell me you didn't bring extra water either."

Chester looked rather embarrassed. "Well . . . I didn't think . . ."

"No, you certainly didn't," Gunther answered angrily. Banging his fist against the back of the car, Gunther paced to the front of the vehicle. "So now what do you propose we do?"

"We could wait awhile and see if anyone comes along," Rainy offered. "It's always a possibility that the

Indian agent for the Hopi villages will need to make a trip back or forth."

"It's going to be at least one hundred and ten degrees this afternoon. Do you really want to stand around here and wait to see if someone chances to come along?" Chester said, taking out his anger on Rainy.

Rainy put her hands to her hips. "Do you have a better plan?"

"We should probably walk to where we can get help."

Rainy laughed. "And where would that be? It's at least fifteen miles back to Winslow, and that's the closest place we'll get a tire repaired or replaced. You didn't even think to pack water. Good thing I brought a jug, or we'd all die of thirst."

"You have water?" Gunther questioned. "Why didn't you say so? I'm absolutely parched."

Rainy smiled and walked back toward the car. "I'm sorry, Gunther. You should have said something sooner." She passed by the older man and patted him on the arm. "Why don't you take it easy over there in the shade. I'll bring you the water."

Gunther ignored her kindness. "I just want a drink; I'm not an invalid."

"Of course not," she said, understanding his frustration was with Chester and not with her.

Rainy reached into the backseat and pulled out her bag. She didn't bother to bring out her own canteen but rather brought the jug Daisy had packed for them. Leaving the food as well, Rainy came to where Gunther stood, still fuming over their situation.

"Look," Rainy said softly, "the heat of the day is going to be upon us soon and we really should do what we can to make ourselves more comfortable. Last night you mentioned bringing a tent. Maybe we can use it, along with the car, to make some shade before the heat gets too intense. Then we can just ration out the water and take it easy. Come nightfall, we can all hike back to Winslow—or I'll hike it on my own. I know the way and I can probably cover the distance in half the time."

Gunther's expression registered contempt. "I need to get to the Hopi village—not to Winslow."

Rainy shrugged. "Well, I can't help you there. However, I can walk back to Winslow, borrow a spare from the Clarkson Company, and get someone to bring me back in the morning."

"Oh, this is hopeless!" Chester declared.

"Be quiet," Rainy and Gunther answered in unison.

Rainy saw Chester take a step back. Without warning, the wind lifted his fedora and sent it sailing across the road. Rainy almost laughed at the willy-nilly manner in which he ran to catch the wayward hat.

Ignoring Chester's curses and Gunther's growling disapproval, Rainy went to the trunk that was lashed on the back of the car. Opening it, she frowned. It was empty except for a small satchel. She turned, shaking her head.

"Where's the tent? Where are the tools?"

By this time Chester had come back, hat plastered firmly on his head. "I left them all back in Winslow. I didn't figure we'd need them."

Rainy had lost her patience. "Are you crazy? This is the kind of thing that gets people killed." She looked at Gunther, who was already wiping his face and neck with his handkerchief.

"Gunther wanted the space. . . ."

"Shut up, Driscoll. I've had enough of your lip. You were stupidly irresponsible. I specifically told you to pack the tent on top of the car if no other place. Instead you strip the car down, leave the spare tire, the water, the tools, and the only hope we had for any decent shelter from the sun."

"We have the car."

Rainy shook her head. The situation was going from bad to worse. "Look, the car is going to heat up, but maybe if we use it sparingly for shade we'll be all right."

"Well, that's just great," he muttered.

Realizing there was little to do except ask for God's intervention, Rainy whispered a silent prayer. After a moment she turned back to Gunther. "We'll need to watch out for snakes and the like."

"I'm walking back," Chester said, slapping the lid down on the trunk.

"You're hardly in any condition for such a thing. You'll be dead in a matter of hours," Rainy said without emotion.

"By all means, let him go," Gunther muttered.

Rainy shrugged. "Do as you will, but we'll be better off staying right here."

Gunther agreed and reluctantly Chester finally settled down. Rainy took a drink and sat down in the backseat to think. Gunther sat in the front passenger seat. He leaned over the seat and shook his head.

"My niece has married an incompetent fool."

"He's just not trained," Rainy said, trying to be kind. "Are you hungry, Gunther? I picked up some lunch for us this morning."

He smiled. "Always keeping one step ahead of the need, eh? Too bad you didn't think to pack a spare tire as well." He shook his head as if still in disbelief over Chester's actions. Finally he looked at her and nodded. "Yes, I'm quite hungry."

"Good," Rainy said. "We need to ration the food out, so I'll only offer you a sandwich for now." She dug into the bag and pulled out the packet Daisy had made. "I have roast beef or ham and cheese."

"Ham and cheese will do nicely."

She handed him the wax-wrapped sandwich. "I guess I should call Chester and feed him too." Gunther said nothing so Rainy took up another sandwich. Precious Daisy. Bless her for packing a hearty lunch.

"I have a roast beef sandwich for you," Rainy announced as she approached Chester, who was pacing. "You really should try to conserve your energy and stay cool."

He snatched the sandwich from her hand. "There isn't any place out here that's cool." He unwrapped the offering and looked back to Rainy. "Where'd you get this?"

"A friend packed a lunch for me to bring along."

"What else do you have?"

"Nothing for now. We need to ration our food." Chester grumbled but started munching on the sandwich.

Rainy worried as she made her way back to the car. *Maybe I should separate the food and hide some away.* Chester wouldn't be likely to listen to her should she protest his actions. She quickly shifted a few things around and left the bulk of the food, including most of her mother's cookies, inside her bag. She placed the rest of the packet given her by Daisy atop her bag.

"Gunther, would you care for one of my mother's cookies? I think we can splurge and have a cookie with our sandwich."

"Perhaps later. I assure you, I understand only too clearly the need to ration our meager fare."

Rainy leaned back in the seat and felt the heat drain away her energy. She lowered the straw hat down over her eyes and slept.

It seemed like it had only been minutes when she awoke to hear Gunther and Chester arguing behind the car. Groggy from the overheated car, she strained to make sense of their words.

"You are without a doubt the reason we're stranded here," Gunther declared. "You're stupid, Driscoll. You have no common sense and you don't think any further than what interests you at the moment. How completely foolish to leave basic survival items back in Winslow."

"I resent you calling me stupid. I'm not stupid. I just thought you wanted as much space as possible for those articles. Have you forgotten our real mission here? Under the circumstances, I believe I've shown far more sense and intelligence than you have. After all, you brought Rainy Gordon along."

Rainy's brows knit together as she pushed back her

hat. She tried to remain still as she edged closer to the open door. She had to catch everything they were saying.

"Rainy will keep the Hopi from asking too many questions. They respect her. She'll be our ticket to success."

"She certainly wasn't our ticket to success at the university."

"You were the fool who put the stolen artifacts in her desk. You were supposed to put them in her father's desk, but no. You ruined a perfectly good plan to get rid of Raymond Gordon once and for all, but you had to do things your way."

"I thought I could press her into marrying me. Lucky for your niece my plan failed."

"I hardly see it as luck that you and Bethel have married. . . . What in the world?"

Rainy was barely aware she'd climbed from the car until she found the duo looking at her with as much surprise registered in their expressions as she felt must surely be in her own. She stared open-mouthed at Gunther and Chester.

"How could you have betrayed my father like that?" she asked Gunther. "He's cared for you like a brother."

"Oh, this is rich," Gunther said, slamming his fist against the car. "Now do you see what you've done?"

"Me?" Chester protested, pointing at the middle of his sweat-soaked shirt. He'd long ago discarded his jacket, but not Gunther.

Now Rainy saw the reason why. Gunther pulled out a revolver he had been hiding under his coat and waved it in the air. "You, my dear, have stumbled into something you should not know about."

"You're stealing from the Hopi. You've been stealing from the Indians all along—haven't you?" She backed up a pace and tried to swallow down the dust in her dry throat.

"This is a messy affair," Gunther said, shaking his head. "I had hoped to spare you the details. You've always been kind to me, even if your father did steal my job with the university."

"How can you say that?"

Gunther's face contorted. "I say it because it's true. He took the position that was rightfully mine. I was left with whatever I could get. Begging leaves a bad taste in my mouth."

Rainy felt light-headed at the thought of what Gunther was saying. "So you just pretended to be a friend to my family? For what purpose?"

"For the purpose of getting rich," he declared. "Chester immediately understood my goals because his desire was also to get rich. Now with the economy falling apart in bits and shreds, we have to hurry to secure our future."

"By stealing?"

"By whatever means are necessary."

Rainy felt sick. She clutched at her stomach as nausea overwhelmed her. "You let me be blamed for the university situation. You ruined my career, my dreams. Chester threatened me several times, then turned around and promised me the moon—including a position with National Geographic—all if I became his mistress."

Gunther scowled at Chester but said nothing. Chester, however, appeared eager to stay on Gunther's good side.

"She's lying, Gunther. I wouldn't do anything to hurt Bethel."

"I don't trust you any farther than I can throw you, Driscoll. You'd been nothing but a greedy pain in the neck since I took you on. I'm sorry you ever married my niece. Miss Gordon may be naïve and overly simplistic in her religious notions, but she isn't a liar."

"But I'm telling you—"

"I don't want to hear it," Gunther said, holding up his hand. "We have a bad situation here and I need to decide how to resolve it."

Chester moved away to the edge of the road while Rainy tried to process all that she'd just been told. How could this be? How could her family have so clearly misjudged Gunther's character?

Chester began to shout. "Look! I see a car!"

Rainy could only pray the vehicle would take them to safety and get her away from Gunther and his gun. She felt weak in the knees. *Maybe the heat has done more to me than I thought.*

She moved toward the car. "I need a drink of water."

Gunther didn't try to stop her. He went instead to stand beside Chester. The gun was cleverly concealed behind his back. Rainy had the water jug midway to her lips when it dawned on her that Gunther would probably force the people in the other car to give up their vehicle. *What can I do to keep them from being harmed?* Her mind raced as what looked like a black touring car drew nearer.

Oh, God, please help me, she prayed. She quickly drank from the jug and replaced it as the touring car came within a few hundred yards. Rainy made up her mind then and there to warn the people in the car.

Racing across the short distance, she yelped in pain when Gunther reached out and yanked her back. Her ankle burned from the violent twist Gunther gave her. "Where do you think you're going?"

"I won't let you hurt them." She tried to fight him, but by now the car had stopped in front of them and Gunther had raised his gun to her head.

She grew still and looked across to find a shocked Sonny and Duncan staring back at her from inside the car.

CHAPTER TWENTY-SIX

Duncan wanted only to remove Rainy from harm. Seeing her there, blue eyes wide with fear, gun to her head, made him less than a patient man. He got out of the car without even waiting to see if Sonny had some kind of plan.

"What do you think you're doing?" he asked Gunther.

"Stay back. You don't want to hurt her, do you?"

Rainy tried to pull away, but Gunther held her tight. Seeing her struggle made Duncan desperate to free her. "Let her go."

"I don't believe you're in a position to give orders, Mr. Hartford," Chester Driscoll declared.

Duncan waited for Sonny to come around the car. With a smile the auburn-haired man shoved his hands in his pockets and struck a nonthreatening pose. "What's this all about, Gunther? Get too much sun today?"

"He's the one who's been taking the artifacts," Rainy declared, trying to balance on one foot. Duncan could see that she favored her left side. He wondered how badly she was hurt and whether or not she could run for cover if need be. "He and Chester are the ones who planted those Indian pieces in my desk and then blamed me."

Sonny frowned. "Why would you do that, Gunther? You're like an uncle to us. I thought you were our friend."

Gunther laughed and his pockmarked face contorted. "I did what I had to do to earn your father's trust. I never intended to cause Rainy harm. Chester took matters into his own hands and ruined my plans to see your father dismissed or, better yet, jailed. But that's not important. Right now I'm hot and tired and I want to leave. And you, Sonny, are going to take me where I want to go."

"Sure, we can all pile in the touring car."

Gunther shook his head. "No. Not all of us. Just you and me and Chester." He shoved Rainy into Duncan's waiting arms.

Duncan quickly shielded her with his body as Rainy cried out in pain. He didn't know what to think of the strange matter of Gunther Albright being responsible for the thefts. He really didn't even know the man, although he'd had a couple of minor encounters with him through the university.

Duncan looked to Sonny, who seemed to think the arrangement acceptable. "That's fine, Gunther. We can leave Duncan and Rainy here. I can come back for them later."

Gunther raised his gun again and pointed it straight at Duncan. "I can't have witnesses. I'll have to leave the state now as it is. But I won't be pursued.

Your sister knows too much, and while I've always liked her, I can't have her sending the police after me."

"Ah, Rainy won't say anything," Sonny assured in his very matter-of-fact manner. "Will you, Rainy?"

"I'll do whatever it takes to keep you from hurting Sonny," Rainy declared from behind Duncan. She tried to pop around in order to see Gunther, but Duncan refused to let her and held her fast.

"See?" Sonny continued. "She'll be a good gal because she doesn't want you to hurt me. That's an even trade."

"Hardly," Gunther said. He seemed to consider the matter momentarily. "She said we're about fifteen miles from Winslow. Is that a fair assessment?"

Sonny nodded. "Easy fifteen."

Gunther sighed. "Very well. Take us to Winslow. We'll deal with things from there." He moved closer to Duncan while Chester went to the car. "If you say one word of this to anyone—if you walk out of here and send the authorities after me—I'll not hesitate to kill Sonny. Do you understand?"

Rainy peered around Duncan and this time he didn't attempt to stop her. "We understand. We won't do anything to endanger Sonny's life. Please don't hurt him."

"Sonny will be my insurance against problems. If either one of you does anything to cause me grief, Sonny will pay the price. Just remember that." Gunther gathered his things and then, on what seemed to be a whim, picked up the water jug and took a long drink before emptying the rest of the contents onto the parched ground. He shrugged at Duncan as if offering an apology, then made his way to the car. "Let that be added incentive."

Duncan wanted nothing more than to run to the car and knock the man to the ground. The rage inside him threatened to interfere with rational thought. Only having Rainy at his side kept him from risking everything.

"Sonny will accompany me back to my home," he said from the car window. "He will go with me as long as I feel there's a threat from either of you. Knowing what's in store for me if I'm caught, I won't care one whit about adding his murder to my list."

Rainy ripped away from Duncan. She tried to rush for Gunther but fell to her knees when her left leg collapsed beneath her. "But, Gunther, the theft of a few articles—articles that you may still have in your possession—well . . . that's hardly as bad as murder."

"My dear," he said as Sonny put the car into gear, "you don't know the half of it. It wouldn't be my first murder."

Duncan saw Rainy pale as she tried to get to her feet. "Gunther, please."

The old man ignored her and motioned Sonny into action.

Sonny turned the car around and headed back to Winslow while Rainy and Duncan watched in despair. Duncan went to her as soon as the car headed south. He slowly helped her to her feet and opened his arms to her. Rainy fell against him in tears. "Oh, Duncan, what are we to do?" Her sobs pierced his heart and broke the anger he felt.

Duncan pushed back her straw hat and dabbed at

her sweat-soaked brow with his handkerchief. "We will pray first, and then we'll assess the situation and see what action might best suit our purpose."

"I can't even think clearly. I doubt I can pray with any real eloquence."

Duncan smiled. "God doesn't much care how we sound." He let his Scottish brogue thicken. "He loves us with an everlastin' love—no matter how eloquently we pray. Good thing too. I've always been better with ancient artifacts than with words."

Rainy nodded. "I've been praying and I'll keep praying, but I'm so afraid." She paused and her expression grew thoughtful. "You could walk out in a few hours, when it's not so hot," Rainy continued, wiping at her tears with the back of her hand. "That was my original plan, but now my ankle is twisted and I know I can't walk far."

"Are you all right otherwise? They didn't hurt you, did they?"

Rainy shook her head. "Chester worried me, but he didn't touch me. I didn't even twist my ankle until you showed up with Sonny. Though it hurts a great deal, I have to admit my pride smarts, too, from being so foolish and not recognizing Gunther's involvement."

"Ah, anyone could have missed that. He was just an old man."

"And he seemed to actually love my mother and father," Rainy said, looking dumbfounded. "I just can't believe this. How could he have deceived people so completely?"

"It's easy to deceive the ones who trust you and

love you," Duncan said. "They aren't looking for any reason to be suspicious. I'm sure if Gunther only offered kindness and a congenial manner that your parents probably believed him to be a good friend."

"They did," Rainy agreed. "That's what hurts so much."

"Well, don't give it another thought. Gunther will get what's coming to him. Mr. Richland isn't about to let this situation go unpunished. Sonny and I learned from Bethel Driscoll that Chester was headed out here to work with his uncle. We put the pieces together then and there, and I wired Mr. Richland with the information. My guess is that even now, Richland has alerted the law enforcement officials and will have a plan in place to deal with Gunther and Chester."

"But what about Sonny? If they go charging in there with the police, Sonny may get killed."

"Sonny's a smart man. Give him credit, Rainy. He can deal with this. He did exactly what he wanted to do—he got Gunther and Chester away from us and headed back to Winslow, where he knows there's bound to be help."

"I suppose so," she said reluctantly.

"I know so," Duncan said encouragingly. "Right now we need to figure out how we can help Sonny— and ourselves. It's too bad Gunther poured out the last of the water."

"Oh, he didn't!" Rainy declared. She pushed away from Duncan's side and hobbled to the car. Opening the door, she pulled out her canteen. "I had a feeling Chester would try to pilfer our meager supplies. Little did I know it'd turn out this way."

"No, you couldn't have known," Duncan said, coming to stand beside her. "No one suspected Gunther. Chester seemed suspicious, but he appears to be nothing more than Albright's lackey. That's why you can't blame yourself in any of this. Even I had it figured to be Jennetta or Phillip—never you."

It was as if those two little words changed everything between them. Duncan caught the expression on Rainy's face, then watched as she tucked the canteen back inside the car. "We have some food too. One of the Harvey Girls packed fruit and cheese and pie, along with sandwiches. So if you get hungry we have plenty. Oh, and my mother sent cookies."

She moved away from him in her awkward manner, but Duncan wasn't about to let it go at that. "Rainy, I never thought you were guilty. I have to admit there were times when the evidence seemed completely against you, but I still held on to the belief that you had nothing to do with it. Even when the Indian Affairs man told me about your mishap at the university, I never believed you were responsible."

"You knew about the university? Even before I told you?" She searched his face for the truth.

He reached out and touched her cheek. "I knew."

Rainy shook her head. "I can't believe all of this is happening. What if Gunther tries to hurt Sonny? I can't bear the thought of it." She stepped away from Duncan and struggled to the road again. She looked to the south for several minutes, shading her eyes with her hand. "Sonny's just about to get everything he's ever wanted. He's been given his dream job—a geologist position with the government." She turned back

to Duncan. "Did you know that?"

Duncan nodded, feeling terrible for the trembling in her voice. If he didn't take her mind from Sonny, he feared she might well begin another onslaught of tears.

"I wanted to tell you the truth about what happened with the investigation," he said softly, "but it wasn't the only reason I came here with Sonny."

Rainy lowered her hand and looked at Duncan. "What other reason was there?"

"I wanted you to know how I feel about you."

He crossed the distance between them, and before he could give Rainy a chance to protest he took her in his arms. "I don't care what else happens—I have to tell you how I feel."

Rainy nodded. "I'm listening."

At least she didn't fight him. The fact that she allowed him to embrace her gave Duncan hope. "I was a complete idiot not to make my feelings known to you that first night you asked me to share your supper table at La Fonda. I had cared about you from afar, and those feelings only grew more intense up close. I love you, Rainy. I know that without any doubt or hesitation. I love you and I want you to be my wife."

Rainy cocked her head to one side. Her expression suggested she was waiting for something more, but Duncan had no idea what it could be. He'd already spilled out his guts—told her what was in his heart.

"Please just tell me I haven't totally ruined my chances with you. Please tell me there's still a chance for us. I need to have hope."

Rainy raised her head and looked from side to

side. "Hope doesn't seem to grow in abundance out here in the desert. We're stuck out here, my ankle is swelling as we speak, and Sonny is traveling with a madman who holds a gun. And in the middle of all of this, you proclaim your love and devotion."

Duncan grinned. "It'll make a great story to tell our children and grandchildren."

"Duncan, we have to make it out of here before we can talk about getting married, much less the rest of your plans."

"We'll make it out of here all right. Especially if you say yes to my proposal."

"Oh, and why's that?" Rainy questioned. "How does my saying yes help us get out of here?"

Duncan tightened his grip on her. "Because then I'll definitely have something to live for."

Rainy shook her head. "Your timing is the worst."

"I know."

"I mean, I plan to leave for Scotland in a few days."

Duncan shook his head this time. "I wouldn't have let you go."

"I'd already convinced myself I could never have you," Rainy admitted. "You know how I was praying for a husband."

He shrugged. "And here I am."

She looked at him for a moment and sighed. "I don't know what to do with you. You drive me positively mad. One minute I understand you—the next you seem like a stranger."

"Spend the rest of your life getting to know me," he encouraged.

"If we don't get out of here, it may well be a short lifetime." She grimaced and tried to shift her weight.

"Look, we need to get you off your ankle." He scooped her into his arms and carried her back to the car. "I know it's hot, but you need to rest. I'll put you in the backseat and then help you elevate your foot."

The look on her face was one of pain and worry. Pausing as he placed her inside the car, Duncan bent down to meet her gaze. "We're going to make it out of this, you'll see. I know God didn't bring us this far to let us die here."

"And just where did God bring us?" Rainy questioned.

"He brought us to the truth." Duncan kissed her lightly on the forehead. "The truth about the missing artifacts, the university thefts—and the truth about how we feel about each other. That is, unless you've changed your mind."

Rainy shook her head. "I didn't change it—I tried to change it and Phillip Vance tried to help me change it, but there was always something about you. Something in the middle of all my thoughts and feelings. There were times I wanted to run up to you and tell you everything and beg you to marry me."

"You wouldn't have had to beg, sweetheart. I would have willingly complied."

He touched his lips to hers ever so gently. He wanted nothing more than to kiss her for a long, long time, but there was work to do and he knew their survival depended on it. Pulling away, he whispered in her ear.

"Marry me, please."

She opened her eyes and looked up. "If we get out of here alive, I'll gladly marry you."

He grinned and backed away from the car. "You've given me a challenge to be sure, but now I have a reason to fight. You'll see how stubborn we Scots can be."

"I'm Scottish myself, or have you forgotten?"

He laughed. "Nay, I've not forgotten it, lassie. I'm countin' on it."

Rainy thought about his words as she watched him walk away from the car. He was counting on her stubbornness. For what? To survive? To make it through the pain? She knew her tenacious behavior had gotten her into trouble on many an occasion.

She watched Duncan scrounge for materials to build a fire. He hoped someone would see the smoke and come in search of the problem. She could only pray his plan worked.

Oh, Father, everything seems wrong. She grinned at the sight of Duncan. *Well, not everything,* she admitted. *I'm quite happy with your choice of a husband for me, but everything else seems quite hopeless. Please, Father, help us to right these wrongs. Save us, Lord. Save us from the desert isolation and heat. Send the cooling breeze of the evening. Help us get to safety.*

She prayed over and over while Duncan worked. He paused only long enough to take the tiniest of drinks and then he was back to work.

"He's a good man, Lord." She whispered the words as Duncan tried to set fire to the odd pile of fuel he'd collected. Her suitcase and clothes were among the sacrificed articles, as well as the trunk that had

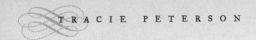

been on the back of the car.

At first the fire seemed unwilling to take, but then, much to Rainy's relief, the flame caught and began to consume some of the smaller, drier pieces of brush. Thick billowing smoke from the clothes and trunk filled the air.

"Well, at least that much has worked," she said with a sigh. "Now, if someone will just see it and come to help."

CHAPTER TWENTY-SEVEN

Rainy shifted uncomfortably in the backseat of
the car. She'd tried to sleep through the chill
of the desert night, but it seemed impossible. Her
dreams were laced with wild images of Gunther and
the desert. At one point she found herself in a dry
field of overripe corn. The full moon overhead shone
down nearly as bright as the sun and the corn with-
ered on the stalk. Rainy tried to save the corn by
watering it but found her water ran out after only a
few stalks. Then, in frustration, she tried to pick the
corn but instead the pieces turned to Indian treasures and Rainy stood holding first a piece of jewelry
and then an intricate pot. People pointed at her,
some accused her, and with a start, Rainy awoke to
feel her hips sore and her ankle swollen and stiff.
Realizing her situation, she wanted only to have a
good cry.

Sitting up, she tried not to disturb her aching leg
any more than she had to. What a rotten twist to her
situation. *If I could have kept myself from injury, we might
have walked to safety.*

353

Opening the car door, Rainy eased to the edge of the seat and looked out at the night sky. The stars were soothing to her. In the midst of such madness, they seemed to offer her something stable and consistent. She recognized several constellations, remembering how she and Sonny would sit until late into the night as children, watching the skies, talking about God and what they would do when they grew up.

"Oh, Sonny," Rainy whispered so as not to wake Duncan in the front seat, "I pray you're safe."

Thoughts of Sonny refused to leave her mind. She wondered where he was and whether or not Gunther had given up on the idea of forcing Sonny to travel with him. She thought of Sonny's dreams and plans for Alaska and tears came to her eyes.

I thought I was strong, Lord. I thought I could handle just about any test or trial. I thought the only real problems I had were finding a husband and clearing my name—both very selfish ambitions.

Now I sit here, unable to help anyone or to do anything, and I've never been more frustrated. I've always relied on my education and wits. I've always felt ever so self-sufficient and capable. But I'm not, Lord. I'm not. Please show us what to do. Please help us to get out of this mess without harm coming to anyone.

She worked her way back into her sleeping place and tried to get comfortable. Just when she thought it impossible to fall asleep, Rainy was once again dreaming of the dry desert lands.

Hours later Rainy woke again, this time with the distinct feeling that something was happening. She feared for a moment that Gunther had returned, but after craning her neck to see, Rainy was relieved to find their campsite still deserted.

"It's nearly sunrise," Duncan murmured from the front seat.

Rainy could see a hint of light and color on the eastern horizon. "What are we going to do? Our signal fire hasn't brought any help, and the roads have been deserted all night."

"Someone's bound to come through here," Duncan offered. "Aren't the harvests going on in the area? Aren't people bringing crops in for sale? Moving cattle or sheep—that kind of thing?"

"We can't count on that. This isn't exactly the main road." Rainy straightened up and leaned against the car door to ease the tension in her back. "We've used almost all the water in the canteen. I still can't hope to walk very far, but you could get to Winslow and—"

"I'm not leaving you here," he said, sitting up to look over the seat at her.

"But we don't have any water."

"We can drain the radiator and use what's there. I don't know what it will taste like, but we can try to filter it with a piece of cloth."

Rainy realized it was a good idea. "That would give you enough to take in the canteen."

Duncan's jaw tightened. "I said . . ."

Rainy reached out and touched his hand. "I know what you said, Duncan, but if you don't go for help, we may die out here just as Gunther planned." She looked out the window to the horizon. "It'll be fully light before long and the heat may become unbearable. If you leave now, you could get to Winslow before the worst of it and get back here with help before the afternoon heat becomes too stifling."

Duncan sighed and gripped her hand tightly. "There has to be another way."

Rainy shook her head. "But there's not. We've only got a bit of the food left. Enough for one meager meal, but that's it. Look, if we're going to survive this, we both need to make sacrifices."

"But if Sonny manages to ditch Gunther and Chester, he'll know where to come to find us. I really think we should stay here with the car."

"But Gunther and Chester know where to come too," Rainy reasoned. "You have to see that there's no other way. Right now you're in good shape. You've had food and water and rest." She smiled and added, "What little rest could be had." Sobering again, she continued. "But, Duncan, hours from now that won't be the case, and if no one shows up and Sonny still can't get to us, we'll gradually grow weak and sick from the lack of water."

She saw Duncan's look of resignation and knew he finally agreed. "All right," he said. "I'll go."

"Good. You'll be back before you know it and then we can help Sonny. I only hope we're not too late," Rainy said, feeling her emotions go topsy-turvy on her again. "I just hope he's all right. We used to be close enough to sense when the other one was in danger, but I can't sense anything at all. You don't suppose that means . . ."

"Don't even say it," Duncan said. "You know better. Sonny is a survivor. He's not going to be defeated by the likes of Gunther Albright and Chester Driscoll. You'll see. He's probably already figured a way to get himself out of this. Remember, we sent word to Richland and told him where we were headed and what you were doing. Did you let any of your Hopi friends know that you were coming?"

"Yes, I sent a message with a courier. The group was only going as far as Canyon de Chelly, but she promised to take it over after the tour was completed. I'm sure Istaqa knew we were on our way to see him."

"Good. When you didn't show up, he probably began to check what happened. Maybe he would have even called La Posada."

"It's possible—if the phone lines are working. The system isn't always the best out here."

"I understand," Duncan said, nodding. "But between Istaqa knowing and Richland being apprised of the situation, someone is bound to come to our rescue and to Sonny's."

"I hope so. I couldn't bear it if . . ."

Duncan smiled reassuringly. "Nothing bad will happen. Trust God to have this under control. It'll work out. You'll see."

Rainy wanted to see. She wanted to have hope, but even as Duncan bustled around outside the car, preparing for his walk to Winslow, she was losing faith. Soon she'd be alone, and though she couldn't tell Duncan, she was terrified. What if Chester Driscoll came back for her? Once Duncan was gone, she'd be defenseless.

She couldn't tell Duncan her fears. He'd just insist on staying at her side, and Rainy knew their only hope

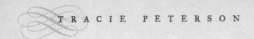

was in his walking to Winslow. She sighed and reached for one of her mother's cookies.

"Oh, Mother, I wish I'd listened to your apprehensions. I know I'm in this fix because of my pride and determination to control everything. I should have listened to you and given thought to what you had to say." She took a bite of the cookie to ease the rumblings in her stomach, but the dry texture only made her more thirsty. Funny how water didn't seem all that important when there was plenty of it.

She heard Duncan working to drain the radiator and wondered how awful the water would taste. It would be better than dying of thirst, but the thought still caused her to shudder.

I should never have tried to keep this from Dad. He wouldn't have allowed me to leave with Gunther. Had I not tried to sneak around, I would be safe at home and Sonny wouldn't be in danger. Her regret threatened to eat her alive. This must have been what her father had tried to teach her so long ago about obedience. If Rainy had obeyed, she'd be safe now. Instead, she'd endangered the lives of not only herself but Sonny and Duncan as well.

Glancing up, Rainy noticed a hint of dust on the horizon. She strained her eyes to make out the forms of several riders on horse and mule.

"Duncan!" she cried. "Riders are coming."

Duncan came around to where she sat. "Where?"

Rainy pointed to the north. "I think they may be Hopi." Struggling, she got out of the car and hopped around to the front. Duncan came up to support her. "Yes! I think it's Istaqa."

Rainy began to wave wildly while bouncing on her right foot. "Istaqa!"

The man at the front of the entourage waved and Rainy relaxed against Duncan. "He sees us. We're going to be all right."

"I already knew that," Duncan said with a grin. He pulled Rainy close. "I couldn't possibly lose you now."

Rainy looked deep into his eyes. Without hesitation she stretched up on her tiptoes and kissed him on the mouth. "I never knew what an optimist I was marrying."

"You didn't know you were even marrying me until yesterday."

"Hmmm. Well, maybe my heart knew."

"And maybe it was just the seductive spell of the desert and the harvest sky," Duncan whispered.

She grinned. "Or maybe the spell woven over me by one very handsome Scot."

"Hmmm," he said against her ear, "maybe."

She stood in Duncan's supportive embrace as Istaqa and six other Hopi riders and two extra mules came to a halt in front of the broken-down car.

"Una sent me out. She said you must be in trouble, otherwise you would have let us know why you didn't come to us yesterday."

"You don't know the half of it," Rainy said. "My brother is in real danger. The man I was bringing to you turned out to be the very man who's been behind the artifact thefts. Gunther Albright was a good friend of my family, but apparently he's been stealing what he could for some time."

Istaqa eyed Duncan suspiciously. He nodded as if

in greeting, then turned his attention back to Rainy. "This Albright man, he has your brother?"

"Yes. Sonny and Duncan showed up yesterday, and Gunther forced Sonny to take him and his partner, a man named Chester Driscoll, back to Winslow. I twisted my ankle; otherwise Duncan and I would have walked to Winslow last night."

"Would you have any water you could spare?" Duncan suddenly asked. "I'm afraid Albright dumped most of ours, and the prospect of drinking radiator water isn't very appealing."

Istaqa signaled to one of his companions and a waterskin was handed down. Duncan helped Rainy drink first and then drank his fill before handing the bag back to Istaqa.

"I don't know when anything has ever tasted so good," Rainy commented. She grimaced at the throbbing pain in her ankle. "Can you get us to Winslow?"

"I'll take you there," Istaqa replied. He turned to the man at his left and gave instructions in Hopi. The man immediately brought up the two extra mules, then motioned for three of the other men to follow.

"I'll send my companions back to alert our people. If this man you speak of is waiting for you in Winslow, or if he's on the trail up ahead, we will need to know that others can get the word out." Istaqa's square-cut black hair blew gently in the breeze as his dark eyes narrowed. "I will make sure this man is stopped. I will see your brother safe."

Rainy felt a deep love for her friend. The compassion he felt for her and Sonny was very evident. "I know you will."

"This is ridiculous!" Gunther Albright paced back and forth as Sonny worked to dig out the car.

"I can't help it, Gunther. Those patches of sand get me every time—just ask my sister."

Sonny hid his grin as he bent over the log he was using to try to free the tire from the sand. He wasn't trying too hard, however. After spending the previous afternoon driving in circles, Sonny had managed to get them stuck in the sand. He calculated they were only about five miles from Winslow, but Gunther had no idea where they were and neither did Chester.

"We'll die out here if you don't dig us out," Chester said, his voice in a panic.

"We aren't going to die, Chester," Sonny answered as he eased up and pretended to reassess the situation.

"Some of us may if you don't figure a way out of this mess," Gunther declared. "I didn't come all this way to spend the night in the middle of nowhere, yet that's what you've forced upon me. Now that it's getting light, I expect you to dig us out of this hole and get us to Winslow."

"I'm working on it, Gunther. I don't want to be out here any more than the rest of you," Sonny said in a serious manner. He stared Gunther in the eye. "After all, you've left my sister and friend to die. I want out of here every bit as much as you do." He saw that the older man was exhausted. Gunther had refused to sleep, fearful that Sonny might somehow free the car and leave without him knowing it. The old man wouldn't even leave the car unless Chester was sitting in it for insurance. Now Sonny knew they were both ready to drop, and he planned to use that to his advantage.

"I don't much care what you want. Get back to work. I don't intend to spend even another hour here."

Sonny went back to the pretense of digging out. He walked to the edge of the road and picked up a few stones and put them in front of the car tire. Seeing that he was working, Gunther went back to where Chester sat in the shade of some scraggly mesquite.

"This is a fine mess you've gotten me into," Sonny heard Gunther say. He lowered his voice then, however, and Sonny couldn't hear any further comments. He watched from the corner of his eye as Gunther eased onto the ground and leaned back to rest. He pointed to Sonny and said something to Chester. Sonny could only imagine that he was instructing the man to keep watch. Chester nodded while Gunther pulled his hat down over his eyes. With great reluctance, Chester got up and walked to the car.

"Don't try anything stupid, Gordon. I'll be sitting here in the car watching you the whole time."

"You do that, Driscoll. I'll feel a whole lot safer just knowing you're on guard."

Chester frowned but nevertheless crawled in behind the wheel of Sonny's touring car.

Sonny grinned again and got down on the ground. He dug around the wheel and glanced every so often over to where Gunther dozed. It wasn't long until he heard snores coming from the front seat of the vehicle as well. When he was certain that both men were asleep, he jumped to his feet and hiked out across the desert toward Winslow.

At a good lope, Sonny knew he could make the distance in a little over an hour. He was in good shape and had an ample supply of water in the canteen he wore on his hip. He also felt confident that God had provided this moment for him. He was rested and alert, having slept through most of the night. He could do this. He would do this and he would rescue Rainy and Duncan before it was too late.

The day was still rather pleasant by the time Sonny walked into Winslow. He went immediately to the town marshal and explained the situation.

"We've already had word from some Indian Bureau man named Richland," the marshal told Sonny. "I've had my men out searching the area, but they were told over at the hotel that Albright had already left the area."

"Yes, he'd taken my sister and headed north to Hopi country. Albright and Driscoll are stuck just northeast of town. I can lead you there. My sister and friend, however, are stranded about fifteen miles north, just off the main road. They've been there all night and they don't have water."

"Everything's going to be all right," the man said without emotion. His calm was maddening to Sonny, who could think of nothing but his sister dying from heatstroke.

The marshal rounded up two cars and a deputy and motioned Sonny to the front seat of his own car. "We'll take Albright and Driscoll into custody first, then go on ahead and find your sister."

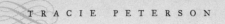
Sonny hated the delay. "Isn't there another car I could borrow? I hate to leave her there any longer."

"Try not to worry. This won't take long."

"But Albright has a gun. He may not come willingly."

The marshal shrugged and smiled. "Gun or no gun, he doesn't have much of a choice. I can leave him to the desert until he's more cooperative."

Sonny nodded. "Let's get to it, then."

CHAPTER TWENTY-EIGHT

*T*o Sonny's amusement, Gunther and Chester were still asleep when he returned with the marshal. The men were so confused and disoriented as they awoke that they were easily taken into custody.

"If I could get a hand from your deputy," Sonny said after the men were secured in the backseat of the marshal's car, "I could get this car out of the sand." The marshal nodded and motioned his deputy to give Sonny assistance.

Sonny maneuvered a long pole into a position that would give them the best advantage. He and the deputy worked for several minutes until Sonny was confident that the car was about to be freed. "Okay, just give it a little gas."

"You know," a familiar voice called out, "we're never going to stick to our schedule if you keep getting us stuck in the sand."

Sonny dropped the pole and whirled around. Spying Rainy and Duncan on muleback with Istaqa at their side, he felt the world suddenly go right. "You're safe—you're here!"

Rainy laughed. "Of course, silly. And you're stuck in the sand as usual. Why the Harvey Company ever hired you to drive for them is beyond me."

"I guess they hired me because of my dashing good looks and dreamy eyes. Remember, the part about the eyes was particularly important."

Duncan got down from the mule and came to where Sonny stood. "Can I give you a hand with this?"

Sonny breathed a sigh of relief and slapped his friend on the back. "Yup, then you can buy me breakfast and we'll talk about your wedding plans."

Duncan looked surprised and glanced back at Rainy. "Wedding plans?"

Sonny nodded, giving Duncan a most serious expression. "You spent the night in the desert with my sister. Now you have to marry her."

Duncan shook his head. "No, I don't *have* to marry her. I *want* to marry her. And she said yes when I asked her to do just that."

Sonny met Rainy's pleased expression. "She had her hat set on getting a husband—she prayed night and day about it. You didn't stand a chance, you know."

Duncan sighed and shrugged. "Life is hard." He grinned up at Rainy and winked. "Might as well suffer it with someone who's as pretty and sweet as your sister."

"My sister—sweet? Haven't you learned about her temper yet?" Sonny questioned. "Then there's her—"

"That's enough, Sonny," Rainy interjected. She threw him a cautionary glance, then turned a sweet smile on Duncan. "He doesn't care about my flaws. He loves me."

Sonny nudged Duncan with his elbow. "We'll talk later."

Duncan nodded. "To be sure."

In Albuquerque, Rainy recovered from her twisted ankle and planned her wedding. Her parents decided to delay the trip to Scotland long enough to see their only daughter wed and to help the university out of a terrible bind for their fall schedule.

"The board was rather stunned to learn that Gunther Albright was behind this mess. They thought him to be the most mild mannered and even tempered of any of their professors," Rainy's father told her as they gathered around the breakfast table.

"He certainly had us fooled," her mother stated as she deposited a plate of scrambled eggs smothered in salsa.

Rainy still shuddered at the memory of Gunther's gun at her head. "I still can't believe he could be so cruel to us—especially you and Dad. You treated him like a brother."

Her father nodded and took up the Bible for family devotions. "He was a wolf in sheep's clothing. The Word warns us of people like that. People who come claiming to be one thing when they're really something else."

"But don't you feel as though all your kindness to him was a wasted effort?" Rainy asked. She took the plate of eggs and served her father a generous portion before serving herself. Handing the bowl to her mother, she waited for her father's answer.

"I guess I don't feel it was wasted. Gunther will remember that we were kind to him. He'll remember that I came to him in jail and forgave him for everything—including the fact that he threatened your life and that of Sonny's. That was probably the hardest part of all."

"Yes, to be sure," her mother replied. "But it was what God would have us do. I wouldn't trust Gunther again or allow him another opportunity to repeat his actions, but I can forgive him."

"I feel I have so much to learn," Rainy said with a sigh. "I've been so angry with Chester and Gunther. I've tried to just let go of my feelings, but it's hard."

Her father covered her hand with his own. "It will probably take time."

"But it didn't take you all that much time. It's only been a week and a half and you're willing to forgive."

Her father nodded. "I've learned from past experience that the sooner I deal with a grievance, the sooner I recover my life. The longer I let the matter remain in turmoil and bitterness, the more time I lose. It's a part of maturity and growth. It'll come to you in time—with each situation like this that you have to work through and forgive. The important part is that you be willing to let God work through you and use you in this. He can help you—if you really want to forgive Chester and Gunther."

Rainy nodded. "I know that you're right."

"Well, I have the last of my things loaded in the

car," Sonny announced as he bounded into the dining room.

"Then come have breakfast before it gets cold," their mother chided.

Rainy looked to her brother and grinned. "So the great adventure begins."

"A little later than I planned, but instead of stopping in California, I'll go right on up to Juneau, where I'll meet up with my friends."

They joined hands as Rainy's father led them in a blessing. "Father, we thank you for the food on our table and the bounty we enjoy. We praise you for the many blessings we've been given—for Rainy's name being cleared and her safe return and for Sonny's safe return and the realization of his dream in Alaska. We thank you for these things and so many more. Amen."

"Amen," the family murmured in unison.

Rainy was reluctant to let go of her brother's and father's hands. "I'm going to miss you both so much." Her eyes misted with tears. "But at the same time, I'm so excited about the future God has shown each of us. I just want you all to know how much I love you."

She met her mother's gaze from across the table and knew deep within her heart that if anyone understood, her mother did. After all, she had married and, as a young bride, had left her homeland and family to come to America. She knew what it was to be separated from those she held most dear.

Sonny leaned over and kissed her on the cheek. "I love you too. Now stop being all sappy. I'm starving."

They all laughed, including Rainy. Somehow in that one silly moment, she knew everything would be just fine. They were a family—and no matter the distance in miles, their love would always keep them close.

———

"So tell me the truth, Mom. What do you think of Duncan?"

"He's a wonderful man," her mother said as she put in the last stitches on the hem of Rainy's wedding dress.

Rainy toyed with her veil and hugged it close. "He is wonderful. Oh, Mom, I'm so happy. I thought this day would never come."

Her mother smiled. "I know. I feared you'd grow impatient and take whatever you could just to get married and have a family. It's always best, however, when we hold out for what God has in mind. You never would have been happy married to a movie actor."

"I know," Rainy said thoughtfully. "I thought about that the other day. I tried to imagine the parties and the travel—the big house and servants. I know I would have been miserable. I think Phillip definitely cared about me, but I don't know that he could hope to understand me. Duncan understands me."

"That's because he shares your love of God and your passion for the Southwest. You both love archaeology and digging for pieces of history. When you can share those kinds of things and understand each other's needs, it can't help but make for a good marriage."

Rainy nodded and exclaimed in joy as her mother

held up the ivory dress for her inspection. "Oh, Mom, it's beautiful!"

Rainy's mother had worn the gown when she'd married Raymond Gordon in 1895, and it had been the height of fashion. Edrea had taken the dress and restyled it in a manner better fitting to the 1930s.

Rainy fingered the satin and marveled at the changes. Her mother had taken the pinafore lace from the bodice and worked the high neckline into a soft, molded scoop. The full muttonchop sleeves were cut down to make a sleeker line.

"I can't believe it's even the same dress," Rainy said as her mother turned the gown to reveal the back.

"The lace for your veil was taken from the train," her mother explained. "I think it looks quite nice, if I do say so myself."

Rainy embraced her mother, careful not to crush the gown. "It's wonderful. I love it so much—especially knowing that it was first worn by you."

Her mother held her tight for a moment. "All of your life you'll remember this. When times are good, you'll remember it with a fondness and joy that just blends naturally into everything around you. When times are bad, your thoughts will be uplifted by the memory of your wedding day and the anticipation you held for your future."

Her mother pulled away and put the dress aside. She motioned Rainy to sit with her on the bed. "Darling, I want you to know how proud I am of you. I know how hard it was for you to face the accusations at the college and not hate your adversaries. I know, too, it was equally difficult to deal with Gunther and Chester's actions."

"It isn't easy," Rainy said softly. "But just as Dad said, it's a process. I'm trying to work through it a little at a time. Day by day."

"That's the wisest thing to do. After all, Jesus told us to take up our cross *daily*. There's a reason for that. Some people try to take care of life's struggles in bigger chunks and some people never try at all. But I'm a firm believer that you should take everything one step at a time—even forgiveness. You'll need to remember to do likewise when Duncan upsets you or changes your plans. It isn't always easy to live with another human being, but the situations that develop between husband and wife are even more difficult than those that develop with parents or siblings."

Rainy knew her mother spoke with great wisdom, but in all honesty she couldn't imagine her mom and dad ever arguing or feeling strife toward each other. "But you and Dad never fought—did you?"

Her mother laughed softly. "Oh, mercy, but did we fight. I didn't know how to be patient back then and, well, this may come as a surprise to you, but when I first met your father, I wasn't interested in God. I didn't know anything about the love of Jesus or His sacrifice for me."

"I guess I didn't realize that," Rainy said, trying to remember if she'd ever heard her mother speak of her coming to salvation. She'd just always imagined that her mother had loved God from childhood, just as Rainy had.

"I wasn't the best of souls to share time with," her

mother continued. "Ray was such a sweet boy—so mild mannered and giving. He worked with his father on their sheep farm outside of Edinburgh. He loved working with the sheep, loved spending long hours in the fields. I, on the other hand, preferred the parties and fun that could be had with my friends."

"It doesn't seem at all like you."

"I've changed. The love of God changed my heart. I fell in love with your father because he was the only person who truly loved me for myself. He didn't care if I was dressed up in satins and lace. He only cared that I belong to him—and to God. He talked to me long and hard about the Bible and why we needed a savior. But my family was well-to-do, and while we hadn't really turned our noses up at the idea of church and such things, we were hardly a God-fearing people."

"Why have I never heard this before?" Rainy questioned. "I remember you talking about Grandma and Grandpa both being powerful witnesses for Jesus."

"And they were, in their old age. Your father helped us all to find Jesus for ourselves, but even after I prayed to be saved from hell, I still had a great deal to do to work on my personality and attitude. I had to learn that there was more to life and relationships than money. It wasn't easy. I was used to buying what I needed, and sometimes that included my friends."

"I can't imagine you like that." Rainy reached out and grasped her mother's hand.

"Where did you imagine your temper came from?" her mother teased. She hugged Rainy close and smoothed back a stray piece of red-blond hair.

"When the doctor told me he was certain I was to have twins, I prayed that you'd both be boys. I feared having a daughter. I was afraid she'd be just like me—ill-tempered, rushing to conclusions, spoiled. Then when you were born, I was overjoyed. I had a son and a daughter. Because the delivery had been so difficult, I knew you were all I would ever have. But you know what? You were enough."

"Was I that much trouble?" Rainy asked, sitting up. She looked quite seriously into her mother's tender expression.

"No, you were that much love. You were wonderful, Rainy. I could never have hoped for anything better. You'll always hold a special place in my heart. I just want you to know how complete you made my life."

Tears came to Rainy's eyes. "I love you so much—Daddy too. I don't know what I'll ever do without you two."

"You'll come and visit us. Who knows? You might even fall in love with Scotland."

Rainy nodded. "I've come to believe in these last few months that anything is possible."

———

A month later, Rainy smoothed the satin of her mother's gown and prepared to become the wife of Duncan Hartford. The butterflies in her stomach told her that she was not nearly as brave as she presumed. Licking her dry lips, Rainy whispered a silent prayer for strength and peace.

"I know I'm doing the right thing, Lord," she whispered as she caught her reflection in the mirror. "I just need you to stay with me every step of the way—I don't want to mess this up."

Her father soon came for her, and before she knew it she was walking down the aisle.

Lamont Hartford smiled at his son and soon-to-be daughter-in-law. "Dearly beloved, we are gathered together . . ."

How special, Rainy thought, *to have Duncan's father officiate our wedding.* She could see how much it pleased Duncan. If only Sonny could have delayed his trip to be at her wedding, the day would have been perfect— but it was perfect enough. Sonny had his own life, and she was happy he was in the interior of Alaska with his friends and a new job. She knew she held his love— even from three thousand miles away.

"Who giveth this woman to be wed?"

"Her mother and I," Rainy's father answered. He leaned over and kissed Rainy soundly on the cheek. "We love you so much," he whispered, then left her in Duncan's care—for the rest of her life.

Rainy felt a lump form in the back of her throat. The seriousness of the moment seemed to weigh down on her. *I know I'm doing the right thing.* She drew in a deep breath. *I've never been more sure of anything.*

"Rainy Gordon, wilt thou have this man . . ."

Rainy's eyes filled with tears as she corralled her thoughts and looked at Duncan's questioning gaze. She felt his reassurance as he squeezed her hand. "I will." *I will have this man for my husband and I will love him for all of my days.*

Duncan gently pushed the ring onto her finger, then kissed her sweetly as Duncan's father declared them man and wife. Rainy thought she might faint dead away from the intensity of the moment, but before she knew it she was being whisked away for a picture.

"You're beautiful," Duncan whispered in her ear as they allowed the photographer to pose them. Rainy was arranged in a high-backed chair while Duncan stood directly behind her.

The photographer fussed with her dress, positioning the folds of the material first one way and then another. Rainy leaned her head up to catch sight of her husband. "You don't look so bad yourself."

Duncan lightly fingered the lapel of his dark suit. "Anything to please you."

Rainy giggled. "I'm going to remember you said that."

"Miss Gordon—I mean, Mrs. Hartford, I wondered if I could speak to you for just a moment."

Rainy looked up to find Marshall Driscoll standing just beyond the photographer. She stiffened but felt Duncan's comforting touch as he gently rubbed her shoulder.

"What can I do for you? I'm rather busy."

"One more moment and we'll be finished," the photographer promised. He went to his camera and Rainy waited in silence for the moment to be forever captured.

All the while, Mr. Driscoll stood to one side watching. It rather unnerved her, but Rainy knew there was nothing she could do. To her relief her father and mother soon joined them. Her father held out his hand and shook Marshall Driscoll's hand and smiled.

Rainy couldn't help but feel a sense of curiosity and even frustration. What was this man doing at her wedding, and why was her father welcoming him?

The pictures were taken and the photographer soon gathered his things and left. Rainy remained seated, uncertain of what else to do. She watched her parents with Driscoll and wondered how they could possibly be so accommodating to this man.

Seeing that Rainy was watching him, Driscoll left her parents and crossed the room. "I'm sorry for the intrusion," he said, "but I had to come."

"Why?" Rainy asked.

"Because I wanted to apologize." Suddenly his expression suggested defeat. He lowered his gaze. "I'm sorry for what Chester . . . what he put you through. I knew about some things and presumed others. I knew you weren't guilty of the thefts at the university, but I couldn't bring myself to get to the bottom of it and expose Chester. He never confided in me— at least not to the extent that I knew what he was up to these last months."

Driscoll seemed most contrite for what had happened and Rainy's anger faded. "It was kind of you to come and apologize."

"That's not all," her father said, joining them. "Marshall has asked me to stay on with the university permanently."

Rainy perked up at this. "And what did you tell him?"

"I declined," her father said. "I told him that my plans were set for Scotland and we would only delay long enough to get teachers in position for the classes

Gunther's dismissal left open. Then I told him that I had a very qualified daughter who would probably love to work at the university—especially in the areas of archaeology and Indian history."

Rainy looked at Duncan, who beamed her a smile. She shook her head in disbelief and looked to Marshall Driscoll. "And what did you have to say about that, Mr. Driscoll?"

"I thought it a wonderful idea. I've already released a letter to the board exonerating you of all guilt and accusations. I've made it quite clear that my son was to blame for the mishap three years ago. My son and Gunther Albright." He paused and drew a deep breath. "We're prepared to offer you a position."

Rainy nodded. A part of her wanted to jump for joy and immediately accept whatever position Driscoll might offer but another part couldn't have cared less. She turned to Duncan and reached for his hand. "My husband and I will discuss it and I'll let you know."

Marshall Driscoll nodded. "I hope very much you'll join us."

With that said, he allowed Rainy's parents to lead him from the room. Rainy got to her feet and turned to face Duncan. "So . . . what do you think?"

"I think I love you more and more by the minute," he said, pulling her close.

"No, I already know that part. What do you think about Mr. Driscoll's offer?"

Duncan's expression grew thoughtful. "Is that what you want?"

Rainy studied her husband for a moment. She

thought of all the time she'd spent fretting over the university and what might have been. She thought of how desperately she'd longed to clear her name. God had worked out all of the details—freeing her from the stigma of being a thief, giving her a husband to love her. Without a doubt, everything seemed much clearer now.

She slowly shook her head. "No. No, it isn't what I want at all. I want to have your children and spend my life enjoying your company."

He slowly grinned. "I think I can arrange both."

She laughed. "I've seen your determination when you set your mind to a thing. I've no doubt you can accomplish whatever you decide is worthy."

He nuzzled her neck. "So you won't mind terribly that I've talked to the National Geographic Society about a husband-and-wife team who can provide them extensive research on the Hopi and Navajo Indians?"

Rainy's eyes widened. "Truly? What did they say?"

"They were very interested."

"Oh!" She couldn't help pulling away to give a little jump and clap her hands. "I can't believe you did that. This is wonderful!"

Duncan picked her up and whirled her in a circle. "I always want you to be this happy."

Rainy reached up and ran her fingers through his wavy black hair. "I love you, Duncan Hartford." She heard his sigh and joined it with her own.

Later that night, long after everyone else was asleep, Rainy and Duncan strolled in the garden together. Rainy wore a flowing nightgown and robe of white lawn, her strawberry blond hair flowing down to her waist. She felt like a princess in a fairy tale and Duncan was her prince.

Looking to him, she smiled warmly at the sight of him in his loose open shirt and gray trousers. They held hands as they walked. Words seemed unnecessary. He was everything she'd ever wanted—loving, giving, and kind. *What a wonder it is to be wife to this man,* Rainy thought.

She smelled the fragrant scent of her mother's honeysuckle—so sweet and delicate. A friend had brought her the plant from California and her mother had babied the bush until it grew strong and supple. There were other flowers—some in pots, some planted around the courtyard walk and walls. There was so much of her mother here in this garden. So much of Rainy's past was here as well. The garden had always been a comfort to her.

"I'll miss this place," Rainy told Duncan. "Even when I was in Santa Fe working for the Harvey Company, I knew I could come here anytime I wanted. Mother worked absolute wonders with this garden, and now she'll go away and the new owner will never know how much effort she put into it."

Overhead a full moon shone down on them, lighting the path as if it were day. Duncan put his arm around her shoulders and whispered in Rainy's ear, "I have a surprise for you. I worked out the details with your father and . . . well . . . I bought this place."

"What!" Rainy pulled away and caught the amused expression on his face. "You honestly did?"

He shrugged. "You seemed to like it so much, and I figured we'd need a place to come when we were not out on a dig. Does it please you?"

She laughed and hugged him tight. "You know it does. Oh, thank you, Duncan. I don't know what to say."

"You've already said it. You told me that you love me, and that's all I'll ever need."

"I agree," she said, stretching on tiptoe to kiss him, "and I intend to say it often."

"Just so long as you mean it each time."

Beneath the harvest skies God blessed their union with a deep abiding peace and satisfaction. Rainy believed that nothing would ever be more wonderful than these first moments with her husband. *Sometimes,* she thought, *to have the very best, you must let go of the mediocre that you hold to so tightly.* She'd let go of her desire to control her life—she'd let go of her plans for helping God answer her prayers and she was learning to let go of her doubts and insecurities. Together, Rainy knew that she and Duncan would be able to face most anything. And with God at their side, Rainy knew there was nothing they couldn't accomplish.

It was a new beginning.

A starting place for all the dreams they would share.

Snuggling against her husband, Rainy had no room for doubt. The future was much too promising.

> "Mr. Morris lets us see the intricate patterns in the minds of the characters while they make changes that can enhance or destroy their lives. He never ceases to amaze me with his unique individuals who face difficult choices if they are to honor God."
>
> —*Rendezvous magazine*

A Grand Series of Faith and History!

Epic in scope, Gilbert Morris's HOUSE OF WINSLOW series is nothing less than the compelling story of the forces and people that shaped American history. Each book has a plot that sweeps you away with characters whose lives are examples of heroism, courage, faith, and love.

The Leader in Christian Fiction!

BETHANYHOUSE

11400 Hampshire Ave. S., Minneapolis, MN 55438 • www.bethanyhouse.com